ALSO BY

AHMET ALTAN

Endgame
Like a Sword Wound

LOVE IN THE DAYS OF REBELLION

Ahmet Altan

LOVE IN THE DAYS OF REBELLION

Book Two of the Ottoman Quartet

*Translated from the Turkish
by Brendan Freely and Yelda Türedi*

Europa
editions

Europa Editions
214 West 29th Street
New York, N.Y. 10001
www.europaeditions.com
info@europaeditions.com

Copyright © 2001 by Ahmet Altan
First Publication 2020 by Europa Editions

Translation by Brendan Freely and Yelda Türedi
Original title: İsyan Günlerinde Aşk
Translation copyright © 2020 by Europa Edition

Library of Congress Cataloging in Publication Data is available
ISBN 978-1-60945-619-1

Altan, Ahmet
Love in the Days of Rebellion

Book design by Emanuele Ragnisco
www.mekkanografici.com

Cover image: Franz von Stuck, *Mary von Stuck in a Red Armchair*, 1916.
Copyright © Mondadori Portfolio/Akg

Prepress by Grafica Punto Print – Rome

Printed and bound in Great Britain by Clays, Elcograph S.p.A.

LOVE IN THE DAYS
OF REBELLION

Index of Characters

Osman

A middle-aged man who lives alone in modern-day Turkey except for his frequent visitors from a century ago, who bring along their personal versions of a family history that only the dead can remember and tell.

His Majesty the Sultan

Sultan Abdulhamid II, born in 1842 and reigning since 1876, rules the Ottoman Empire from his palace on the Yıldız Hill overlooking the Bosphorus.

Sheikh Yusuf Efendi

Osman's great grandfather. The leader of a prominent *tekke*—a monastery of dervishes—in late 19th century Istanbul, whose wisdom is sought by people from all corners of the vast Ottoman land.

Reşit Pasha

Personal physician and a confidant of His Majesty the Sultan.

Mihrişah Sultan

An Ottoman princess related to the Khedive of Egypt and the estranged wife of Reşit Pasha.

Hüseyin Hikmet Bey

The only child of Mihrişah Sultan and Reşit Pasha; trained as a lawyer in Paris he is now recovering from a self-inflicted wound at the French Hospital in Salonica.

Mehpare Hanım
The daughter of an Ottoman Customs Director and a two-time
divorcee, who has a daughter from her first husband, Sheikh
Yusuf Efendi and a son from her second husband, Hüseyin
Hikmet Bey.

Constantine
Mehpare Hanım's Greek lover with whom she has taken up
residence in Salonica.

Rukiye
The daughter of Mehpare Hanım and Sheikh Yusuf Efendi.

Nizam
The son of Mehpare Hanım and Hüseyin Hikmet Bey.

Hasan Efendi
A former commissioned officer of the Imperial Navy; both a
loyal disciple and son-in-law of Sheikh Yusuf Efendi.

Binnaz Hanım
Sheikh Yusuf Efendi's daughter who married Hasan Efendi.

Ragıp Bey
Osman's grandfather. An officer in the Ottoman Army, child-
hood friend of Hasan Efendi, and son-in-law of Sheik
Yusuf Efendi.

Cevat Bey
Ragıp Bey's brother and a leading member of the Committee
for Union and Progress.

Dilara Hanım
Poland-born and well-travelled widow of an affluent Ottoman
Pasha, she now resides in Istanbul alone with her teenage
daughter.

Dilevser
Dilara Hanım's daughter.

1

Some nights he woke to the footsteps of the ants crawling across the Persian carpet.

These wasp-waisted ants with trembling joints and shiny black knuckles were the last creatures to walk across these carpets that had been woven centuries ago in dark, damp rooms in mountain villages and grown worn and faded, and even though no one heard them, their footsteps echoed in Osman's tranquil soul, which had freed itself from time and the world, and made him tremble in fear.

He struggled out of the bed in which his grandmother had once gone to the most obscure and isolated corners of lust to seek the keenest pleasures human flesh could taste, stepped on the wooden floor that had been worn out by constant cracking, waited a while as he fought to gather strength from this ragged firmness, then shuffled wearily out of the room.

In his grandfather's long nightshirt, which was worn out here and there and had long since lost its whiteness, he lit all the lamps in the living room and saw not the ants he'd expected but his dead, swaying restlessly in their transparent, slippery bodies.

His dead were prisoners of time, they walked as if nothing could have stopped them during the time that had stretched before them when they were born and the moment death had intercepted them, they'd been trapped in time between birth and death. When they went backward they could go no further than their births and when they moved forward they couldn't move past their deaths; now they had to wander forever between the moment of their birth and the moment of their death. Each time they told their unchanging life stories, which were frozen between two precise dates, they tried to change the unchangeable with the words by adding new details and events.

They chose to tell their stories to their young relative Osman, who'd cut himself off from life while he was still alive but could not grasp hold of death, and who'd crippled himself by falling into a deep and dangerous timelessness where the past and the future mingled.

Osman couldn't remember when he'd begun speaking to his dead. As he tried, with the strange, dark intellect that didn't help him find peace or achieve success, to drag himself through a life that was wracked with foppish whims and strange sexual fantasies, poisoning himself and those around him, he'd suddenly wearied and retreated to his grandfather's old mansion.

He didn't know whether his dead had brought him here or whether he'd found them after he arrived. He escaped into the past with his dead and freed himself from indecision, pain, and frustration by wandering through the astounding tunnels of history. His small inheritance was enough to meet his daily needs, and he hid from his daily pain by observing the pain of the past.

People thought him mad, and for his part he thought people stupid. Seeing the past lives of the dead so clearly reinforced this opinion. Perhaps this was the main reason he loved the dead who told him these stories.

Whenever they saw Osman alone in that dusty old mansion, his beloved dead streaked toward him with an irresistible power like candle flames in a room where the windows had been left open and began speaking to him in weak, broken voices that resembled their transparent bodies.

They all had terrifying secrets.

To keep these secrets he clenched his fists passionately as if he was holding a fire in his palms, then, unable to bear the burning of what he had to conceal he became gripped by the need to reveal at least part of it by opening his fists.

Among the secrets they revealed were murders, uprisings, betrayals, sinful loves, and painful longings; their narratives were full of conflicts, lies, and omissions because they tried to conceal these secrets even as they revealed them.

Osman felt a sense of secret superiority when he witnessed the combination of their desire to reveal and their desire to conceal.

They all began speaking at once as soon as they saw him.

He'd learned to choose one, focus on that voice, and listen only to it amidst all the wailing narratives. This was a skill peculiar to those who have lost track of time, and destiny, which grants something in exchange for everything it diminishes or diminishes something in exchange for anything it gives, had granted a gift that couldn't be appreciated by anyone who hadn't broken his bonds with time.

That night when he woke in fear, he chose Hasan Efendi, the most entertaining of his dead; despite the fragility of death there was a grandiosity in Hasan Efendi's voice that was reflected in what he was relating, the tremulous roar of the thousands who'd filled the square, a quaking terror of the future sensed under the shouts of joy. Osman followed the voice into a crowd of the long-forgotten dead who'd gathered under fluttering black banners.

Hagia Sophia was surrounded by thousands of fezzes that rippled like a ruby-red sea. Reflections of the winter sun glinted on the long bayonets of the soldiers waiting to one side, on the brocaded uniforms of the Sultan's guards, the white scarves of the Albanian guards, and on the shoulder-length keffiyeh of the Syrian *Zühaf* guards.

After thirty-three years of tyranny, the crowd that had gathered to celebrate the opening of parliament couldn't fit into the square and thousands had climbed onto the roofs, buttresses, pillars, minarets, and domes of Hagia Sophia, which for centuries had witnessed a long string of rulers from Byzantine to Ottoman times, riots, heads dangling from the branches of trees, executions, massacres, and coronations, and which, with quiet dignity, kept what it had seen to itself.

As he glanced around and engraved the smallest details in his mind so he could tell his Sheikh about it in the evening, Hasan Efendi, in his green turban and long black robes, stood alone and as still as a statue at the very top of Hagia Sophia's magnificent dome, just beneath a giant silver crescent, he seemed perhaps more impressive than the crowd itself as he stood alone at the very top like a black silhouette etched on the sky.

At the edge of the square were the troops in khaki uniforms that had been brought to Istanbul after the Third Army in Salonika had revolted against the Sultan and Caliph of all Muslims especially to keep the mullahs loyal to the Caliph from stirring up trouble and shouting, "Sharia will be lost!" These soldiers, who were not satisfied with their cartridge belts and who'd filled their pockets with extra bullets, stood with a terrifying determination to persuade all who saw them to fall into step with the new order.

Hasan Efendi, who was fiercely loyal to the Caliph and to sharia, and who'd never liked the reformers, told Osman later, with a sarcastic and almost mischievous grin that didn't suit a dead man, "It was God's doing, in less than four months these soldiers who'd been sent here to protect the abolition of sharia were rebelling and shouting for sharia, and hundreds of them were cornered in the streets of Istanbul and put to the sword by their own comrades."

The square was full of black banners, embroidered in silver

thread with Koranic verses about the military, that served as a dark, proud reminder of how important both religion and the military were in this society.

The square and all the streets leading to it were filled with people from the four corners of the empire, Thracian shepherds, seamen from the islands, Arabs from whom wafted the spicy smell of their mysterious peninsula, Jews who had migrated from sacred cities, Montenegrins with pistols in their cummerbunds, Bulgarians and Kurds, Kirgiz, Gypsies who sang and danced constantly, and Tatars with high cheekbones.

Again and again the people in this mixed crowd took out their guns, restrictions on the sale of which had been lifted after the proclamation of "liberty," and fired into the sky, the sounds of gunfire mixing with the liberty marches.

As the crowd seethed, intoxicated by its own voice and zeal, there was a rumbling sound that was difficult to identify from a distance; people immediately understood what the rumble meant; it was the Sultan's carriage, accompanied by mounted lancers.

Those who saw the carriage began to frantically shout, "Long live the Sultan!" as if they hadn't just been applauding constitutional monarchy and singing songs of liberty to celebrate the end of tyranny.

The Sultan's physician Reşit Pasha looked at the Sultan and saw that since the day his own army had limited his powers when he'd believed his power was limitless and divine, he seemed older and less healthy than he really was, his face was pale and lined despite the blush they applied to his cheeks when he went out in public, so, to cheer him up he called out in a low voice to the Sultan, who was sitting with his head bowed as if he didn't hear the crowd that was cheering him.

"Your subjects are happy to see you, your majesty, look at how they're cheering you."

The Sultan looked up slowly and gave his physician a slightly patronizing and resentful look.

"Do you still believe in this kind of cheering, doctor? They also cheer the people who want to send us to our death."

As the Sultan feared an assassination attempt, his carriage raced through the crowd in the square and the streets at top speed, sparks flew from its wheels as it passed. When the carriage passed, the crowd parted like the Red Sea miraculously parted when Moses touched it with his staff, to make way for "The Caliph," thus both showing their respect and saving themselves from the carriage that would clearly slow for nothing.

There'd been fear of an attack, but the trip passed without incident, except that when they were near the old palace an old woman in black waved her feeble arms at the carriage and shouted, "Give me back my sons!" but no one could hear her over all the noise.

When the horses, who were covered in lather from galloping without stop since they'd left the palace gates, stopped in front of the parliament building, the band that had been waiting played the Hamidiye March to greet the Sultan.

The irritable cavalrymen encircled the carriage to keep the crowd at bay: surrounded by a crowd that was shouting, screaming, singing marches, and charged with a shared enthusiasm, the Sultan, with the rancorous resentment of those who have lost power suddenly, slowly got out of the carriage and walked to the large gate without looking at anyone.

As he shuffled along, a power emanated from this slumped-shouldered man who was able to respond to the conflicting feelings of the crowd who needed to either hate or love someone and who satisfied their perpetually hungry emotional world with his presence; the six centuries of history he had inherited and the 1,003-year-old religion of which he was Caliph illuminated his presence, which was stained here and there, with a divine light, and the mere sight of him deeply affected people in a compelling manner.

As he walked along that corridor, those in the parliament hall sensed the approaching Sultan's presence as if they'd smelled a sharp scent in the air, the loud murmur of talking voices lowered decibel by decibel, and the Sultan entered a completely silent hall.

Most members of parliament, looking too polished and conspicuous, like brand-new patent leather shoes, in their pitch-black frock coats and red fezzes, felt ill at ease and indeed even frightened in this hall; among the black frock coats, as if to prove this was an imperial parliament, were the Yemeni members in their green and purple keffiyeh, Arabian members who covered their heads with shawls that were tied back with black camel-hair bands, hodjas with white turbans, and members in military uniform.

Landowners wearing medals and gilded, flamboyant clothes sat next to the podium, in front of them was the Shaykh al-Islam, dressed completely in white, and the ulema in their emerald green robes beside him. Next to the Muslim clergymen were gigantic, robust patriarchs with long beards and pitch-black robes, lined up like pitch-black sarcophagi brought up from a crypt.

Everyone in the hall rose to their feet when the Sultan entered.

The Sultan, in his loggia, stood leaning on the sword he'd placed against the floor and looked around the hall for a long time. Without moving a muscle in his face, the man who'd held all the power looked at those who held it now, intimidating them with his gaze, his stance, and his silence. After a member of parliament read the Sultan's speech declaring constitutional monarchy, prayers were recited and at that moment the sound of cannon fire filled Hagia Sophia square. Artillery units on the Bosphorus and warships in the Marmara Sea had fired their cannon. The birth of constitutional monarchy was proclaimed to the empire and to the world with a one-hundred-and-one-gun salute.

The Sultan left the hall as he'd arrived, shuffling slowly; he quietly climbed into the waiting carriage as if none of what was going on had anything to do with him and reclined on the soft cushions.

In the carriage, the Sultan's physician looked at his pale face and asked anxiously if he was tired. The condescending smile that the doctor knew so well appeared briefly on the Sultan's face, then he answered tersely, "I'm fed up."

The Sultan didn't speak until they'd reached the palace.

That night the seven hills of Istanbul glowed like bundles of flames, all the lights were on in the palace and the mansions of the princes and pashas; those who in fact felt a deep sorrow feared being seen as avoiding the celebrations and participated in this fiery demonstration as prisoners of the terror that raised its head whenever this old city celebrated.

The old city walls, illuminated by torches, mosques, churches, ships, and waterfront mansions fixed their fiery eyes on the sky, and the red lights of the city and the shadows of centuries-old temples were reflected on the Golden Horn, which pierced the city like a curved dagger, and on the Bosphorus.

On that December night on which the cold of winter made itself felt, sheikh Yusuf Efendi, who'd been invited to the celebration but hadn't attended, wrapped himself in his fur-lined robe and strolled through the *tekke* garden in Unkapanı, looking at the burning lights, listened without comment to Hasan Efendi describe the events without bothering to conceal his anger at the way the Sultan of the empire and the Caliph of the world had been treated, he spoke with an angry bitterness without actually expressing what he felt.

As Hasan Efendi related what had happened, the bright lights of the city were suddenly extinguished and the city sank back into its accustomed darkness, there were no lights except for the trembling flames of the oil lamps inside the tombs of the Sultans and the saints' shrines.

In that darkness, the Sheikh shivered as if he sensed what was going to happen in the city, and, saying that it was getting cold, went inside.

2

The sisters at the French hospital showed a special tenderness and consideration to the polite patient with the soft gaze who, for whatever reason, looked like a pansy with the purple rings under his eyes and who spoke superb French. They often came to his bedside to ask how he was, hold his hand, say a few encouraging words, and sometimes, as the nights grew longer, they'd pull up a chair and read to him from books they'd borrowed from the hospital library.

Sister Clementine, who was said to have been a baroness once, spent more time than the other nuns with this patient whose education could be heard at once in his voice, and she clearly enjoyed talking with him about literature, writers, people, weaknesses, religion, and sometimes, when no one else was around, even politics. The sisters had either learned his tragic story or he'd touched their spirits with the otherworldly look in his large, chestnut eyes, and they were swept up in an ardor in which they saw him as part brother and part lover, they often spoke among themselves about Monsieur Hikmet; they each felt a secret pain, an inexplicable sorrow, at the thought that this patient who had recovered enough to shave himself would soon be discharged.

Even though he'd pointed the gun, which he was using for the first time, directly at his heart, by the grace of God his hands had trembled and he'd shot himself above the lung and shattered his collarbone; as Hüseyin Hikmet Bey later told

Osman, "You can't imagine what a sad embarrassment it is to fail to die."

He'd wanted to kill himself because of the inconsolable pain of knowing full well that he could never be reunited with the woman he loved, his wounded pride that the woman he loved had chosen another man, and the disappointment he'd experienced in politics, and to all this pain was added the shame of not being able to die. As Hikmet Bey lay in his hospital room listening to the moaning of patients in other rooms, the whispering of the nurses, smelling the disinfectant the janitor added to a bucket of water to mop the floors, he knew the importance of warm affection to the healing of his soul, which was more badly wounded than his body, much more clearly than he had when he was healthy. He didn't know how the desire to see Sister Clementine's hair, which he'd decided was a chestnut red, had seeped into his gratitude for the interest she'd shown in him.

Despite the nurses' tenderness, the vibrant harmony of past balls, Paris nights, love affairs, and sin that he could sense in Sister Clementine's voice even when she prayed and the anger that betrayal inevitably causes, he couldn't get his wife Mehpare off his mind.

Despite his bitterness, desperation, and sense of abandonment, or perhaps because of them, he dreamt of this beautiful woman every night, he muttered her name during bouts of fever, and thought no one but this woman could ease his agonizing loneliness. Like any man who's been betrayed, no matter how angry he was he secretly believed that the only person who could relieve his pain was the person who'd caused it, and he allowed himself to dream; he waited for Mehpare Hanım to come back, for her to enter his hospital room one morning, concealing the shame on her face with a distant look, and ask his forgiveness.

When she didn't come, he didn't distance himself from

Mehpare Hanım, on the contrary he felt more strongly bound to her. He'd loved his wife since the day he met her, this love, like many others, had not been nourished and strengthened by happiness, but by doubt and desperation, over the years it had become part of his personality, of his very being; he couldn't get over this love, moreover, he didn't want to.

When this longing became unbearable and started to break not only his soul but his body, he prayed to God, like a patient in pain begging for morphine, for the ability to forget, but his soul rebelled against his body's entreaties, he remembered Mehpare Hanım at her most beautiful, the way she combed her hair, the way she held his hand on the way to their bedroom, and, realizing that to forget her would completely erase her from his life, at that moment, like anyone who was in love, he couldn't countenance even the thought of forgetting. He loved someone who was far away, someone who wouldn't come to him, and the only connection they had was the love he felt; the moment he forgot, this connection would vanish, and Hikmet Bey couldn't bear to even imagine this. He would be unable to let go of this love unless it left him one day without his knowledge.

In fact, Hikmet Bey was not the kind of person who needed to suffer in order to love; when he loved, he loved with all his soul, with all his being; an impediment, a sense of longing, desperation, a game, or a betrayal couldn't increase his love, when he'd fallen in love with Mehpare Hanım he hadn't held back even a drop of his soul, he hadn't kept aside anything for himself, he'd felt no need to hesitate. With the childish purity and innocence that was sometimes seen in well-raised men, he'd gone to the very limit of love: there was nothing beyond these feelings, nothing but death; and he really had tried to cross this boundary of death when his love wasn't returned, but, as he himself said, "Unfortunately, I didn't succeed."

He remembered that day in shame; the people who'd rushed

into the room when the gun went off, the shouting in the mansion, running, footsteps, the sad, frightened looks on the children's faces, the rushing servants on the edge of tears, the annoyed, derisive look on Mehpare Hanım's face, about which Hikmet Bey said, "Even remembering it is painful." They carried him to the carriage by the arms and legs like a sack and placed his bloody body on the seats. He heard the driver shout and crack his whip, felt the pain in his chest, murmured, "Mehpare . . . " and then passed out. Later he told Osman, "I remember that I wanted to say something, to call to her, I was going to tell her something; they operated on me at the hospital, after I came to, I thought for days about what I was going to tell her, but, strangely, I couldn't remember."

The palace doctor's son had been brought to the hospital with a serious wound and had been abandoned there like a miserable outcast, neither his children, his wife, his mother, nor his father came to see him, and even the Committee friends with whom he'd shared a common fate lost themselves in the joy of their success and chose to forget their friend who'd shot himself because his wife betrayed him. If he'd died, many of those who didn't visit him in the hospital would probably have gone to his funeral, but he hadn't, and it had become his destiny to live with the humiliated shame of being a "cuckolded man" rather than have a tragic end.

On account of the influence the Sultan still had, Reşit Pasha received daily updates on his son's condition from the governor's office, and as soon as Mihrişah Sultan learned her son would recover, she sent a telegram to her daughter-in-law, whom she'd never loved, telling her to send the children to Paris immediately; the strange thing was that this woman who hadn't even gone to visit her seriously wounded son surprised everyone by not only taking her grandchild, but Mehpare Hanım's daughter from her marriage to sheikh Yusuf Efendi as well.

Sheikh Efendi didn't want his daughter to live with him; he accepted Mihrişah Sultan's taking her with restlessness and a heavy heart about his decision. Even though he was known as "the protector of the abandoned," even though he never hesitated to help strangers or intercede on their behalf, he couldn't be there for his own daughter, he couldn't take his own flesh and blood under his protection, adding one more sin to the many he'd committed since the day he'd first seen Mehpare Hanım, no one knew the reason, he shouldered this heavy sin without giving any explanation to anyone. Later Hasan Efendi, pitying his Sheikh, told Osman, "He could have taken her in if he wanted, but he wanted her to stay with Mihrişah Sultan; his daughter constituted a link to both Mehpare Hanım and Mihrişah Sultan, who'd charmed him with her beauty when she'd come to the *tekke*, it wasn't because he didn't want his daughter, it was because he didn't have the strength to cut this bond, he left her with that whore."

After sending her two children to her mother-in-law, Mehpare Hanım closed up the mansion in Salonika and moved to her Greek lover's large mansion in the middle of the vast vineyards in Khalkidiki to escape the gossip and to live her love in peace. On the day she arrived there, she erased Hikmet Bey and what they'd lived together from her mind with the selfish ferocity seen in women who leave the man they don't love to be with the man they do love, indeed she did this with an inner peace that's difficult to explain.

With the uncanny intuition that lovers have, Hikmet Bey sensed that he'd been forgotten, what was more depressing was the knowledge that he wouldn't have been forgotten if he'd died, and this gave him one more reason to regret that he'd lived.

Despite the pain he felt, there was no bitterness in his heart; in the mystical manner seen in those who return from the brink of death, he tried to understand each of the people close to him and found excuses for them not having visited him even once. Perhaps he no longer had the strength to be angry, perhaps because he had humiliated, denigrated, and shamed himself so much more than anyone else that he didn't even take secret offense at what they did. He just felt a deep repentance. He realized that a failed suicide attempt was more dishonorable than never having attempted suicide.

While the Muslim community celebrated the opening of parliament, the Christians, especially in Salonika, were swept up in the excitement of the approaching Christmas season; despite the soberness of the nurses and doctors, there was a cheerful flurry of activity in the hospital, everyone had begun buying little presents for their acquaintances. Hikmet Bey couldn't find anything to be cheerful about, so in desperation he borrowed from the happiness of others as he watched the preparations for Christmas from his bed with a bitter smile.

Two days before Christmas, when Sister Clementine was doing her rounds in the deserted hospital as the patients slept, she went into Hikmet Bey's room and saw that he was still awake, and without attempting to conceal her pleasure said, "Are you still awake, Monsieur Hikmet?"

With a broken smile that suited his pale face, Hikmet Bey replied, "I couldn't fall asleep." Sister Clementine straightened the bedsheets and pulled the blanket up a bit and said, "Tonight will be cold, cover yourself well." Hikmet Bey said, "If you have the time could you sit with me a bit?"

"Aren't you going to sleep?"

"I'm not sleepy, somehow I can't sleep at night, and even if I do fall asleep, I wake up again and again."

Sister Clementine pulled a chair up next to the bed and sat down.

"Would you like me to read to you?"

"If you have the time, I'd prefer to talk."

Sister Clementine sat with her knees together, her hands

resting on her lap, both of them were aware of an undulation in her voice that had nothing to do with the innocent manner in which she was sitting.

"You'll be leaving us next week, Monsieur Hikmet. What will you do when you get out?"

"I suppose I'll go back to Istanbul."

A shadow passed across Sister Clementine's face.

"Have we bored you so much that you want to flee at once?"

Later Hikmet Bey told Osman, "I think it was that night, as I was conversing with that tall nun, that I realized for the first time that women are attracted to men who fall into the position of being despised by other men." Osman noticed that he spoke of Sister Clementine without using her name, referring to her only as "that tall nun" as if she was of no importance to him, but he didn't point out this sly omission and attributed it to Hikmet Bey's inhibition.

"By no means, not at all," Hikmet Bey replied to her reproach. "In any event there are a lot of things I have to take care of here, when I said I would be leaving I meant after I've wrapped everything up."

"Do you miss Istanbul?"

"I suppose I have, I think I miss approaching the harbor in a ferry more than I miss Istanbul itself, the odd smell the city has, the buzzing . . . When I think of Istanbul I think of the harbor, as if I don't remember anything else . . . What about you? Do you miss Paris?"

Sister Clementine sighed, then leaned toward Hikmet Bey with a playful smile, "Don't tell anyone, but I miss it terribly."

Then she added, "The head nurse would be furious if she heard that."

"Why?"

"Oh, because the city is a worldly place, it means that I miss the world, we're supposed to have left all that behind."

There was a silence.

"I miss Istanbul, but I'm not sure I miss the world, no, I can't say I've missed the world, I've even grown accustomed to this place, to the hospital; if they weren't discharging me I'd stay here, far from the struggles and problems of life."

"Don't say that, Monsieur Hikmet. Just as it's inappropriate for us to miss the world, it's inappropriate for you not to miss it, you're a young man, you need to live your life."

"I'm not young anymore, Sister Clementine, I'm not trying to hold on to my youth, I don't miss it . . . from now on life is pointless for me; when you no longer have anything to hope for your youth has ended too; what can I hope for, nothing . . . From now on life is just something I have to endure, indeed, if you can believe it, it's like a prison sentence . . . "

Smiling like an aristocrat who'd learned to smile through the deepest pain, as if he was mocking himself, Hikmet Bey said, "They've put me in solitary confinement, as they do to convicts who try to escape; when you try to escape you lose all your privileges, I will carry on my life as someone who couldn't escape, who was caught attempting to escape."

Sister Clementine held Hikmet Bey's hand.

"Why are you talking like this, why are you being so pessimistic? I would never have thought you would give up so quickly."

"Quickly? Do you think I gave up quickly? I gave up very late, too late, I should have given up earlier . . . Someone who gave up in time might get the chance to bounce back, but anyone who gives up too late doesn't have a chance . . . I didn't give up quickly, I was late, Sister Clementine, too late, about ten years late."

Sister Clementine spoke in a slightly reproachful manner and with a spiritual maturity, earned through years of hard work, that obliged mortals to be respectful and keep their distance.

"Monsieur Hikmet, when we know that life doesn't end with death, that it begins again in a better way, how can you decide that your life has ended in this world, that your life is over when you're still in your prime. I know that this is held just as much a sin in your religion as it is in ours."

This time he really smiled a genuine smile.

"Ah, I wish that were my only sin . . . But I committed much more pleasurable sins, sins that are more difficult to forgive. You can be sure that this sin is much more innocent than my previous sins."

Every time the word sin is uttered between a man and a woman, whoever they are, it creates its own fire and charm, it penetrates the thickest uniforms, cloaks, and clothing worn against it, it reaches the indelible experience of sin and the pleasure derived from it and moves the soul with its ungodly power. The same thing happened this time; for a brief moment, the coquettish shadow of Paris evenings and sinful experiences, whatever their nature, that she'd tried to forget passed across Sister Clementine's face, but she regained her spiritual composure so quickly that it could have seemed he'd only imagined it. However, Hikmet Bey, despite being wounded in body and soul, was familiar enough with the shadow of sin to recognize it at once.

Instinctively, as if she wanted to protect herself, Sister Clementine reached into her deep pocket and took out her rosary beads.

"Everyone is a sinner, Monsieur Hikmet, that's why we seek redemption, this is why we work to avoid sin, we pray daily, we entreat God to not allow the smallest, seemingly most innocent sin to taint our lives. Don't forget, the most dangerous sin is the simplest and most innocent; a person can decisively close his soul to the greater sins, but it's the small sins that find a chink in our armor and make their way in."

For the first time since he'd arrived at the hospital, Hikmet

Bey looked carefully at Sister Clementine's face, he looked at her as a man looking at a woman and tried to see what was concealed behind the wimple that looked like swan's wings, the pale blue habit of coarse cloth, the white apron, rosary beads, mature and understanding smile and clasped hands. With the instincts of a man familiar with women and bedroom games, like a purebred hound catching its prey's scent, he caught the scent of a woman, there was a woman hiding in there. She had a slightly bulging forehead that shone like ivory, blond eyelashes that reached her temples, an aquiline nose that gave her an aristocratic look, thick, blond, almost yellow eyelashes, dark, almost navy-blue eyes, and thick lips. Later Hikmet Bey said, "It wasn't a face I wouldn't notice, that meant I'd never looked carefully before, when I looked at her all I saw was her habit, her wimple, her rosary beads; it didn't occur to me that there was a woman behind them."

Hikmet Bey never told anyone, but he remained faithful to the wife who'd left him for another man; if he'd known he wouldn't be mocked for it he would have told people, he would have said he wasn't being faithful to his wife but to his love. Moreover he'd never decided to or even wanted to be faithful, it was just that he didn't want to look at another woman with desire.

That night for the first time he looked at Sister Clementine with the awareness that she was a woman, and with desire. Once he'd said, "Destiny created me to amuse itself." And he was probably right, the first woman this man who was loyal to the wife who'd abandoned him became attracted to was a nun who had rejected her womanhood.

Osman, who was suspicious of everything and didn't trust either life or the dead, didn't think this was a coincidence; for Hikmet Bey, who couldn't stand to be alone and without a woman, to choose a woman he could never be with meant he was still trying to remain loyal to his wife without realizing it.

Still, one of the strong bonds that tied Hikmet Bey to Mehpare Hanım had been broken; like all loves that can't be nourished by hopes or dreams, this love showed its first sign of weakness and received its first wound when he took interest in another woman. The first sign that the bond of melancholy servitude was weakening saddened him deeply, but this didn't diminish his interest in Sister Clementine.

He controlled his desire to touch her by keeping his hands under the blanket and clasping them the way she did; unable to see the entreaty in his own eyes, he asked a strange question that later surprised him, "Do you like to dance, Sister Clementine?"

The nun with a beautiful face tilted her head to one side, looked at him as if she wanted to say something, then put on her spiritual smile and stood.

"Go to sleep now, Monsieur Hikmet, it's late."

Hikmet Bey waited for her to turn and say something before she went out the door, but she didn't.

Before Christmas, the patients who'd left the world of the healthy and the happy due to illness, pain, and injury felt a desire, of which they were secretly ashamed, to participate in the celebrations of the healthy during the holiday season. The wealthy gave money to the nuns to buy gifts for their fellow patients and the nuns, while the nuns bought gifts for the poor out of their own pockets.

On Christmas Eve they organized a small party in a hall on the ground floor that the nuns used as a cafeteria, and that smelled of boiled meat, coffee, and medicine. They made sherbets and bought cookies and put a large pine tree in the corner, and a chorus of nuns sang carols.

For the first time since he'd arrived at the hospital, Hikmet Bey got dressed, put on a tie, and became Reşit Pashazade Hüseyin Hikmet Bey. Despite the black rings under his eyes and the pallor that would remain on his face for the rest of his life, his stance, his expression, and the way he straightened his tie while speaking to the head nurse proclaimed that he was no longer a forlorn, wounded patient who needed tenderness but an Ottoman aristocrat who managed to carry the pride in which he had been steeped since childhood under all circumstances.

In his striped, black suit, with the bottom button of the vest left open, his starched shirt, his pearl-grey tie-clip, newly polished shoes, and newly re-shaped fez, he was no longer the wounded man who hadn't managed to commit suicide and who everyone pitied, the unfortunate man whose wife had betrayed him, the patient with the childish expression who made all the other patients thank God that they were in better shape, and had suddenly become one of the leading Committee members of Salonika, Hüseyin Hikmet Beyefendi, the son of the Sultan's physician. Of course it wasn't the way he was dressed that impressed those who saw him, they'd all seen a handful of people who were wealthier and more elegant than Hikmet Bey; what impressed them was that this man who, while he was lying in bed in his nightgown, had looked at everyone as if he needed some kind of help but didn't even know what kind of help, had, as soon as he got dressed, or rather as soon as the expensive fabric caressed his skin, suddenly regained his past, his family, his identity, and his wealth, which he unconsciously believed he'd lost when he came through the hospital door covered in blood, he once again became aware of who he was and of how much power he had; when Hikmet Bey remembered his power, everyone else was also reminded of it by the self-confidence that emanated from him.

His suit of English cloth, sewn by French tailors, had done more to help him pull himself together than any of the medications he'd been given. The nuns, who met people from every social stratum, noticed at once the aristocratic effort he

made to conceal his disdain for this small party and the understanding expression he assumed when talking to people not of
his class, and even though this didn't diminish the tenderness
they felt toward him, their behavior revealed that their friendship was now a more distant one. Sister Clementine was the
only one who felt closer to Hüseyin Hikmet Bey as he was in
his new clothes.

She went over to him, smiling her spiritual smile.

"Can you come here for a moment, Monsieur Hikmet, I
want to show you something."

They found a quiet corner and Sister Clementine took a
package from her pocket and gave it to him. For a moment,
probably because of his clothes, he'd forgotten where he was
and who he was talking to; he took the package, said, "Merci,
madame," and opened it calmly.

Inside was an 1808 edition of *Abelard and Heloise*, of red
leather that had turned brown and with some of the yellow letters on the spine missing. Hikmet Bey was familiar enough
with antique books to realize that this book had been pur-
chased from a collector, and for a considerable sum of money.
Sister Clementine had wanted to give an expensive gift to the
man who'd reminded her of her past, and she did so with a
book that looked ordinary and cheap.

Hikmet Bey leafed through the book with genuine joy and
let her know he knew its value without putting her in a difficult position.

"An 1808 edition . . . That must have been difficult to find
in Salonika."

"I saw it at a friend's house and bought it . . . Have you read
it?"

Hikmet Bey replied with a smile that childishly lit up the
face the nuns thought looked like a pansy.

"I was innocent once too. Like everyone else, I read the stories about lovers who could never be united before I read the

stories about lovers who separate, like many of my friends I discovered the pleasures of touch on my own, but this book taught me about the terrifying pleasure of not being able to touch."

He paused and looked into the nun's eyes.

"Thank you, thank you so much . . . I'll keep this for the rest of my life, it's such a lovely gift."

Then, unable to contain himself, he added, "Very innocent as well."

The nun's large, shiny forehead flushed for a moment; Hikmet Bey realized he'd embarrassed her and he felt embarrassed by this, so he hurriedly took the gift he'd bought from her out of his pocket and gave it to her.

"I got something for you too."

Sister Clementine made an exaggerated effort, struggling with the gilded ribbons on the package, and didn't look at him.

It was a copy of Baudelaire's *Fleurs du Mal*; the title was embossed in gold on the cover of the morocco-bound book, and Sister Clementine's name had been embroidered on the bottom. Next to Sister Clementine's expensive but humble-looking gift, Hikmet Bey's gift seemed too showy; he felt he needed to offer an explanation.

"I couldn't get out of the hospital so I had to order it, they made it a bit too showy."

Sister Clementine leafed through the book as if she hadn't heard what he'd said. When she looked up it was as if, as a Christmas gift, God had granted her the right to behave like a woman for a few minutes, and she put the persona of Sister Clementine aside, took back her real name, and became Baroness Roucheau of the Paris salons. For her the real gift was not the book but Hikmet Bey himself, who without condemning her had given her the chance to revive a past that had never fully died despite being overlaid with a new identity, prayer and rosary beads.

She smiled like a woman and not like a nun.

"My gift was very innocent, monsieur, yours was very sinful."

The reply was given not to the nun but to the baroness.

"We need both of them, madame, in order to be wounded and in order to recover."

"Why would we need to be wounded?"

"In order to recover, madame."

That Christmas Eve Sister Clementine allowed a sinful miracle to occur through the intercession of two soft, chestnut eyes and relived the past for a moment, then immediately went back to being a nun. Perhaps people could kill themselves and their identities once, but it was impossible to do so twice; after having eradicated a baroness, she didn't have the strength to eradicate a nun. There, that night, she realized this with pain and with a regret, who knows, she might never be able to confess that for a few minutes she'd relived a past that she'd long forgotten and she accepted this reality with the resignation that being a nun had taught her,

"Please sit down, Monsieur Hikmet, don't tire yourself."

"Thank you, Sister Clementine, tonight I recovered. After all, I'm being discharged tomorrow."

As Hüseyin Hikmet Bey told Osman later:

"For those who live with deep, sharp pain, it's almost impossible to find a great happiness that will make them forget their great sorrows; even when the possibility of happiness is present, those oppressed by a suffering that's difficult to bear can't find the strength and courage to open the door, they even remain silent so this unexpected visitor will go away; the talisman that will revive a melancholy person and make them smile again is hidden in small, sudden, brief moments of joy."

He discovered this truth that Christmas Eve in the hospital cafeteria whose smell would cause him to make a face when he remembered it. That a woman had changed her identity for him even for a moment, their brief but unforgettable chat had become an exit, a bridge to life for Hikmet Bey, who had recently been lying in an iron bed with grey rails in a room painted snow-white, believing his life was over, taking himself to account and blaming himself mercilessly like any honest man who has lost.

The next day he woke in a good mood; he ignored the pain he still had in his shoulder, stretched in his bed like a little boy, got up, and looked into the mirror on the wall, happily looked at the pale face that for some while had been reminding him of bad times, and then dressed carefully. He said farewell to and thanked each of the nuns in turn, except Sister Clementine, who'd vanished, went to see the hospital director and made a generous donation to the hospital, then climbed into the carriage that was waiting for him and left the hospital.

Even though it was the end of December, it was a warm, sunny day. As he left the hospital's well-kept garden he turned to take a last look at the large, yellow, rectangular building with its smooth façade. He set out for home with a wound in his shoulder that for the rest of his life would ache in damp weather, a deathlike sorrow that would never disappear, and a small but lively delight that would conceal them.

When Hikmet climbed agilely out of the carriage and went into the house, he stopped for a moment, he'd been on the point of going to the master bedroom as usual to change into his house clothes but realized he didn't want to go there, he didn't want to go to the study where he'd shot himself either; he was confused about where to go and stopped in the large entrance.

Then he realized what was missing, the sound of Mehpare Hanım's heels as she came to greet him, the children's laughter, the nannies talking, the servants whispering, the accustomed sounds of the house were gone. The servants who'd gathered in the kitchen were silent, they'd been awaiting his return with a fear whose cause they couldn't find.

At that moment Hikmet Bey realized the extent to which his life had been emptied, in his own words, he realized it when he was faced with that "horrible silence." It occurred to him to turn around, leave at once, spend the night in a hotel and never step foot in that house again, but when he saw the butler looking at him, he made a last effort to pull himself together, strode into the hall, and said, "Tell them to bring me a coffee please, Latif."

The entire house had been cleaned thoroughly, the floorboards had been scrubbed, there was a smell of soap and lavender one only encounters when moving into a house that's undergone major cleaning.

There was no human smell, none of the smells of cooking and furniture that seep into the walls over time, and which make a house a home; the smells had disappeared like the sounds, the house had lost its memory like someone who'd received a head injury.

For Hüseyin Hikmet Bey the house was at the same time familiar, he knew the rooms, the corridors, the furniture, the view from the windows, and alien, he couldn't find any of the familiar sounds or smells, or signs that left traces on his soul rather than in his mind's eye.

The mansion was more difficult to bear like this. In this house full of memories he could tolerate remembering and reliving the pain, in a new house with no connection he could spend his life trying to forget the past, but it was difficult for him to stay in a place that was at the same time so familiar and so alien.

He walked angrily past the study where he'd shot himself five months earlier. Like every other room in the house, it was perfectly clean, but there was a dark and resistant bloodstain, turned brown over time, where he'd fallen after shooting himself. He looked at the stain for a moment, then opened a drawer, took out a sheet of paper, sat at the desk, and wrote a short letter to his mother in French that began, "Chére Maman."

"I'm out of the hospital. I'm well. I'm leaving for Istanbul at once. Please send the children there. I kiss your hands."

He put the letter in an envelope, sent it to the post office, had his coffee, then told Latif to pack his bags and make a reservation for him for the next day on the Istanbul ferry.

He wanted to get away from Salonika and from this house as soon as possible, to go to Istanbul and forget the past.

The following day he boarded the Istanbul ferry.

As he leaned on the railing and looked back, he realized he wasn't leaving a city but a woman he knew he'd never forget. The woman he loved would remain there; he was removing the possibility, which had been nourishing his dreams, of meeting her at a social event or on the street, or rather he supposed he could do so just by boarding a boat. He would carry the woman he'd expelled from his life in the depths of his soul, moreover with an even stronger longing.

He did not yet know this.

3

Major Ragıp Bey wrapped himself in his thick, grey military greatcoat as he walked from Galatasaray to Taksim through the newly falling snow, and just as he was passing the Odeon, the famous beer hall's large door opened and three tipsy young officers spilled out, followed by a cloud of condensation that smelled of alcohol, women's perfume and white almonds. It was only just past noon, but apparently the officers from the Salonika units that had been sent to the capital to prevent possible riots had already started drinking.

An angry expression appeared on Ragıp Bey's face.

These young officers had listened to the Beyoğlu adventures of more experienced officers during long watches on Macedonian nights and had turned them into unattainable fairy tales with the new details they added to their dreams each night, and now, in Istanbul, with a fearful hunger in their souls from those nights of isolation, they were throwing themselves into the Greek whores' beds and becoming regulars of the dens of iniquity. The barracks had been left under the command of sergeants and inexperienced officers, drills and training had been abandoned, and lack of discipline reigned.

What was most frightening was the fierce hostility between the officers from the Committee and those who remained loyal to the Sultan; just the other night two officers had pulled guns on each other during a political argument, and Ragıp Bey had only been able to avoid bloodshed at headquarters by intervening at the last moment.

The Major, who disliked chaos and was close to hating what he'd seen in the past few days, berated himself for not rebuking these three officers, and he walked through the increasingly heavy snow with a fury fanned by his psychological makeup, which tended to rapidly amplify even the slightest sense of anger.

Just then, through the snowflakes that were getting into his eyes, he saw an old man, who he later learned was a carriage driver, whose expression reflected shame about his helplessness rather than fear. At the time he didn't even think about it, but later, every time he thought about the event that would change the course of his life, it always struck him that the first person he noticed was the one who had the least significant role; at that moment he wasn't even able to think this. He looked around to see why the man was reacting this way, he saw a woman whose veil was open and who was trying not to show her fear as she looked around for help, and the nasty grins of the two hoodlums who were pulling off her abiya.

He didn't hesitate, he strode up to the man who was pulling at her abiya, grabbed him by the throat, and pushed his head back. The hoodlum, who had just smoked hashish and thought himself much larger than he was, looked in surprise at the man who'd grabbed him by the throat and reached for the knife under his armpit, but the strange smile had already appeared on Ragıp Bey's face as, almost cheerfully, he punched the hoodlum in the face as if he wanted to feel the man's nose as it broke beneath his knuckles.

When he saw that his friend had collapsed and that blood was pouring from his nose, the other hoodlum reached for the gun in his belt, but when he saw Ragıp Bey reach for his gun he stopped, either because he thought his opponent would be too quick or he didn't have the nerve to engage in gunplay with an officer in the middle of Beyoğlu, mumbled through his moustache, and helped his friend to his feet.

With the animallike naturalness often seen in the under-world these hoodlums inhabited, he submitted to someone more powerful without any wounds to his pride, he walked away with his friend, who pressed a large scarf to his nose, to seek weaker prey, leaving bloodstains on the pavement.

After he was sure that they'd really gone, Ragıp Bey turned and looked at the woman; there was no sign of the gratitude, fear, or admiration he'd expected to see in her eyes, on the contrary she looked pleased, as if she'd enjoyed what she'd seen. Later Ragıp Bey would notice that this woman, whose name he would learn was Dilara, wasn't afraid of men no matter what they did, that she saw their braggartly weakness even when they were at their most violent and aggressive, and that she treated them like puppets created for her amusement, but what would really surprise him was that Dilara Hanım always did this in a kind and respectful manner and was able to conceal the mockery that lay beneath.

Ragıp Bey hadn't beat up the hoodlum to impress her, but nevertheless, when he didn't see the admiration he expected in the woman's eyes, he felt angry, as if his actions had been met with ingratitude. As for the woman, she touched Ragıp Bey's arm lightly and, in a strong and vibrant voice that evoked a sense of trust and respect in all those who heard it, and with a slight accent that made her words more effective, said:

"Thank you for rescuing me, I don't know what would have happened to us without you."

Even though he found the gratitude in her voice that he hadn't found in her eyes, Ragıp Bey felt uneasy; he'd never encountered a woman with a voice like that, but like all men, he instinctively recognized something in the woman's voice that suggested the end of male dominance and that each step he took from here would lead to captivity, and he was astounded; this was not a familiar feeling for him.

"It was nothing," he grumbled, "these hoodlums are

getting out of hand these days, it's our job to get them back in line."

Then, as if to indicate that the conversation was over, he nodded and tried to walk past her, but she wouldn't let go of his arm.

"Which way are you going, sir?"

Ragıp Bey looked at her as if to say he found the question inappropriate.

"I didn't catch that, ma'am."

The woman acted as if she didn't understand what he was implying.

"I asked which way you were going."

Ragıp Bey answered reluctantly:

"I'm going to Akaretler."

The woman smiled as if she found his irascibility amusing.

"Oh, what a coincidence, I'm going to Nişantaşı, I can give you a lift, the driver can drop you off after me."

Ragıp Bey rejected this offer decisively.

"No need, don't trouble yourself, I'll walk, I need the fresh air."

Dilara Hanım squinted her eyes, frowned, and pursed her lips, from her manner it was clear she didn't take his attitude or his words seriously.

"No need? How can I let you walk in this weather, who looks for fresh air in bitter cold like this, if you keep dragging this out the cold is going to make me sick as well."

The snow was getting heavier, Ragıp Bey would look ridiculous if he insisted on walking, Dilara Hanım had forced him to make a choice between looking ridiculous and looking indecisive. He didn't want to prolong this strange discussion in the falling snow, so he made a face and said, "Let's go then." They got into the carriage, and Dilara Hanım hunched on the edge of the navy-blue velvet seat.

"It's ice-cold in this carriage too."

They didn't speak at all until they'd reached Taksim Square, as they passed through the square the interior of the carriage had warmed a bit and the windows had become misted over from the passengers' breath. Dilara Hanım opened the upper part of her abiya as if she was alone in the carriage; it was the first time since they'd met that Ragıp Bey got a good look at her face.

Her braided hair was the color of the shiny horse chestnuts that used to fall into the garden and emerge from their thorny green pods when he was a child. Her face was illuminated by a strange light that set her apart from everything around her, as if someone was shining a light on her from some hidden corner; she was wearing neither blush nor eyeliner, this natural look, as if she'd just washed her face with lots of fresh water, sheltered an innocence that was at odds with her disdain as well as a lust that was at odds with her innocence. Her eyes, under eyebrows that were a little uneven at the ends and gave her face a mocking expression, bulged a bit in a way that reminded him of paintings of the Virgin Mary he'd seen in Germany, under her perfect, Slavic looking nose were small but fleshy lips that looked as if they'd been drawn by hand; it was difficult to decide whether her face was beautiful or not, but one still wanted to look at it.

With every movement of her face, when she raised her eyebrows or pursed her lips, her expression changed; when she leaned back, raised her eyebrows, and looked straight ahead, she looked like a reserved lady one would hesitate to speak to, when she leaned forward slightly and smiled she had a flirtatious air that would make any man feel it would be easy to chat with her.

The humble sturdiness of the carriage, which had clearly been brought from Europe, the softness of the velvet seats, the respectful manner of the driver who was clearly accustomed to working for wealthy households, her attire, the fabric of her abiya, and the emerald brooch on her collar hinted at wealth and breeding in a way that was not recognized at once but that commanded respect.

Dilara Hanım wiped the condensation from the window with her hand, the snowfall had become much heavier; the streets were deserted and the houses and pavements were becoming covered with snow.

"And you wanted to walk in this weather, you would have frozen to death, God forbid."

Ragıp Bey, who had been lost in contemplation of her face, was startled as if he'd been caught doing something inappropriate. He was seized by the disquiet and unreasonable anger that proud poor men feel toward wealthy women. He realized that the woman was interested in him, but instead of the self-confidence that such obvious interest would make him feel, he felt humiliated, because he thought she was showing her interest so openly because she looked down on him.

As if getting ready to give the order to attack, he tightened himself and squared his shoulders, raised his head, and took shelter in the only place he could, his manhood. He was about to say that he was used to weather like this, when he suddenly realized how laughable he was being. As he slowly unbuttoned his grey greatcoat, he looked up with the mocking smile that appeared on his face when he hit someone he was fighting.

"Thank you, I owe you my life."

At first she frowned with the surprise and anger of a woman who was accustomed to confusing men with her mockery when she in turn was mocked, and, with the secret delight they feel when they've attained something they sought, she tidied her hair, assumed the distant, respectable lady expression, then the lines of her face softened and she let out a little laugh.

"Please, anyone would rescue a freezing officer in Beyoğlu."

With this little laugh she let out, with the secret guidance are women use to show men they are attracted to how to impress

them, she was telling Ragıp Bey know how he should behave
without actually telling him. Ragıp Bey had understood this as
soon as he heard her laugh.

He had regained the defiant self-confidence, which women
recognized at once, of men who were proud of their power and
who were sure that in the end all women, whether rich or poor,
beautiful or ugly, hardheaded or scatterbrained, would utter
the same cries of pleasure.

Dilara Hanım realized that this man had a capacity for the
kind of violence she'd just witnessed when he broke a hoodlum's nose without hesitating, that it was not something that
had been brought out by a street fight and that it could come
out anywhere at any moment; oddly, she hadn't noticed it during the fight, but only when he mocked her.

Just as Ragıp Bey recoiled from her mockery, she recoiled
from his savagery, just as he was attracted by the charm of her
mockery, she was attracted by the charm of his savagery.

Like any woman who has intuited that the man she is with
could touch her profoundly, she first pulled back and became
the distant lady only so that she could move closer.

"Where are you stationed?"

"At Taşkışla."

"So, you're one of the soldiers who came from Salonika."

He replied with the same pride that all the officers who'd
come from Salonika felt involuntarily.

"Yes, I came from Salonika."

"You're one of the people who made our father the Sultan
angry."

Ragıp Bey looked at Dilara Hanım to see if she was serious,
but when he saw the same mocking smile he realized she was
joking.

"In fact one of those who made him very angry."

Ragıp Bey took out his cigarette case but stopped before
lighting a cigarette.

"May I?"

"By all means, but we've reached my house, we'll have them make hot tea for us, you can have your cigarette with tea."

This time Ragıp Bey didn't decline the invitation, he put his cigarette case back in his pocket; meanwhile the carriage had entered the mansion garden and stopped in front of the marble steps that led up to the large front door; as they left the carriage, the snow was falling in large, heavy flakes.

The door was already open when they got out of the carriage, and a butler in a black frock coat and a Greek servant in a white, lace cap came rushing out to greet them; they entered the house, Dilara in the lead followed by Ragıp Bey. In the large vestibule, as the servant helped her take off her abiya, Dilara Hanım calmly gave orders.

"Bring us tea in the living room, and don't forget to bring cognac and cakes."

Through a door to the left they entered a large living room where a fire was roaring in the fireplace and the windows looked out onto the garden.

"Please sit, I'll be right with you."

Alone in the living room, Ragıp Bey went and warmed his hands over the large logs that crackled as they burned.

He watched the red, yellow, lilac-tongued flames move across the logs; first the flames touched a log then retreated, then they touched it again, moved over it like red water, then retreated again; watching it, it seemed as if the fire would never ignite the log, it would keep moving over it and then retreating, then suddenly a tiny flame appeared on the side of the log. When the other flames retreated, it continued burning, then another tiny flame appeared on the other side and then the log was burning.

As he watched the game the flames were playing with the logs, he felt he'd warmed up enough and moved away from the fireplace, he glanced at his reflection in a crystal mirror with a gold-leaf frame hanging on the opposite wall, walked past two winged armchairs, went to the window, and looked out at the garden.

Large, heavy snowflakes continued to fall. The bare trees were covered in white, and the dark, stagnant water in the pool had started to freeze around the edges.

As he contemplated the sad loneliness of the garden in winter, Ragıp Bey suddenly felt alone, alienated and fragile. He remembered walking in fear on a snowy morning like this after beating a Pasha's son and feeling as if he no longer had a future. He left the window, went back into the warmth of the room, and sat in one of the large armchairs.

There was a settled warmth in the living room that gave a sense of security; he lit a cigarette and left it in the crystal ashtray on the coffee table; a book in German had been left open on the coffee table, he picked it up, it was Goethe's *The Sorrows of Young Werther*. As he was leafing through the book the door opened and Dilara Hanım entered, followed by the servant bringing the tea. Ragıp Bey put the book down in a hurry as if he'd been caught doing something forbidden.

The servant placed the tray on the long coffee table in front of the sofa then left them alone, and Ragıp Bey looked at Dilara Hanım.

"So, it seems you know German."

"Yes, why do you ask?"

Ragıp Bey gave the shy smile he always gave when the subject of books came up.

"I saw your book . . ."

Dilara Hanım looked around in surprise.

"My book?"

When Ragıp Bey picked up the book and showed it to her she smiled.

"My daughter Dilevser is reading that."

"Why did you laugh, don't you read books?"

"Of course I do, but this book is more suitable for a young girl than for a woman of my age . . . As the title says, it's about a young person."

Dilara Hanım stopped as if she'd made a gaffe and offered an explanation.

"The title of the book, *The Sorrows of Young Werther*."

Ragıp Bey nodded.

"I saw that."

"Oh, do you know German?"

Ragıp Bey answered as if it wasn't something important:

"I spent some time in Germany once, I was serving with a German regiment."

As she poured tea and passed it to him, Dilara Hanım asked:

"How long were you there?"

"Almost three years."

"That's a long time, did your wife accompany you?"

"I wasn't married at the time."

Dilara Hanım looked at him as she poured cognac from a cut crystal decanter into a large tumbler.

"You'll have some cognac, won't you, it'll warm you up in this weather."

"I will, thank you."

"Did you like Germany?"

"They're good soldiers."

Dilara Hanım smiled.

"Not everyone in Germany is a soldier, or did you never leave the barracks?"

Ragıp Bey remembered the unforgettable love he'd lived in Germany.

"Of course, they're good people, I enjoyed my time in Germany."

Dilara Hanım poured cognac for herself as well.

"I didn't like it much, they seemed a bit too cold to me, a bit too, how should I put it? A bit too calculating."

"Why were you there?"

"My husband and I went to a spa, to Baden-Baden, in fact Baden-Baden is a lovely place, have you ever been there? It's so green, it's a fun place, but still, I don't know, it seemed to me as if there was a severity under that fun."

"What does your husband do?"

"Unfortunately he passed away some time ago, he was much older when we married, and we used to go to Baden-Baden for his health."

It grew dark outside, the playful red of the long-tongued flames was reflected from the crystal mirror into the living room. Every time Dilara Hanım moved in the dimly lit room with the white seen through the large window behind her it created a pleasant illusion, it was as if he was watching rippling red silk. As he lost himself in this silky undulation, whose softness could be sensed from a distance, silence reigned in the living room.

Dilara Hanım rang the silver bell next to her, and when the servant appeared she said, "It's dark in here, light the lamps."

And at that moment Ragıp Bey understood the reason for the uneasiness he'd felt since he entered that house: in this wealthy and respectable mansion, the servants didn't find it odd that their mistress brought a stranger home and drank cognac with him. Apparently guests like this were common here.

He put his cognac down on the coffee table.

"I should be on my way."

"I won't hear of it, look how heavily it's snowing, wait for the weather to improve, the driver will take you wherever you want to go, but right now it's snowing too heavily for the horses to move; and why are you always in such a hurry to leave, ever since the moment we met you've wanted to leave. Do you find me so boring?"

Ragıp Bey rushed to say, "By no means. I don't want to impose."

The woman had an openly inviting manner, but at the same time, perhaps because of the mocking tone in her voice, or the confidence that came from being wealthy, she also seemed distant and inapproachable, and seeing these two conflicting manners confused him, because he expected women to adopt a single manner that he could understand.

Dilara Hanım picked up the crystal decanter, looked at Ragıp Bey, and asked, "Would you like some more," and when he nodded yes she poured cognac first into his glass and then into her own.

In every movement she made there was the refined, educated elegance of a woman who'd been born and raised in the palace, but there wasn't even a trace of the insincerity women from the palace almost always had. She commanded respect without effort, wandered at will through the respect she'd created, and confidently amused herself with her guest. She didn't have the latent fear aristocrats usually have of people from lower classes, she could consort with men of any class without hesitation; she was sure no one would touch her if she didn't want them to, though she didn't know why, and indeed had never thought about it.

They continued their conversation slowly and gently, in harmony with the snow falling outside the window, and like any man and woman meeting for the first time, they talked about their lives and their past, or rather Dilara Hanım talked and Ragıp Bey listened.

Dilara had been born in Poland as the daughter of a German small landowner, had taken music lessons from her mother, who was the daughter of a patriotic Polish teacher, had discovered a taste for literature, and from her father had learned to keep people at a distance and to manage them with her glances. At thirteen she was abducted in a raid on her village and became part of a group of that was sent as a gift to the harem of the Ottoman palace; in the harem she was ostracized because she was more intelligent and less beautiful than the other women, and when she was eighteen she was given away as a bride to an elderly Pasha from Crete. The Pasha truly loved his young wife, took it upon himself to complete her education, got her to take oud lessons, taught her French himself, received permission from the Sultan to take her to Europe, where he travelled often because of his poor health, brought her to the most beautiful cities, where they stayed in the most comfortable hotels, gave her the life of a European woman, then departed the world, leaving her a large fortune. Since then Dilara Hanım had lived a calm, safe, and secure life in that mansion with her daughter.

She didn't tell Ragıp Bey that, that unlike many Ottoman women who were widowed at a young age, she didn't forget her womanhood, but had casual affairs with handsome men who were not from her circle so as to avoid gossip.

During a moment of silence she watched the snow falling into the garden.

"Snow reminds me of my childhood, I can't decide whether or not I like it."

"Snow reminds everyone of their childhood."

The crackling of the fireplace and the light of the lamps reflected in the mirrors stood in contrast to the shadowy white darkness outside, the atmosphere caressed Ragıp Bey softly, and he kept putting off the idea of leaving that had remained in a corner of his mind.

Dilara Hanım rang the silver bell, and when the servant appeared asked calmly:

"Is dinner ready?"

"Yes, ma'am."

Dilara Hanım turned to Ragıp Bey.

"I've had dinner prepared, the carriage will take you after we eat."

Ragıp Bey tried to decline, but even he realized that he did it weakly.

"I don't want to impose, let me be on my way before it gets too late . . . And there's no need for your carriage, I'll hail a cab."

As she stood, Dilara Hanım spoke in an authoritative and mocking tone that he'd never heard in a woman before.

"Major, your attitude is bordering on rudeness, your insistence on leaving is close to insulting, don't throw it in my face that I'm so boring, dear."

He muttered, "By no means . . ." then stood and followed her, but inwardly he was angry at the way she pressured him; he couldn't stand up to this odd woman, and, what was worse, he himself was having difficulty deciding whether to stay or go.

They entered a large, well-lit room, in the center was a large table covered with a white tablecloth, the table had been set for three, and there were silver candelabras. Ragıp Bey glanced around for the third person, it was just the two of them, he gave her a questioning glance and she smiled.

"My daughter will be joining us."

As soon as she said this, the door on the side opened and a girl of about seventeen or eighteen came in; because of her upbringing she tried to conceal her displeasure at having a male guest at the table and, showing the politeness she'd been taught to show even to unimportant people, said, "Welcome" reluctantly, then sat and waited for her food without looking up. Dilara Hanım didn't pay attention to her daughter's manners, to the way she responded negatively to the presence of a male guest, she accepted her daughter's near rudeness with nonchalance. It was only Ragıp Bey who was disquieted by this behavior, he felt like a piece of furniture that had been placed in the house by mistake.

For a time they ate their soup in silence. That he managed to sit in silence with two women without trying to win their hearts, that he adopted such a cold and even angry attitude, caused both women to feel he was challenging their authority and the secret sovereignty that women were supposed to have at the table.

Dilara Hanım responded to this defiant silence with her own silence, but in spite of her indifference the young Dilevser didn't have the patience to remain silent. He was different from all the men who'd been there before, he didn't have the unstated but importunate conceitedness of a man who'd been invited by a woman, and she found his long face and nonchalant stance interesting.

"Are you a colonel?" she asked suddenly.

Her emphasis made it more than clear that she disdained any military rank, whether it be high or low.

"No," he said.

As she was bringing her silver spoon to her mouth, Dilara Hanım paused suddenly and, without raising her head, glanced at Ragıp Bey and her daughter before continuing with her soup.

"What are you, then?

"I'm a major."

"Did I unwittingly say something offensive?"

"Not at all, why would you say anything offensive to me?"

"You speak as if you're angry."

Dilara Hanım listened to their exchange without interrupting, she was curious about how Ragıp Bey would handle her daughter's tactlessness.

"No, I'm not angry, I'm just not accustomed to this type of conversation."

Dilara Hanım decided to interrupt because the conversation had lost its focus and might go in the wrong direction, so she gave Ragıp Bey an attractive smile, though it was difficult to tell whether it was tender or mocking.

"What type of conversation are you accustomed to?"

"The type of conversation officers have among themselves."

"And what are they like?"

"Just what you'd expect, we talk about the nation's problems and about military matters."

As she reached for the salt, Dilara Hanım quipped, "That is, matters that women don't understand."

"Please, I didn't say that, though I do imagine ladies wouldn't relish that kind of conversation."

"Does this nation belong to gentlemen alone, Ragıp Bey? Why wouldn't ladies relish talking about these matters? You yourself saw it just a little while ago, when the nation starts going down the drain, men reach for our veils first; if men understood the nation's problems as well as they say they do we wouldn't be in this situation, our finances wouldn't be in the hands of thieves and our streets wouldn't be controlled by thugs."

Thus time Ragıp Bey was genuinely surprised and was unable to conceal it; it was so unexpected for him to hear a woman talk about finances that he opened his eyes wide in near horror.

Dilara Hanım continued in a serious tone:

"Why are you so surprised? You don't even realize that your surprise itself is a kind of insult; all men are like that, I know; this isn't about you, but to tell the truth I'd like to meet a man who thought differently . . . Look, when Dilevser's father died I went to the Ministry of Finance and the Ministry of War to have the Pasha's pension transferred to her, I saw for myself what a mess things were there and I wasn't able to get a penny out of them, in the end I said, 'To hell with it,' and let it go; if we didn't have any income we would have been dependent on strangers, we would have had to open our arms for men in exchange for money like the poor women on the streets."

Ragıp Bey blushed deeply and simply murmured, "Please."

"Why are you embarrassed, Ragıp Bey, isn't this the reality of life, don't you see the women I see, you might not visit them yourself, but your fellow officers who came to save the capital certainly visit them, I know they do, and they never think about how these women ended up in that position . . . I've travelled all over Europe, you've been there too, you've seen it, I have firsthand experience of what developed nations are like; I'm not blind, I saw, I'm not deaf, I heard, I'm not stupid, I think, I argued with people who understand these things, I read books, the Pasha, God bless him, was a very open-minded person, he wanted me to see and learn. If you ask me what I learned, all developed nations have set their women free, there, men and women stand shoulder to shoulder, a nation that keeps its women imprisoned at home can't and won't develop."

Dilara Hanım put down her spoon and continued, "Without women, Ragıp Bey, there is no nation, look at this nation's streets, there's no need to think deeply about it, you can see it right away, a nation where there are no women in the streets is a poor nation in every sense, like ours. Poor women, all of them are prisoners in their own homes today, you may be free, but at best yours is the impoverished freedom of a guard who wastes his life in prison."

This time Dilevser, feeling sorry for Ragıp Bey, interrupted.

"Mother, if you keep talking like that, we'll end up sending Ragıp Bey away hungry, he hasn't eaten a bite since you started in on him."

Her mother looked at her and then smiled.

"Excuse me, Ragıp Bey, I'm not giving you a chance to eat, perhaps this is why you don't allow us to talk, because we talk so much when we do."

Ragıp Bey had never met a woman who talked like this, even in Germany he never met a woman who compared men and women and blamed men.

"Please, you speak well, I learned something from what you said."

"Now I'll allow you to eat in peace, we can discuss these matters another time."

Once again Dilara Hanım had implied that they would see each other again, that she'd simply decided this, she wasn't the least bit shy about her inviting manner. As Ragıp Bey said to Osman later, "The most impressive thing about her was that she wasn't ashamed of the things other people are ashamed of."

Dilevser served Ragıp Bey some more food.

"My mother never stops talking about this, she's very sensitive about equality between men and women."

"Equality between men and women?"

"That's impossible, isn't it, Ragıp Bey, equality is impossible."

In spite of himself, Ragıp Bey reacted without thinking.

"But men go to war, we fight and die."

"Who are you fighting for, Ragıp Bey, who are you dying for? Is fighting and dying the only way to prove your manhood, is war a manhood contest among men, or do you fight for those who've been left behind, that is, for women?"

Ragıp Bey fell silent, and Dilara Hanım kept after him.

"Why don't you answer?"

"When you're under siege, Dilara Hanım, you have to think carefully before making a sortie, if you don't, as I just didn't, it ends in disaster, so if you don't mind, I need a chance to think."

"You're not under siege, you're among friends."

"I'm accustomed to enemies, Dilara Hanım, it will take some time to become accustomed to friends."

Dilara Hanım knew how far she could go in provoking men, she knew instinctively when to stop, knew when she was discomfiting them and how to ease this discomfiture with a smile. She realized that if she kept it up, Ragıp Bey would become genuinely frightened of her, he wouldn't be able to bear this fear and he'd flee.

If she was going to frighten a man like this she would do it after he was so attached he couldn't leave and not on the first day they met; moreover this officer was one of the few men who could respond to her naturalness, which could be considered terrifying, with the same kind of naturalness, who didn't try to appear to be more than he actually was, he wasn't ridiculous like those officers who'd spent their lives in the mountains and tried to pretend they were sophisticated, even when the conversation was getting the better of him. Even though he'd lost the argument, the way he accepted his defeat earned him both women's admiration, and it was always important to Dilara Hanım to feel that her daughter admired a man.

Ragıp Bey didn't say a word about himself, about what he'd experienced in Macedonia, the skirmishes he'd been in, his heroic past, his house, his wife, his father-in-law, who was one of the most famous sheikhs in the empire.

When, after having a last cognac with his coffee, Ragıp Bey climbed into the carriage that had been readied for him and left the mansion, he was even more of a mystery than he'd been when he arrived. Both women sensed the manly confidence concealed beneath this officer's silence and realized he wasn't like the men who'd come to the mansion before him. By saying nothing, Ragıp Bey had told these women much more about himself than he'd intended, they were much better than men at understanding these kinds of things; it was to this that he owed being invited to dinner two days later.

On the deserted, snow-covered streets, where the gas lamps augmented rather than alleviated the loneliness and silence, he sat in the carriage listening to the wheels roll through the snow and the deep sound of the horses' hooves, he felt as surprised, awed, and frightened as a shepherd who'd met a mythical creature who changed her appearance every time her reflection appeared on the river that flowed through the forest, now as a water fairy, now as a mermaid and now as a dragon.

In his world, courage, determination, and prowess were valued over cleverness, bright ideas, and precise observations, he'd always earned the admiration of both men and women without any effort, as if it was his natural right. He earned admiration without even trying to, and women desired him. He'd seen the same look in Dilara Hanım's glances that night, but instead of pleasing him, this desire felt more like an insult. He knew enough about woman to realize that Dilara Hanım wanted him not as a man, but as a plaything, that she didn't care at all about his feelings and desires, that her desire contained no admiration or passion. Dilara Hanım had chosen Ragıp Bey the way a pampered woman showed the shop assistant the dress she liked in the window, she'd pick him up like a trollop she found in the street, take him into her bed, and then send him packing when she tired of him.

It excited Ragıp Bey to experience two contradictory feelings that usually aren't experienced together in love games, being desired and being defeated, he wanted to get closer to this woman, but he also wanted to mistreat her.

A feminine fragility was added to the famous, manly anger that terrified and intimidated everyone who met him for the first time, he wanted to take Dilara Hanım in his arms and show her the pleasure of womanhood and the aggressiveness of manhood, but he also wanted her to caress him lovingly, a miracle occurred on that snowy night, the feminine fragility that conceals itself in the deepest, darkest corners of every man woke with all its weakness, powerlessness, helplessness, wanting to be loved; tender, impatient, and full of lustful expectation, Ragıp Bey was dragged into the mystical landscape called love, which no man could survive without the guidance of a woman, where there were no maps and where people forgot everything they saw as soon as they passed it.

Like every woman who knows how to impress men and subjugate them, Dilara Hanım had quickly awakened Ragıp Bey's feminine side, the feminine side that men who have never even sensed its existence must wake before they can fall in love, and this triggered his desire to be loved.

In just a few hours his destiny and his life had changed, an unhappy but peaceful man had become a restless man who dreamt of happiness.

4

One morning as Hüseyin Hikmet Bey found himself arriving in Istanbul, which from a distance looked like a large, soft, scalloped lace with all its domes, minarets, towers, hills, and woods spreading over snow-covered hills, he saw seabirds scooping struggling fish that gleamed with phosphorescence from water that had paled with the falling snow, white doves fluttering noisily from mosque court-yards, shadows with red fezzes that looked like drops of blood that had fallen onto white wool when a coy woman pricked herself as she was crocheting, and the long, black *caiques* that moved through all that whiteness like some kind of black magic, inhaled the fragrance of Persian tobacco from the coffee-houses that lined the shore and the mixed scent of tar, human sweat, daffodils, and chrysanthemums from the flower fields on the hills, and shivered.

He felt that this city, which until then had been an enter-taining place to stop as he migrated to another land, had become his home, that no matter what happened he would never be able to move away, that wherever he went he would end up returning, and though the adventurer in him was sad-dened to realize that the days of eager travelling of his youth were over, he felt the peace of knowing he had a homeland.

As he made his way down to the quay through the women from first class, with their silk abiyas, soft clouds of scent hang-ing in the air, and soft furs, he saw something he'd never hoped for: His father was standing beside the carriage waiting for him. Reşit Pasha had come to meet his son. He felt more sadness than joy to see his father waiting for him; then at that moment he realized it would take either great joy or great sorrow for traditions to change suddenly.

Reşit Pasha wore the tired and understanding expression seen on the faces of those who had lost the wealth, power, fame, or a personal trait that had set them apart and made them superior to others. His face had not become more lined, but it was as if the lines had deepened, and the slowness of his movements and the darkness in his eyes suggested that while he had resigned himself to his fate it had cost him the sacrifice of a good part of his power and of his faith in himself.

As father and son looked at each other as men with opposing world views and from opposing camps, and who hadn't quite adapted to the camps they'd joined, they each felt an odd sorrow; each knew the other was suffering, and each was more saddened by the other's distress than he was by his own.

Hikmet Bey bowed and kissed his father's hand with a more genuine respect than usual; Reşit Pasha did something he'd never done before, he hugged his son, hugged him as if he was a small child.

"How are you?"

"I'm well, thank you, how are you, you're looking well."

Reşit Pasha found it unnecessary to mention his worries about the future and even his fear that his life might be in danger.

"Yes, I'm fine."

After a brief pause, he asked in a hesitant tone:

"And how are you?"

Hikmet Bey realized his father was asking about his wound but didn't want to talk openly about what had happened. He sensed that if he glossed over it now in such a hesitant tone it would remain between them like a ghost they never mentioned, so he answered openly:

"My wound is completely healed, it aches a little when it's cold but other than that there's no problem."

"Good, come, let's get into the carriage, we can talk on the way."

They climbed into the carriage, the driver loaded Hikmet Bey's luggage into the back, and they set off. On account of the snow the usual noisy crowds were absent and the streets seemed deserted. Hikmet Bey wiped the condensation off the window with his buckskin gloves, but all he could see outside was whiteness.

"I rented a mansion for you in Nişantaşı, we had to do everything in a hurry so there might be a few things missing, you can work all of that out with the housekeeper, it's a nice, quiet place with a large garden."

"Thank you, that was very thoughtful of you, I really do need quiet . . . I sent a telegram to my mother asking her to send the children, I want to have them with me."

A smile appeared on Reşit Pasha's face.

"Your mother isn't going to send the children."

Hikmet Bey sat up a little in his seat.

"I don't understand."

The Pasha shook his head as if he was speaking about a spoiled child.

"She's coming herself, and of course she's bringing the children. She sent word to say that she wanted to see that old man having his nose rubbed in it with her own eyes. The old man, you may have guessed, is his majesty the Sultan."

For his father to have repeated his mother's mocking words about the Sultan showed that the effect of constitutional monarchy had spread even to the palace.

"How is the Sultan?"

"How do you think he is, he's distressed about being betrayed by the very army he put so much effort into building, it seems to have aged him suddenly."

"Please don't do this, father, you know as well as I do that he's been bathing this nation in blood for years, that he's destroyed the lives of so many officers and intellectuals, please don't speak of him as if he's an innocent old man, we only did what had to be done, and indeed as far as I'm concerned it wasn't enough."

The Pasha didn't seem to want to engage in this argument, indeed he even seemed secretly pleased that his son was on the winning side even if he was on the losing side.

"I don't want to argue with you about this, Hikmet, but don't forget, this man you say has blood on his hands gave us everything we have, even if no one else feels this way I have a debt of gratitude to him and I'll never forget it."

Just as his father was secretly pleased that his son was on the winning side, Hikmet Bey was secretly pleased that his father hadn't changed sides, that in these tumultuous times he hadn't sold out his former master to save his life.

"How are things in the city?"

"Very chaotic, the Sultan isn't in control of the situation, you know that parliament has opened but no one is in control of the situation, your friends thought about proclaiming constitutional monarchy but they didn't think about what to do next, I could go as far as to say the declaration of constitutional monarchy was more of a surprise to them than it was to the Sultan, they're not prepared in any way to govern the country, everything is even more out of control than it was before . . . I'm afraid this can't last long, dark and evil days are coming, if you ask me."

"Dark for whom?"

"For everyone, Hikmet. Believe me, for everyone."

Silence reigned in the carriage, neither of them wanted to upset the other by getting into a pointless political argument.

"Anyway, never mind all that now, whatever happens we'll all see it together, let's go directly to my house, the housekeeper had all your favorite dishes prepared, they'll move your things into your mansion while we're eating."

Hikmet suddenly worried about his father.

"Are you alright?" he asked in a low voice.

The Pasha sighed, looked at his son, and gave him a smile that was slightly nonchalant and full of fatherly love.

"I'm getting older, Hikmet, I no longer expect anything from life, I have nothing to console myself with, after all these years of living with the Sultan it's as if I've started to resemble him, when he suddenly got old, I got old too, but I don't think I'm upset about this, on the contrary I'm happy about getting older, about feeling as if I'm a guest in this world, I don't care about the issues that used to be important to me, maybe this is what old age is like, who knows."

Hikmet Bey realized his father was trying to embrace old age in haste to pull himself aside before life itself pulled him aside, but even though he'd fought for the abolition of the palace his father was a part of, he couldn't stand to see Reşit Pasha accepting old age and changed the subject.

"Did my mother say when she was coming?"

"You know how your mother is, she could be waiting for you when you get home, she might have said she was coming at once and not appear for years . . . To tell the truth I don't know when she's coming, but don't worry, she'll be here before long, she hasn't forgotten that the Sultan exiled her, she won't let that go without taking the chance to tell the Sultan, 'You see, you sent me away, but here I am, I'm back.' She'll be here soon."

Reşit Pasha fell silent and closed his eyes, he seemed to be hesitating about what he was going to say.

"In fact this isn't a good time for her to come here, I didn't want you to come either, these are dangerous times, the whole empire is restless, new uprisings are on the point of breaking out in Arabia, Kurdistan, and the Balkans, no one has any power here in the capital, even your committee is split into two factions, one of them is establishing a new party, there are going to be new showdowns here."

Hikmet listened, and like all children he thought his father was exaggerating, but what he would experience within a few months would show him how right he'd been.

That night Hikmet Bey stayed at his father's mansion. When he saw how much the housekeeper and his now quite elderly Ethiopian nanny had missed him, how much they loved him, and how sorry they were for him, it wounded him to realize how he'd hurt those who loved him and once more he felt humiliated by what he'd had to experience.

His father tried to conceal the pain he felt for him, he knew how wounding this was for a man because he'd lost his wife too. Only a few times did Hikmet Bey catch his father looking at him in helpless sadness, as if he was looking at a cripple who'd lost part of his body.

They ate in silence as they were accustomed to do: the cooks, under the stern and rigorous supervision of the housekeeper, had prepared the most distinguished Ottoman dishes for their Pasha's son. Hikmet Bey ate like a child who'd come home from boarding school, gorging himself on pilaf with cream, seared cutlets, and Kayseri dumplings so tiny that forty could fit in a spoon, and his father, who was trying not to let on that he was examining his son as a doctor examines a patient, was pleased.

Over coffee they chatted like friends in a way they'd rarely done before: they didn't mention Mehpare Hanım, they gossiped about Mihrişah Sultan, Reşit Pasha loved to make witty remarks about his ex-wife, as well as about the Pashas' greed and bad manners. They talked about how Bulgaria's declaration of independence while the Ottoman empire was experiencing the turmoil of constitutional monarchy, the ceding of Bosnia-Herzegovina to the Austro-Hungarian Empire, and the annexation of Crete by the Kingdom of Greece might lead to war in the Balkans.

They both took care to avoid domestic politics; if Reşit Pasha was upset that his son was a member of the organization that had overthrown the Sultan, he didn't let on; perhaps he was pleased that his son had chosen to struggle for liberty rather than live off the treasury as other Pashas' sons did, but he didn't say so.

They both felt the most important thing was to be honest and ethical, and the only way they could be honest was by completely opposing the other's ideas. They accepted that destiny had toyed with them like this and had made them experience such contradictions.

Towards midnight Reşit Pasha announced that he was going to bed.

"Your room is ready too, the housekeeper will help you."

Hikmet Bey told him to let the housekeeper sleep, he knew where his room was, but the Pasha either didn't hear him or pretended not to; he left the living room without answering, walking with the cheerful liveliness he experienced whenever he passed through the harem, no matter what was going on in his life.

After his father left, Hikmet Bey lit a cigarette and looked at the Bosphorus, flowing pitch-black under the falling snow; now for the first time, being with his father brought him a sense of peace, and he felt secure in the house that, as a child, he had always associated with missing Paris and being bored with where he was.

After finishing his cigarette he stood, went to the living-room door to go to the room in which he hadn't slept for years; as he made his way toward the door he remembered the happy, carefree days of childhood and for a moment thought about the shame and torment that weighed him down; he remembered reading Faust when he was young, and smiled at the thought that he would have to make a bargain with the devil to undo what he had experienced. Later he would tell Osman, "Sometimes you want to bargain with someone over your destiny, but as God doesn't bargain, who else can you bargain with except the devil?"

That night there was no devil to bargain with either, or, at least until he passed through the living-room door he thought the devil would have no interest in him.

As he passed through the living room door, the housekeeper, who'd been napping in a chair by the door, stood, rubbed her eyes, and picked up the oil lamp beside her.

"Why didn't you go to bed, I haven't forgotten where my room is, do you think I have amnesia?"

There was the same gleam in the housekeeper's eyes as when she used to give Hikmet candy when he was a child, she didn't pay attention to what he'd said, and she answered as she made her way down the corridor.

"Oh, my dear Hikmet Bey, how could I go to bed before settling you in your room, you're a strange one, do you think I would leave you in the living room like an abandoned sack and go to bed?"

They made their way down the corridor to the sounds of waves striking the boathouse, the windows rattling in the wind, and the creaking of the wooden house, which seemed to increase at night. As he made his way down the dim corridor he heard the same sounds he used to hear as a child, when he used to worry that the "bath mother" his Ethiopian nanny had invented to frighten him might jump out at him; he noticed that this fear that had been instilled in him as a child was still there, even though it had diminished he still felt a tingling in his spine; the childhood he'd thought he'd lost had not vanished completely, there were still traces of it in the walls, the corridors and the sounds of the house where he'd lived so long ago.

When he reached his room, the housekeeper partly opened the door and made way for him. He bade her good night, and she replied, "Just call me if you need anything, I'm awake, now good night, my brave young man."

After the chilly corridor, he felt the warmth of the pinkish-green, pot-bellied glazed tile stove burning in the center of the room; as he looked around the room, he saw the girl waiting for him by the window; he went back to the still partly open door, threw it open, and shouted for the housekeeper.

As the housekeeper made her way down the corridor she answered softly, without bothering to turn around or hide the mockery in her voice.

"A gift from his excellency the Pasha."

For a moment Hikmet Bey stood in front of the door, at a loss for what to do; the housekeeper had already reached the end of the corridor and had disappeared from view, there was only the faint light of the oil lamps that had been placed at intervals but that provided little illumination. Then, as there was nothing else to do, he went in and closed the door.

The girl was wearing shiny white baggy trousers of ruffled silk that ended just above her ankles, a white tunic of the same cloth that came to her knees, a thick, silver Circassian belt around her waist, and white, flat heeled, pearl-embroidered shoes that left her pink heels exposed. Her thick black hair, rubbed with musk, and with a line of glass beads on the ends, fell over her shoulders; right away Hikmet Bey noticed the greyish-blue eyes under her long, black eyelashes and her shiny, black, violin-bow eyebrows that became thinner at the ends and that almost met in the middle. The mist of the bath-house she'd clearly just left still clung to her, and the flush on her fine-boned cheeks was from hot, soapy water rather than from shame; she clasped her thin-fingered hands just below her belly and bowed her head.

At another time Hikmet Bey would have been angered by

this imposition and found it insulting to be given a woman as a gift, but he had become accustomed enough to desperation to realize it was his father's desperate attempt to alleviate his son's suffering even though he knew he was being pathetic; he accepted the gesture without anger, and indeed with the gratitude of knowing someone was worried about him. In addition to his tolerant maturity, there was a part of his body that had not touched a woman in months.

He walked toward the stove.

"What's your name?"

She had a harmonious voice, it sounded as if she was singing.

"Sir, they told me you were to call me whatever you wanted."

"Don't you have a name? Is it up to me to name you?"

"No, sir."

Hikmet Bey didn't insist, he realized she would insist on doing as she'd been told, it was clear she'd been told that if she pleased the gentleman it would save her life. The poor girl was ready to relinquish her entire past to save her future, she'd give him her name, her past and her body, and if he wished, Hikmet Bey would take care of her and make her life secure. The bargain was open and clear. Hikmet Bey made a face, but then accepted the bargain that had been made for him.

He sat on the bed.

"Then let your name be Hediye."

As soon as he sat, she came over to him, knelt, and began taking off his shoes. He hurriedly pulled his feet away.

"Please stop."

She rose to her feet in fear and gave him a pleading look.

"Come, sit next to me. I can undress myself. Where are you from?"

"I'm Circassian, sir"

"That's clear from your beauty."

He felt the mortification of being a woman's absolute

master, but at the same time he felt a boundless excitement that was open to any kind of desire. Having a woman without making any effort and knowing that this was not his privilege alone, that it had nothing to do with his past, his intellect, his knowledge or his personality or any of his adventures, none of his pain had anything to do with the girl sleeping with him, and knowing that someone else could have slept with the girl that night stripped him of his past and all the values that made him Hikmet Bey and transformed him from someone who had gained his place in society through his own efforts to a man who had only been created at that moment.

His body was tingling, and he noticed that his hands shook slightly with the strange embarrassment of knowing that a woman who had no interest in his past or his future would give him all she possessed that night without question and without evasion, and this aroused a physical lust that was unconcerned with thoughts or feelings.

When he'd slept with prostitutes in Paris in his youth he'd always felt both a wretchedness that was like falling off a cliff and a pleasure that was like rising up to the sky, untrammeled by any moral or emotional concerns, and the tension of being pulled in opposite directions gave him a boundless and unnamable animalistic gratification to which he didn't give much thought.

Suddenly the room seemed too bright.

"Please douse the lamps, except the one by the bedside."

Hediye sensed that Hikmet Bey desired her; when she stood, her hips were level with his face; summoning nearly all her power to her body in a way that only women can do, she walked slowly, confident as she extinguished the lamps that the powerful light emanating from her body would touch the man's flesh. As the light dimmed, the brilliance of her white silk clothes increased, and when there was only one lamp left burning she turned and sat next to Hikmet Bey.

The large, tiled stove burned hotter and hotter, trembling from time to time as coals settled and the constant sound of the waves and currents of the dark waters of the Bosphorus crashing against the boathouse echoed through the deserted corridors of the waterfront mansion.

After most of the lamps had been extinguished the room sank into the dimness Hikmet Bey wanted, everything lost its true form in this shadow realm, all of the furniture, the stove, the consoles, the mirrors, closets, and carpets flowed out of their forms and beyond the boundaries that constrained them in the light, flowing into each other like melted glass, they gained such a magical mobility that they could seem completely different each time you looked at them.

In this warm, dim room in which shadows grew larger, Hikmet Bey could change form just as the furniture did, from the pale, pansy-faced aristocratic patient of the nuns in Salonika to the "perverted" Pasha's son seeking "deviant" pleasures among the red-gartered prostitutes of the Paris brothels.

There was no one in the room but himself to feel ashamed before; in his mind, which was shutting down in the fog created by his increasingly impassioned desire, all feelings including shame vanished. He told Hediye to undress and lie naked on the bed and looked at her for a while. He told her to open her legs, close them, then open them again; he undressed without taking his eyes off her body, touched one of her small feet, then took both feet in his hands, kneeled at the foot of the bed completely naked, and rested her feet against his cheek.

It snowed until morning, and throughout the night they tried everything Hikmet Bey had learned from the prostitutes in Paris as well as what he and Mehpare Hanım had discovered together. From her first man, Hediye learned many pleasures and games many women in that city had never known, never would know or even hear of, moaning sometimes in pain and sometimes in pleasure, she did whatever he wanted of her and in addition managed to derive pleasure from everything she did; she understood how women who were cast aside by day could bind a man to them at night.

As black-cloaked muezzins climbed the minarets, white with snow, that had been erected like long fingers pointing to God, to recite the morning call to prayer and announce to the city that a new day and a new prayer time had arrived, Hikmet Bey, like every sinner who has made love to someone other than the person they loved and derived pleasure from it, came to the painful realization that the person he loved could also derive pleasure from someone else, he thought about Mehpare Hanım as he fell asleep, his weary body satisfied by pleasure and his mind tormented by jealousy. He wondered what Mehpare was doing at that moment and, realizing he didn't want to know, pressed himself against Hediye's warmth and drifted into unknowable dreams in which his face once again resembled a pansy.

When he woke in the morning he felt stronger than he had for some time, it was as if he had regained the pride and the manhood he'd lost; when he turned in bed and stretched like a big cat, he saw the woman who'd given him so much pleasure sitting in a chair by the head of the bed. She was wearing a long velvet navy-blue dress with a raised collar that was fastened with a button and the same silver belt she'd been wearing before. The dark rings under her eyes were traces of the previous night; it was probably because of the color of the dress that these rings also seemed navy blue and this gave her face a weary but somehow more meaningful expression; when she saw he was awake she smiled and it surprised him to see her smile, for some reason it had never occurred to him that she could smile at him, that they could have this kind of relationship.

"Would you like me to bring your breakfast or would you prefer to have it in the dining room, sir?"

Hikmet Bey was ashamed to have breakfast in his room with Hediye as if they were newlyweds.

"Tell them to put breakfast out for me in the dining room."

"As you wish, sir."

When Hediye left the room he dressed hurriedly because he was shy of her returning and seeing him naked. He was tying his tie when she entered.

"They're preparing your breakfast."

After hesitating a moment, and with the natural closeness only women could show when sharing privacy, she said, "They've lit the fire in the bathhouse, aren't you going to wash?"

He worried that the inhabitants of the waterfront mansion would make fun of him, so he answered angrily:

"No, I'll bathe when I get to my own home, there's no need now."

"As you wish."

"Is the Pasha here?"

"They left early this morning, sir."

Hikmet Bey relaxed, he didn't want to see his father this morning, he realized his father was also reluctant to see him; both of them felt they shouldn't see each other for some time so that they could digest their complicity.

He didn't touch the olives with thyme, the jams, the cheeses brought specially from the four corners of the empire, hard-boiled eggs, pastries, honey that smelled of flowers, fresh cream, and butter which had been prepared for him and hurriedly drank his tea as Hediye and the housekeeper stood watching him, then he turned to the housekeeper.

"Tell them to get the carriage ready, I'm going to look at my new house."

"The carriage is ready, Hikmet Bey, we can go whenever you wish."

"Where are we going?"

"To the mansion in Nişantaşı."

Hikmet Bey grumbled angrily like an overindulged son of a Pasha.

"I know that, what do you mean when you say we're going."

"The Pasha ordered me to stay with you for a while and get the house in order."

Then she nodded toward Hediye.

"She's coming with us."

Hikmet Bey realized that dragging his feet was only going to make things more difficult.

"Then get ready as quickly as you can."

"We're ready, we'll just put on our abiyas and we can leave."

The two women hurried out of the room so as to not annoy him further, Hikmet saw the hurt in Hediye's eyes, but tried not to pay any heed; the poor girl realized that the man who had shared everything with her the night before wanted to go away and leave her there.

The two women returned a few minutes later in their abiyas and carrying bundles, they got into the carriage without speaking and remained silent all the way to the mansion in Nişantaşı; they were frightened by Hikmet Bey's irritability. The house-keeper realized he was irritable because he was ashamed, but Hediye wasn't in a position to understand this, she thought he didn't like her.

The two-story stone mansion was situated in a large garden, a pebbled driveway led to a large door, there were five steps leading to the door, there was another, similar two-story stone mansion, surrounded by low walls, on the other side of the garden, but Hikmet Bey didn't even look at it, he had no intention of being neighborly.

The interior of the mansion resembled that of the one in Şişli where he'd lived with Mehpare Hanım, or at least that morning Hikmet Bey thought it looked similar to his old house; the servants had cleaned the house, lit all the stoves, and built fires in the fireplaces before the master's arrival, it was nice and warm in the house.

As soon as Hikmet Bey entered the house he tersely ordered a fire to be lit for his bath, when they told him this had already been done he became even more irritated. He found fault with everyone and everything, striding through the house in a rage that made the servants' knees tremble, commanding them to move one piece of furniture after another and then, when the footmen and maids picked the furniture up to move it, angrily telling them to leave it where it was. He was aware that his irritable manner was unbecoming, but he couldn't control himself.

In the end he went to take his bath and let the inhabitants of the mansion breathe a sigh of relief; the large, marble-floored room was filled with lavender-scented steam, the Italian bathtub had been placed under nickel-plated faucets from Austria. He undressed and was about to step into the tub when Hediye entered, bowed her head, and asked in a wounded voice if he needed anything.

In her heavy, navy-blue dress she looked odd in that steamy room, and when he looked at her he involuntarily remembered how she looked naked and the pleasure she'd given him the previous night; when he remembered this he suddenly wondered what Mehpare Hanım was doing at that moment, but remembering Mehpare didn't keep him from desiring this girl, nor did desiring this girl help him get Mehpare off his mind. It was as if he was tangled in a chain, as he desired the girl he remembered Mehpare Hanım more often and became even more jealous, but he couldn't stop desiring that girl.

He spoke as if he was rebuking her.

"You'll get sweaty here in that dress."

She could have interpreted these words in two ways, she could either leave so as not to sweat or she could take off the dress; Hikmet Bey left the decision to her, for some reason he was ashamed to express his desire openly. Hediye wasn't sure of what he was saying, of what he wanted, she stepped forward through the steam and looked at his face; that morning she sensed she could only ascertain what he wanted from his expression rather than from his words.

In spite of his shouting, his anger, the way he spoke to everyone as if he was scolding them, there was a pleading expression in Hikmet Bey's eyes. This morning he was ashamed to tell this girl, who was prepared to do anything he wished, what he wanted, perhaps what made him bashful was the thought that the footmen and maids would know about their relationship and that what happened between them would become public knowledge, it disturbed him to realize that after all he'd lived through the only woman in his life was a Circassian concubine and that everyone knew about it.

Hediye started to unbutton her dress, but as she did so she couldn't resist taking her womanly revenge, she unbuttoned the little buttons with maddening slowness, using this slowness to show him that even in a relationship in which she had no voice only a woman could master herself and create a space for herself, even if it be insignificant, to pay him back for the hurt of wanting her so much when they were alone and humiliating her when they were with others. Hikmet Bey realized what she was doing and noticed that she was displaying an unbecoming artlessness, he smiled and decided there and then to not treat her badly in front of others, and as she undressed he realized that this was in fact what constituted his bad behavior.

He smiled.

"You seem to be having trouble taking that off, do you need my help?"

"I can take it off myself, sir."

"Why do you call me sir every time you open your mouth?"

"That's what I was always taught."

Hikmet Bey bowed his head toward the bathtub.

"Ok, then, let's take it off, sir."

This little joke worked right away and Hediye unbuttoned her dress very quickly. Hikmet Bey was truly surprised when he saw that she wasn't wearing anything under the dress.

After that, he treated her like a lady and made the servants treat her the same way; Hediye demonstrated that she deserved this treatment by not changing her attitude and her respectful manner. Hikmet Bey felt that the bond between them was strengthening every day; this wasn't love, he was still in love with Mehpare Hanım and would never love Hediye in the same way, but it seemed as if this young girl had become part of his body, he always wanted her with him, he liked being with her, bathing with her, sleeping with her, joking with her, it wouldn't have been easy to give her up, at times he surprised her and made her happy with expensive gifts, and was always curious if Mehpare Hanım had experienced the same kind of thing.

There was no one in this enormous city from whom he could get any news about Mehpare Hanım, her relatives had already passed away, he couldn't have asked them even if they were alive, indeed it was impossible for him to ask about the wife who'd left him for another man. He wanted to know what Mehpare Hanım was experiencing, he couldn't overcome his curiosity even though he knew it would hurt him, that it would sadden him, that it might even distance him from Hediye, who lately had been the greatest joy in his life.

At that time there were only two people in the capital who knew what Mehpare Hanım was experiencing with that Greek womanizer in Khalkidhiki, one of them was Hasan Efendi, who never forgot that beautiful woman even when everyone else did, as if he wanted to demonstrate that enemies could be more loyal than friends, and who gathered information about her in ways that only he knew about, and the other was sheikh

Yusuf Efendi, who knew everything Hasan Efendi knew. They both knew that Mehpare Hanım was very happy and didn't care what the world thought, and this caused them as much pain as it would have caused Hikmet Bey if he'd known.

5

T hree days after celebrating the New Year in Khalkidhiki, Mehpare Hanım returned to Salonica with Constantine, believing that the gossip would have subsided by then, and Salonica greeted the beautiful woman with the smell of eucalyptus trees, which had been sharpened by winter rains.

Despite being controlled by Muslims, the city breathed in Christian smells such as the scent of flowers from the gardens of the wealthy neighborhood where it seemed the silence would never be broken, the smell of beer and fried calamari from the beer halls that lined the shore, the smell of seaweed and the sea along the shore, the smell of cocoa, milk, and vanilla emanating from the patisseries, the smell of cognac and women from the *cafes chantants*.

The declaration of liberty was felt more strongly here than it was in the capital, political life was being experienced with such enthusiasm that it seemed as if it could turn into a fair-ground fight at any moment.

Minority communities and socialist and liberal parties organized meetings and congresses to draw up their own roadmaps of the new life they assumed would be established in the empire. For their part the Committee members who had left their mark on the city were bewildered and disquieted even though they had become legendary throughout the empire, they were frightened by the power they'd seized so suddenly, this power weighed heavily on their shoulders, and they couldn't come to the fore in governing the nation.

There was such a dangerous uncertainty in the nation, no one could bring themselves to seize the reins of power, everyone feared their hands would be scalded and they would pay for this with their lives; even though there was a sultan, a cabinet, a parliament, the Committee for Union and Progress, which had brought about the declaration of constitutional monarchy and that was considered powerful, and political parties of various stripes, no one was governing the nation and short-term decisions were dragging the nation toward disaster.

The liberty that had been greeted with celebration was turning into an angry and impassioned anarchy that presaged a bloody future presided over by an administration unaccustomed to governance.

In those strange and confusing days, as the empire experienced an irritable joy on the eve of bloody tumult, no one noticed Mehpare Hanım settle into her Greek lover's large mansion outside the city. Just like the empire itself, she was experiencing the freest, most enthusiastic, most restless, and happiest days of her own history.

Her life had never been so uncertain, her future had never seemed so uncharted, but, perhaps for the first time, she was not frightened by this uncertainty, on the contrary, it intensified her desire to live, her desire to cling to life like someone clinging to a branch on the edge of a cliff.

The wild restlessness of her flesh had always suffocated a soul that had been pampered by the confidence of knowing she had always and would always be loved, this restlessness grew within a discomfiting silence, meeting no obstacles and turning her into a nervous, irritable, and selfish person who constantly sought to satisfy her flesh. Now, for the first time, she'd met a pampered, selfish man who was as accustomed to being loved as she was and who gave the impression he could slip through her fingers at any moment, she learned about jealousy, worry, the fear of loss, and that the soul that had always been comfortable and satisfied confronted the hungry flesh that always expected to be satisfied, and it experienced the same painful hunger as the flesh for the first time.

The new restlessness that had become a part of her life broke her body's insatiable dominance and created an equilibrium and balance between her flesh and her soul and, strangely, this equilibrium calmed her, yes, she was more restless than she had been in the past; now she was curious about where Constantine went, who he met, when he returned, whether he had other women in his life, was he tired of her, and she struggled to make out the meaning of the man's every move, every glance, every change in tone. She no longer had any tolerance for other people, she didn't just pay attention to her man in bed but at every hour of the day, she wanted no one but him, she wanted to be alone with him all the time.

All of this brought her a kind of unhappiness she'd never known, as well as a kind of happiness she'd never known. Despite the small disappointments and worries she was pleased to experience this happiness she'd never known, for the first time since the unfortunate day she'd married sheikh Yusuf Efendi, she left the bedroom and spread out into salons, gardens, and cities.

With an almost animalistic instinct, Constantine nourished her happiness and her unhappiness in the same manner, he allowed both of these feelings to run side by side, never allowing either to pass the other, as if he was driving a two-horse carriage.

On the days he walked next to her among the trees in the garden, holding her hand as he whispered his love to her, embracing her from time to time, and leaning her against a tree trunk for a long kiss, he entertained her with talk about ancient Greek philosophy, poetry, mythology, and other topics she'd had no idea he was knowledgeable about, as well as about his childhood, in a voice that was occasionally as deep and vibrant as that of an Olympian god and occasionally as loud and boastful as that of a young Greek tough down by the harbor. Sometimes after a night during which he always added a surprising new element, a new touch or word or pain to their love games, his soft touch and strong embraces alternately manly or womanly, making her feel deeply the music of one skin touching another, she would wake happy and grateful only to find he had disappeared, causing her to pace fretfully, full of doubt and melancholy, wondering where her man had gone.

He turned their relationship into a grand voyage, full of surprises and adventures, that had no destination yet always promised the arrival in an ever-peaceful harbor.

Mehpare Hanım, who could never confine herself to a single feeling, was constantly distracted and dazzled by excitement, by the storm of changing feelings, she never had the time to be bored by any one feeling, neither happiness nor unhappiness, joy nor sorrow, yearning nor being reunited.

She found happiness in this pain she had newly encountered and that was nourished by doubt and worry; this beautiful and witty woman who was afraid of boredom and distress was capable of deriving pleasure from pain.

The secret of her being able to transform worry, doubt, and jealously into pleasure was the hidden confidence she had that she could turn the tables on Constantine and could wrap him around her little finger as she had other men; this confidence allowed her to submit to pain without doubt, and unlike many people, she didn't flee from pain, indeed on the contrary she feared that this pain would end and that the turmoil of the intoxicating tides in which she lived would run its course.

After many years of living in security, what she needed now was restlessness, doubt, and disquiet; as she told Osman once, "Everyone seeks what they lack, even when what they seek is something others fear finding."

Even though from afar it might have seemed as if Mehpare Hanım was the one who was being scarred, and indeed she was, it discomfited Constantine, who had never encountered anything of this kind, that she desirously abandoned herself to pain and jealousy and derived pleasure from it, and this prodded him to nourish his emotional outbursts. He had difficulty understanding why Mehpare Hanım didn't flee from pain the way other women did, why she didn't try to pressure him into establishing a more secure life or try to prevent the flings he was having.

He had the impression that in this game he always enjoyed playing with women there was a secret plan he couldn't see, and he thought Mehpare Hanım was concealing this, even though it was he who created the doubt and uncertainty in their relationship, he fell into doubt because she didn't complain about her doubt, when he left Mehpare Hanım at the mansion and went into the city, he couldn't take his mind off the woman who was waiting for him, and, when he returned, even though this was something he'd never done before, he questioned the footmen carefully, trying to learn whatever he didn't know, he tried to discover whether she'd had any visitors or if she'd gone out, and when he learned that she never left the mansion he began glancing rancorously at the handsome footmen and the well-built, pretty-faced Albanian gardeners.

For Mehpare Hanım to have submitted unconditionally did not comfort the man who had subjugated her, indeed it disquieted him considerably; if she had protested, complained, reproached him, asked him not to go into the city he would have felt better, but she did none of these things. She enjoyed her suffering, and it was impossible for Constantine to understand this; like all men who think they understand women very well, he was surprised to encounter behavior he'd never seen before in a woman and it shook his confidence.

Mehpare Hanım had managed to captivate a man even as she was submitting to him.

These two people, who until then had enjoyed their power and dominance in love games, one admiring her own beauty and the other admiring his own attractiveness, noticed their own blind sides and weaknesses and experienced the unique taste and excitement of living as slaves to each other, and from time to time they went out among other people to catch their breath and refresh themselves, but because in the Muslim quarter, particularly among the Salonica Committee members, Mehpare Hanım was seen as "a whore who'd run off with an infidel," they had to socialize with foreign dignitaries and wealthy local Greeks.

As usual, Mehpare Hanım stirred waves of admiration in these circles as well, she was always surrounded by men, they listened to the accented French that swept them up in preposterous fantasies and breathed in the mysterious air of her Ottoman levelheadedness which did not allow her to forget her upbringing even when she was in a crowd despite having left her husband. They all secretly wondered, as they always did when they met a woman who'd left her husband, whether she might do the same thing with them the next time, they were surreptitiously making advances toward her, and this wounded Constantine with a jealousy he could not confess to.

At these gatherings, at some point in the evening the men usually discussed politics and occasionally the women became absorbed in their own gossip; then the men and women would gravitate together and return to their accustomed topics, literature, concerts, rising sopranos, the mansion someone had bought recently, stories about travels.

Mehpare Hanım had no interest in politics, and when men began discussing these matters she walked away with an air of disdain, but the victorious tone of their discussions lately, their joy about Greece annexing Crete, the way men and women celebrated together, the way they mocked the Ottomans, the Sultan, and the Committee disturbed her for the first time and made her feel that she was in a foreign milieu. Until then she had divided people into male and female, rich and poor, but the anger she felt when she listened to these discussions led her to realize that there were many more divisions among people.

One night as they were returning from one of these parties, an inevitable argument occurred. Mehpare Hanım rebuked Constantine in an irritable tone.

"What is all this about Crete? . . . aren't you a bit too over-joyed that the Greek government took over an island, don't you find these discussions a bit strange, I don't know, a bit frivolous?"

"What does this have to do with frivolity, why should it be frivolous to feel joy when people are freed from slavery?"

"Why should it concern you that the Greeks have taken over an island, aren't you an Ottoman subject?"

"I'm an Ottoman subject, but I'm Greek, Greek blood runs in my veins."

Constantine usually chose to speak only about light topics with women, and she was infuriated when she heard this.

"Why are you talking about blood now, I used to think you were fonder of wine than blood, did you just discover this blood in your veins, you've never talked like this before."

Constantine wanted to pull her to his side in a friendly manner rather than argue with her.

"Mehpare, the Ottoman Empire has oppressed us so much . . . "

Mehpare Hanım replied fiercely to his friendly tone.

"You don't seem so oppressed, you have your vineyards, your garden, your winery, your wealth . . . Don't you think you're being a bit ungrateful?"

"Wealth isn't always enough, have you ever been humiliated when they call you infidel or Greek *palikari*, have you ever been despised, have you ever felt like a questionable infidel? Have you ever felt that, no matter how rich you are, the poorest Muslim or the most immoral Turk is valued more than you are, is considered more trustworthy than you are?"

Mehpare Hanım shook her head.

"I've never seen anyone treat you badly, I think you're exaggerating a bit."

"You couldn't understand, you've never been looked at that way, you've never been despised or intimidated."

"What do you mean? I go through that at every party we go to."

"What are you talking about, everyone treats you as if you're one of us, they flock around you."

"Isn't this an insult? I'm not one of you, and I feel that if I say this you'll all reject me."

"Now you're exaggerating," he said, caressing her hair tenderly. "Let's drop the subject, politics is not our concern, at least there's no room for politics between us."

That night the conversation ended there, they changed the subject, but both of them sadly realized there was a division between them that they'd previously been unaware of.

They took particular care not to bring the subject up again; only once, when mustachioed men in black suits began visiting the mansion more frequently at night and she saw the hostility with which they looked at her and how impatient they were for her to leave the room, did Mehpare Hanım warn the man she loved.

"Constantine, I don't know exactly what you're up to, but don't even think about being heroic, that's not your thing."

Constantine laughed.

"That means you know all about heroics too."

Mehpare Hanım nodded in an adult manner.

"I was married to a hero who received that kind of guest at night."

Constantine didn't like the subject of Hikmet Bey being brought up, but he pretended not to care.

"So? What happened?"

"He shot himself."

Constantine laughed again.

"He didn't shoot himself because of these visitors, his heroic act was to be with you, and he paid the price."

She sensed something derogatory in these words, so she looked at him and waited for him to continue. Constantine realized he'd crossed a line.

"My heroism is of the same kind, Mehpare, I too am with you and I'll pay for this with my life, I assure you that you're the only danger in my life."

Mehpare Hanım didn't answer, she never brought the subject up again, even though it occasionally worried her she never said so, she just realized that there was an estranging element between them and realized in surprise that there could be more in a relationship between a man and woman than love and lovemaking.

Even though she didn't really care about any of these things, after realizing she'd been so angered by the Christians' joy and that religions, states, and borders could find a place for themselves in even the most private human relationships, she stopped going to parties and shut herself up in the mansion. When Constantine didn't go to the city she carried on her former life with him, and when he did go she either walked in the garden or sat by the fireplace to write letters to her son and daughter, who were with her former mother-in-law.

Nizam, her son from Hikmet Bey, was quick to forgive his mother, especially after his father recovered from his wound, and replied to her with very warm and amusing letters in which, even though they were never more than a page long, he talked of his life with Hanım Sultan and his life in Paris, which he was clearly happy about, in a way that made his mother smile. Nizam, who was able to adapt right away to any new environment, adapted to social life in Paris, became the favorite of the girls at school, and was soon even able to steal kisses from them during the breaks. He was always respectful to his grandmother, he always managed to ingratiate himself with people, and moreover he didn't do this out of lowly opportunism or as a sycophant with a hidden agenda because in fact no one was that important to him and he didn't take anyone seriously enough to upset them, including himself. For Nizam, life was fun and anything that spoiled this fun seemed silly and meaningless. His fellow students were the children of wealthy bourgeoisie and aristocratic families, and he made friends with the more sexually adventurous of them, going to cafes with them after school to drink a glass of red wine and talk about girls and women; having a very wealthy and famous princess for a grandmother, being handsome, witty, and quick, and having the ability to act as if the weight of life was easy to carry soon made him a favorite at school.

Rukiye, however, wasn't as quick as Nizam to accept what had happened to her stepfather and the way her mother had left him; her replies to her mother always had a note of distance and resentment. Just as Nizam's letters amused her, Rukiye's letters saddened her. Her rare letters made Mehpare Hanım feel the unstated blame and she realized her daughter hadn't forgiven her.

She hadn't made many friends at school, her standoffishness kept her friends at a distance, and her response to anything she didn't like made her attitude clear; despite her honesty and openness, indeed perhaps because of them, she attracted everyone's attention as a mysterious and pampered oriental princess, but she kept everyone at a distance.

The only relationship she established, and she didn't know whether it was friendship or love, was with Boris, the self-contained son of the Russian philosophy professor

Koncharov, who had sorrow in his plum-colored eyes and who brushed the pitch-black bangs from his right eyebrow with a patient movement of his hand.

For the first time she experienced the delicious and slightly acrid taste, like that of wild berries, of feeling an interest in another person without talking about feelings, just strolling through this vague and nameless place between friendship and romance.

Like all rebellious children who occasionally act out impudently, she went to the Koncharov house to satisfy her desire to be sheltered, she couldn't find this satisfaction in the father she'd never forgiven for abandoning her, in the mother she'd never forgiven for abandoning her stepfather, or in her step-grandmother, who never showed emotion no matter how much she loved. Almost every day she and Boris walked through the streets, even in rain and snow, and then, numb with cold, went to his house and ate the ham sandwiches Madame Koncharov prepared as she waited impatiently for Professor Koncharov to leave his study and come join them.

Professor Koncharov, who was six feet tall with broad shoulders and long, wavy white hair, resembled a steppe lion; when he talked to the children about philosophy, life, the Russian Revolution of 1905, the Paris Commune, social classes, philosophers, and the small weakness that emerged in their daily lives and stood in such contrast to the extraordinary books they'd written, he spoke in a sonorous voice that was difficult to tame, pleased by their intelligence and interest.

Rukiye impatiently asked every question that came to mind, even those that might seem childish or even stupid, as if she wanted to learn everything she could possibly learn from Professor Koncharov, and he always answered her immediately. As her admiration for and attachment to Professor Koncharov grew, so did her attachment to Boris.

One afternoon as they were drinking cocoa, which

Professor Koncharov laced with cognac when Madame Koncharov wasn't looking, she asked one of her usual difficult questions, "What is philosophy, Professor Koncharov?" and this made him laugh out loud. It was clear that she'd expected a short, clear, and open answer. Koncharov, who was accustomed to such questions from young people who believed life was in fact very simple and easy but that older people overcomplicated things, lit one of the strong, tasteless Russian cigarettes he had such difficulty finding and said, "Now look, Rukovna . . . "

Like many professors who are in fact undercover actors, Professor Koncharov was fond of the sound of his own voice as he launched into a tirade, explaining that philosophy sought the answer to a very simple and ordinary question such as "what is life?" which because it was so ordinary pointed out the ironic meaninglessness in which human fate was imprisoned and which mesmerized with the splendid despair of the knowledge that the answer could never be found, but that even as it pursued unanswerable questions it asked other answerable questions and opened the way for science, which contrary to philosophy always found what it sought, he uttered a sentence Rukiye would never forget, and that changed the course of her life.

"Philosophy is religion's restless brother."

Rukiye, who had been listening to the professor in silence so as not to miss a single sentence, suddenly interrupted.

"Professor, do you hold philosophy to be equal to religion?"

Rukiye, who had always distanced herself from religion because of her anger at her father the Sheikh and who as she belittled religion also belittled her father in an attempt to free herself from the legendary fascination in which he was swathed, was surprised to hear religion mentioned in the same breath as philosophy.

The professor knew that Rukiye's father was a sheikh and also understood her reaction to religion and pursed his lips as he always did when he was thinking.

"My child, when you lie on the grass on a summer night and look up at the stars, if it's not simply a romantic summer activity like songs or dances that make the night more enjoyable, if you really look at the stars and actually see them, then the gates of the sky open to two destinations, religion and philosophy . . . Religion connects the creation of this splendid universe to God and finds peace, this is why religion offers peace and security, because it has found the answer to the question mankind is most curious about; but philosophy, as I just said, is religion's restless brother, it is not satisfied with any answer it finds, and each answer leads to a new question."

Professor Koncharov sensed the pain underlying her rejection of religion and that by rejecting her religion she was rejecting her father, and continued talking to ease the disquiet that comes from rejecting one's father.

"My dear Rukovna, one should avoid simplistic judgments; we don't have to be religious, we don't have to believe in God, but we do have to ask why religion exists. If we're trying to understand life we have to understand all of its aspects. I would like for God to exist, if there was a power everywhere to which we could submit our destinies with peaceful hearts, then life would be easier, and it's true that religious people believe that there is an authority that will quietly judge their lives."

He smiled the smile that suited him so well.

"You can see that this is a kind of drug, you can see the peace it gives people, but men of religion seem to me to give peace to others, I learned a lot from them in my youth. To tell the truth, even though I'm not a believer I'm not very opposed to the idea of religion; if we live a life we don't understand we can expect to be granted peace by a being about whose nature we have no idea. If we're skeptical about God's existence we must also be skeptical about God's nonexistence. We don't know if there is a God but at the same time we don't know that there isn't, so belittle belief in God's existence as much as you belittle the belief that God doesn't exist. Because just as you don't need to believe in anything, you don't need to be frightened of believing in something."

That night Rukiye didn't say a single word until they reached Mihrişah's mansion, which was surrounded by a fence of yellow-gilded iron bars that looked like spears, and Boris shared this silence with her. They parted in front of the house with a brief farewell.

Like all young people who enrich their intelligence with knowledge, Rukiye had, in order to protect a personality that had not yet completed its development, long since made the choice between keen faith and keen disbelief. She'd chosen unbelief, the only weapon she had, to take revenge on her father, and with the fire of youth had taken this to the point of belittling men of religion and indeed even insulting them.

Now after hearing Professor Koncharov, who she admired and held in high esteem, and with whom she'd replaced the faith she'd torn from her soul, her confidence in her own ideas was shaken.

Sheikh Efendi, who she'd erased from her mind, suddenly came back to life with his entire legend, power, the admiring lights that surrounded him, and she felt small, oppressed, and powerless before the sudden appearance of this glorified person who she'd considered an enemy.

When she belittled the father she'd never once seen, she also belittled her loss, but if this father was someone important this loss would be greater. After her conversation with Koncharov, she had to belittle the professor as well in order to belittle her father, and if she did this she would truly become an orphan; because the professor was like a sweet-smelling and magical liquid that filled all the empty spaces in her life, at that time to give up on him would be too dry, too rotten with both loneliness and insecurity.

With the fragility of young people who are inclined to feel completely powerless and alone when the smallest conflict with a loved one arises, to the same extent that when they encounter someone they love and trust they feel secure and at ease believing they possess this loved one's power, Rukiye felt alone, vulnerable, and even an unwanted burden. To realize that someone she'd belittled might be very strong eroded her self-confidence.

As she climbed the stairs to her bedroom she encountered Mihrişah Sultan, the tails of her red dress sweeping down the stairs, clearly on her way out for the evening. As the Sultan passed she asked, as always, how Rukiye was, but then she suddenly saw the fear, desperation, and loneliness in the young girl's pale face. That young girl was incapable of concealing emotions she didn't even know she had.

"What happened, what's the matter?"

"Nothing, ma'am."

Mihrişah reached out and took Rukiye's hand with a gentleness she would never have expected.

"Come with me."

As they descended the stairs together, Rukiye tried to object.

"You'll be late, ma'am."

"It doesn't matter, Rukiye."

They entered the large living room to the right of the entrance hall and sat next to each other in the armchairs in front of the fireplace. As Mihrişah Sultan took off her long, white gloves and gently touched Rukiye's hair, the tenderness she felt for this young girl, whose paling face suddenly reminded her of her father the Sheikh, helped conceal her lack of experience in comforting children.

She realized from the state Rukiye was in that she'd been shaken by a pain that was out of the ordinary, and she was surprised to realize she felt a similar pain, though she didn't understand the reason.

Either Rukiye's resemblance to her father reminded her of the love she'd once felt for Sheikh Efendi, and traces of which she still carried, or she'd encountered such clear sorrow in a child who felt neglected, or the damage to her soul caused by concealed repentance for not showing her son love and tenderness suddenly broke down the walls of her selfishness when she saw another child in pain, or the need she felt within to love someone unconditionally, which was awakened by the selfish loneliness that was occasionally depressing even for her, or for some reason we'll never know, she felt an unmeasurable love and tenderness when she saw the pain emanating through the cracks in Rukiye's self-confidence.

She caressed Rukiye's hair silently and softly as if she was caressing herself, then took the girl's hand as she closed her eyes to conceal the tears that had suddenly begun to form. She held Rukiye's hair and her hands.

They sat together in silence, losing track of time, experiencing the unique pleasure and trust of loving like a mother and being loved like a mother.

That evening in front of the fireplace, these two women, one young and one growing old, who almost never showed their feelings and who were always distant toward each other and everyone else, experienced a silent and exhilarating adventure that neither had ever imagined, expected, or foreseen.

Rukiye, who since childhood had born, her sense of abandonment and loneliness without even confessing it to herself, wept with her head on Mihrişah's chest as she'd missed being able to do since childhood, not trying to hide her tears or even stop them, trembling and sobbing as Mihrişah Sultan stroked her hair.

For her part, Mihrişah Sultan, who had always been indifferent to the feelings of others, and indeed even mocked them, experienced for the first time the strong pleasure of sharing the feelings of someone who'd been hurt by her own loneliness, of being a shelter and a consolation for that person.

That night they became a grandmother and a granddaughter in the truest sense, they loved each other in a way that would never diminish.

One careless word from Professor Koncharov had caused Rukiye to establish a new relationship with Mihrişah Sultan and to see her father Sheikh Efendi with new eyes, had changed the course of her life and led her to carry her future to another city, to another man, to another terrible sorrow.

6

D ay by day the area around the mosques, which with their round domes and slender minarets made the Ottoman capital's magnificent skyline look like God's signature on earth in Sufi calligraphy, was becoming more crowded.

The unemployed, the poor, the destitute, the hungry, the fool-saints; in the shady stone courtyards of these historical buildings, each of which reflected an earlier reign, they dressed in shabby clothes, hungrily waiting for the soup with rice and chickpeas that the soup kitchens would distribute, their angry murmuring steadily growing louder as they expressed their grievances and dissatisfaction.

This crowd had been oppressed for years by severe tyranny, they'd had to keep their mouths shut and had been poisoned by their own silence, but now they were finding the opportunity to speak for the first time; they hadn't decided where to direct their anger, they hadn't even really thought about that, and because they were not yet prepared to commit the sin of expressing anger at His Majesty the Caliph, the shadow of Islam on earth, they forgot what they'd suffered during his reign, saw constitutional monarchy as the source of their current tribulations, and directed their anger at the Committee.

Hasan Efendi, who hated the infidels of the Committee who'd rebelled against the Caliph and Sultan of the World, left the *tekke* toward noon and wandered through Istanbul from one mosque to another, he was a big man who seemed as if he could never eat enough and he had a tremendous appetite, he ate at three or four different soup kitchens and as he did so he chatted with the people around him and gathered intelligence for the Sheikh.

Even though he sensed that his Sheikh didn't support the Sultan, his upbringing prevented him from confronting him about or even mentioning the subject, his odd conception of loyalty enabled him to remain loyal to both the Sultan and the Sheikh and he hoped that one day the Sheikh would come to share his opinions.

Recently a fool-saint named Blind Ali who loitered in front of the Fatih Mosque had caught his attention. He was partially paralyzed, could only walk with the help of two people, was blind in one eye, and wore a greasy turban, and as soon as he appeared in the courtyard people gathered around him.

Blind Ali began by saying, "There have been revelations," as if he was in a state of ecstasy, then went on to say, "The saint has been seen under the curtain," implying that he was the saint who had appeared.

Hasan Efendi went to the mosque early again that Friday, took a zinc plate of food, knelt next to a distressed-looking man who was eating at the far end of the courtyard, and said, "Peace be with you." In the slowly falling snow the man shivered as he ate, his hands were trembling from the cold, his spoon kept clinking against his plate, and each time he lifted his spoon to his mouth some of the pilaf fell back onto his plate.

The man had no coat, robe, or cloak and his fez, which had been blackened by dirt, had clearly not been re-blocked for years. Over his singlet he wore a dirty shirt with tattered cuffs and a navy-blue broadcloth vest that had probably been given to him as charity. His torn shalwar had been inexpertly mended with white thread, and under a rip that hadn't been mended his skin was raised with goose bumps, arousing a sense of compassion mixed with disgust in everyone who saw him.

"Are you here for Friday prayers?"

"Yup, for Friday prayers."

"I haven't seen you around here before."

"No, I've never been here before, they say a saint appeared, and according to what people say, Blind Ali Hodja saw the Prophet Mohammad in a dream."

The man finished his pilaf, trembled as he put his plate down, folded his arms across his chest, and lowered his voice.

"They say they're going to raise the green flag."

Hasan Efendi frowned.

"Against His Majesty the Caliph?"

"Heaven forbid . . . Against the masonic infidels who rebelled against our Caliph."

The man gave Hasan Efendi a pleading look.

"If only I had a little tobacco."

"If I had any I'd give you some, but I don't smoke, I freed myself from that addiction a long time ago. Don't think I was a light smoker, when I was in the navy I smoked like a chimney, but in the end I didn't see that it was doing me any good, toward the end, I swear to God, I coughed so much when I woke in the morning the sailors thought the engines had been fired up."

Hasan Efendi leaned in toward the man as if he was about to tell him a secret.

"It's not good for your manhood, you should quit. Look, since we're talking, where are you from, who are your people?"

For a moment the man seemed to have forgotten who he was and where he was from, then, as he remembered who knows what distant dreams, a happy and indeed arrogant smile appeared on his face; anyone who saw the man dressed the way he was would have difficulty believing that a man in his state could smile like this, that this expression could exist in his vocabulary of smiles. But the smile didn't last long, it gave way to a weighty melancholy and he sighed deeply.

"Oh, brother. Even I'm surprised to remember who my people are and where I'm from and even I suspect I invented it. Of course I wasn't always as you see me now, I've been in better shape, I've had better days, but that's all in the past now, all that's left of the great forestry inspector Kamil Bey is Kamil the tramp who lives like a dog in front of soup kitchens."

The man thought to himself for a while.

"In fact I'm from Uşak, my father was wealthy, after I married I became a forest warden, in time I was promoted to forestry inspector for Aydın province, which includes the Denizli, Menteşe, Manisa, Aydın, and Izmir districts. When I came to Istanbul during that period I went to express my gratitude at the Forestry Ministry. The minister received me, I thanked him and was about to leave when he told me to see the undersecretary before I left. To cut a long story short, I said fine and went to see the undersecretary, he received me graciously. As I was leaving he gave me a piece of paper with measurements on it and said, 'Have three Uşak carpets made to these measurements and send them to me.' I agreed. These weren't small carpets, they were for large halls, anyway, I went to Uşak, looked around, found three of the best quality carpets, and borrowed money to buy them. I put the invoice and the cost of transport in a sealed envelope and sent it with the carpets. How stupid I was, I didn't even realize I was being asked for a bribe. I started my job, a month passed, no money arrived, my debtors started pressuring me, I wrote one more letter to the ministry asking for my money. I got a paper in the mail saying I'd been discharged in recognition of my disability. I was meant to have bribed them and then got the money back in bribes from the foresters; how could I have known this, brother? I was unemployed and deep in debt, and I couldn't find a job because I'd been labeled unskilled. I sold everything and paid my debts and moved to Istanbul. You can see the rest of what happened, three years ago my wife left me too."

"Where did she go?"

"How should I know, brother, maybe she went to her father's village, maybe she went bad, in any event she was barren. That's the way it is, if you can't feed a woman she leaves, a man who can't put food on the table isn't seen as a man. That's how it is, I was left all alone, living a dog's life . . . I don't have two pennies to rub together, I live in a room in Tophane, I sweep the floors in return for my lodging, I eat at soup kitchens."

The man suddenly fell silent, his hands were turning blue from the cold, he put his hands under his arms and looked around; while they'd been talking the courtyard had filled up, a ragged-looking crowd in faded robes, turbans yellowed with age, misshapen fezzes, and threadbare shalwar had begun to gather in front of the mosque.

In place of the peace one would expect to emanate from the courtyard of a house of worship, a smell of anger and restlessness spread out amid the falling snowflakes. The crowd began to surge, they saw Blind Ali, helped along by two people, murmuring something they couldn't quite make out, then they all went into the mosque and took their places for prayer.

After the prayers were over the congregation didn't disperse, they remained in the courtyard as if they were waiting for something but didn't know what it was. The crowd was silent. The snowfall grew heavier. Seagulls who'd flown up from the Golden Horn circled above the crowd in hope of food.

Suddenly the crowd parted, Blind Ali was carried out of the mosque and placed on the coffin rest by the door, he squinted his only eye at the crowd, and the trembling that might have seemed pathetic in anyone else seemed at that moment like the otherworldly power of a divine shadow.

On the marble coffin rest, on which a new body rested every day at noon, his blind eye, crippled body, and angry courage made him seem like a solution to the hungry, desperate people who'd gathered in the snow.

He shouted to the crowd in a barely intelligible voice that sounded like water bubbling from a dark well.

"Believers, there have been revelations. A saint has been seen under the curtain."

Even though everyone else was shivering from the cold, Blind Ali's shirt was open, it was as if the cold didn't touch him.

"We want a shepherd," he shouted, "every flock needs a shepherd. The flock lacks a leader. Sharia commands that we go to His Majesty the Caliph."

Suddenly green flags emblazoned with Koranic verses rose above the crowd. Blind Ali was taken from the coffin rest and carried to the front of the crowd, and amid shouts of "God is great!" and "There have been revelations!" they left the courtyard and began marching toward Yıldız Palace. There was nowhere else they could go, nowhere else they could take shelter; they wanted someone to save them from this poverty, this abasement, so they went to the Caliph, the only savior they'd ever known. They'd forgotten that the very same Caliph had failed to save them for years, they had to forget in order to have hope.

The Sultan, whose intelligence-gathering organization had collapsed to a considerable degree, was unaware that a mob had set out from Fatih Mosque and he and his physician Reşit Pasha were examining the new pistols he'd lined up on the table.

"Look at these, doctor, how beautiful they are."

The Sultan picked each of them up and weighed them in his hand, he pointed an unloaded pistol at the wall and pulled the trigger. It was clear that it delighted and amused him to touch them and play with them. Suddenly he stopped and gave Reşit Pasha a mocking look.

"You don't like these very much, do you, doctor?"

"I'm not that interested, Your Majesty, perhaps because of my profession, I never had much interest in weapons."

"That is, you say you're a doctor and that you save lives instead of killing, but that we like weapons because we kill, is that how it is?"

Reşit Pasha was no longer as frightened as he'd once been of the Sultan, who no longer had the power over human life he'd once had, but he was ashamed and panicked about having been disrespectful, he didn't want to seem like someone who was disrespectful when he wasn't frightened.

"I beg your pardon, Your Majesty, that's not what I meant to say."

"Don't worry, doctor, a sultan is not a physician, we know how to kill, and we kill when it's necessary, to be a monarch is to constantly make the choice between life and death, sometimes you have to kill one person to keep another alive, yes, every Sultan has knowingly or unknowingly killed, but you keep some people alive. A good Sultan isn't one who never kills, there are no Sultans like that, a good Sultan is one who makes the right decisions about who to kill and who to keep alive. It's impossible to keep people alive without killing, doctor, even God, perish the thought, can't do this, so how could we possible succeed?"

The Sultan put the gun he'd been holding back on the table and thought for a while.

"They call us a bloodsucker, stop, don't object, I'm telling you what they say. But they praise our ancestors . . . When our ancestors went to war they gave orders that people be killed, we, at least, avoided wars, we didn't allow Muslim sons to die in battle, were we wrong? Should we have gone to war and let thousands of our native sons die? Would they have loved us then? Would they not have insulted us then?"

The Sultan was defending himself, as he'd become accustomed

to doing in recent months, not to try to say anything to the opposition, he'd made lists to convince himself he was right and put himself at ease, it was as if he thought that if he himself believed he was right, others would believe this too. Later Reşit Pasha told Osman, "He wanted to be his own judge and jury, he didn't want to leave this to others, but when he saw that this was getting more and more difficult he tried constantly to prove he was right so he could better resist the judgements others would make."

The Sultan picked up another of his weapons and changed the subject abruptly.

"Have you ever fired a gun, doctor?"

"I fired a gun once when I was young, but I missed."

The Sultan smiled confidently

"Bragging is not an attractive trait, but I'm a good shot, ever since I was young I've been able to hit whatever I shoot at."

"No doubt, my Sultan, everyone knows this, the whole world knows what a good shot you are."

"This gun you see, doctor, it's the only thing in life you can trust to keep you safe, it will never betray you, one day a woman from your harem who you take to bed could betray you, the brother you grew up with could betray you, but a gun will never betray you. Even when you're a sultan there can come a time when a gun can save your life, a gun can save both a sultan and an empire. How many of our ancestors were killed in their quarters by useless ingrates, if they'd taken the precaution of carrying a gun they might have changed history, but they didn't do this, they expected others to protect them. You can't entrust your safety to others, doctor, look, no one can take my life in this room, if you ask me why, I always carry two guns in my pockets, I'll kill anyone who comes to kill me, sometimes you can change your entire destiny if you gain five minutes."

The Sultan put the gun back on the table.

"Let's go try out these guns."

As they were leaving the hall to go try out the guns, they heard a commotion outside; at that time the Sultan was particularly suspicious of any unusual noise and he looked around anxiously and asked loudly what was going on.

"There's a crowd gathered outside, Your Majesty, they want to see you."

"Send for the chief clerk Ali Cevat Bey."

Ali Cevat Bey came rushing in, his face flushed.

"You summoned me, Your Majesty."

"A crowd has gathered outside and wants to see us, go take a look and see what's what, find out what they want."

Ali Cevat Bey went out in front of the palace and saw that a crowd of roughly a thousand people had gathered; they were all grumbling, shivering impatiently in their misshapen fezzes and dirty turbans, waving their green flags.

The chief clerk approached Blind Ali, who was in front of the mob.

"What's going on, what do you want?"

As Blind Ali began to speak in his bubbling voice, the murmuring of the crowd died down.

"The taverns must be closed, photography must be prohibited. Muslim women should not be allowed out onto the street."

Ali Cevat Bey didn't understand what the man was saying. He asked a turbaned young man with a red face and scraggly beard who was holding Blind Ali by the arm.

"What does Hodja Efendi want?"

The young, red-faced man got straight to the point.

"We don't want the constitution."

The chief clerk returned to the palace, but his quick arrival and brief presence had encouraged the crowd and they shouted that they wanted to see his Majesty the Caliph, and tramps in the vicinity heard the noise and joined the crowd.

The Sultan asked Ali Cevat Bey what they wanted.

"They don't want the constitution, Your Majesty."

The Sultan replied without letting on whether he was pleased or angry.

"Then they should go to whoever wrote the constitution."

"Sir, the crowd is growing larger, perhaps if you showed your blessed face, I don't think they're going to disperse without seeing you."

The Sultan knew that if anything happened, the Committee would blame him, so he made his way to the reception chamber to disperse the crowd before it grew larger, the window looking out onto the square opened, and the Sultan's head appeared.

They raised Blind Ali toward the window.

"My Sultan, we want a shepherd . . . No flock can be without a shepherd. Sharia commands that Muslim women not go outside uncovered, that photography should be prohibited, that the taverns and theaters should be closed. Have no fear, my Sultan, there have been revelations, the saint has been seen under the curtain, have no fear!"

The Sultan pretended not to hear people telling him to his face to have no fear.

"The necessary commands will be given, the dictates of sharia will be obeyed, be at ease, Hodja Efendi."

The Sultan turned to his physician in distress.

"Oh, doctor, the fool-saints have appeared, this is an omen of the apocalypse, there's trouble coming for us. Who stirred this man up and sent him here, did the Committee put him up to it, are they betting on being able to say that the Sultan is stirring up the reactionaries and then put the blame on me?"

"Why are you saying this, Your Majesty, your subjects were troubled and ran to you, they wanted to see your blessed face and hear your voice."

"But my subjects applauded the Committee too. As I've always told you, doctor, don't trust the crowds, never trust them. Whenever crowds appear in this nation, someone dies. That's the way it's always been and that's the way it will always be. May God bring this to an end before anything distasteful happens."

Blind Ali had no idea of what was being said about him. This was the most magnificent day of his life, he'd made the crowds follow him, he'd made the Sultan come to the window and show his face. This crippled body that had been humiliated and pushed was full of joy as the crowd carried him down from Yıldız Palace on their hands as the Sultan's spies, the Committee's spies, the police chief's spies, the official police, and the guards in front of the Beşiktaş police station looked on and composed the reports they would write.

Even though Istanbul was being neglected, it was not so neglected that a protest would go unnoticed. At that time neither Blind Ali nor the people carrying him on their shoulders knew that there was a price to pay for seeing the Sultan's face, and that Blind Ali would pay this price by hanging from the gallows; even if it was only briefly, success had made the desperate crowd forget their troubles and gave them a reason to feel important, and, as usual, they would be satisfied with this.

As the crowd dispersed slowly to houses that were dimly lit by feeble oil lamps, damp single rooms, isolated shacks, unkempt madrasa cells, and coffeehouses through dark, narrow streets, Hasan Efendi, once again feeling hungry, headed for the *tekke*.

His Sheikh and his dwarf wife, the sheikh's third daughter, were waiting for him and no matter how far afield he wandered or what he experienced it was his destiny to return to the *tekke* to find his Sheikh, the light of his life, and his wife, the darkness of his life, to experience joy and distress there in the same place, under the same roof.

It was dark and the snow was falling faster. The *tekke* on the shores of the Golden Horn, with its tall cypress trees, quiet courtyards, illuminated windows, incense-scented walls and the warmth one felt on passing through the door, awaited its guests like a haven and accepted all who came.

Sheikh Efendi, who had a pale, transparent face, a black beard and long black hair with a streak of white in it, was sitting alone in the *zikir* room reading the Koran as usual. When Hasan Efendi entered he raised his head slowly, looked at Hasan Efendi, and gestured for him to sit next to him.

In this shadowy hall that smelled of agarwood, Sheikh Efendi's face seemed to glow with a white light and his black eyes, misted with his own sorrows, seemed to understand everything; Hasan Efendi was deeply impressed by this in the same way that others were impressed with the patience of this person who could only ease the restlessness of his own soul by giving peace to others, who was always ready to listen to people's troubles, his quietness wrapping him like a shawl to cover the storms within, the great faith that helped him carry the disappointments of life with a melancholy derision, a voice like water from a sacred spring that refreshed all who heard it, the humility of the belief that he could only approach God by getting closer to people, his legendary power, was able to make Hasan Efendi rise above the turmoil of his life with a single glance, and once again he calmed his son-in-law with a single glance and caused him to forget his weariness.

His strength refreshed, and in a quiet tone appropriate for the hall they were in, Hasan Efendi began to relate the events he'd witnessed. As usual, Sheikh Efendi stared straight ahead as he listened, expressionless, as if he was thinking about something else and only once, when Hasan Efendi said, "Ali Hodja," when he was referring to Blind Ali, did he frown slightly and raise his head.

"Excuse me?"

Hasan Efendi continued talking as if he didn't understand why Sheikh Efendi was angry.

"Ali Hodja . . . Ali Hodja."

The Sheikh looked at Hasan Efendi's face, the pace of the clicking of his prayer beads increasing slightly.

"It seems as if they've made all the tramps pashas and all the fool-saints hodjas."

Hasan Efendi said nothing, afraid to go too far, and waited for Sheikh Efendi to continue; without realizing it, the Sheikh shared some concerns with the Sultan, with whom he never agreed on almost any subject.

"When God is going to punish someone, he first takes away the person's mind, then makes him blind, if madmen are appearing as leaders it's a sign that our minds have been taken away and that we're blind. Let us pray that today this poor, sinless crowd won't pay for the Ottomans' sinful money and all the blood they've shed."

Then, as if he was issuing Hasan Efendi a warning, he said:

"It's clear that death is at the city gates, who will it take, who will it leave unscathed, after this, everything is darkness, everyone's life is at risk, everyone from the Caliph to a stableman in Sütlüce. We have no part in the power struggles of the world, if anything is to happen to us, let it happen as we follow our own path. We have nothing to gain from the conflicts of this world, nor do we have anything to offer . . . Warn everyone, no one from the *tekke* will have any part in this, I am responsible for every one of them, if I lose even one of them I will have to account for it on judgment day."

When Hasan Efendi was sitting with the Sheikh, everything seemed bright, as if he was sitting next to a light, but as soon as he left the hall his soul darkened and he felt a deep disquiet. In fact he too wanted to join the crowds that were demanding sharia, to shout, he wanted to find himself an enemy, he might not be able to rebel against his destiny and change it but he could find something else to rebel against and change, yet the Sheikh would not allow this. He had to carry on with the heavy weight he felt in his soul.

As he neared the harem his anger and sense of oppression increased, when he entered his room he found his dwarf wife waiting for him in her nightdress with her hair down and falling over her shoulders. When she saw her husband enter the room, when she saw that he nearly filled the room with his bulky body, she gave a smile that seemed devious to Hasan Efendi, though someone who knew more about women might have thought it reflected selfish lust.

Unlike her sister, who had married Ragıp Bey, Binnaz Hanım was fond of physical pleasure, every night she waited for her husband with the smile of a hunter waiting for his prey, certain that he would catch it. After putting Hasan Efendi to bed, this small woman got to work, moving all over his body, arousing him each time, she took what she wanted from her husband but also truly gave him pleasure, though there was an aspect of this pleasure that he found repugnant. Even though the pleasure was fleeting, the disgust had a permanent side, the more pleasure he experienced the more disgusted he felt, and this disgust seeped deeper into him.

As usual, when he saw his wife waiting for him he grew angry because he felt that, as always, someone was going to force him to do something he didn't want to do.

"You're still up, Binnaz Hanım?"

Every night he never failed to ask the same question, and his wife always gave the same answer.

"I waited for you, Hasan Efendi."

When he received the same answer again, he grumbled through his moustache as usual.

"You needn't have."

Binnaz Hanım didn't mind her husband's grumbling, all that mattered was for her to get what she wanted; this tiny woman had a determination and willpower that no one would have guessed she had, when she wanted something, whether it was great or small, she did whatever it took to get what she wanted and reach her goal. Belittlement, contempt, even insults—no one but her parents had the power to insult the Sheikh's daughter and even they could never change her mind. Once she'd learned to carry the heavy load of being a dwarf she learned not to care about the feelings of these large, healthy, good-looking people who differed from her, she took revenge on them without caring about them enough to even realize that it was revenge. She wasn't one of them, so their rules didn't apply to her.

Her husband came into this room every night unwillingly, angry and grumbling, but she knew how to make him do what she wanted, she usually solved his ill-tempered stress with a simple question, and once again she asked the same question.

"Have you eaten?"

Binnaz Hanım could withstand hunger and sleeplessness without complaint in spite of her tiny body, she could go days without sleep or food, but in spite of Hasan Efendi's robust body and gigantic appearance, he could not withstand sleeplessness or hunger; in the strange and tragic coupling of a dwarf and a giant, the one who seemed stronger in mind and body was in fact the weaker one. As his mother-in-law, who loved complaining about her sons-in-law out of the sheikh's hearing, used to say about Hasan Efendi, "The camel is big but a colt was able to lead it."

When Hasan Efendi heard his wife's question he realized he was hungry, he hadn't eaten since lunch.

"I haven't, I'm starving."

"I'll bring you something at once."

Binnaz Hanım jumped out of bed, put on her tiny slippers, put a shawl over her shoulders, and darted off, she'd already had a tray prepared for Hasan Efendi, after a servant brought the tray to the door she brought it in herself; the tray was

almost bigger than her and fully loaded but, as her mother
used to say, she had the strength of a demon, she could lift a
weight that large men couldn't lift, she would just pick it up
with her short arms and let out a grunt.

She put the tray on the table; Hasan Efendi, who had
undressed and put on his nightshirt when his wife went to the
kitchen, sat at the table, and Binnaz Hanım got back into bed
and watched this big man eat. There was something in Hasan
Efendi's appetite that she found arousing, watching him eat
gave her an almost sexual pleasure; once again that strange,
lustful smile appeared on her face.

At first Hasan Efendi ate quickly but later he slowed, he
wanted to delay going to bed for as long as possible, but eventually he finished his meal and had to go to bed. As soon as he
got into bed and pulled the quilt over him, Binnaz Hanım blew
out the oil lamp and disappeared under the quilt, and as soon
as he felt her tiny hand reaching under his nightshirt he tried
to stop her in an angry but hopeless tone.

"Stop, woman, I'm tired."

Binnaz Hanım didn't care.

"You don't get tired, my lion, could a brave man like you
ever get tired?"

Hasan Efendi tried to push Binnaz Hanım away, but he was
ashamed to do this and couldn't do it decisively, this huge man
wasn't strong enough to push away the tiny woman on top of him.

"Just a minute," said Binnaz Hanım, "stop for a minute, my
lion, leave yourself to me."

Hasan Efendi struggled a little, then left himself to her, he
didn't complain about his wife moving all over his body,
touching his genitals, and pulling up his nightshirt with her
tiny hands even though he felt disgusted, as if a wet reptile
was crawling all over him; as usual this disgust gave way to a
reluctant pleasure, then into a blind, deaf carnal lust that was
without love, and indeed without desire.

He did what his wife wanted like a mating animal, without kissing her once, without smelling her neck or even her hair. He ground his teeth in his sleep all night, tossing and turning, his anger not diminishing even in his sleep, but Binnaz Hanım, for her part, fell into a peaceful sleep.

Hasan Efendi set out early the next morning, there were lively discussions in all the *tekkes*, lodges, mosques, and coffee-houses about what Blind Ali had done. Although they did not disapprove openly, seasoned hodjas, members of religious brotherhoods, and strictly observant Muslims made it felt that they disapproved of what Blind Ali had done and said it wasn't appropriate to become involved in a power struggle between the Sultan and the Committee, that it might lead to a conflict in which Muslims killed Muslims. Those who were desperate, hungry, seeking shelter and an authority they could trust, those who hoped to benefit from this power struggle, supported Blind Ali enthusiastically. It seemed as if the Muslim community was split in two.

The palace and the Committee's members of parliament and military officers put their spies into action in the capital, they watched what was going on and tried to predict the political outcomes of this event; the palace was anxious and the Committee was angry.

A few days later, when they became alarmed that if no measures were taken, these religious mobs flocking to the palace to support the Caliph would grow much bigger, the Committee had Blind Ali arrested. Immediately the loud discussions in mosque courtyards became whispers. However, this uprising on the part of the devout poor was not yet keen enough for them to risk their lives; they concealed their anger beneath prayers and curses, but these whispers were more dangerous than loud discussions, they now grew in darkness like seeds planted in the soil.

Blind Ali's trial proceeded very quickly, at first the defendant arrived in court with an air of indifference, tried to frighten the judges, and shouted about revelations in his bubbly voice, but later he became meek and fewer and fewer of his supporters gathered in front of the court. Everyone had smelled the smell of death.

Toward the end of the trial Blind Ali said that he had nothing to do with politics and that he had simply been reminding the Caliph of the dictates of God and of sharia, but the judges no longer listened to him, even though they realized he was just a pathetic madman, they couldn't set him free once he'd appeared before the court; the decision had been made when Blind Ali was sent to trial.

The sour-faced judge announced his ruling and broke his reed pen.

"Death by hanging."

At dawn on a snowy day much like the day Blind Ali was carried out the gate of Fatih Mosque on his followers' shoulders, Hasan Efendi was among the crowd that gathered to watch his execution. The sky was the color of cold iron, bluish snow was falling, and the morning frost stung the faces of all present. When a red glow appeared on the other side of the Marmara Sea, the prisoner was brought in by a squad of gendarmes; he was in handcuffs and he seemed smaller, he was wearing an execution shroud that swept the ground and there was a placard on his chest proclaiming his death sentence. Two gendarmes seized him by the arms and dragged him up to the gallows.

Blind Ali looked at the crowd with his single eye and there was a strange expression on his face, it was as if he was pleased these people had gathered and wasn't really aware of what was happening. As the gendarmes dragged him along he suddenly saw the gallows, that ominous noose, the trestle beneath it, and the gypsy executioner waiting for him, he stopped in his tracks; that palsied and crippled body resisted so strongly that the two strong gendarmes could no longer drag him; when the gendarme captain barked an order, a few soldiers with rifles on their backs rushed forward, holding their rifle butts with one hand to keep them from hitting their backs, and grabbed the prisoner's arms. Blind Ali's feet swung in the air as they brought him up to the gallows like an old sack.

It had taken six gendarmes to bring him up to the gallows, but the gypsy, licking his lips as if he was about to have a good meal, seized him by the shoulders and had no trouble lifting him onto the trestle beneath the noose, the madman no longer had the strength to resist, he seemed to shrink and wrinkle and in the end was nothing more than a trembling wretch. He said something, but no one could make out what it was, they heard nothing but a strange bubbling sound.

The executioner placed the thick noose around Blind Ali's neck.

A terrifyingly complete and deathly silence reigned in the square, the only sound was the predatory shrieking of the hungry birds who took flight from the Golden Horn.

They asked whether he had a final wish.

Blind Ali tried to say something, but no intelligible words emerged from his mouth.

When the signal was given for the executioner to carry out the execution, Blind Ali shouted loudly enough for everyone in the square to hear him.

"There have been revelations!"

The executioner kicked away the trestle. For a moment Blind Ali remained suspended in the air, he seemed to grow taller, as if he was being stretched, his feet kicked a few times, his entire body was wracked by spasms, then suddenly he relaxed and fell still. His motionless body started swaying at the end of the rope.

The crowd dispersed in silent fear.

The death that had been waiting at the gates had entered the city.

7

Later Ragıp Bey told Osman, "It was a strange feeling, it was years before I could put a name to it."

Ragıp Bey was living the most unsettled period of his life; every day in a different way his soul was pressed by alien and uncertain emotions that left him helpless, and the life he thought he knew so well was constantly presenting him with secrets he couldn't unravel.

He escaped his wife's flesh, which smelled of prayer and incense and seemed alien to human flesh, by telling her that he had to remain at the barracks, then went to Dilara Hanım's mansion, leaving his mother and his wife, two rigid and uncompromising women, alone together to fester in their hostility to each other.

Dilara Hanım welcomed him gracefully every time, served drinks, had the servants prepare the most delicious food, she never asked why he hadn't come sooner, how long he would stay, or when he would come again, she conversed softly with him as if she wanted him to hear the softness of her voice even more, she talked about places she'd seen, people she'd met, books she'd read, and she played the oud and sang. She created a warm, pleasantly scented, and secluded world for Ragıp Bey that always reminded him of candles, the yellowish-red of the burning logs, she made him feel he was master of this world, then she made love to him with a selfish appetite that at times made him feel ashamed and at times annoyed him, but that always made him feel he could never find greater pleasure.

The next morning a fire would be lit for his bath, he would put on clean underwear from a drawer that had been set aside for him in one of the walnut closets and his uniform, though he was never certain when it had been ironed or who had ironed it, at the breakfast table he sat across from Dilara Hanım, who did not seem worn out from the previous night, her red hair tied up in a bun, wearing a polite smile, and exercising her silent authority by commanding the servants with her eyes rather than with words, he ate his breakfast to the smell of the tea wafting from the samovar that purred like a well-behaved cat and Dilara Hanım's perfume, which permeated the entire house, then he would leave the reddish light of this peaceful and happy world and be greeted respectfully by the elderly driver as he climbed into the carriage that was waiting ready at the door.

This peaceful happiness lasted until they reached the street, the pleasant-smelling warmth of the house would be replaced by the cold of the snowy city and he doubted the reality of what he'd experienced the night before, of what he'd done and of their lovemaking; he wanted to return at once, look at Dilara's face, and believe again that he had touched her naked body.

This sudden break from the dream world destroyed everything he'd experienced there, it did not allow what had been experienced to accumulate, did not allow one experience to connect to another smoothly, it created a thrilling void between that moment and the previous night and caused him to feel as if he was leaving that void; that void pushed the images of the previous night far away, made them unreachable, and caused him to worry deeply that he might never experience these images again.

According to Ragıp Bey, the strange and nameless feeling he'd mentioned to Osman was this jarring break he experienced almost every time and the worry that ensued.

After the carriage left the street he felt something was missing, thought that a sentence that had been uttered hadn't been uttered, he felt as if Dilara Hanım hadn't uttered the last sentence and had stopped talking at the end of the conversation.

Ragıp Bey didn't know if there'd been a sentence like this, or what it had been if there had been, but the feeling of that unspoken last sentence covered his soul, it erased every sentence he'd heard, it emptied his memory and rendered everything that had been said meaningless.

Every time he went to the mansion it was to hear that missing sentence, and every time he left without hearing that sentence he felt a void, felt that something was missing.

The strangest thing was that what connected him to Dilara Hanım wasn't all of the sentences that had actually been uttered but the unspoken missing sentence about which he knew nothing; one day if he heard the sentence or he thought he heard the sentence, if he didn't leave the house with that void, that break, that missing thing, it was as if he would not come back to the mansion, or if he did, he would not embrace Dilara Hanım with the same desire, with the lust of someone who wanted to be sure that the body he touched was real.

During a significant period of his life, Ragıp Bey was the prisoner and pursuer of a sentence that did not exist, of something that was missing, of a void, and he ached with the anxiety of knowing that he was attached to a void.

The perfect unhappiness of his marriage and the nameless missing thing in his relationship with Dilara Hanım led Ragıp Bey to seek consolation in his work and pay more attention to military discipline and obedience.

While other officers spent their time discussing politics and enjoying the entertainments Beyoğlu had to offer, he drilled his unit to make it perfect, he didn't tolerate even the smallest mistake in his command, a slightly untidy bed in the dormitory, an unpolished boot, a loose button on a uniform, the slightest impertinence, he was hard on the junior officers and sergeants, but the efforts of a single officer didn't mean anything.

It pained Ragıp Bey to see that the army was on the verge of losing all discipline, the privates had no respect for or trust in the officers, they saw that officers with differing political views hated each other, the soldiers in Istanbul, and particularly the units from Salonica, took advantage of the lack of discipline and began adopting a rebellious attitude.

There were robed and turbaned mullahs at the headquarters gates, and even within them, most of them never left the Taşkışla barracks where the troops from Salonica were quartered, they took advantage of the officers' indifference and whispered and prayed with the sergeants who were now in control of the soldiers. Young officers and mullahs looked at each other with hatred when they encountered each other at the headquarters gates, but they said nothing; neither side could predict which side the privates would take when a conflict arose. As is usually the case when political will vanishes, the officers who believed they were the secret masters of the empire were facing off against the hodjas.

Despite how tough he was, even Ragıp Bey couldn't prevent the mullahs from wandering around within his unit, he was afraid there might be unpleasantness, but he was aware that trouble was coming.

Once when he was having a heart-to-heart talk with Ibrahim Izzet Bey, one of the officers he trusted, he brought up the subject of the mullahs.

"What's going on, there are men with turbans everywhere, this looks more like a religious institution than a military headquarters."

İbrahim İzzet Bey sighed deeply.

"If I trusted the soldiers I would drive those reactionaries out at bayonet point, but to tell the truth, brother, I don't trust the soldiers, as long as these men are wandering around here holding Korans I doubt they would listen to us. Not long ago a friend told one of these mullahs off, but the sergeants defended him so fiercely he had to back down and walk away, when I say he walked away, he actually ran away, but I don't even want to say this. He's not a coward, we fought off a lot of Bulgarians together in Macedonia, quite a few times I saw him go into the bandits' caves alone. He's not afraid of death, thank God none of us are like that, he was afraid of being beaten up by his own soldiers, that would be a disgrace worse than death."

Ragıp Bey made a face.

"When the army starts tolerating this kind of disgraceful behavior, there's no telling where it will lead; I hear things that make me hate the people I hear them from; soldiers are reciting the Koran with mullahs in one room, in another room young officers are being entertained by a belly dancer, on top of that soldiers are pulling guns on each other because of the struggle between the Committee and the Sultan . . . We've lost the soldiers' respect and it will be difficult to win it back. I'm afraid this won't end without bloodshed, in the end we're going to have to shoot our own soldiers."

Less than a week after this conversation, what Ragıp Bey had feared came to pass. One morning as he was writing out the drill schedule he heard a commotion outside, there was shouting and swearing and a general tumult unusual for a military headquarters; he tightened his bandolier and threw his greatcoat over his shoulders.

Two groups of soldiers were facing each other with pointed guns, one group was led by young officers and the other by three burly sergeants.

The senior sergeant was shouting like a hoodlum in a street fight.

"You want to send us off to Arabia while you stay here and fool around with cotton-soft women. We fought in the mountains of Macedonia, a lot of us were killed there. We're not going anywhere, enough is enough, let someone else go. No one is strong enough to get us out of Istanbul. We'll go above your heads to the Caliph, to our father the Sultan."

An irritated young officer tried to control his anger.

"Sergeant, this is the army, we all obey orders here, don't turn this place into a madhouse. You've received your reassignment orders, get ready, then get going, otherwise this isn't going to end well."

The sergeant had no intention of backing down, he seemed sure that no one could touch him.

"If we were scared of cowards we'd be cowards, mister officer, no one here is afraid of trouble. From now on the only way we leave here is on a stretcher, we've made up our minds, we won't take even a single step. Let them cancel the reassignment."

"Sergeant, you're inciting the soldiers to mutiny, this is a very serious charge, I'm warning you for the last time, get your soldiers in line, obey your orders."

"It's not going to be that easy, mister officer, we want to see our father the Sultan. We're not going into the deserts of Arabia on the orders of some Masonic officer . . . Let's see if you can make us go."

It was snowing, snow had accumulated on the two cannon in the corner and their dark mouths had become blacker, the snow on the rooves of the headquarters buildings took on a leaden color as they reflected the grey of the sky; soldiers in grey coats squinted against the snowflakes, pointing rifles at each other and waiting anxiously to see what would happen.

There was a brief silence, the young officers felt they were approaching the point of no return; after a few anxious moments of hesitating between the obligation to maintain discipline and their anger at this insubordination and having to take responsibility for shedding blood, one of the young officers shouted, "Sergeant get your soldiers in line and obey your orders at once. Now leave headquarters immediately and form ranks in front of the gate!"

"We're not going anywhere . . . We want to see our father the Sultan . . . "

The officer turned to his soldiers and commanded them in a stern and decisive tone, "Load and aim!"

The barracks suddenly filled with the unnerving sound of gun mechanisms, a few birds took flight from the rooftops in fear.

As Ragıp Bey was stepping in to intervene, one of the sergeants shouted, "God is great!" and at the same moment the young officer shouted, "Fire!"

Two of the sergeants fell on their faces and the third fell on his back as if they'd been cut down by a scythe, they fell without moving, five of the soldiers behind them fell in a twisted heap, the others threw down their rifles and raised their hands.

Ragıp Bey rubbed his forehead for a moment then rushed over to the young officers.

"Arrest the soldiers who surrendered, get the wounded to the infirmary immediately."

Meanwhile more officers came running from every corner of the barracks; Ragıp Bey saw that a young lieutenant had ordered the feet of the three dead sergeants to be bound.

"What's going on, Lieutenant, why are their feet being tied?"

"I'm going to hang them in front of the gate, Major. As an example for anyone else considering mutiny."

Ragıp Bey made an angry face.

"Are you crazy, Lieutenant, these are your own men."

"You saw what they did, Major, they mutinied against the army."

The other young officers gathered around the lieutenant, they supported their colleague, it was clear they wanted the

sergeants to be strung up in front of the gate, they seemed prepared to disobey superior officers as the sergeants had just
done; Ragıp Bey put his hand on his pistol just in case.

"This isn't some rowdy fairground, this is the army. We
have rules about life and death here, Lieutenant!"

Without waiting for the lieutenant's answer he turned to a
nearby captain.

"Send news to the Army Commander Muhtar Pasha at
once, bring the bodies inside, post sentries to guard them.
Don't let anyone in without my express order. Tell the guards
that anyone approaching the bodies without my orders is to be
shot."

The major realized that the young lieutenants' inexperience
would inflame the soldiers even more and that if they dragged
this out, things would get worse, he ordered the soldiers to
carry the bodies inside at once and for the wounded to be
brought to the infirmary.

Ragıp Bey shouted at the top of his voice.

"Disperse . . . Everyone go back to their own units, no one
is to leave headquarters. The Pashas will arrive soon to conduct an inquiry."

Only then did the officers realize the enormity of what had
happened, they dispersed wearily, concealing their anger and
disquiet.

That night Ragıp Bey left headquarters to go to Cağaloğlu
to see his brother Cevat Bey, who'd come to Istanbul with
other leading Committee members who'd been especially chosen for this assignment.

The two brothers hadn't seen each other for some time and
embraced affectionately, and felt glad of the security of having
a brother they could embrace freely and lovingly during this
struggle they'd become involved in.

"How are you, Ragıp?"

Ragıp Bey looked at his brother and saw that his gaze was

sterner, that there were more lines on his forehead, and that an authority resembling old age had settled in his young face.

"Thanks, brother, I'm fine . . . You seem well too."

"How is Mother? I haven't been able to see her for a while, I've been so caught up in this turmoil that I forgot to even go visit my mother."

"Mother is well too, I can't go see her very often either, most of the time I'm at headquarters."

Cevat Bey looked at his brother's face as if he was trying to find something concealed there.

"How's the wife?"

"She's fine too brother, she sends her regards."

Ragıp Bey cut the niceties short and got straight to the point.

"Did you hear about what happened today, brother?"

Cevat Bey made a face.

"I heard . . . Disgraceful . . . The sergeants died, didn't they?"

"Yes they did. What's going on, where's all this heading? There's no discipline left in the army, we can't get the young officers away from the women."

Ragıp Bey fell silent, even as he was saying this he remembered Dilara Hanım's face and blushed, but he hadn't been neglecting his duties so he continued.

"Headquarters is being run by the hodjas, the sergeants and privates listen to them, they hate Committee members more than they hate Bulgarians. Three sergeants died today, more will die tomorrow, don't you people see what's going on?"

Cevat Bey sighed and smiled.

"Are you hungry?"

Ragıp Bey realized he was very hungry, and also that his brother was smiling because he remembered their mother's question.

"I am hungry."

"Let's eat first, and then we can talk."

As they ate pilaf with chickpeas and tahini they talked like children about old friends and acquaintances, Ragıp Bey's mansion's garden and memories, school and their neighborhood. Over coffee Cevat Bey stroked his moustache and continued from where he'd left off as if there'd been no interruption.

"Everyone's aware of what's going on, but they have trouble making decisions: I told Talat many times that it won't work this way, that we should overthrow the Sultan and take over the government, but—between me and you—they don't dare, and indeed they may be right, no one's ready to take positions of authority. Let's say we took over the government, who would we put in the cabinet, won't they be disappointed when they see the men behind the legend of the Committee? Who would be minister of public works? Who would be forestry minister, who knows enough about any of these things? In fact these things aren't too difficult to learn about, but as far as I understand Talat is in fact afraid that we'll get involved in power struggles and fall out with each other, and if you think about it, it's not so far-fetched. So, you could ask if it's better that way, no, it isn't, you'd be right about that, it's not clear who's governing the country."

Cevat Bey lit a cigarette.

"To tell the truth, we were caught unprepared, as if declaring constitutional monarchy would solve everything and there would suddenly be peace and prosperity. Our constitutional monarchy is like an old woman praying to saints, I guess we saw it as a kind of prayer, we would pray for it and God would solve everything. But it doesn't work like that, so despite Talat's misgivings, I still say the same thing, we have to take over the government, we left the nation ungoverned, it's our responsibility. It's almost reached the point when people will say it was better under the Sultan, they're saying this, don't you read the newspapers they're putting out, they curse the Committee every day, as if we were the ones who'd been oppressing the nation for thirty years, as if we were the ones who impoverished them, as if we were the ones who tyrannized them."

Cevat Bey stroked his moustache and put out his cigarette.

"The person behind all this is that devil they call the Sultan, he stirs up the religious fanatics and then they go stir up the soldiers. That useless Dervish Vahdeti has established a reactionary society called the Mohammadan Union Society, I read about it a few days ago, the entire fiftieth regiment signed up as members. We have to stop these fanatics and reactionaries at once, otherwise what happened today will start happening every day, this nation's children will start killing one another. We have to start with the mullahs in the madrasas. Don't worry, we're also thinking about what to do, some of our friends are saying we should draft the madrasa mullahs into the army, we'll take them and give them military training."

"Do you think these mullahs who've been exempted from military service are just going to agree to this, won't they put up a struggle?"

Cevat squinted his eyes, and there was a cold glint in them.

"They'd pay the price, Ragıp, a lot of them would be killed. Perhaps it would be better that way, perhaps we need to settle accounts. We have nowhere else to go, after that these mullahs and the Sultan who's stirring them up will step back or we'll send them to their maker. I don't see any other solution, this isn't the time to be soft, the weakest link is the one that's going to break."

"A lot of blood will be shed, I'm not reluctant to engage in this, you know me, but making soldiers kill each other is a big price to pay. More and more people in the army are supporting the mullahs, the officers who didn't go to military schools and the sergeants listen to them and see us as infidels.

Sometimes I wonder if this was what we wanted constitutional monarchy for."

"They say that if blood must be shed it will be, Ragıp. Should we hesitate to shed blood and let the nation slip back under the tyranny of the evil Sultan? Don't worry, we'll take precautions. This nation is our responsibility, we can't and won't shirk this responsibility and we will stand against anyone who moves to betray it. Of course we don't want the people of this nation to die, but if they have to die in order for the nation to be saved, then they will. We all owe our lives to this nation, if we have to we will pay, perhaps with our lives, perhaps by taking the lives of others, but one way or another we're prepared to pay the price."

Ragıp Bey finally brought up the topic he was interested in.

"What's going to happen to the army, have your people thought about this as well? The army is going down the drain, brother, you might not see it because you're involved in politics, but I'm there, the soldiers are no longer soldiers, there's no obedience, no discipline, no respect, no real training, no morale, no equipment, no weapons, the sergeants talk back to the officers, the officers despise the sergeants. God forbid, but if this army went to war it would be destroyed. What are you going to do about the army, everything from top to bottom has to be changed. You know I've seen the Prussian army, compared to them we're like a leaderless flock, this army makes me ashamed to be a soldier, I'm worried my soldiers will start to be insubordinate. Let me be more specific, when officers summon a sergeant or a private to headquarters, they load their guns before letting them in. The Pashas do nothing, they're not aware of what's going on, I tell you, brother, if you can't fix the army right away the future is dark for us."

Cevat Bey seemed pained by what he'd heard.

"We know about the state of the army, Ragıp, we're going to work on that too, Enver has ideas about this, but everything takes time, we'll rejuvenate and renew the army, but first we have to crush these mullahs, then we can turn our attention to the army."

Even though his brother insisted he stay the night, Ragıp Bey left toward midnight, saying he had to get back to the barracks; the snow was falling in large, heavy flakes, he stood in front of the door and listened, there was no sound, the city had fallen into a silent, innocent sleep; streets, houses, and rooftops were covered in white; this white silence reminded him of the fairy tales he'd heard as a child. Compared to the events of that day, the night really was like a fairy tale, peaceful, calm, and carefree, like a child who forgets at night what he's experienced during the day, but Ragıp Bey knew the city would wake the following morning, the white would be polluted, and the peace would vanish.

What Cevat Bey had told him didn't put him at ease, on the contrary he was even more concerned; even Ragıp Bey, who was always stern and uncompromising and who could kill a man in the blink of an eye if he had to, found something frightening in his brother's severity. He felt as if they were preparing for events they would not be proud to have lived through, like any officer who loves his job, he was not afraid of death or killing, rather he feared he would be ashamed of what he would do.

As he walked through the snow along that dark and deserted street, the first thing that came to mind was to go see his Sheikh, he needed his calming voice, his air of not being concerned with worldly affairs, his prayers that proclaimed God's existence, but he thought it was too late, although even at that hour Sheikh Efendi would have woken, sat next to him, and listened to what he had to say without asking any questions, he didn't have the heart to disturb him.

Ignoring the cold and the snow that was accumulating on his fur cap, he walked at a leisurely pace down Babiali Hill. In front of the prime minister's office, weary sentries waited like dark shadows, they'd only just been put on sentry duty by the sergeant of the guard and hadn't fully woken yet, they might even have still been dreaming as they stood there. Ragıp Bey realized that some of them would die in a bloody fight that they would never really understand; he knew they would die but it was not in his power to save them, he doubted he could even save himself; death was approaching everyone step by step and it was not certain who it would take.

Sheikh Efendi had once told Ragıp Bey, "Death always surprises people."

"We're not surprised by the night, by the day, by weddings or wars, but we're surprised by death even though we've been dying ever since we were created. Even as he creates us the creator tells us he will take back the soul he has created, but even though people can prepare themselves for everything, they can't prepare for death. Perhaps this is the grace of God, if you ask why, well, otherwise people wouldn't be able to enjoy the lives they lived. God tells people they are going to die, but he doesn't allow them to believe it, he allows people to live as if they were never going to die. Who else could have the power to make people manage to live with such a terrifying reality?"

Ragıp was confident enough of their friendship that he objected in a joking manner.

"If God has the power to kill, why doesn't he have the power not to kill, Sheikh Efendi?"

"Of course he has enough power, but if there was no death how would anyone appreciate the value of life? We started, the end is certain, we will end . . . Infinity is nothing for mortals, Ragıp Bey, ask yourself if you would like nothingness."

Then, softening his voice even more, he added:

"For us, eternity begins after death, it only gains meaning then. The world is too small to contain infinity, neither this world nor those living in it can grasp the meaning of infinity, we're not strong enough, perhaps when we leave this world and go to the next we'll see that an endless life has meaning, but not here, here everything beautiful owes its beauty to being ephemeral."

As he walked past buildings that had been turned into shadows by the sparse gaslights, he was still thinking about what Sheikh Efendi had said.

"The Sheikh said that death gives life meaning and even beauty, but he's never seen how these young men killed in a skirmish will experience that beauty and that meaning. He's never seen bodies torn apart, severed arms, and the bloody whiteness of gouged eyeballs or heard the moaning of wounded soldiers . . . He might know about life, perhaps even about life after death and the next world, but he doesn't know about death, we know death, we've seen it. What he said was true, we're also always surprised by death, but, to tell the truth, we've never ascribed meaning to it because we've never seen any meaning in it," he said later.

When he reached Eminönü, the wind from the sea made the night even colder, the condensed breath from his nose had formed tiny icicles on his moustache.

There was no one around, no carriages or *caiques* in sight. That night as usual the capital was like a deserted ghost city; Yeni Camii, with its large dome and its minarets reaching toward the sky, stood on the shore like a pitch-black giant opening its hands and beseeching God; the mosque made Ragıp Bey suddenly feel very alone and very small.

He jerked his bandolier into place and put his hands in his greatcoat, and, as he became whiter from the snow, crossing the bridge like a white ghost moving through the darkness, he decided to go to the barracks.

He heard the snow crunching under his feet, dogs barking here and there in the distance, the lapping of the waves, and his own breathing. The cold moved from the soles of his feet and spread throughout his body, he was so cold he could think of nothing but a warm room, a stove to sit by, and this longing for warmth made him think of Dilara Hanım and the mansion in Nişantaşı.

Indeed lately, whatever he thought about inevitably ended up reminding him of Dilara Hanım. His world was like a small village with a single square, wherever he set out from he ended up in the same square, with this red-haired lady, and he wondered what she did and who she saw when she wasn't with him.

The thought that Dilara Hanım might see other men made him feel a tightness in his chest, it hurt his pride whenever he thought about it; even though he avoided confessing this to himself, he was aware that he was jealous. What bothered him most was how accustomed the staff were the first day he went to the mansion; he thought about how other men had been welcomed into that house and more would come after him and he didn't have the power to do anything about it, then occasionally as he became aware of this helplessness he would begin to hate Dilara Hanım and swear never to see her again, but he could never keep his oath.

He only felt peace when he saw Dilara Hanım and when he was with her, because it was only when they were together that she had no chance to be with other men, when he was with her both his love and his hate diminished, when they were together he felt as if it would be easy not to be with her, but as soon as they parted, both love and hate began to dominate him. He carried within him two contradictory feelings about the same person, and his soul, unaccustomed to carrying even a single feeling where women were concerned, was wearied and disquieted.

Lately it was as if the feelings he had about the nation and the army had been nourished by his feelings for Dilara Hanım, the pain, anger, and desperation he felt for that woman was reflected in every aspect of his life and made him unhappy and uneasy about every aspect of it. Dilara Hanım had altered his untroubled nature and his untrammeled soul and he'd become an anxious person.

He was so absorbed in these thoughts and in the anger they aroused that he picked up his pace, walking not as if he was trying to get somewhere but as if he was attacking an enemy.

He was no longer conscious of the cold, he was aware only of the darkness and the silent whiteness, his back was perspiring, when he looked around he saw he'd reached the barracks, he hadn't even been aware of his surroundings, from the dry thorns in his trouser cuffs he must have strayed from his path and passed through fields and gardens.

There was something sad and isolating about the way it was snowing, as if the snow was concealing those with secrets. Suddenly he worried about what Dilara Hanım was doing at that moment, what was she doing at that moment in a secluded room in a mansion in this silent, snow-covered city; was she offering another officer cognac that she'd warmed in her palm, had she let down her red hair so that the yellow light of the fire could play on it, was she speaking in her husky voice about one of the strange and mysterious novels she'd read, was she pulling someone onto herself the way she had with him? The thought of another man touching her was enough to drive him mad; he felt a strong desire to make love and a strong desire to kill, the two feelings were similar, and they were directed at the same person.

If he'd fallen for a whore in a Galata brothel he'd be strong enough to keep her to himself and not let anyone approach her, but he felt he was powerless to keep a lady from being flirtatious.

These wealthy ladies were like a maze of corridors in which all the doors had been closed; he couldn't find a way in when he wanted to enter and couldn't find an exit when he wanted to leave, the power that drew him into the maze or drove him out of it was not his own.

He began walking decisively, he'd decided where he was going and this decision put him at ease, even though he'd walked so far in the cold he didn't feel tired. Not making a decision about Dilara Hanım had made him tired, had made him uneasy about everything without realizing it, and now making a minor decision concerning her had revived him and made him stronger.

He walked at the same determined pace until he reached her street, he walked without stopping, listening to the wind in his ears, but when he reached the end of her street he stopped suddenly. He thought it would be inappropriate to frighten the inhabitants of the mansion by knocking on the door at this hour of the night, he decided to walk past the mansion and return to the barracks. Even though he wasn't going to knock on the door, he wanted to pass near her, to feel the warmth of the woman he knew was within those walls.

He turned down the street slowly, almost dragging his feet, feeling the cold and aware of how far he'd walked; on both sides of the street were large, snow-covered gardens and unlit mansions.

The white of the snow illuminated the sky, that light descended on the rooftops as snowflakes; as soon as the snow touched the rooftops it lost its lightness, then settled on the cobblestone street like white shadows.

Ragıp Bey walked down the deserted, snowy street, he planned to walk to the end and turn back, but then as he was passing Dilara Hanım's mansion, he saw a red light glowing at the intersection of the dull lightness of the sky and the whitish darkness of the street, there as a light on in Dilara Hanım's window.

What he felt at that moment was almost the same as what he'd felt the first time he was shot during a border skirmish; he felt first as if a strong hand had picked him up and thrown him backwards, then he felt a pain in the upper part of his chest, the pain spread like corrosive smoke and took his breath away, he felt dizzy, weak in the knees, he could no longer see, and he collapsed, angered at the thought that this would sideline him from the battle and that he would be humiliated.

When he saw that light, he felt the same sharp, physical pain he felt when he was shot, mixed with this physical pain was the same sense of humiliation at being sidelined from the battle. Snow had filled his mouth and his nose, he could barely breathe, he leaned on a nearby wall.

Anyone else might have left at once and spent the rest of his life troubled about what might have been happening in the red light of that bedroom on that snowy night, suffering from all the things he imagined, but it was not in Ragıp Bey's nature to quietly accept defeat, or to quietly accept being sidelined from the battle. Despite the strong attachment he felt to Dilara Hanım, despite how indecisive and confused he'd become, he could not countenance her turning him into a wretched victim, an underdog.

After leaning on the gate to catch his breath he brusquely brushed the icicles off his moustache and went in through the iron gate to the crunching of the pebbles that had turned to ice under the snow, reaching the thick wooden door and pounding on it with his fist.

Soon he saw a trembling light in a window on the ground floor.

He heard the servant's timorous voice:

"Who's there?"

"It's me, Ragıp. Open the door."

When the door opened he heard Dilara Hanım's voice from the stairs.

"Who is it?"

"It's Ragıp Bey, ma'am."

The door flew open. He glanced at the sleepy servant who had a coat draped over his shoulders, then turned at once to look at Dilara Hanım, who was standing halfway down the stairs leaning on the bannister, and the first thing he saw was her hair. Her hair was tidy, it was still tied up.

At that moment he realized in shame that his hand was on his holster and that he'd been pounding on Dilara Hanım's door as if he was pounding on the door of a Galata brothel. He stood in the doorway looking at the woman he loved, knowing that she had the right to berate him and that he would deserve it if she did.

Dilara Hanım told the servant to make tea and to rekindle the fire, then descended the stairs.

Ragıp Bey was unable to come in through the door, he stood on the doorstep with his face flushed with cold and shame, his long greatcoat covered with snow.

Dilara Hanım came over to him and took his hand.

"Why are you standing there, come in. Your hands are cold, you're cold, a tea will warm you up."

Ragıp Bey murmured, "I was late getting back to the barracks, I couldn't find a *caique* to get home." Dilara Hanım didn't even listen to his excuses and acted as if it was completely normal for him to come at that time of night.

"Take off your coat, did you walk all the way in this weather?"

She helped him take off his greatcoat and seated him across from the fire, to which the servants had added fresh logs. They'd brought the samovar and had prepared a tray of food in case he was hungry. Dilara Hanım poured tea and added a little cognac to it.

"First drink this to warm up. Have something to eat, too, you must be hungry."

Ragıp Bey drank his tea in silence, his body was ice cold and he felt a strange pain as he began to warm in front of the fire, he didn't touch his food, and when Dilara Hanım realized he wasn't going to eat she poured him a glass of cognac and put some tea next to it.

Now, sitting next to Dilara Hanım in front of the fire, those long, cold streets, the snow, what he'd felt as the snow flew into his face and eyes, the pain he'd felt in his chest when he'd seen the light in her window, none of it seemed real anymore, it was as if he'd never walked those streets, as if he'd never worried, as if he'd never been jealous. His mood warmed and melted just like his cold body, he just felt slightly ashamed deep down, as well as a strong gratitude to Dilara Hanım, not for welcoming him the way she had, without blame, questioning, or pushing him for explanations, but for being alone in her room at that time.

They drank their cognac in silence.

When they'd finished, Dilara Hanım stood.

"Let's go to bed if you wish, you must be tired."

Dilara Hanım sensed that he was ashamed and didn't once mention how late it was.

They blew out the lamps and climbed up to the bedroom together.

The bed was made, there was only a small indentation that seemed to have been made by her body, and one of the foreign novels Dilara Hanım liked to read was open next to the bed.

That night, in contrast to their usual habits, they made love very softly, very slowly, feeling each other's bodies with love and tenderness rather than with lust; perhaps that night for the first time lovemaking became a reflection of love and gratitude rather than an aim in itself, rather than enjoyment and pleasure.

He learned that just as there are different kinds of lovemaking with different women, one could make love to the same woman in different ways, depending on changing feelings; for the first time he held a woman's hand and kissed her hand with love while making love, for the first time between bouts of lovemaking he laid with his head on a woman's chest; for the first time he felt the body of a woman he was making love to as of it was his own body. Perhaps it wasn't as fiery as their previous lovemaking, as burning, as capable of making them feel lightheaded enough to forget everything outside the bed, but it carried the lovemaking out of bed, every touch created a deep and permanent love and attachment.

On that cold night, as the city surrendered to the snow, Ragıp Bey learned to trust a woman and to feel gratitude to the woman who had taught him this.

Later he told Osman, "The sweetness of trusting the woman you love is something you can't find anywhere else, anyone who experiences this becomes enslaved to it."

But the following morning, after leaving the house happy as usual, he once again began to worry that a sentence was missing.

8

At that time Reşit Pasha spent most of his time at the palace with the Sultan, so it fell to Hüseyin Hikmet Bey to find the right waterfront mansion for Mihrişah Sultan, who was impatient to come to Istanbul.

Hikmet Bey, who had lived a secluded life of exile in his mansion reading books and spending time with Hediye since he'd returned from Salonika, and who hadn't seen his friends from the Committee who were now in power, accepted this duty happily, realizing that he missed being in the streets and seeing people.

One day when he was out looking for a waterfront mansion he ran into Selim Bey, a childhood friend from Kanlıca, and he realized that his short friend with his symmetrical face, a fiery man who loved to talk about politics and women, had hardly changed at all. He embraced Hikmet Bey in a friendly manner that he hadn't seen in any of the friends he'd met recently and invited him to his waterfront mansion, which was next to that of the Sultan's nephew, which had a hundred and twenty-seven rooms.

Hikmet Bey wondered if his friend knew about what had happened to him, but nothing could remain a secret in the capital, and gossip about people connected to the palace spread particularly quickly, it was almost impossible that Selim Bey, the son of Cypriot Mustapha Pasha, hadn't heard that doctor Reşit Pasha's son had shot himself because of his wife.

When they entered the waterfront mansion Hikmet Bey

regretted having accepted the invitation, the mere thought of meeting Mustapha Pasha, a friend of his father who he'd known since childhood, or his wife, confused him. He realized he was not yet ready to meet people, to speak to them, to see the look of pity in their eyes. He thought about coming up with an excuse and fleeing, but Selim Bey put his arm through his as he walked quickly and bantered about the members of the Committee; if he'd stopped for a moment Hikmet Bey would have excused himself and left, but Selim Bey never stopped talking.

He gave orders to the servants who greeted them then without letting go of Hikmet Bey's arm, he rushed him down the long corridors toward his quarters in panic at the prospect of meeting someone at any moment. Hikmet Bey's face was pale with a fear he found meaningless and that he was ashamed of, there were beads of sweat on his forehead, they finally arrived at Selim Bey's quarters without encountering anyone and sat on benches by one of the large windows that looked out over the Bosphorus, which was flowing grey-green under an ashen sky, then Selim Bey looked at his friend in surprise.

"How are you? Is anything the matter?"

"Thank you, I'm fine, we walked here from the woods a bit quickly, it must have tired me out, I haven't been out of the house for quite some time."

Selim Bey studied his friend's face, and Hikmet Bey slowly caught his breath and managed to free himself from the strange and meaningless fear that had taken hold of him suddenly.

"They'll bring us tea now, we'll catch our breath, I suppose I talked too much when I ran into you, sometimes the way I talk makes people feel seasick, when they listen to me they feel like they're on a ferry in stormy weather."

Hikmet Bey laughed.

"Not at all. I'm already feeling better."

After the tea arrived, Selim Bey asked the first question he needed to ask.

"What were you up to around here on a winter day like this, were you on your way to visit someone, am I delaying you, if it's something you can't talk about, just go, I won't ask any questions."

"No, it's nothing like that, my mother is coming here from Paris, we need to find a waterfront mansion for her, I was tired of sitting around at home, looking for a house has given me an excuse to be out and about, when I ran onto you I was about to go ask the tobacco merchant on the pier whether there were any vacant waterfront mansions in the neighborhood."

"You're looking for a waterfront mansion for Mihrişah Sultan?"

"Yes."

"You know what they say about being in the right place at the right time, it just happens that the place next to us is vacant, like ours, the woods behind it stretch as far as the top of the hill and there's a six-or-seven-room lodge up there for summer . . . It would be perfect for Mihrişah Sultan."

"That's wonderful, Selim, I'll go talk to them right away."

Selim grabbed Hikmet's arm like a spoiled Pasha's son who believed that everything in life would turn out well.

"Hold on, what's the matter with you, we'll tell our butler to go talk to them and handle it and we can talk here in the meantime."

He immediately called the butler, gave him instructions, and then went back to talking about politics and what the Committee was up to. "Do you see anyone from the Committee?"

"I don't see anyone."

"But you're probably aware of what they're up to, while we were celebrating getting rid of one tyrant, a hundred more tyrants took over, they don't tolerate even the slightest criticism, they resort to threats and blackmail at once."

He suddenly stopped talking to avoid saying anything insulting.

"Are you still with the Committee?"

"I'm not sure, Selim, perhaps I was never really a staunch supporter of the Committee, that's how it seems when I look back, I just wanted to get rid of tyranny and breathe some freedom."

After a brief pause, Hikmet Bey added:

"I think that what I really wanted was to make this place like Paris, but now I see that's not as easy as I thought it was. A childish dream . . . "

"Isn't that what we all want, in fact, don't we want this wreck of a nation to be like the cities we see in Europe? But in order to do this we have to get rid of any kind of authoritarianism. I was talking to a friend recently and, strangely, he gave the example of France just as you did, he said they overthrew the tyranny of the king by rising up themselves and shedding blood, this is true deliverance, you can't seek deliverance at the hands of soldiers the way we do. In short, it can't happen without the people."

Hikmet Bey shook his head in despair.

"But the people here don't act, Selim."

"Do you know Ahmet Samim?"

"From time to time I read his column in the newspaper."

"He's a dear friend of mine, you'll like him when you meet him, he and a few other friends like him try to enlighten the people by writing articles, but the Committee rains threats on them every day. Still, no matter what happens we have to say what's going on, we have to communicate the truth to the people through articles and speeches."

Hikmet Bey suddenly started to laugh. Selim Bey was slightly offended.

"Did I unintentionally say something funny?"

"No, no, it wasn't anything you said. Something else came

to mind. When my father was the palace physician and I was a clerk for the chamberlain, one day a childhood friend, the son of a pasha, told me that we had to tell the people what was really going on at once, and I, despite being from a family that supported the palace, joined the opposition, now the people I joined have won the fight and seized power, another childhood friend who's also the son of a Pasha comes and tells me that we have to tell the people what's really happening at once and calls me to join the opposition. Life keeps putting me among the people holding power, and the sons of pashas keep convincing me to join the opposition. And it's always the sons of pashas who talk to me about the people. So Selim, can you swear to me that you wouldn't laugh about that?"

Selim Bey laughed as well, then became serious again.

"In this country, can any honest person have any destiny except to be in the opposition, Hüseyin Hikmet Bey, son of Reşit Pasha?"

Hikmet Bey became serious too.

"To tell the truth, I don't know, Selim. I keep wondering whether I deserve to be considered honest. I wonder what I've done to deserve considered being honest."

"You were born honest, Hikmet . . . There's nothing else you can do. That's your destiny, whether you deserve it or not. It's some people's fate to be honest."

There was a silence.

"Come on," said Selim Bey, "let's go see my parents, we'll eat together, you can stay the night and we can talk a bit."

Once again Hikmet Bey felt a sudden sense of panic.

"I haven't socialized for a long time, it's been quite some time since I've taken part in conversation at the dinner table, I don't want to be a bore for your parents, in any event, if we rent the place next door we'll be seeing a lot of each other, tonight, if you'll excuse me, allow me to go back home without meeting anyone."

Selim Bey realized that Hikmet Bey was truly uneasy and didn't insist.

"As you wish. Then come tomorrow morning so you can see the place next door in the daylight, I do hope we'll have the honor of having Mihrişah Sultan as a neighbor. Anyway, let me tell them to get the motor launch ready so they can take you back to the other side."

After giving the orders for the motor launch to be readied, the two of them left the waterfront mansion together, then stood in silence listening to the Bosphorus currents until the launch with green and red lights on the sides appeared in the darkness. Before getting into the launch, Hikmet Bey asked after Selim Bey's brother.

"He's fine . . . You know he's in Paris, but he'll be return-ing soon."

"Give him my regards, I'd love to see him too."

"I hope you will . . . I'll be expecting you tomorrow morn-ing, I'll have the key sent over, if Reşit Pasha would be kind enough to come as well he could join us so he can see it too."

"I'll send my father word when I get home."

"Sometime this week I'll invite a couple of friends I'd like you to meet, let's have dinner together. There's no reason to go wild, they're all good people and I'm sure you'll like them."

Hikmet Bey didn't beat around the bush.

"Fine, fine, it would do me good to see a few people."

They embraced before he boarded the launch. Selim Bey stood on the shore watching the back of the launch until it dis-appeared from view, and Hikmet Bey was pleased at having received a friendly embrace that he'd needed for a long time.

Despite the chill and the harsh Bosphorus wind on his face, he stood in the back of the launch. Selim seemed to be feeling the same kind of excitement he himself had felt when he joined the Committee, and he guessed that he'd joined some kind of opposition movement.

There was something brotherly in the friendship he'd offered Hikmet, and from experience he knew that this kind of brotherhood could only be found in opposition groups rebelling against those in power; his first period of working with the Committee had been the best time of his life, they'd prepared for their rebellion with a common sense of anger and fear, they'd entrusted their lives to each other. Now Selim Bey had given him the hope that he could experience this again; even though he never left the house, he knew that the Committee had become authoritarian and corrupt and that they'd been incapable of governing the nation since they came to power. Nor could he forget the despicable way they'd left him out in the cold without even daring to take his side, how they'd silently distanced themselves from him for fear of being tainted by scandal, if the same thing had happened to any of them he wouldn't have abandoned them, or at least he thought he wouldn't have.

The lights on the far shore were getting larger, there were lights here and there in the woods, which looked like a black engraving, he held his fez with one hand so it wouldn't fly away and held the collar of his coat closed with the other.

Suddenly he remembered his fear of meeting Selim Bey's family; this fear showed him that the wounds to his soul had not yet recovered, had not yet healed, that the shame of a failed suicide and his longing for the woman who had left him still remained, together with all the humiliation.

Sometimes he forgot Mehpare Hanım, a few days would pass without her coming to mind, then suddenly he remembered her with a burning pain, at times like this there was nowhere he could take shelter, neither in a job nor in a fight nor with friends.

He called Hediye, rested his head on her lap, and remained like that for hours, he tried to find closeness, if not consolation, in the warmth of her body, tried to withstand the loneliness that engulfed him.

Hediye, who'd become accustomed to the sad look in his eyes, to his sudden silences, and to the way he embraced her without lust, sat still and in silence for hours; she already knew that after resting his head in her lap for hours he would erupt with lust like a volcano, embrace her, and drag her to bed. Although she guessed she was replacing another woman, she never voiced this and never complained about it.

She greeted him at the door when he got home, it was clear his lateness had worried her but that she knew she had no right to express her concern; for whatever reason, she was always afraid something would happen to Hikmet Bey. She took his coat in delight.

"You must be cold, sir."

"Yes, I am a bit cold. It's cold outside."

"Would you like to eat right away?"

"Yes, in fact I'm hungry. Did you know that cold makes you hungry?"

They went into the living room together, Hikmet Bey sat in front of the fire, and Hediye remained standing.

"Have a seat, Hediye, why are you on your feet?"

"Let me go and tell them to prepare the food, sir."

"Tell the housekeeper to come, I want to send news to my father."

"Certainly, sir."

Hikmet Bey told the housekeeper to send a man to his father with the news that he'd found a waterfront mansion next to the Cypriots in Kandilli and that he wanted his father to come look at it with him the following morning.

"Tell him to go at once, if my father isn't home he's to wait for the answer and then come."

Like every other pasha in those troubled times, Reşit Pasha was walking on eggshells, he was afraid of hearing bad news, but also of being arrested, exiled, or worse at any moment; no one knew who would be next, when even the Sultan was in a perilous position, everyone feared for their lives, when he was told that a message had arrived from his son he said he hoped everything was well then went to see the messenger in fear of hearing bad news.

He relaxed when he heard the message.

"Tell Hikmet Bey that I have to go to the palace in the morning, I'll pick him up at his mansion at noon, tell him to wait for me."

The Sultan sensed that the Committee was looking for an excuse to dethrone him and diminish his political influence in a way that everyone would see, so he spent most of his time engaged in carpentry, talking with the doctor about medical advancements, and telling stories about his youth, and most of the stories he told Reşit Pasha surprised him.

Some days earlier when they'd been talking, somehow the subject of rabies had come up.

"Once," said the Sultan, "I personally wrote a letter to Monsieur Pasteur inviting him to come to Istanbul, unfortunately he didn't come, he couldn't, if he'd come we could have found the solution to the rabies problem before anyone else."

"The famous Pasteur, Your Majesty?"

"Yes, doctor. At the time he wasn't as famous as he is now, but I'd heard about his work, I wanted so much for him to come, establish a hospital and continue his work here, but what can we do, it wasn't in the cards."

Then he complained about the doctors he'd sent to study in Europe.

"I noticed, Pasha, that some of the doctors who never went to Europe are better and more skilled than those who studied there. And as for those who studied in Paris, I don't expect anything from them. I know all too well that those who go to Paris abandon themselves to pleasure and don't spend any time studying. I saw Paris when I was a prince, even at night it's like daytime, you can't take your eyes off the debauchery.

When we first went to Paris, Münir Pasha was a clerk at the embassy, later when I became Sultan I brought him to the palace, I liked him, he was a good man. He used to say that there wasn't a single night in Paris that he went to bed before dawn. But when he was still in his thirties and forties he had no manhood left. He abused it so much . . . I'll never forget, I was sitting with the diplomats, I needed a pen so I asked Münir Pasha for his, he dropped a pillbox as he was taking his pen out of his pocket and he said, 'Winter is coming, we have to stay strong, the doctors gave me a pep pill.' We laughed at this for a long time. That's how it is, Pasha, everyone who's lived in Paris needs pep pills when they're still young. What a shame it is."

He paused and lit a cigarette and then, as it was his habit to change the subject abruptly, he launched on the subject of drinking.

"And they drink a lot. I saw the king of England, it would be difficult to find anyone who had as much tolerance for drink as that king, he adds cognac to the strongest beer, but he still doesn't get drunk, he has such a high tolerance for alcohol. My father Sultan Mecit drank as well, he was a victim of drink and sexual excess, he passed away at a young age. Drink is the reason my brother Sultan Murat went mad. You don't know this, but the famous Namık Kemal led my brother astray, they used to drink *rakı* till morning. Namık Kemal was my close friend as well. I told him several times that he would be the death of my brother and that he shouldn't encourage him to drink so much, but neither he nor my brother listened to me."

The following morning, after days of snow, the weather was clear, a bright winter sun changed the city's face, it was as if everything had become cheerful; Reşit Pasha woke early and went to the palace, he was brought to the Sultan at once, and the Sultan complained as if he was late.

"Where have you been, doctor, I've been waiting for you,

look, the sun is out, I've been in the doldrums for days, I've been sitting still for so long I feel I've put down roots, I thought we might walk in the garden while the sun's still out but you weren't here, this is how the weather in Istanbul is, it's not dependable, it could cloud over before we have a chance to get outside."

The doctor was surprised.

"Are we going out into the garden, Your Majesty?"

"Why are you surprised, doctor, don't we need to move around a bit, walking is good, doctor, it helps the circulation, strengthens the heart, come, let's walk, are you dressed warmly enough, if not they can bring you a fur, don't get cold."

"I'm dressed warmly, Your Majesty, I won't get cold."

"Let's go, then, I'll show you my hoatzin birds, you've never seen anything like them."

Reşit Pasha had never walked in the palace's back garden, which covered the entire hillside, it was adorned with a variety of trees and flowers brought from the four corners of the world and was green and colorful even in winter. It was as if they had arrived in another climate, even the snow on the branches had been cleaned off and it was as if a season had been provided to match the bright sun, it was as if this garden was kept magically warm while the rest of the city lived through the cold of winter.

The guards and gardeners disappeared and watched from their hiding places; they knew how dangerous it was to encounter the Sultan suddenly when he was strolling in the garden; once a gardener encountered the Sultan and took the opportunity to request something of him, but the Sultan was terrified of being assassinated so he took out the pistol he always carried in his pocket and shot the gardener. Reşit Pasha had heard that this was one of three murders committed by the Sultan, who had sent thousands into exile; in addition to the gardener he'd killed with his own hands, it was said that he also had one of his favorite eunuchs hanged; once, this eunuch shot another to death during an argument in the palace; the man went to the Sultan for protection and confessed to the murder.

When the Sultan asked him what he'd used to kill the other man, the eunuch showed him the pistol in his pocket.

The Sultan could not forgive anyone taking out a gun in his presence, so he had the eunuch arrested at once and he was hanged in Beşiktaş early the next morning. He also sent Mithat Pasha, who'd brought him to power after his uncle's abdication by drafting the Kanun-i Esasi, into exile in Ta'if and had him strangled in prison there.

Reşit Pasha had never had the courage to ask the Sultan about these rumored murders, he didn't know whether or not the rumors were true but he believed the Sultan was capable of shooting someone who appeared before him suddenly; this was the terrifying reality for those in the Sultan's retinue.

They walked among thick-trunked trees that were thousands of years old, red pines, sandalwood trees that exuded magical and alluring scents, beds of golden tulips, multicolored fields of hyacinths with leaves like droplets, orchid hothouses, roses that bloomed even in winter, and reached a stream that was clearly man-made, the streambed had been lined with fine sand and shiny flat stones and there was a boat.

"Come, doctor," said the Sultan, "let's take a boat ride."

After helping the Sultan into the boat, Reşit Pasha sat beside him and saw that there were no oars, when the Sultan saw the pasha looking for the oars he smiled with pleasure, as he did whenever he surprised someone.

"Don't look for the oars, doctor, this boat doesn't have any . . . Look, it has pedals, you have to step down on them. Have you ever used pedals?"

"No, Your Majesty."

The Sultan loved knowing things that other people didn't know and spoke confidently about whatever he knew.

"It's easy, just do what I do, you'll catch on right away."

The Sultan and his physician pedaled, and the boat started moving along the stream, on both sides of the stream were miniature copies of the ferry stations of the Bosphorus, each an exact copy, each chiseled building with its own sign and brass bell.

"Let's go see the hens and the roosters first, let's see if you've ever seen such beautiful roosters."

The Sultan brought the boat to the shore and they got out together.

There were perhaps thirty thousand hens and roosters in a coop almost as large as a mansion. They were not like any hens or roosters the pasha had ever seen; some were snow-white, some had bright green and red feathers, some had long necks, some had crests, some were tiny, some had sharp spurs, some were speckled, some were entirely red, and others were entirely brown.

As they approached the coop, thousands of hens and roosters began to crow as if they were greeting the Sultan, there was cackling, flapping, and all manner of noise, the Sultan, who was always frightened by any kind of noise or sudden movement, looked at the animals with a loving smile.

"Look at them, doctor, what a commotion they make . . . These white leghorn chickens lay eggs as big as my fist, I eat one every morning, you know me, I don't eat butter at breakfast, fat slows you down, but eggs strengthen the body, you definitely should eat an egg every morning too, doctor."

The Sultan clasped his hands behind his back and started walking along the front of the coop, speaking to each of the hens and roosters in turn, it was as if he was sure they could understand him.

"How are you, my girl, is that big bantam bothering you,

how are you, your voice is a bit feeble today, are you ill, you don't lay eggs anymore, have I broken your heart, are you angry at me . . . "

As he listened, the pasha bit his lip to keep from laughing, he thought the Sultan had hired a detective to keep tabs on the hens.

When the Sultan turned to him just then he had trouble suppressing his laughter.

"Doctor, you should talk to animals, even to plants, these poor creatures can't speak, but by God they understand what we say, all animals understand what we say, they know whether we're angry, sad, or ill, and like all of us they need affection and love. Let's go see the other animals, it's been a while since I've visited them."

The doctor was heading toward the boat when the Sultan stopped him.

"There's no need for the boat, the animal cages are at the foot of the wall, let's walk, we can take the boat later."

They walked side by side along a path of snow-white pebbles, it was as if each pebble had been cleaned and polished individually, and as they approached the garden wall, which was as high as a building, Reşit Pasha heard, roars, bellows, and growls the like of which he'd never heard before, the animals had smelled them approaching.

First they saw the peacocks, they opened their netlike wings and cried at the top of their lungs in their ugly voices, which didn't match their beauty, which was like a rainbow shining under the sun.

"It's impossible for people to understand the creator's deeds, he gives with one hand and takes with the other, look how beautiful they are, but what about the sound they make, it's unbearable, and think of the tiny, plain mockingbird that can fit in your hand, you can't get enough of listening to it, God gave this bird beauty and gave the mockingbird a beautiful

voice. He never gives everything to one being, neither to a bird
nor to a sultan . . .

Then he saw zebras watching them timidly with their large
eyes as if they were ready to flee at any moment, when they
moved together their black and white stripes were as dizzying
as a pinwheel spinning quickly; as Reşit Pasha, who'd never
seen a zebra, looked at them in surprise the Sultan informed
him:

"These animals only live in Africa, we had trouble getting
them here. Whenever I come across a picture of an animal I've
never seen in a foreign magazine I can't resist, I order one at
once, I'm interested in these animals, I want to have one in my
zoo so I can see them in person."

A little later they reached the lion cage, and the lions tore
the air with their terrifying roars. Two lions paced up and
down in the cage with solemn irritability, taking no interest in
the visitors; nearby was a cage in which two yellow and black
striped tigers lay on the floor. The Sultan stopped in front of
the tiger cage.

"They call the lion the king of the jungle, doctor, if they're
the kings of the jungle, these are the queens of nature, there is
no animal more beautiful than them, they're both strong and
beautiful, look at their lines, look at their eyes. If you look carefully you can see the work of God everywhere, did you know
that lions and tigers are never found in the same place, one
lives in Africa and the other in India, if you ask why, if these
two animals lived in the same place they would tear each other
apart, they would kill each other until there was only one left,
then they would become extinct. If you ask me, it should be
the same way for people, each of us on a separate continent.
You see what happens when we live next to each other . . . "

They passed deer, antelope, wolves, foxes, lynx that were
slightly larger than cats, panthers, and giraffes, they examined
each species and were surprised by each of them; the Sultan

showed off how much he knew about them and expressed his admiration for them; Reşit Pasha saw that he was truly fond of animals and was surprised at how this man who was always cold and distant toward people could find a place in his cold and unaffectionate nature for the love of animals.

The biggest surprise for Reşit Pasha, or rather the most frightening experience, was the area where the dogs were kept. There were hundreds of dogs in the cages, but not a sound came from them, not a growl or a bark or a howl, and they remained motionless, they maintained a silence that was more terrifying than any sound an animal could make.

Their appearance was as terrifying as their silence, they were unlike any dogs the pasha had ever seen: There were furry boxers, miniature Dalmatians, Dobermans with short legs, oversized lapdogs . . . each of these strange creatures resembled something other than what it was.

When the Sultan saw how surprised the doctor was he explained.

"You can't find dogs like these anywhere else in the world, I breed dogs and come up with types no one has ever seen before, but, as you see, they're all mute, I couldn't find a solution for this."

As they hurried past the dogs that would haunt Reşit Pasha's dreams for years, it was clear the Sultan was not happy with the results he'd achieved.

They moved away quickly and went to see the guinea pigs, which were kept apart from all the other animals, they were such a pure white that they glistened like snowballs in the sun.

"You see I'm very fond of these animals, their whiteness always touches me, they seem so innocent, don't they, doctor?"

A few months later the pasha would realize how sincere the Sultan was when he said he loved those animals, when he was sent into exile he left behind his jewelry, thousands of gold coins, valuable watches, prayer beads, and his collection of weapons without complaint, but he insisted on taking his Siamese cats and one of his two white guinea pigs.

"They really are beautiful, Your Majesty."

"Come on, doctor, let's have some coffee. You're not cold, are you?"

"No, Your Majesty."

They walked through the trees until they suddenly came across a shack that looked like a rural coffeehouse, it had a thatched roof and there were low tables and short stools out front. The pasha was even more surprised to see a rural coffeehouse in the palace garden; he'd known this man for so many years, but during this hour-long stroll he'd seen so much he'd never seen before, he realized there was so much about the Sultan he didn't know, and that it was not easy to grasp his essence.

They sat on low stools under the thatched roof and pulled their coats around them, a plump man who looked like a stereotypical rural coffeehouse owner came out and greeted them as if they were ordinary customers, saying, "Welcome, gentlemen."

"What would you like?"

"We'll have two coffees," said the Sultan, "but I want them frothy, don't boil them too much."

"As you wish, sir."

There was an ashtray with a pack of cigarettes and matches in it on the wooden table. The Sultan was a heavy smoker, all the ashtrays in the palace had a pack of cigarettes and matches in them so he wouldn't have to look for cigarettes, and these cigarettes and matches were the only sign that this rural coffeehouse belonged to the palace.

The Sultan was unable to leave the palace and live like other people, so he'd had a rural coffeehouse built in a corner of his garden in order to bring a little bit of the outside world into his palace. The only person in that large palace, indeed in the entire empire, who was allowed to treat the Sultan like an ordinary person, and indeed who had been ordered to do so, was the man who ran this coffeehouse; his job was not to make coffee, it was to make the Sultan feel he was going to a coffeehouse as an ordinary person, and the Sultan enjoyed this game like a child even though he knew he was the one who'd invented it. Later Reşit Pasha told Osman, "He could be so childish, it was impossible to believe this was the man who governed the entire empire with absolute authority."

As they were waiting for their coffee, the Sultan, as was his habit, brought up a subject and started talking.

"As I told you when we were looking at the peacocks, doctor, God never gives any creature everything completely, he always limits something, people who look at us think, the great Sultan, he has everything, he lives a happy life, however there is pain and suffering in our life as well, but we are not allowed to complain. There's no one in the world who doesn't suffer, who doesn't get sad, there are probably many people who have no idea what my life is like. They imagine I'm a man who never experiences pain or suffering, that I'm a man who's sat in a cage like a bird all my life."

He stopped talking when the coffee was brought out, when the coffee man left he continued after taking a sip of coffee.

"When I was a prince I went one day to my brother's house in Çengelköy to swim in the sea. One of my men came to tell me that my little daughter was ill and that I was needed at the palace. I got out of the sea at once, got into a boat, and set out for Dolmabahçe Palace; when they saw me approaching, many of the palace staff gathered on the quay. When I saw this I grew even more worried. I was impatient to reach the quay, I tried to go into the palace but people blocked my way. As I was trying to force my way through them, Marco Pasha came out, told them to let me through, and said they should tell me the truth. He turned to me and told me my daughter had been in an accident, part of her body had been burned, every possible medical measure had been taken, it was up to God and his mercy whether she would recover. When I heard this I fainted. When I came to a while later I rushed to my daughter's room, they'd put the poor child in bed and wrapped her in cotton . . . part of her face was uncovered."

The Sultan took another cigarette from the pack in the ashtray and lit it.

"I kissed her face, it was as if she was waiting to see me before she died, doctor, she opened her eyes and looked at me, I think she smiled when she saw me. Then she let go. I was beside myself for days. Later I looked into what had happened, her mother was busy with something, the child was unattended, she found some matches and started playing with them, a match ignited, her tulle silk dress caught on fire, they ran to her when they heard her screams but they arrived too late."

He sighed deeply.

"Do you know, doctor, that I built the Şişli Etfal Hospital in honor of that child, so others wouldn't experience the pain of losing a child."

He inhaled, puffed out his cheeks, and blew smoke rings, then watched them drift away.

"Why are we talking about this? How strange it is, doctor, when a person is sad he can't think of anything to cheer himself up, but he remembers earlier sufferings, it's as if sorrow attracts sorrow."

He waved his hand slightly and said, "Whatever," as if he was answering someone.

"The coffee's good, isn't it, doctor?"

"Yes, Your Majesty, and it's frothy."

"They make really good coffee here. If you're finished, let's go, otherwise we'll get cold, it's not good to sit too long in cold weather."

He left a small coin next to the coffee cup as if he was in a real coffeehouse.

"Good day, coffee man, your coffee was delicious, my compliments."

"Good day, gentlemen, I hope to see you again."

They walked through the trees and reached the bank of the stream, got into the boat, and paddled back the way they'd come; the Sultan was silent on the return trip, and as Reşit Pasha found it inappropriate to speak when the Sultan was silent, he said nothing.

When they got out of the boat, the Sultan started talking as if the pasha was aware of what he'd been thinking all that time.

"Trouble is coming, doctor, the like of which has never been seen. God help us."

"Why do you say that, Your Majesty, everything has been sorted out, thank God."

"Nothing has been sorted out, doctor, you know that as well as I do, but you don't want to upset me; the nation is boiling deep down, it can't keep going this way for long, there's nothing we can do, the only thing I can say is that I hope God ends this well . . . "

With a sadness that surprised even himself, Reşit Pasha realized that the Sultan had grown older; he had an attitude of resignation, he observed what was going on, he saw where it was heading, but instead of struggling against it he resigned himself. It was as if he was slowly preparing himself for the day he would leave the palace, like a prisoner accepting his sentence, he was saying farewell to his palace, to his garden, inwardly hoping that what was coming would happen as soon as possible.

Perhaps this wasn't so, but Reşit Pasha recorded this stroll through the garden in his memory as a farewell visit; he was also touched by the sorrow in the Sultan's voice and in what he said. Later he told Osman, "In fact I knew that the Sultan had a changeable nature, at the time I knew that if conditions had changed in his favor he would change instantly and become a powerful fighter again, but still, his moods had a strong impact on me, upset me."

That day Reşit Pasha left with sense of sorrow; he wasn't able to come up with a precise analysis of his feelings for the Sultan, was he frightened, was he angry, did he love him, was he grateful to him, perhaps he felt all of these things simultaneously.

Their relationship contained all the complex feelings that existed between master and slave; Reşit Pasha didn't know when or how this had happened, but he sensed that his life had become connected to the Sultan's, he was also aware that this feeling was not mutual, if Reşit Pasha was the one who was defeated the Sultan would carry on with his life without being too upset, but if the Sultan was defeated it would shake the doctor's life deeply. The pasha didn't find this disparity between them strange, even though he'd been defeated he was still a sultan and he was a subject, he'd never questioned the Sultan's divine authority and it was too late to start doing so now. That the person to whom he'd bound his life had grown older made him older as well, his defeat meant his own defeat.

He arrived at Hikmet Bey's mansion without having been able to overcome his disquiet. When Hikmet Bey saw his father, he immediately asked if anything was the matter.

"How are you, is anything the matter? You seem upset."

"This morning I strolled through the palace garden with the Sultan."

Despite his sadness, he was secretly proud of having had this privilege bestowed upon him.

Hikmet Bey waited in silence for his father to continue.

"He was like a melancholy old man, his mood made me sad as well, I think that when I see the way he's aged, I see that I've also aged."

had fallen in love with very beautiful women, both of them had been abandoned, neither of them could get over their love, it was almost as if they had built their lives around this pain in order to be able to forget it.

The winter sun shone on the garden, giving it a bluish tint as flowers poked through the snow, the icicles hanging from the trees, on the point of melting, gave off a bluish mist; the flowers with the larger tufts reflected a whitish purple in the sun, this edged the blue of the garden with purple in some places and white in others.

Reşit Pasha took a long look at the garden; Hikmet Bey was cold and wanted to get into the carriage, but he had to wait because his father didn't move.

Whatever it was that Reşit Pasha had been thinking about, he suddenly turned and put his arm through his son's, as they walked toward the carriage he spoke as if he was murmuring.

"It's not worth it, Hikmet."

At that moment Hikmet Bey didn't take heed of what his father had said, but for the rest of his life, whenever he encountered something beautiful he remembered this passing statement that hadn't meant anything to him at the time and to which he now attached great importance; this was perhaps the most unforgettable statement his father had made to him.

When they got into the carriage both of them, and particularly Reşit Pasha, suddenly cheered up; the blue mist of the garden had dissipated the heavy atmosphere between them, they seemed younger and almost giddy; throughout the trip they talked about palace gossip, the bad manners of the Committee members, the tragicomic romantic adventures that sometimes spilled out of the pashas' mansions.

They were still cheerful when they arrived at the waterfront mansion. If Hikmet Bey had allowed it, the Pasha would have looked at every single room in the house, but he told his father that there was no need and that all the rooms were in good condition.

Reşit Pasha took his son at his word, but warned him mockingly, "Look, if your mother finds any faults she'll make life hell for you, are you sure every part of the house is suitable for her?"

"I'm sure, Father, I think Mother will like this place. What do you think?"

"Yes, it's nice, you found a good place."

He stopped, looked at his son, and laughed as he added, "Sometimes you surprise me, are you becoming a man of the world? You did this job well."

Hikmet Bey would never have guessed that such a simple compliment would make him so happy, the pasha's cheer and satisfaction reflected on his son as well.

Before they went back, they sat at a coffeehouse on the shore and looked out across the sea as they had coffee together as father and son, and Reşit Pasha told his son amusing stories about his own childhood.

Later Hikmet told Osman, "I've probably never seen my father that cheerful. I don't know if the strange beauty of the garden touched him, or if he was happy because Mihrişah Sultan was returning, I was never able to figure that out."

9

As it prepared for a bloody and unforgettable uprising whose effects would be felt for a century, the capital, focused on its own problems within a frightening chaos, noticed Mihrişah Sultan's arrival despite the inwardly seething military barracks, the dank rooms within the thick walls of the madrassas where thousands of dirty tricks were paving the way for disaster, the fear and alarm that increased daily in government offices, Committee meetings where angry shouts echoed off the walls, the panic in the mansions of the wealthy and powerful whose concern about the future deepened every day, and the rage that burned toward the point of explosion in the muddy neighborhoods where poverty and desperation continued to grow.

It was as if everyone suddenly fell silent and the entire city watched the red-haired lady and her long-faced granddaughter debark the Marseilles ferry with her negro servants in matching uniforms, chests filled with silk clothing that took twenty carriages to transport, and her French ladies in waiting, each of whom was uniquely beautiful.

It pleased her to enter a city as if she was entering a salon, making everyone stop and look at her, and even though she had to create a larger spectacle than had been necessary on her previous visit to Istanbul to turn people's heads, she got what she wanted, and despite the discontent exhibited by Rukiye, who disliked displays of any kind, she made this complicated city talk about her, at least for a while.

The mullahs talked about her lack of religion, the officers talked about her beauty, the merchants about her wealth, the women about her clothes, and the denizens of the palace about her lack of tact. In that strange and complicated time, it was as if the city settled down for one night, as if animosity was forgotten for one night.

As for Sheikh Efendi, he sat in the *zikr* room and listened expressionlessly as Hasan Efendi told him about her arrival. Hasan Efendi told him in detail about Mihrişah Sultan, her servants, her ladies in waiting, and Rukiye, though he didn't mention her long face and preferred to say she looked healthy.

When he'd finished he said that Mihrişah Sultan "would probably visit the *tekke* soon."

All Sheikh Efendi said was that their door was open to everyone, but he felt, with great shame, that he wanted to see her as soon as possible. However, what the Sheikh felt was unlike the kind of longing other people felt. He had pledged his loyalty to God at a young age, when he was still a child, and he'd sworn to avoid everything that God and religion considered a sin; in order to remain loyal and keep his oath, he had to avoid missing anyone he was forbidden to miss, and he was not allowed to miss, think about, or imagine any woman other than those in his harem.

Sheikh Efendi was so sincere in his faith and in his loyalty to his religion that when he wanted to see a woman he wasn't supposed to miss, when he felt a desire like this, he did not even accept that it was a desire, a longing, and far from accepting this, his soul declined to notice that he felt this. He realized that there was a sinful desire growing within him, and even though he was unable to name this desire precisely, he knew of it from the deep pain he felt and from the way this sinfulness was shaking his conscience.

The desire never emerged as a clear, obvious, and observable feeling, that desire was concealed even from Sheikh

Efendi himself, all he felt was the pain of an unrequited desire and the shame caused by his doubt about the source of this pain.

Perhaps what was stranger was that Sheikh Efendi, who used to be impatient to see her, who used to miss her, and who now successfully concealed from himself that he'd missed Mihrişah Sultan, had in fact previously made a great effort to miss her without even realizing it. He struggled to miss a woman he could see occasionally rather than missing his former wife Mehpare Hanım, who he knew he would never see again, in this way easing slightly the sorrow of carrying an impossibility in his life, he'd made a great effort to replace Mehpare Hanım with Mihrişah Sultan, but all of these feelings and efforts made him like a person who sensed the sun was behind the clouds, indeed who knew it was there, but who could not see the sun when he looked at the sky. Sheikh Efendi's feelings were concealed behind the clouds generated by his own beliefs, there was no other possible way, he couldn't voice this desire even when he was alone with himself, he couldn't accept its existence. He struggled to both create and destroy his feelings for Mihrişah Sultan and to conceal both of these efforts from himself. He had to carry all of this turmoil without letting anyone, including himself, sense it.

To do what was almost impossible for a human being, to not be satisfied with not gratifying his desires but to conceal their very existence from himself even as he felt them, to transform these desires into a nameless and uncertain feeling, to accept that even imagining a reunion was a sin did not negate the feeling he had. It transformed the desire into a nameless sorrow and Sheikh Efendi, wearied by all this effort, was now unable to free himself from the sorrow that penetrated his soul further by the day or of the guilt, he became a melancholy person who was ashamed of his melancholy.

That night he woke shouting.

His wife woke as well, she looked at Sheikh Efendi, who was sitting up, covered in sweat, and asked what the matter was. Sheikh Efendi was evasive.

"Nothing, I was having a nightmare but I don't remember it."

Then he put on his cloak, went down to the *zikr* room, which was illuminated by a single candle, and began to recite the Koran aloud. The only thing that calmed his soul a bit was reciting the Koran, to listen to God's voice and feel its existence, then his own existence became smaller and less significant in the face of divine power, and so his pain and his sins diminished slightly.

Without realizing it, he always recited verses that talked about hell; in fact his suffering, shame, and fear of sin had nothing to do with the fear of going to hell, if he believed that he would pay for the sins he carried in his soul by burning in hell, he would be relieved by the thought of having paid for his sins even if God were to appear suddenly in that dark hall illuminated by a single candle, open hell in front of the Sheikh and throw him into the flames.

Like everyone who truly believes, Sheikh Efendi did not fear God's anger and wrath, what he really feared was to make the Creator ashamed of what he'd created, to fall from his grace and believe he did not deserve God's love and compassion anymore. He was in love with God, and his sinful desire for a woman, moreover a woman who was forbidden to him, was so shameful and scorching because he saw it as a betrayal of his true love.

He didn't tell anyone about the dream he had that night, he didn't even allude to it, it was only one day years later that he told Osman about the dream he'd never forgotten.

"I saw Jesus Christ in my dream, he was climbing the hill with his cross on his back, I was watching him from one side, there were two women with me, I don't remember their faces, they mocked Jesus Christ. Then, because it was a dream, I became the one who was carrying the cross, I was both the person watching and the person carrying the cross, then I felt myself being pulled by the arms and nailed to the cross, I felt that pain, when I woke I looked at my palms, as sleepy as I was, I saw blood, I remembered that dream for years and always thought that perhaps there really was blood on my palms when I woke."

For his part, Osman didn't remember the pain experienced by his great grandfather, who was so frightened of sin, but he did remember the lie he'd told, he was sure that his great grandfather remembered the faces of the two women in the dream, but the sheikh hadn't wanted to admit this even after he was dead.

That same night, Osman's other grandfather Reşit Pasha also woke up in a sweat, but he knew what he'd seen and didn't try to conceal this from himself. As usual he saw Mihrişah Sultan completely naked and was consumed by the terrible longing that occasionally comes to and unsettles people who carry a love that has diminished but that will never burn out.

He put his Damascene sweater on over his nightshirt, went to the *selamlik*, and sat on a sofa next to the window in the hall overlooking the sea. He was accustomed to these sudden longings, the sudden combustion of a love; he knew it would pass, but until it did it would be harrowing. Each time they appeared, these longings left behind a wearier and sadder man.

Just as Sheikh Efendi reached for the Koran to alleviate his desperation, he too reached for his book, *Naima's History*, which was always left open next to that sofa; just as God's voice made Sheikh Efendi aware that his pain was insignificant and that he was powerless and inadequate, Reşit Pasha saw his transience and insignificance when he listened to the voice of history.

To see that so many of the people flowing through the pages of this history book, this terrifying multitude of dead people, whatever the things or events they'd found important, whatever loves or hates they'd experienced, were now lost in eternal darkness with whatever feelings they'd had, whispered to Reşit Pasha that he was a very insignificant part of this great current and that one day he too would vanish into eternity.

Listening to the sound of the unceasing and bitter late winter wind that whipped up the waves that crashed against the waterfront mansion, he felt smaller and less significant with each line and each page he read. At that moment, the only consolation he could find for the pain he suffered on that lonely, blustery night, the only remedy, was to see the void waiting for each person and to realize that life and indeed he himself were temporary.

In order to recover from their dreams about Mihrişah Sultan, to calm their longing and desire for this beautiful woman and at least slightly ease their suffering, each man sheltered either in God or in history according to his own temperament. Like seriously ill patients, they struggled to decrease the value and the weight of the pain, they waited for morning with the same burning anguish, completely unaware of each other.

When morning seeped into the darkness, it found both of these men weary, wounded, and pale. With the help of God and history, they'd been able to quiet themselves, gather the sorrow that had overflowed from their souls, and hide it deep within themselves. No one saw how much they'd suffered the previous night, only those who saw the pallor of their skin and the dark rings under their eyes might have guessed that Sheikh Efendi and Reşit Pasha had had a bad night, and those who saw this weariness saw something holy in it; they thought the Sheikh had spent a sleepless night in prayer and the doctor had been up tending to a patient. They would have been correct in this assumption. The Sheikh had indeed spent the night in prayer and the doctor had spent the night tending to a patient, but the reason for the prayer and the identity of the patient were other than what they'd thought; as is often the case, the reality that people saw contained a lie as great as the reality despite all of its reality. As Reşit Pasha said later, "No reality is real enough."

Mihrişah Sultan, however, was not even aware of the sinful storms she'd caused in the souls of these two men. She didn't care about Reşit Pasha's suffering, she felt for him the selfish anger and contempt that women feel for men they don't love but who insist on loving them, and she couldn't believe that Sheikh Efendi would suffer in this manner. Despite her confidence in her own beauty, the strange untouchability that Sheikh Efendi wrapped himself in when he met another mortal, the power that reflected the strength of his faith, made it impossible for her to even imagine that Sheikh Efendi could suffer over a woman.

She would go visit him as soon as possible, Yusuf Efendi, with his black cloak, white forelock, almost transparent pale skin, and symmetrical face, was the most unreachable man she'd ever met; there was an impossibility emanating from the Sheikh's being that attracted every woman who saw him. Most women retreated in the face of this impossibility, frightened of committing the sin of tempting a man of religion, but women like Mehpare Hanım and Mihrişah Sultan, whose being centered almost completely on their own beauty, could not resist the temptation of trying to penetrate the Sheikh's soul.

For Mihrişah Sultan, Sheikh Efendi's presence in the city had become part of its charm, and just as she'd made the whole city look at her even in these complicated times, she wanted to make the Sheikh look at her and to shake him up just as she'd shaken up the city.

After she'd settled into the waterfront mansion in Kanlıca, where life was quiet and uneventful, with a splendor that made the young women and maids in the neighboring mansions gather by their windows and provided new material for coffee-house gossip for days, she sent a message to her son, calling him to come see her.

As Hikmet Bey had guessed that his mother's arrival would be ostentatious, that she would have planned a show to take revenge on the Sultan for having exiled her from the city, demonstrating that he no longer had any power over her or over the city, he hadn't gone to the harbor to greet her. Hikmet Bey had neither the power nor the desire she had to use crowds as a mirror to reflect her own beauty and power.

Therefore he waited to see her until she'd moved into her waterfront mansion.

The first meeting between mother and son since that awful incident took place amidst the running butlers, panicked servants, rushing housekeepers, French handmaids who looked at everything in surprise and gasped frequently, unpacked chests, and furniture being moved, was not at all as they'd expected. Mihrişah Sultan looked her son over carefully and said, "You look well," then kissed him softly on the cheek. In this unaccustomed manner, her habit of not allowing any incident to outshine her own being, her anger at her son for having attempted suicide on account of another woman, and the slight distaste she had for men she found weak also played a part; she couldn't overcome these feelings even in the case of her own son.

For her part, Rukiye embraced her stepfather with all her strength and pressed him into her chest. She embraced that man who had become accustomed to not being loved with a submission that gradually made him sadder and sadder, like a small child.

Rukiye truly loved Hikmet Bey, and everything required for a perfect love was contained in her love: she appreciated his knowledge, his kindness, his unexaggerated politeness, the courage he had in both politics and love and that no one noticed, his honesty, and the way he kept his pain to himself. She'd observed him for years, and with her natural instincts and the understanding that had been deepened by her conversations with Professor Koncharov and the novels she'd read, she decided that Hikmet Bey deserved every kind of admiration. When this admiration was enhanced by the compassion she felt for people who'd received blows they didn't deserve, the guilt she felt for her mother's sake, and her own strong and determined nature, it turned into an almost motherly love. She saw her stepfather almost as a son and wanted to protect and console him. During that brief but powerful embrace, both of them felt that love and accepted their new relationship, and this acceptance increased and strengthened their love even more.

Mihrişah Sultan, who had never been fond of displays of affection, practically dragged Hikmet Bey from Rukiye's arms and said, "Come, there are people I'd like to introduce you to."

Nearby, the French ladies in waiting, who responded to this magical city, whose colors, smells, people, mosques, and sea views had transported them at first sight into an oriental fairy tale, watched with delighted surprise as the Sultan and Hikmet Bey approached them. They were all very beautiful, and even though Mihrişah Sultan had never once spoken about what he'd gone through, they knew all about it. Family secrets that were never spoken of explicitly wandered through houses like ghosts without being seen or even heard with a persistence no one could understand, people learned of them without even knowing where or from whom they heard about them, and Hikmet Bey's story was one of these silently disseminated family secrets.

Like the nuns in Salonika, the French ladies in waiting were also impressed by the adventure and pain of this pale, handsome man who'd shot himself because of a woman. As they laughed among themselves with the giddiness seen in many who find themselves in a new life in a new city, they suddenly, when they saw Mihrişah Sultan and Hikmet Bey approaching, with amazing rapidity that anyone who didn't witness it would find difficult to believe, stopped being frivolously childish and became solemn ladies; they wore mature smiles on faces flushed with youthful merriment and a mysterious gaze that could be described as melancholy replaced the mischievous look in their eyes as they tidied the unruly forelocks that had escaped their buns and fell over their shiny foreheads, they stopped waving their arms in circles silently as they excitedly pointed out to one another everything they saw, clasped their crumpled handkerchiefs in their hands, curtseyed slightly, and greeted those who were approaching them with a small nod; Mihrişah Sultan introduced her son to each of the young girls, who were all from the leading aristocratic families of Paris.

Suddenly encountering again the strange and impressive combination of politeness, innocence, and mischievous coquettishness that he'd seen in his youth in the aristocratic young ladies he'd met in Paris, Hüseyin Hikmet Bey felt two contradictory and indeed almost opposite feelings. While his soul, traumatized by betrayal, suffering, and sorrow was refreshed and rejuvenated by these girls' very existence, by their laughter and clever witticisms, the overwhelming desperation and weariness brought about by comparing his current condition to their youth made him feel old. For the first time he thought about old age; for a moment he was shaken by the repugnance and enormity of what he felt and stumbled slightly.

What saved him was his mother's mocking voice.

"Hikmet, you're not going to pay these ladies a compliment they'll never forget by fainting, are you?"

When Hüseyin Hikmet Bey looked at his mother's face and saw her stunning beauty and seemingly eternal youth, he realized how strange his anxiety about old age was and pulled himself together.

Mihrişah Sultan went over next to the window and turned to Hikmet Bey.

"Can we see that old fool's palace from here?"

Hikmet Bey, who had pulled himself together, smiled malevolently.

"Are you asking about His Majesty the Caliph's palace, Mother?"

"Is there any other old fool who has a palace in this city, or at least a palace as big as his?"

"On a clear day you can see it from here, but you can't see it today."

These meaningless exchanges that are only encountered at family reunions, small clashes that no one cared about, teasing, secret concerns that were unspoken but felt, a deep, established, and well-rooted love felt in the emphasis on a word, the encouraging jokes of French ladies in waiting, all of this softened the sorrow that had come to dominate his personality, his existence, and his very fabric, and, even if only briefly, allowed room for merriment, and as soon as this merriment emerged, a Parisian lothario, a witty gentleman, a spoilt child, and an arrogant son of a pasha appeared, sometimes in order and sometimes individually, and trotted out amusing utterances in French that, like an unforgettable childhood memory, never got rusty and always remained light and fresh, and, unlike his adult and sober Ottoman, reflected the flirtatiousness of a carefree young man.

This banter pleased Mihrişah Sultan because it indicated that her son could "forget that woman" and recover and it amused the hot-blooded French ladies in waiting, but Rukiye, who loved his pain more than anything else and who always wanted to see the mature sorrow in Hikmet Bey, was saddened by it.

When dinner was announced, Hikmet Bey was speaking with the French ladies in waiting about Paris, learning from them about developments in the city he'd fallen in love with, mocking their ignorance as he answered their questions about Istanbul, telling sardonic anecdotes about old pashas that made them burst into laughter, occasionally telling them about a mysterious murder, ghosts wandering the city streets at night, and legends about how the Prophet flew over the city when Mehmet the Conquerer took it, smiling at their wide-eyed response.

Despite how much everyone moved around during the course of the conversation, Mademoiselle de Lorenz, one of the most attractive of the girls, managed to stand next to Hikmet Bey or to sit in the armchair next to his, and all the while he smelled her jasmine perfume, which made him feel as if the warmth of her body was touching his, causing him to experience an unnamable excitement.

The dinner was a full Ottoman feast, with different flavors refined from Armenian, Greek, Arabian, Kurdish, and Turkish cuisines in a variety of consistencies and colors, a true adventure had been prepared for the French palate; Circassian chicken, pilaf with cream, the cold dishes that were brought to the table glittering like gold, lamb stew that smelled of thyme and melted in the mouth, sherbets and pastries with pistachios and walnuts were brought to the table to the surprised gasps of the French girls. The wine served with these dishes lent a French atmosphere to these Ottoman flavors. Everyone spoke only in French, this harmonious language reminded Hikmet Bey of his youth, and also of how much Mehpare Hanım had loved it.

At one point Hikmet Bey turned to his mother.

"Do you know, anything that reminds me of Paris makes me excited and happy, makes me forget all my troubles."

Rukiye interrupted with a long face, as if the merriment at the table bothered her.

"But you never come to Paris."

Mihrişah Sultan smiled with her usual mocking coldness.

"Perhaps he doesn't want to forget his pain."

Mademoiselle de Lorenz, who had managed to sit next to Hikmet Bey at dinner as well, leaned toward him and whispered in a tone that no one else could hear, as if this was a sign of an intimacy between them that set them apart from everyone else at the table, asking, "Are you really so fond of your pain?"

Hikmet Bey nodded, embarrassed by this public display of intimacy and troubled by this embarrassment.

"Be assured, mademoiselle, that I'm not fond of my pain, I know it too well to be fond of it. Don't pay attention to what my mother says, she likes to mock me, or rather she likes to mock all men, and besides, I'm no longer devoted to my pain."

The girl was truly surprised by this.

"You were once devoted to your pain?"

"Sometimes pain seems as if it's part of the person who caused it, detaching yourself from the pain feels like detaching yourself from that person. Anyway, to speak of pain with a young lady such as yourself would be to risk being boring, and this is a risk I dare not take. Let's drop the subject, what do you think of the food, do you like it?"

Mademoiselle de Lorenz looked into his eyes just long enough to let him know she'd understood, smiled, and nodded as if she wanted to change the subject.

"I've never eaten such delicious food in my life, but if I ate it for a month I'd be plump enough to enter the harem."

Then, with provocative emphasis, she asked the question all French women he met inevitably asked.

"Do you have a harem as well?"

"No, I don't."

"Why not?"

"I couldn't find a harem suitable for me."

Mademoiselle de Lorenz paused as she struggled to understand what he meant, and frowned as if she was offended.

"You're making fun of me."

Hikmet Bey smiled.

"Yes."

"Have you no shame, Monsieur Hikmet. You're using my ignorance to mock me."

"I'm just teasing you. No. I really don't have the kind of harem you asked about, the kind of harem you imagine only exists in the Sultan's palace, and perhaps the palaces of a few viziers. Not everyone is cut out to deal with such a large crowd of women."

Once again Mademoiselle de Lorenz adopted a provocative manner.

"Would you like to have been cut out for that?"

"Occasionally. And would you like to live in a harem like that?"

The girl imitated Hikmet Bey's voice when she answered.

"Occasionally."

Just as Mihrişah Sultan had hoped, the dinner continued as a merry and jocular feast during which Hikmet Bey regained his former personality and self-confidence. As he spoke to the others at the table in French that was increasingly brilliant, he told stories as if he was hungry to speak, he answered questions asked out of curiosity, and thoroughly enjoyed the pleasure and confidence of making women laugh, he flattered Mademoiselle de Lorenz and made the other girls jealous, his joyful voice and his health pleased his mother; his levity annoyed Rukiye and after they had coffee he looked at the darkening sky and said that it was time for him to go.

"With your leave, Mother, before the weather gets any worse."

He politely declined Mihrişah Sultan's invitation to stay the night. He embraced Rukiye affectionately. He bade farewell to the girls and said he hoped to see them again. He smiled when Mademoiselle de Lorenz said, "I hope you visit your mother often," and he replied, "You'll see for yourself how devoted I am to my mother," then, after kissing Mihrişah Sultan's hand in gratitude, he left the waterfront mansion feeling he'd regained his strength.

When the launch that had picked him up from the pier reached the other side, he got into the carriage that was waiting for him and hunched in a corner, as he moved away from his mother's waterfront mansion, her grandeur, Rukiye's love, Mademoiselle de Lorenz's attention, and the French ladies' admiring laughter, he was like a shadow getting smaller as it moved away from the fire, the youth and confidence in his soul faded, and he retreated back into his loneliness, injury, hopelessness, and desperation.

The past would not release him and he could not reach the future. The owner of the pain from the past was far away and as for the future, it seemed meaningless and unattractive enough to lose its promise even during a short voyage by sea.

He walked wearily into the mansion in Nişantaşı. The household had gone to bed, and apart from a few lamps at the head of the stairs, all the lights had been extinguished. The enormous mansion seemed as if it had been abandoned, indeed, in Hikmet Bey's words "it was as if it had died." In a panic similar to anger, he almost shouted as he rebuked the housekeeper who opened the door for him.

"Turn all the lights on, what's going on with this house, you've turned it into a mausoleum, I never want to see this place so dark again. The lights are going to burn all night!"

The housekeeper couldn't reply that for as long as she'd known, the lights had been extinguished every night, with the submissiveness of a flunky she swallowed the rebuke and, as if it was her fault, said, "As you wish, sir," then she angrily woke all the servants in the house, it was the same kind of anger she'd seen in her master, and had them light all the lamps in the house one by one.

As he climbed the stairs he saw the footmen rushing about to light all the lamps, being careful not to raise their voices as they called to each other, and when he realized that he'd caused a sudden flurry of activity in the mansion, a smile like that of a naughty child, and that did not match his mood, spread across his face. It amused him that people were rushing about like this because of a single command he'd given, that they were taking his ludicrous command seriously, and even though he was ashamed of waking everyone in the middle of the night, this did not keep him from feeling like a naughty child.

When he reached his room he forgot about this brief amusement, and once again he was weighed down by the knowledge that he could not build a new bridge from the past to the future. He had the feeling that every glimmer of hope he had would turn him into a sadder and more anxious man.

He opened the door and went into his room.

A large tiled stove was burning in the center of the wide bedroom, as the room was dark, the red glow of the fire was reflected outwards like a thin, rectangular line from the bottom of the engraved iron door, that rectangular line turned into a mouth, and the rounded stove turned into a creature from a fairy tale.

Hediye stood next to the stove in a tight, shiny, sky-blue dress that reached her ankles; she had probably heard his approach. She peered at Hikmet Bey from under her eyelashes, there was a strange urgency in her eyes, a panic. As usual she looked him over thoroughly, as if she wanted to know in a single glance that he'd returned home in good health, that nothing had happened to him while he was absent from the house, that he hadn't lost an arm or a leg, that he had not been wounded or shot. As soon as she was certain that the man had returned home in one piece a smile appeared on her face, though it disappeared again quickly. With the surprising instinct of a woman who is attached to a man, no one knows how, she knew that Hikmet Bey was angry.

The light of the red flames that appeared under the stove's door illuminated the skirts of her blue dress and created a purple halo, a fiery mixing of blue and red just above her soft, white, flat-heeled, buckskin shoes, but it didn't stop there, it climbed up the shiny folds of her dress, as far as her chest, with a mysterious undulation. Hediye undulated in a vague shimmer in the darkness like a curl of flame that had broken free from a large fire, the motionless white of her face, barely visible, was in strange contrast with her body, which seemed to be undulating because of the play of light.

For a moment Hikmet Bey looked in surprise at the unexpected movement of light in the dark room, when he saw her in the middle of the dark room, which didn't reveal her beauty and indeed concealed it, he became aware once again of her beauty, which he'd become accustomed to, and indeed more aware than he had been. If he had seen her in daylight he would not have been as moved as he was. This young girl who always effaced herself, who behaved as if she didn't have an identity, a personality, who even behaved as if she had no being and who in this way even made her beauty almost invisible, seemed to Hikmet Bey to have a new identity, to have gained a new personality, to have become a new person in these moving blue, red, and purple lights, the beauty concealed from Hikmet Bey in daylight appeared now in the darkness.

When Hediye moved toward him and away from the stove, the lights on her blue dress disappeared, as if her body had melted into the deep darkness, though the shadow of her white face became more apparent.

She went up to Hikmet Bey and touched his arm lightly.

"Sit down, sir."

Hikmet Bey sat on the edge of the bed.

Hediye kneeled and took off his shoes, then undressed him in her usual manner.

"You're cold, sir. If you'll allow me, I'll rub you with lavender water."

When Hikmet Bey didn't answer, she poured lavender water into a silver bowl from a bottle she'd prepared earlier, with the sound of the water being poured into the bowl, it was as if a lavender mist had spread through the room with the red light from the bottom of the stove. The smell entered with the red light through his half-open eyes and moved into his body, taking him to a land he didn't know and couldn't see, but which he believed was beautiful.

"Would you like me to light the lamps?"

"No, *merci*, it's fine like this."

Hediye started rubbing Hikmet Bey's wrists. When the cool water touched his flesh in that hot room, his entire body felt chilled. She rubbed his arms and shoulders. She made Hikmet Bey lie in the middle of the bed and then climbed onto it and knelt, her feet were bare because she'd taken off her flat-heeled shoes, she was still wearing the ankle-length dress, and as she moved, her lower legs appeared and disappeared. She was to Hikmet Bey's right, she didn't move to his left side to rub his left shoulder, she reached from where she was to the left, and as she rubbed, her breasts brushed his face slightly.

Both of them played their parts calmly and with loyalty, as if rubbing Hikmet Bey's shoulders at that time of night was their real purpose. As he did with all the women who entered his life, Hikmet Bey taught Hediye that there were also games involved in lovemaking and showed her how to derive pleasure from playing them. Now both of them were playing a game they knew well, as the game dragged on they felt their desire increase, but at the same time, with concealed obstinacy, they each waited patiently for the other to give up first. They both knew from shared experience the kinds of rewards patient lovemaking gave to those who were patient.

Besieged by a temptation that penetrated his flesh a bit more with each passing moment in that red, lavender-scented darkness, as hands rubbed his shoulders, breasts touched his face, bare feet touched his legs, and the hardness of the legs he sensed through the silk he touched with his fingertips, Hikmet Bey hadn't much chance to continue and win this contest of obstinacy with Hediye, who had been trained to constantly control herself and her feelings, and both of them knew this.

Hediye enjoyed transforming from a powerless slave to a powerful mistress, and Hikmet Bey enjoyed transforming from a strong and decisive master to a weak man who had lost his willpower; master and slave changed places as day and night change places. Both of them were aware of how light and time affected their personalities. One of them was pleased to seek the power she needed and the other was pleased to seek the slavery that was familiar to him.

Neither of them knew how long this game took, but in the end Hikmet Bey seized her by the waist and pulled her on top of him and the warmth under the silk covered his body. Hikmet Bey's hands impatiently tried to unbutton Hediye's dress but somehow he couldn't find the buttons, Hediye watched for a while without moving and with a smile that was invisible in the darkness, then unfasted the straps on her shoulders, then in every cell of their bodies they felt the intoxicating touch of the human body and the warmth generated when two bodies touch each other and that makes everything beyond it seem cold and alien.

The red light from the slit at the bottom of the door of the stove now reached the foot of the bed, from there it climbed, losing its sharpness as it spread, moving over the folds of the blue silk dress crumpled in a ball under Hediye's feet, reaching the bed as a shadowy red light; this did not lessen the darkness but changed its color and made it slightly reddish; in this pale light Hediye's body, like a silver fish, became brighter, and Hikmet Bey disappeared beneath her completely.

Hediye's face was above Hikmet Bey's, when she lowered her head toward the man, her long hair poured over the pillow in all directions like a black waterfall, two faces were lost under the undulating cover of her soft, shiny hair, and their breaths mingled. Hediye touched her lips lightly to his; Hikmet Bey had taught her to kiss on the lips, at first she'd found it strange and had even tried to avoid it a few times; she didn't know about kissing this way. As Hikmet Bey said to Osman, "At that time, who was there in the Ottoman Empire who knew about kissing." Then she discovered the crisp, fresh taste of lips, unlike that of any other part of the human body, she liked to touch them with her tongue, to take little bites, to take his lips between hers and suck them like an aromatic fruit. They began to kiss passionately for a long time, enjoying it fully, as if they'd gathered their entire bodies into their lips, feeling each touch throughout their bodies; kissing like this drove them mad with excitement. As Hikmet Bey said later, he didn't enjoy kissing any woman as much as he enjoyed kissing Hediye, not even Mehpare Hanım, no other woman had been able to bring all of her passion and desire into her lips as much as she did.

It gave Hikmet Bey immense pleasure to feel a woman's entire body in her lips, it was as if he was being swept up in an otherworldly adventure, those kisses bore the weight of whatever he'd experienced, protected him and sheltered him from reality; as he grasped her waist and pressed her body against his, he murmured with gratitude and excitement.

"You are my only truth, Hediye."

Even though he said this in the ardor of making love, he believed what he was saying and Hediye remembered those words for the rest of her life. No gift that the man to whom she'd given her body, soul, and being ever gave her made her as happy as this short utterance. In that bed, for the first time, she believed that she had a special place in Hikmet Bey's life, that she had a special significance for him.

She moved her lips to his ear and made a sound that only someone who heard could understand.

"Ah, Hikmet Bey . . . "

She wasn't able to say anything more; for her to find the courage to utter his name when they were making love was a great and deep declaration of love in the private language only the two of them could understand.

There, they created a love with long kisses and short utterances, a love they could only experience when they made love, and which they pretended didn't exist in all other circumstances.

On that snowy night, as they made love with mad desire in that reddish darkness, neither knew that at that moment plans were being made for a murder that would shake the entire Ottoman Empire, and that with two gunshots the following morning, their lives and everyone else's would change.

10

There were things the dead didn't know either, and, according to Osman, they tried to conceal some truths even after they died, they tried to rewrite their lives in the way they wanted. They assumed a strange silence about the shooting of Hasan Fehmi Bey, the leading journalist of the *Serbesti* newspaper, on the Galata Bridge by an unknown assailant, the first step toward a great riot that would shake the Ottoman Empire, they said they had no knowledge of that murder. Only Ragıp Bey, with his accustomed openness, said, "They went to great lengths to keep the details of the murder hidden, but I heard from friends that it was Abdülkadir Bey who shot the journalist, though I don't know whether what they told me was correct." It was clear from his tone that he believed this was true, and also that he disliked Abdülkadir Bey, one of the notorious Committee gunmen. Osman and all of the other dead believed that Cevat Bey, who was on the organization's central committee, had information about this but, with his usual seriousness he said, "I was in Berlin when the murder was committed, I'd gone there to meet Enver Bey."

They received news of the murder during a spectacular ball at the imperial palace in Berlin, a ball that Enver Bey wanted to forget for the rest of his life and that Cevat Bey could not forget, that he hid among his memories like a burst of controlled laughter and that caused a smile to spread across his face each time he recalled it.

Chandeliers the size of a man emitted thousands of droplets

of light that multiplied in intricate yellowish patterns like water flowing over amber-colored pebbles, creating the sensation of bathing in water made of light. The distinguished officers of the Hassa Regiment in their multicolored uniforms and medals that glowed proudly on their chests like little torches wandered through this sea of light, conversing with beautiful, ivory-skinned women in long white gowns who moved as if they were gliding; an unnamable fragrance composed of hundreds of different perfumes gave a feminine charm to the entire vol-cano of color and light, and Cevat Bey would never see any-thing like this again.

Cevat Bey, dizzied by that magnificent and glamorous night, was so intoxicated by this complex and indescribable scent that it settled in his entire soul and in his entire mind to the extent that he sought it every time he heard the word "woman," he sought this scent that no woman could possess on her own, and like almost everything he sought in life, he could not find this either.

As the orchestra was tuning up, Cevat Bey was trying to talk to Enver Bey in a corner of the hall, but because German offi-cers and diplomats, who treated this young and silent officer as if he was a prince, kept coming over to chat with him and flat-ter him, he didn't get the chance. For his part, Enver Bay was so flattered by the respect he was being shown and the praise that was being showered on him that he didn't pay much atten-tion to Cevat Bey. Cevat Bey wearied of this and started glanc-ing around for friends scattered in the crowd when a palace official approached them and, after greeting Enver Bey respectfully, spoke to them in a low voice as if he was telling them a secret.

"Her Majesty the Princess awaits your excellency in her quarters, sir."

Enver Bey flushed, turned his head, and looked at the man in surprise, then when he realized from his expression that

Cevat Bey was as surprised as he was, he nodded silently and followed the herald. This short man held himself erect as he made his way through the crowd, looking more like a commander going to war than a man who was on his way to meet a woman.

Feeling out of place in this colorful crowd in his grey uniform and red fez and unable to overcome the rocklike tension he felt as everyone else moved about at ease as if they were part of the lights, Cevat Bey retreated to a column, disquieted by being left alone. Hesitating to confess even to himself that he was in awe of this crowd, these lights, the music which had just started, the beauty of the women, the attractiveness of the men's uniforms and feeling the strange sense of deprecation whose source he couldn't grasp and that increased his admiration of these foreigners, he started to watch what was going on around him. Without realizing it, he placed his heels together as if he was standing at attention and clasped his hands behind his back because he didn't know what else to do with them; he realized he was not and could never be part of the merriment that was flowing around him, and worse than this, he sensed that his own country could never reach this level of wealth, splendor, and power that made itself felt even when these people were amusing themselves, though he couldn't identify who or what he should be angry at for this.

At the same time, his thoughts were on Enver Bey. He and all of his friends knew that the princess, the emperor's niece, had taken a liking to Enver and had made advances toward him, but that Enver Bey could not respond because of his strict moral code, and he was curious about what was happening upstairs.

He didn't have to wait long, Enver Bey returned ten minutes later with a confused expression on his face. He was frowning and blushing.

Cevat Bey didn't dare ask him anything, both because of

how angry Enver Bey looked and because he'd been brought up to not ask people about their private lives. As they made their way toward the door, their other friends gathered together in various parts of the hall and approached them, there was whispering as they briefly greeted those around them. They went out the door and into a large corridor paved with marble, and not far from them they saw a beautiful woman in a low-cut dress standing on the flight of broad stairs, shouting and pointing Enver Bey out to Necdet Bey, an official from the Ottoman Embassy in Berlin.

"That man is not human, he's just a puppet, a puppet!"

They all nodded in unison to the princess, whose voice was echoing through the corridors, they walked as if they were in a military parade. It was a long time before they learned what had made the princess so angry, but eventually whispers about what had happened began to spread.

After failing to impress Enver Bey in the crowd as she'd wanted to, she decided to handle the matter alone with him in her own quarters. She greeted Enver Bey in her quarters lying on a sofa in a nightgown that revealed much of her legs and breasts.

Enver Bey stood before the woman in silence and waited for her to speak.

When she realized that this Turkish officer wasn't going to say anything, she was obliged to speak. "I'm quite taken by you, Enver Bey."

When he heard this, Enver Bey suddenly stood at attention, greeted the woman with a click of his heels, then turned his back to her and left the room, driving the princess mad with rage. The Ottoman Embassy in Berlin had to work hard to avoid any coldness between the two nations, emphasizing that this behavior had arisen from Ottoman traditions rather than disrespect for the German imperial family.

When they reached the palace gates they encountered

Hulusi Bey, one of Enver Bey's aides-de-camp, who was out of breath. The young lieutenant gave them the news.

"Sir, today Hasan Fehmi Bey, the lead journalist of the *Serbesti* newspaper, was shot on the bridge."

Enver Bey said nothing, but one of their colleagues, Cevat Bey couldn't figure out which one, said in a dry voice:

"He had it coming."

At that moment none of them could have guessed where this incident would lead. Some were openly pleased and others secretly pleased by the death of this young writer who had criticized the Committee so scathingly, and Enver Bey, for his part, was not at all surprised by the assasination, as if he'd known it would occur.

When they left the palace they went to the apartment that had been made available for Major Enver Bey, who was shown more respect by both the Germans and the staff at the Ottoman Embassy than was usually shown to an ordinary military attache. Cevat Bey, who had come to Berlin to convince Enver Bey to return, once again began to explain the situation to the other officers as clearly as he could.

"It's clear we've made a serious mistake, we sent our most valuable colleagues out of the country, when we sent Enver Bey here, Fethi Bey to Paris, Hafız İsmail Hakkı Bey to Vienna, and Ali Fuat Bey to Rome we thought that we'd solved everything and that we didn't need these people at home, now we're paying the price for this. The reactionaries are gaining strength in the capital, a crank called Derviş Vahdeti has established the Mohammadan Union Society, and even though the military is banned from engaging in politics by a special order, the entire fifth regiment in Istanbul declared that they were joining it. The religious fanatics are objecting to the ministry of war's decision that they have to pass an exam in order to be exempted from military service, saying that this is an insult to religion and trying to provoke the military."

Naci Bey interrupted, acting as if Cevat Bey was defending the religious fanatics.

"Forget about these knaves, Cevat Bey, they're clowns, not men of God, these reprobates don't even know how to read and write, how can an illiterate scoundrel who can't even read the Koran lead the community? They're drifters who took shelter in the madrassas to avoid military service."

Even though Cevat Bey got angry for a moment, he didn't let it show.

"I know this as well as you do, Naci Bey, I was on the committee that demanded a decision be made about this, this isn't what I'm saying, I'm just explaining the situation to you, I'm telling you that the madrassas are in ferment and that religious fanatics are provoking the military. The officers who didn't graduate from the military academy but who rose up through the ranks joined those fanatics as well. As the rumor that they are going to be discharged from the army goes around, they're secretly stirring up trouble in the army, pitting the soldiers against the academy graduates, who they're portraying as infidel freemasons."

Enver Bey, who generally seldom spoke, interrupted in his staccato manner.

"Are there any officers in the German army who rose up through the ranks without studying at the academy?"

"No, Enver Bey, and I'm not saying there should be any in our army, but more than a third of our officers rose up through the ranks without studying at the academy, if they rebel it won't be easy to keep it under control, and what's worse, our younger officers have lost their authority over the soldiers. Most of them began to neglect their duties after constitutional monarchy was proclaimed, particularly those in Istanbul who abandoned themselves to the pleasures of Beyoğlu, most of them don't even show up for duty. The soldiers are almost under the complete supervision of the officers who didn't

188 · AHMET ALTAN

attend the academy and ignorant sergeants, while the senior officers are sitting on the fence, ready to change sides if it suits them. That is, my fellow officers, the army seems to have been left in the cold, the capital is seething, this is why Enver Bey and the others need to return home at once and take control of the situation, otherwise it will be too late."

As usually happens when someone says it will be too late, it was indeed already too late, but, as Cevat Bey later confessed to Osman slowly in a whisper, they seemed content with this. This tardiness would lead to the deaths of a great number of people and leave an indelible and bloody stain on the nation, but it would also allow the Committee to seize the power they'd been seeking so long, and the young officer the German princess had shouted was a puppet would burn himself up like a shooting star that blazed across the night sky.

After Cevat Bey asked for assurance that Enver Bey would return at once if things became more complicated and Enver Bey said, "Fine, fine," with a sardonic smile that reflected his sense of his own superiority as it spread across his handsome face, Cevat Bey sensed, as one always does in these strange moments, that what had been a friendship had turned into something else, into a bond in which one party was arrogant and the other submissive, and swallowed the slight sense of hurt and the anger he didn't allow to show and left Berlin two days later, as Istanbul was preparing for a big demonstration, a funeral, and the beginning of a time when all hell broke loose.

The rancorous reaction to the killing of a journalist by a nation accustomed and indifferent to death, killing, and murder was in itself a sign that the pain and the rancor were about something more than this assasination. It would take countless murders, deaths, and funerals to calm the city that had risen to its feet over this death and restore its peace, for such a great reaction to a single death to be shown in a nation indifferent to death meant that it would be followed by a great deal of bloodshed.

On the day the funeral was held, Sultanahmet Square was like a monster with a hundred thousand heads, the body that carried those heads was invisible, but the muscles that trembled with rancor and itched for revenge were in every corner of the city, in the soil, in the air, even in the waters that surrounded the city. The rumbling that spread throughout the city from Sultanahmet Square, that strange convulsion that shuddered with irritation, seemed not to come from the people but was more like an earthquake that was preparing to ascend to the surface from the very depths of the earth, seeking to destroy everything and rake the city with its claws, an ogre that shook off the fires of the center of the earth as it emerged.

On that late March day, when the promise of the fragrance of spring was felt beneath a fragile winter cold, steam composed of human flesh, warmth, and sweat rose from the crowd in Sultanahmet Square; a cloud composed of the smell of raw leather, greasy linen, and dirty clothes hung over the crowd.

The coffin, draped in green and passing over the hands of a crowd that was rippling with shouts of "God is great," was like an ill-omened box carrying the entire city's soul; when they put it into the ground and covered it with dirt, they would not be burying a person, a critical journalist, but the city's soul, its humanity, and all that remained would be a beastly anger, a savage mass of muscle pulsing with the will to destroy. In a number of different places, a number of different people thought they were the head and soul of this crowd that was preparing to lose its soul and its head, thought they could use their will to influence this body, but they were wrong.

Despite the angry rumbling that filled the entire city, there was no rage in the eyes of those who followed the mullahs whose black robes had taken on a greasy sheen and who wore scimitars in their belts, the crowd who were so thin their bones seemed sharp enough to pierce their yellowed faces, the unemployed, unshaven, with patched clothing and holes in their shoes, there was only the kind of fear and indecisiveness seen in the eyes of those who were hungry, helpless, and didn't know what tomorrow would bring. They could start to flee at any moment, or they could attack suddenly; with an indecisive cowardice that didn't have the power to fly into a rage, there was an uncertainty that made those who saw them want to hide and that was more frightening than the mullahs whose eyes shone with arrogance and confidence as they marched at the head of the funeral procession in their thick robes, those watching the funeral procession felt that the undecided crowd was more dangerous than the determined crowd.

Even in the funeral call from the mosque that day there was no beseeching God for a blessing for a mortal whose soul was being entrusted to him, there was a plea for help for the desperation and misguided anger of the crowd.

After the youthful corpse was taken out of the coffin in its snow-white shroud and placed in the grave and after dirt was shovelled onto it to shouts of "God is great," the crowd dispersed into the streets; they carried their anger, pain, and fear on their backs, diminishing in number on every street as they disappeared into the city. The crowd that had so recently filled the square in such a threatening manner was gone, as if it had died and been buried to be ressurected a few days later; everyone in the crowd was still present in the city, but the crowd was no longer there.

Hasan Efendi also broke away from the crowd he'd been part of, heading for the *tekke* to tell his Sheikh what had happened, and more importantly what was going to happen. The Sheikh knew that Hasan Efendi would bring him all the news and tell him everything he'd learned from his mysterious sources and his intuition; Hasan Efendi also knew that Sheikh Efendi had already learned everything he was going to tell him, but that he would not say this, each was curious about where the other obtained this knowledge and were a bit frightened by this mysterious power, but also felt the security of being close to this power.

They were accustomed to these emotions. They'd been tied up in these emotions for so many years they almost didn't feel them. It was as if one of them had to be lost or incapacitated in order for them to remember this feeling again.

Hasan Efendi found the Sheikh on the shore of the Golden Horn, looking out at the water with a fur draped over his shoulders.

After describing the crowd at the funeral, the way Derviş Vahdeti and Said-i Kurdi wore daggers in their cummerbunds, how angry and agonized the crowd was, and how many sergeants, as well as officers who had risen through the ranks, had attended the funeral in civilian clothes, he passed on the most important information.

"In a few days there will be a mutiny at the military headquarters, the units that came from Salonika won't allow sharia to be lost, they're determined."

Hasan Efendi said this in a tone that seemed to beseech the Sheikh to say something in support of this act. Sheikh Efendi sensed this tone and what was being asked of him, but he waited in silence for Hasan Efendi to continue.

"They will take up their weapons and depart on the path of God."

Sheikh Efendi spoke in a flat, emotionless voice, as if he wasn't objecting to anything, and asked about something that had made him curious.

"Since when have we set out on the path of God with guns?"

Sheikh Efendi looked out over the choppy waters that reflected the purple of the evening sky as if he was waiting for a sign to emerge from them. In spite of himself, Hasan Efendi looked at the water, but there was nothing there except the Golden Horn he always saw.

When he realized that Sheikh Efendi was angry, he continued as if he didn't agree with what he was relating but only passing on what he'd heard.

"They're going to declare jihad."

"Against whom?"

Suddenly Hasan Efendi became excited.

"Against the freemason, infidel officers, against the Committee members. These officers hang pictures of naked women on the walls, in Beyoğlu Muslim women are going around uncovered, adultery is rampant, no one listens to the decrees issued by His Majesty the Sultan, His Excellency the Caliph, against all of this unbelief . . . "

Sheikh Efendi placed his long fingers together, rested them on his chin, and bowed his head; the evening was growing cooler.

"Why did God make us, so many people, such weak and miserable slaves, why did he create and put these miserable, shiftless wretches on this earth, why are we created with all our defects and faults, with a conscience that suffers from our own misdeeds, stumbling over our sins as we try to perform good deeds?"

When Sheikh Efendi fell silent, Hasan Efendi worried that he expected him to answer, he tried to think of an answer, but his mind was so full of the prospect of a mutiny in the military that he couldn't come up with one; in any event Sheikh Efendi continued.

"Is it or is it not a sin to ask why God does anything, no, it isn't, if God didn't want us to ask questions he wouldn't have given us our minds, he would have created us to be like insects and set us free. No, our Lord created us to ask questions, he wanted to populate the world he created with people who wondered about this great creation, and if you ask

why he created us with such defects . . . Yes, he could have
made us perfect if he wanted, and since he didn't, there must
be a reason. Of course there's a reason, why wouldn't there be
one, nothing created perfectly is perfect enough for God. Do
you know what's perfect . . . ? It is the progress toward perfec-
tion, through acceptance of the inevitable, through patience
and suffering, of those created with defects. The progress
made through questioning and searching of the defective
slaves he created as his people reveals the power of our Lord.
Every step we take toward progress, every idea we have to
overcome procrastination, is proof of our Lord's power."

As usual, Hasan Efendi was captivated by the Sheikh's
voice, at first he struggled and flapped about like a bee fallen
in water, then he surrendered and flowed with the gurgling;
he'd forgotten all the feelings he'd had when he came to see the
Sheikh, nothing was left of his rage, of his desire to ask for help
to support the mutiny, of the violent joy at the prospect of
teaching the infidels a lesson.

It was getting dark, the beams of light disappeared in the air
before they could arrive on the earth, the lilac-colored dust dispersed as figures turned into shadows; the Sheikh's hands and
face stood out with a fiery whiteness.

"We don't need guns, mutiny, and violence, all we need is
to think about and work on being better than we are."

When Sheikh Efendi turned slowly, sighed, and started
making his way back to the *tekke*, Hasan Efendi trailed behind
him, they walked in silence as far as the *tekke* door; at the door,
Sheikh Efendi turned to his son-in-law and spoke in an impe-
rious tone that suited him and the fur he was wearing, the
humble tone in which he had spoken a while ago was gone.

"None of us should involve ourselves in this business, guns
are not for us, you need to keep an eye on everyone too, make
sure they don't seduce anyone, particularly the younger members."

The penetrating sound of a *ney* drifted into the cypress-darkening loneliness of the falling, purple-gilded night, the slow, unhurried sorrow of the sacred music that beseeched God pierced the souls of those who heard it, reminded them of their weakness and desolation, and showed the path to God.

Hasan Efendi leaned against the wall and began listening to the sound that played all by itself as if it was passing through the darkness of the night and rising to another realm that was illuminated by celestial light and where night never fell, freeing himself in the falling darkness from the night, the world, his anger, his bitterness and even his own self.

What made him religious, a believer, a man of true faith was neither his anger at the infidels nor the jihad he was preparing in order to walk on the path to God nor his great admiration for the Sheikh; what made him religious was that sound, the strange sorrow he felt when he heard this *ney* playing all by itself.

What made him a true believer was his desire at that moment to be in the presence of God, to thank God for having been created, to express the joy he felt at surrendering with the pure and unique obedience of a slave, and the pain he felt at not being able to fulfill this desire. Because he would only be in God's presence when he died, it gave him peace to feel he loved death more than life, to feel he was prepared to die, indeed to feel that he yearned for death.

When the sound of the *ney* stopped suddenly, he muttered quietly, and as if he believed he would be heard, "Holy God." When he raised his head he saw the Sheikh standing by the door, he too had been listening to the sound of the *ney*. They both realized that they felt the same thing.

When Hasan Efendi moved into the garden as if he hadn't seen the Sheikh, he heard the Sheikh call to him.

"Do you understand now what I was saying to you?"

Hasan Efendi nodded even though he knew he couldn't be seen in the darkness, but he didn't answer.

When he'd moved further away he heard the Sheikh call out again.

"Don't forget to tell Ragıp Bey."

He moved away into the garden without making a sound to confirm he'd heard this command. At that moment he didn't want to talk to a person, not even the Sheikh, he didn't want a mortal to hear his voice; he felt as if he was alone with his God, could not emerge from the feeling that the music had brought him into God's presence. This feeling was not like the fervor, ecstasy, and abandon he felt during the rituals, it was different, quieter, slower, deeper, almost as if it wasn't a feeling, it was a peculiar state that made him something other than what he was, a tree, a leaf, water, that united him with the soil, that caused him to see everything created by God as part of himself, that united him with everything that had been created. He felt this not with his emotions or his thoughts but with his entire body, with his flesh; his emotions were incapable of feeling this, his thoughts were incapable of understanding it, in order to experience this state he needed his flesh, his body, everything he was composed of, his body was lightened as if it was being buffeted by a strong wind, scattering him throughout the world and making him part of a great and infinite whole.

He spent that night sitting under a tree in the garden; perhaps his soul, wearied by the experiences of the day, suddenly found the tranquility it sought in the sound of the *ney,* abruptly released him from this world that seemed so meaningless and low, and gave him the strong feeling that he was part of a great power that had no beginning or end.

That night he did not recite any prayers; no verses came to his mind, he didn't force himself to find a *sura* that he'd memorized; the melancholy sound of the *ney* had opened the path leading to God, and he set out body and soul on this path that had opened before him, scattered to the birds, fish, insects, seas, and algae, he remained all night under the tree, feeling and thinking nothing just like a tree; he needed neither thoughts nor feelings. Later he told Osman, "I discovered true worship that night, that night I discovered the power and love of the true God, I felt as if there was no difference between my body and the tree I was leaning against."

Nobody but the Sheikh saw or understood the miracle that had occurred to this simple man who could turn even his faith in God into the most ordinary and vulgar rage, into a worthless shelter where he nursed his regrets in life.

Had his thoughts and emotions been more developed, what he felt that night would have changed him completely and brought him to terms with himself and with life, would have led him to realize how wrong it was to turn heavenly faith into worldly anger, but this was impossible for him; he would have been lost and out of his depth in a place where feelings and thoughts moved past anger.

He'd seen that there was such a place, he'd been mesmerized by what he saw, but he was unable to stay in this place, and he returned.

After morning prayers he left the *tekke* with the joyful feeling of having been purified, but by the time he arrived at the barracks he was once again himself, and a slave to anger.

At the barracks gate, a private, whose hand, holding his rifle, was red and swollen as if it had been in the cold for hours, stopped him and asked him in an indifferent tone:

"Who are you looking for, haji?"

"I'm here to see Major Ragıp Bey."

"Which Ragıp Bey is this?"

Hasan Efendi became irritated.

"If he comes out here and hits you over the head with a

gannet you'll see which Ragıp Bey, just call in and let someone who knows him look for Major Ragıp Bey."

The soldier, who heard the authoritative tone that had remained with Hasan Efendi from his days as a soldier, didn't hesitate to call in and say there was someone looking for Major Ragıp Bey, and soon a private shuffled wearily up to the gate.

"Are you the one who's looking for the Major?"

"Yes I am, what's it to you?"

"It's nothing to me, if you follow me I'll take you to him."

"Good lord, son, you've turned the core of the army into a village coffeehouse."

They went a little way into the main barracks and he heard the sentry who'd asked him who Ragıp Bey was call to a sergeant standing nearby without feeling the need to lower his voice.

"Sergeant Hüssam, what could this mullah possibly want with that infidel Ragıp Bey?"

"How should I know, if he's come to see Ragıp Bey he must be one of those Committee spies who have a secret religion."

He struggled to hold back the anger that rose in him and grumbled through his teeth as he followed the soldier.

When he entered the office marked "officer on duty" he saw Ragıp Bey hurriedly put the gun on the desk into its holster and noticed the flintlock leaning against the closet behind the desk; he also noticed the joyful light of seeing a friend spread across Ragıp Bey's weary face.

"Hey, Hasan Efendi, I hope nothing's wrong, what brings you here so early in the morning?"

"Only the Lord knows whether it's good or evil, Ragıp Bey. His Excellency the sheikh sent me. Order some coffee so we can pull ourselves together."

As they waited for the coffee they talked about the *tekke*, Sheikh Efendi, "the mother-in-law Hanım," and at one point Hasan Efendi said, "Something strange happened last night."

When he saw that Ragıp Bey had stopped talking and was listening to him, he repeated:

"Something very strange . . . "

Then, not because he was reluctant to talk about his experience but because he didn't know how to describe it, he gave up on finishing what he was going to say and took a sip of the coffee that had been brought by a private with greyish blue eyes and nodded. "Anyway, that's not what I came here to talk about, I have important news for you, His Excellency the sheikh admonished me to tell you."

Stressing for the second time that he'd come on Sheikh Efendi's behalf, Hasan Efendi wanted Ragıp Bey, who he felt looked down on him, to pay attention to what he said and also to ease his conscience by blaming the Sheikh, at least in his own heart, for informing to a member of the Committee, to which he was in fact opposed.

Ragıp Bey had realized he was going to receive important news and had been listening attentively from the start.

Hasan Efendi remained silent for a moment, thinking about how he could say what he'd come to say without giving Ragıp Bey too much information.

"Sheikh Efendi says that you should stay away from the barracks for a few days, and even leave the city if possible."

"OK, did Sheikh Efendi say why? Or should I resort to geomancy to find out?"

Hasan Efendi made a face.

"The way it is . . . "

In the end he realized he wouldn't be able to do this without telling everything.

"The way it is, in a few days there'll be a mutiny in the army, they say there will be a massacre, they're going to kill the officers from the Committee."

"What do they want, why are they going to mutiny?"

"They want sharia, they want the Ottoman Empire to be

restored to the correct religion, they don't want women walking the streets uncovered, they don't want honor to be trampled on, they will restore the people these freemason officers led astray to sharia."

Hasan Efendi suddenly lost control of himself, he was speaking not like a friend who was giving a warning but like a spokesman for the mutineers. Ragıp Bey squinted his eyes and looked at him.

"So, what do you have to say about what's going to happen?"

Hasan Efendi took Ragıp Bey's hand, they'd had many adventures together, they'd got married together to two sisters and had become relatives, he'd always liked him but he disagreed with his ideas.

"Go, Ragıp Bey, stay away from this place for a while."

When he saw that Ragıp Bey wasn't going to say anything, he insisted.

"Go, for God's sake, this time it won't be like anything you've ever seen, there's going to be a lot of bloodshed, there's nothing you can do, there's nothing anyone can do, in a day or two this city is going to rise up and put on its shroud."

"I don't understand, Hasan Efendi, you say they want sharia but sharia is where it always was, if you're talking about His Excellency the Caliph, he's in his palace, he's healthy and wealthy, why is there a need for a mutiny?"

"Don't, for God's sake, is it sharia when women paint their hands and faces like monkeys and sit in pudding shops like window displays? If there is fear of God, how could a Muslim son allow the woman who belongs to him to show herself to everyone like this, you know this better than I do. I'm not talking about you, but the officers who came from Salonika have turned Beyoğlu into a brothel, there is prostitution, adultery, and sin everywhere; men who couldn't recite a verse of the Koran if you asked them to don't know how to shut up when they hear the Charleston. In addition, Ragıp Bey, what is this about making mullahs serve in the army? Is it sharia to oppress these holy men whose prayers lift up the world, to purge all religious officers from the army saying they didn't study at the academy, is this religion, is this Islam?"

Ragıp Bey leaned back.

"Come on, Hasan Efendi, don't talk as if you don't know, as if you'd never been in the army, look at the state of our army, look at the armies of those you call infidels, is it Islam to be defeated in every war, is it sharia to try to fight with a bayonet while foreigners exterminate Muslim children with machine guns? What you say is nonsense, don't be offended, I'm being honest. It's true that our young officers have gone astray to a degree, but the officers you call religious are opposed to any modernization of the army, my dear brother. The Sultan is secretly agitating them, he gets the mullahs to shout, 'Our religion has been lost.' Now tell the truth as your religion dictates, you were in the army, are you happy with the state the army is in, one day soon when the bad Bulgarians and Greeks form an alliance and reach the gates of the capital, will this army be able to protect you?"

Both of them had forgotten the purpose of their meeting, the danger waiting just outside the door, and continued talking about what Ottoman men most liked talking about.

Hasan Efendi stirred in his seat.

"You sum it up well, Ragıp Bey, but what happened to the army that made the infidels tremble for centuries, that led them to be trampled beneath Sultan Süleyman's feet, tell me that . . . I don't have the gift of the gab, but didn't ignoring the dictates of the Koran lead to this? Didn't the nation's prosperity decrease when Selim the Sot ascended to the throne? Does it help to give rifles to an army that has lost its faith, does it help to give cannon to an army like this, does it do any good when the hand that pulls the trigger trembles; what can an army that does not fear God and refuses to serve the Caliph do against infidels except run away? The state of the army is clear to see, even you complain. Why? Because the army relies on Enver rather than on God."

Just as Ragıp Bey was about to answer they heard the sounds of the changing of the guard outside, shuffling feet, rattling rifles, and barked commands, both of them shuddered and turned toward the window as they were reminded of the reason Hasan Efendi had come.

"Whatever," said Ragıp Bey, "God willing, we'll be able to talk about this at a better time. Does His Excellency the sheikh know when this mutiny will occur, did he give you a date?"

"No, but it will happen in the next day or two. He wants you to stay away from the barracks."

"That's not going to happen . . . "

Ragıp Bey thought as he chewed at his moustache.

"Look, Hasan Efendi, this is the best thing we can do, first we bring my wife and my mother to the *tekke*, they shouldn't be alone in that big mansion. Sure, there's the Albanian gardener, but you can't trust anyone in times like these. We'll think about what we're going to do once they're safe."

Hasan Efendi suddenly smiled the way he used to in the old days when they were young. This large-framed man dressed as a mullah had an innocent and childish smile.

"Shame on you, Ragıp Bey, this morning I sent a carriage to the mansion to fetch the ladies, a suite has been prepared for them at the *tekke*, don't worry about them. Let us get you out of town as soon as possible, and stay away for a few days."

The person he'd been angry at a few moments ago and who he'd seen as an enemy had taken precautions to protect his mother and his wife without having been asked to do so; this brotherly friendship suddenly made Ragıp Bey feel happy and surprisingly secure.

"Thank you, Hasan Efendi, we'll get through this with your

help. You keep the *tekke* safe, I'll take care of myself. Give Sheikh Efendi my respectful greeting and my thanks. I'll come by the first chance I get."

They embraced and gave each other their blessings, Hasan Efendi moved toward the door slowly like someone who wasn't able to say everything he should, dragged his feet as if he might turn back at any moment to say something more, he reached the door, paused for a moment as he was opening it, then, whatever he was thinking, opened it quickly and left. When he left the barracks he had the surprising and painful realization that Ragıp Bey's death would sadden him. The guard at the barracks had changed, he looked for the private who'd been at the gate when he arrived, there were a few things he wanted to say to him, but the private had completed his sentry duty and had left.

As for Ragıp Bey, as soon as Hasan Efendi was gone he put on his greatcoat and left. Despite the seriousness of the information he'd just received, he felt a strange joy that made him restless. As he was looking for a carriage to take him to the Committee headquarters in Cağaloğlu, he tried to figure out what this joy was about and was almost angry with himself for feeling this senseless joy at a time like this.

In the square there was a harsh wind that stung whatever it touched, black, lilac, deep pink, green, and purple abiyas filled like balloons with gusts from the ground, men tried to walk sideways as they held on to their fezzes to keep them from flying away. There wasn't a single carriage to be seen. Ragıp Bey raised his coat collar and lowered his head as he strode toward Beyoğlu. He decided to go to Cağaloğlu by way of Karaköy.

It bothered him that his brother had not yet returned from Berlin. If Cevat Bey had been there it would have been easier for him to explain what was going on, he would have been able to convince him of the gravity of the approaching danger, but other Committee members would have trouble believing news that came from a sheikh, they would look for a trap or some kind of intrigue simply because the news came from a man of religion, and they'd laugh at Ragıp Bey for being naïve enough to believe a man of religion.

Later Ragıp Bey, whose anger would not die even after he died, told Osman, "They wouldn't believe anyone except themselves, they didn't even believe themselves, they'd even lost faith in the organization's leaders, each of them followed a different leader and was suspicious of all the others, power had corrupted them." Of course Cevat Bey's comment was deeper: He told Osman, "Because it wasn't nourished by any idea that could control it, the fire of the mutiny got out of control and burned up all beliefs, leaving behind only anger and ambition, for years we experienced that passion of a riot that fed like an opium addict on a constant diet of suspicion and anger, when there was no one left to rebel against, we rebelled against life and embraced death."

Ragıp Bey, who had to wrap himself in his greatcoat when he encountered sudden, swirling winds where the avenue was intersected by narrow streets as he walked past grey buildings with marble statues on their facades and ornamental carvings on their pediments, reached Yüksekkaldırım, passing apartment buildings whose doors were shut tightly as if they sought protection from the wind, beer houses whose windows were frosted with condensation from the breath of the customers, and shops with perfume advertisements in their windows; as he descended to Karaköy, ignoring the weak shouts, dispersed by the wind, of the peddlers who sheltered under overhanging roofs, he suddenly caught the smell of seaweed coming from the sea and felt the cold damp from the water on his face.

There were no carriages in Karaköy either, the street leading to the bridge was deserted except for a few people struggling against the wind and holding their coats and fezzes, and a few steamboats anchored by the shore. He listened to the wind and the roaring of the Golden Horn as he made his way to the bridge, then crossed it, trying to ignore the wind that stung his ears and cheeks like a whip. He wanted to drink tea and smoke a cigarette in a warm room, and while his anger at being obliged to walk through these streets and at the people he was going to talk to, and who would not believe him, continued to grow, the unaccountable and disquieting joy beneath this anger remained.

The joy he felt was such a strange feeling, but it didn't prevent him from feeling other feelings, it wasn't bright enough to leave them in the darkness with its own light; throughout his walk he felt anger, boredom, disgust, worry, and restlessness in turn, these feelings probed him, made their presence felt, but he didn't experience them as fully as he usually did. On account of this inexplicable joy, these other feelings seemed as if they would collapse at any moment like buildings built on slippery slopes, as if they would vanish; even though he could see the reason for these other feelings clearly, he couldn't understand the source of this joy, therefore this joy was not felt as strongly and clearly as the other feelings even though it was more noticeable than the others.

At the Committee headquarters they greeted him with the respect due to him for his formidable reputation in the army and the distinction of being Cevat Bey's brother, but at the same time with considerable aloofness. They brought him to a large room that looked out over the street. He was familiar with some of the people, such as Hakkı Bey, Abdülkadir Bey, Mümtaz Bey, and Müştak Bey, who was sitting by the window and who had a blond moustache and a soft face. An abrupt silence fell as soon as he entered the room; the first to stand was Müştak Bey, with whom he'd once served in Fuat Pasha's retinue, he approached him with genuine friendship and said, "Oh, welcome, Ragıp Bey, how are you,

I hope you bring good news, what brings you here, we don't often see you."

The others, mostly former officers who were now Committee gunmen, were respectful but suspicious, like wild animals when they meet another of their species. They knew Ragıp Bey and he knew them from old "adventures" they'd had; they were all on the same side, but Ragıp Bey was experienced enough to see that they were all checking the guns under their arms. After a brief greeting, they ordered coffee for Ragıp Bey. Then an uncomfortable silence reigned in the room, no one wanted to be the first to speak.

Ragıp Bey already regretted having come, but it was too late to act as if nothing had happened; it was not in his nature to leave without saying anything once he'd come to the head-quarters, if he did it might arouse a cloud of suspicion that would put his life in danger.

Müştak Bey, the only person present who liked Ragıp Bey, was the first to break the silence.

"So, Ragıp Bey, I hope you bring good news."

"I wouldn't call it good news, Müştak Bey."

Ragıp Bey heard the creaking of chairs, everyone shifted slightly in their seats and paid attention.

"I heard that the mullahs are agitating the soldiers and that there will be a mutiny in a few days."

When no one said a word, Ragıp Bey continued trying to convince them.

"I heard this from a dependable source, an old friend who I trust."

In his usual arrogant manner, Hakkı Bey asked, "Where did he hear it from?"

Ragıp Bey had known they would ask this, and when they learned the truth they would mock him behind his back, though not to his face. He took a cigarette out of his case and lit it as he tried to gain time to decide what to say.

"He has friends among the mullahs."

Hakkı Bey leaned back, not bothering to conceal his hatred for Ragıp Bey, whose bravery and fame he'd always envied and who was somewhat distant from the Committee, and smiled with his usual attitude of looking for trouble.

"Does your friend rat on his own friends?"

Ragıp Bey put his cigarette in the ashtray next to him, unbuttoned his jacket, and looked around the room. There was no one present who he could trust except Müştak Bey, and if there was a fight he would at best remain neutral, he wouldn't support Ragıp Bey. The rest of them were merciless, they always held on to their guns as if they were prayer beads, and they always hit whatever they shot at. Ragıp Bey felt a tightening in his stomach.

Now he was preparing to play a game he knew, felt the pleasure of walking at the edge of death, the pleasure that filled his soul every time he tested himself with death; like the other men in the room, he also enjoyed playing with death, he realized that he only felt truly alive when he was close enough to death to touch it, when he saw death as a person of flesh and blood he became acutely aware that he was alive. This was something like a half blind man who only figures as shadows opening his eyes, like someone struggling to breathe and suddenly feeling the air fill his lungs; everything's appearance, light, and smell became sharper, all of the emotions that were usually slightly dulled became sensitized, his soul swelled with the enthusiasm of once again embracing life.

He smiled his famous smile; this was a smile everyone knew; everyone smelled the smell of death, breathed it in, and straightened up; no one moved, but he could sense that everyone's muscles were tensing. Death was like a beautiful woman no one knew who was going to kiss, it frightened them, but when they saw it they became very excited and felt their existence and their manhood.

They heard the creak of the mansion's wooden stairs as someone climbed up and walked past the room, the roar of the fire in the stove, the howling of the wind as it whistled through the eaves, a ferry sounding its horn in the distance, the sound, like breaking glass, of the rain hitting the stone floor of the courtyard, and they heard each sound distinctly and separately.

"I'm not in the habit of going to places where rats go, Hakkı Bey, otherwise we'd see each other more often."

Hakkı Bey, who was angry at Ragıp Bey because he had a reputation in the army and kept his distance from the Committee even though he'd risked his life to fight with them many times, took a step in the death dance that gunmen dance, but if one reason for his dangerous move was his irresistible urge to flirt with death, another was his confidence that Ragıp Bey would not take the second step. He didn't think he would respond to this clear challenge with his own clear challenge, which in this crowd of gunmen would not end favorably for him.

When he heard Ragıp Bey's answer he said, "Think about what you say before you say it, Ragıp Bey!"

Ragıp Bey remained in his seat, he just hung his arm down from the chair and allowed the knife he'd always kept in his sleeve since he was at the military high school to fall into his hand. He knew that if Hakkı Bey moved for his gun, he could hit him between the eyes from his seat before he could even touch his gun. Indeed he'd planned the moves he would make after this; which of them would pull their guns, which of them he'd kill first when they pulled their guns. He decided he would kill Abdülkadir Bey after he killed Hakkı Bey.

"I'm not the one who should weigh my words because I'm not the one who issued a challenge. The person who issues a challenge should weigh his words."

He'd come here to be helpful, to bring news of the coming storm, and now was suddenly looking death in the face because of Hakkı Bey's proud arrogance.

After Ragıp Bey's retort, it seemed there was nothing Hakkı Bey could do but pull his gun, he couldn't countenance this insult, those had been fighting words, there was no other way out, their eyes met, there was no emotion in either man's eyes, neither fear nor anger, they just remained motionless and looked into each other's eyes to know when the other would move.

Just as Hakkı Bey was about to pull his gun, they heard Müştak Bey's soft voice.

"Friends . . . "

Hakkı Bey looked at Müştak Bey out of the corner of his eye without changing his stance. Müştak Bey stood, opened his arms to show he had no intention of pulling his gun, and stepped between them.

"We're about to make our enemies laugh for no reason. Ragıp Bey came here to warn us about a danger, he's telling us that a group of fanatics who organized themselves under our noses is preparing for a mutiny, and instead of taking precautions we're fighting each other. In my opinion, we should let everyone else know, we should look into this to see if there's anything to it, we should inform Talat Bey, if he thinks it's appropriate he can call the members to a meeting. If the soldiers mutiny in the capital, the entire nation will suffer. It doesn't befit us to kill each other in such difficult times, in my view it's time for us to think together, no one here is afraid of death, for God's sake; no one needs to prove anything either, every brave man here has proved himself against the enemy many times before. So why are we behaving like this? Let's sit down and think with clear heads. Fine, there are words that can kill brave men, there are words that can send a snake back into its hole, but there's been a misunderstanding here, how can anyone be enemies under this roof, who could think about insulting each other?"

Hakkı Bey stood motionless, it wasn't clear if he'd been

convinced, he was biting his lower lip, his face seemed tight and frozen, he was looking at Ragıp Bey. Those who knew him felt he could pull his gun at any moment; Abdülkadir Bey considered intervening, their friendship went back a long time, he thought he could get through to him. They were in the organization's headquarters, if these gunmen killed someone who'd come to warn them, and on top of that Ragıp Bey, who was known for his honesty and for the service he'd rendered, it could accelerate the opposition that had begun in the Committee to these gunmen, and the fact that Ragıp was Cevat Bey's brother made the situation even worse.

"Müştak Bey is right," he said in a sedate tone. "In these difficult times it will hurt the organization if there's a fight at headquarters, we have to put the organization before our own grievances. In any event, there's nothing to discuss here."

Hakkı Bey looked at Abdülkadir Bey, but he was still watching Ragıp Bey from the corner of his eye. He nodded toward Ragıp Bey.

"Didn't you hear what he said?"

Abdülkadir Bey realized that the situation wouldn't be resolved unless Ragıp Bey offered an explanation.

"Ragıp Bey didn't say anything to you. Ragıp Bey, do you have a grudge against Hakkı Bey?"

Ragıp Bey answered calmly.

"I don't have a grudge against anyone, if I did, everyone would know about it. I'm not someone who holds secret grudges, everyone who knows me knows this."

At that moment what they both wanted, and the only thing that would make either of them happy, was to kill their opponent; in spite of this desire, neither of them moved for fear of doing something "unbecoming." For either of them to do something unbecoming would mean a loss of respect, and neither of them could countenance this. On account of this, both of them, who'd engaged in this argument out of anger, tried to get out of it with their honor intact, using diplomatic skills that were as familiar to them as shooting skills, using words, refraining from insulting but unwilling to tolerate insults.

Abdülkadir Bey, whose experience had made his skills instinctive, felt he needed to make a move, so he stood and took Hakkı Bey by the arm.

"Come, sit down, Hakkı, there's no need to drag this out, Ragıp said it too, there's no grudge here, don't make people laugh at us."

Hakkı Bey sat down without saying a word, but he was still biting his lower lip. He thought that he should have shot the son-of-a-bitch the moment he stood up, it killed him to have allowed the others to intervene, but there was nothing he could do now, it would be unbecoming to continue. Both Ragıp Bey and Hakkı Bey knew that that they each had a deadly enemy, in those meaningless and dangerous few minutes they'd developed an enmity that would continue until one of them was dead; someday, someplace, there was going to be a settling of accounts and they were going to fight it out.

Ragıp Bey sat in silence, holding his knife, sizing up each of the men in the room. He'd responded to Hakkı Bey's insult, he hadn't backed down, Hakkı Bey's momentary hesitation had made him the hidden winner of the fight, but he knew he would never forgive Hakkı Bey for daring to challenge him and that he would hold a grudge against him. When he thought about the day he would kill this pudgy man, who was as skilled a gunman as he was pudgy, the famous death smile appeared on his face again.

They all had another coffee, then decided to relay Ragıp Bey's news to the leaders of the organization. Abdülkadir Bey said that he had heard similar rumors as well. As they talked, Ragıp Bey realized that they were not that interested in this mutiny, either because they thought it couldn't happen or because they thought it would give them an opportunity to crush the mullahs and the Sultan, they weren't going to take any real precautions; he regretted that his brother wasn't there.

When he left this small wooden mansion that would be the heart of one of the largest empires in history for years and where decisions would be made that would drag the empire to destruction step by step, descended broad marble steps with edges that had been slightly rounded with age, and reached the courtyard, he took a deep breath of cold air. The pleasure of having survived this ordeal and of having taught Hakkı Bey a lesson turned the unaccountable joy he'd felt into cheerfulness; this cheerfulness surprised him and he said, "Good lord," as if he'd just played a joke on himself. He walked as far as Babıali Avenue and found a carriage at the beginning of the street.

A while after he got into the carriage the driver, whose nose had become so blue from the cold that it seemed about to fall off, asked, "Where to, sir?"

"To Nişantaşı."

When he uttered this single word, which surprised him, it was as if someone else had uttered it, he understood the reason for the joy that had been stirring in the depths of his soul for hours like a small fish at the bottom of a river, and that had now turned to delight; he was going to see Dilara Hanım.

The prospect of seeing Dilara Hanım always excited him, indeed it excited him a bit more each time, but this time the joy had risen above every other kind of emotion, even the desire to kill and be killed, as if it had not been touched, as if it had never interacted with the other emotions entwined around it, this delight that was so unaccustomed for Ragıp Bey was not because he was going to see the woman he loved; to suddenly sense the real reason for this delight, this feeling he was aware of without fully keeping its form in mind, like the familiarity of a face seen in the marketplace for the second time without keeping its form in mind completely, made him very angry and ashamed. He realized this delight was the result of having eased his conscience.

He hadn't realized his meetings with Dilara Hanım had made him restless, made him feel a sense of remorse; perhaps he hadn't realized that this restlessness was remorse because he'd never known remorse before. When Hasan Efendi told him he'd brought his wife and mother to the *tekke,* he'd realized he could go to Dilara Hanım without thinking about them at all, without being anxious that they would worry about him, that he didn't need to find an excuse to tell his household, and freed himself from a heavy burden he hadn't known he was carrying; it was because of the relief he felt at getting rid of this burden that he realized he'd been carrying it at all. Moreover, despite the possibility of an uprising, of horrible massacres, the risk of death, threats, and murder that the prospect of an uprising carried, it also gave him a natural reason not to go home and this made him secretly pleased; on one hand he wanted to prevent this uprising, but on the other he wanted it to begin, so that in the chaos he could be as completely free and independent as he'd once been.

Ragıp Bey had always been a strong man; his fearlessness in the face of death, which could be considered a sickness, the way he seemed almost not to believe that death was real, set him apart from other people and encased him in a hard shell, but this power, like all powers, carried beneath it weaknesses and frailties that could not have been guessed. As usual, Ragıp Bey's strength was only nourished by other frailties; now this evening, which smelled of wood smoke, as he huddled in a corner of the cold carriage, whose folding leather roof was being pelted by droplets, passing through city streets swept by an ash-colored wind, he grew angry because an unexpected weakness had appeared beneath his strength. When he entered the realm of women, which he secretly looked down on and didn't understand or even try to understand, his weaknesses and fears

made themselves felt and led him to worry, pangs of conscience, shameful joys, and demeaning delight. He hated to
pay the ever-increasing price for every pleasure he experienced
in this realm. He couldn't figure out how these women caused
him to worry, but this power they never showed openly made
him angry.

He arrived at Dilara Hanım's mansion in Nişantaşı feeling
worn out by his own emotions. As usual, they greeted him with
a memorized politeness and showed him to the living room;
even though he spent most nights at the mansion, the servants
treated him like a guest each time he came, they never allowed
him to feel as if he was the man of the house; in their eyes he
was nothing but a handsome officer who would soon be gone,
and he felt this every time he came.

A little later when the door opened, Ragıp Bey, without
turning around, felt a warmth in his body that told him Dilara
Hanım had entered the room. It happened this way every time,
he could sense Dilara Hanım's presence even if he didn't see
her. Much later, with a meek curiosity that didn't match the
severity of his face, he asked Osman, "Is this thing people call
love the warmth you feel even without touching?" When
Osman realized that Ragıp Bey had asked this not because he
had something to tell but because he was truly curious, he was
even more surprised. He could only murmur that he didn't
know.

When Ragıp Bey turned and looked, he saw Dilara Hanım
approaching him; he now felt an intense longing for her every
time he saw her, for the first time he missed someone when he
was close to her rather than when they were apart.

Dilara Hanım came over to him and took his hand.

"You're cold."

When he heard her voice he was almost filled with gratitude, it was as if he'd heard a number of things he'd wanted to
hear in these words; Dilara Hanım said this in such a way that

with this ordinary phrase she'd also managed to say, "I missed you, I was worried about you, I wanted you." Her face was like her voice, as at that moment, it could express a number of different things simultaneously. On her almost motionless face, which was like the tranquil lake, reflecting the silver moonlight, that he'd come across suddenly while horseback riding with friends in Germany on a full moon night, there was sarcasm, compassion, love, lust, longing for Ragıp Bey, all of these remained together, but if you focused on one of them, that feeling would withdraw into the depths and disappear; this strange flight added a magical motion to her tranquil face, made him want to hold it tightly between his hands.

All he said was, "It's raining heavily."

"Do you want to eat right away or should they make tea?"

"If it's possible, I'd like to have tea first, it will give us a chance to talk a bit. There's something that I don't want to talk about in front of Dilevser . . . "

Without asking what it was he wanted to talk about, Dilara Hanım clapped her hands and told them to bring tea. She'd long since learned not to take what men considered important seriously, but this didn't prevent her from listening seriously to what they said, she'd seen that they occasionally said something that was truly important.

After gesturing to the servant to put the tray on the coffee table, she poured tea into Ragıp Bey's glass.

"Shall we add a little cognac?" she asked with a smile. When Ragıp Bey said, "Please," he didn't recognize in her voice the mockingly compassionate tone that old ladies use when talking to a young relative; if he had, he would have been very curious about what Dilara Hanım thought about him, but he was only curious about her feelings. It didn't even occur to him to be curious about what she thought. Like all men who dismiss the possibility that women could have an opinion of them or make decisions and be led to commit such a betrayal, he would have been surprised to learn that she had an opinion of him.

When one day Dilara Hanım, with a polite smile, told Osman what she thought of Ragıp Bey, he was also surprised, he hadn't expected that much; in any event, Dilara Hanım surprised him more than any other of his dead. The one who shook him most was the one he'd thought would be easiest to get to know and to understand.

It was as if she was protected by a wall of intelligence and elegance between her true identity, thoughts, emotions, and the world, she didn't allow her thoughts to reach people or people to reach her emotions. There was only one passage through this wall, and this was pleasure, but there was a tinge of revenge in the aggressive lust she expressed in bed, in the way she took pleasure from life, it was as if she had an enemy and every pleasure she derived wounded this enemy, but even Dilara Hanım herself didn't know who this enemy was.

Sometimes this enemy was everyone, then she would use sarcasm, intelligence, and wittiness to decimate whoever she was with, sometimes the enemy was herself, then she locked herself in her room, saw no one, didn't smile, was incredibly rude to the helpers and servants she usually treated well and called them names that didn't suit the lips that usually smiled kindly; sometimes the enemy was life itself, and in this case she dragged the man in her life at the moment to bed and made love until morning.

Dilara Hanım's secret anger at an enemy that may or may not have existed was completely unlike Ragıp Bey's easily combustible anger; the same feeling was present in two people as if it was two different feelings. Ragıp Bey's anger was blunt, open, and attacked immediately, whereas Dilara Hanım's never grew sharp, never appeared openly, never frightened people, but constantly made them restless and drew them to her in a mysterious way, people didn't see that anger but the anxiety they felt in her presence made them want to come close to her, approach her, and besiege her with love and attention in order to free themselves from this anxiety and be loved by her.

Once Osman had not been able to contain himself and did something he shouldn't have done, he told Dilara Hanım what he thought of her.

"But it's impossible for you to love anyone."

With her creative sarcasm, Dilara Hanım spoke as if she was saying something very tender to him.

"How banal you are, *mein lieber*, to try to make decisions about people rather than accept that your inability to know people makes you a vulgar and commonplace fool. Of course I loved people, there were even some I loved a lot . . . The point isn't whether I loved them, the problem was that they never realized it. Even when they believed I loved them they had deep doubts. If you were as intelligent as I thought you were, what you could have said was, 'You like to instill doubt in people, moreover you do this as if you're trying to ease their doubts, and for this pleasure you forgo other pleasures that might have been sweeter.'"

Dilara Hanım sat across from Ragıp Bey after she'd poured cognac into his glass.

"Have you warmed up a bit?"

Ragıp Bey stirred his tea before answering, then suddenly raised his head and said, in the calmest, coolest tone possible, "Dilara Hanım, I want you and Dilevser to get away from here for a while." Dilara Hanım was taken aback.

"Why, what happened?"

"Nothing has happened yet, but it will. A bad fate awaits Istanbul, it's possible there'll be an uprising in a day or two, it's not clear where it will lead or what will happen. I probably won't be able to concern myself with you, you two women can't stay here alone."

"I'll go if you come too."

Ragıp Bey shook his head.

"I can't."

"Why not?"

"I'm a soldier, Dilara Hanım, I have to do my duty."

Dilara Hanım smiled.

"Then I can't go either, I'm a woman and I have my duty."

The answer that surprised Osman so much that time surprised Ragıp Bey as well.

"What is your duty?"

"To be where you are."

When Ragıp Bey looked at Dilara Hanım he expected to see a mocking expression, but instead he saw a decisiveness masked by a melancholy smile, and as he later told Osman he believed that "happiness can emerge from a single sentence at an unexpected moment." He felt a gratitude to this woman, for loving him and making sacrifices for him, that he would carry for the rest of his life, and, trying to conceal how pleased he was, gave a deceptive answer about saving her.

"You can't stay here. Things can happen in this city that would be impossible to predict today, this city is famous for its looting, there's no telling when a group of religious fanatics take to the streets, moreover, as a woman, who would defend you, who would protect you? No, I can't allow this."

"Then come with us."

"That's impossible."

After a pause, Ragıp Bey continued in a soft tone that surprised even him.

"I would very much like to come, but it's truly impossible, I can't leave my friends."

Dilara Hanım stood, came over to him and put her hand on his, and addressed him by name, something she never did except when they were in bed.

"Ragıp, how could you think I could leave you behind when you can't leave your friends behind, is that what you think of the woman whose bed you've shared, is that what you think of me."

Ragıp Bey didn't know what to say at first.

"I beg your pardon, of course not . . . How could I . . . But the danger is great, and there's also Dilevser. I'll be thinking about you every moment."

Dilara Hanım stood and let out a cheerful laugh that could almost have been called coquettish.

"I'll take the risk if that's what it takes for you to think about me, if it takes a war for you to think about me, let's get the war started."

Ragıp Bey wished she hadn't laughed like that or made that joke, he wanted her to continue being the way she'd been when she addressed him as "Ragıp," but he didn't say so.

"But . . . "

Dilara Hanım shook her head.

"The subject is closed, Major. Let's tell them to get dinner ready. You must be hungry. I'll have them call Dilevser as well."

Ragıp Bey stood and tried once more to convince Dilara Hanım. "But Dilara Hanım . . . " She put her fingers on his lips.

"Hush . . . Do you want to upset me?"

They couldn't continue their conversation because Dilevser came in just then, holding a book, her place marked by her finger; when she greeted Ragıp Bey, the dreaminess in her voice revealed that she was still lost among the lines of her book, that she had not emerged from the words and sentences in which she was wrapped into what people called the "real" world but that didn't seem lifelike to her.

Later she would think about how her mother's decision had changed her life, made her life real, like a novel, but she didn't know this at the time. However, Dilara Hanım was not aware that by making this decision she was acting in a way that would change the lives of the three people close to her, that would bring jubilation and deadly sorrow. If she'd known what this decision, which Ragıp Bey thought was based on love, and of course it was to a large degree, though in fact it was based on her moral code, her upbringing, a nature that hated to flee, and to a degree on her disregard and her curiosity about witnessing great events, would bring would she have made the same decision regardless, later even she herself wouldn't be able to answer this; "But," she said, "how could we live without our frightful ignorance of the future, if we knew what was going to happen and were able to change it, that might lead to other things happening, I think that in order to be able to carry on with our lives the future must always remain dark."

When Osman looked at all of this, he would have liked to ask Sheikh Efendi, "Is it fair for just one person's decision to alter the course of other people's lives? Isn't it demeaning and frightening to think that a person's future is in the hands of someone he doesn't know?"

But he knew that his great-grandfather would have answered that it was "God's will." Sheikh Efendi would say, "The Lord caused Dilara Hanım to act the way she did in order for everything to happen the way it did, it was God's decision."

He knew that after he said this he would have wanted to ask why God's will hadn't manifested itself in his own life, why the woman he loved hadn't said she would stay with him and alter his destiny, why something like this hadn't happened at least once in his life, and then afterwards, of course, he would sink into the pain brought about by the sin he committed later.

11

When the thin, misty rains departed the city at first light like a delicately undulating, gleaming satin cloth being pulled off a jewelry box, slipping away through dark blue minarets, copper-red domes, and golden crescents that still clung to the groggy shadows of the night, the call of the muezzins summoning the faithful to the first prayer of the day echoed across the hills of the capital, when the calls to prayer all ended simultaneously, a sudden, reverent silence wrapped the city for a moment, as if it had truly witnessed the image of God. In that brief moment of silence, which seemed like an eternity, crystalline reflections of the city like mirages of pure light appeared on the surface of the purple sea.

In that fleeting instant, the capital remained as silent and motionless as if it had been mesmerized by itself.

Then this magnificent silence was broken as suddenly as it had started, the crystal image was shattered by the irregular stomping of soldiers' boots, rifle butts hitting the ground, yelling, shouts of "God is great," curses and terrifying screams and gunshots; disorderly soldiers spilled out of the barracks and attacked their officers at the headquarters, they dragged their captives across the courtyard, hitting their heads against the paving stones, tearing off their uniforms, and shouting "Death to the infidels."

The bloody mutiny, whose consequences would be felt for a long century, began on a sunny, spring morning; the Salonika

battalions, which had been brought to the capital to prevent a
religious uprising, rebelled and demanded sharia, and the city
suddenly became frightened and elderly.

As Ragıp Bey dressed to go to the barracks he realized,
more from the tense, sharpened instincts of those who expect
bad things than from the indistinct sounds in the distance, he
rushed to the window, then turned to Dilara Hanım and said,
"It's begun."

He immediately put on his bandolier and grabbed the
jacket he'd hung over the back of the armchair.

Dilara Hanım, with the coolheaded attentiveness that
women have during major events that agitate men, stopped
Ragıp Bey as he was rushing out the door.

"What are you doing? Take off your uniform, put on civilian clothes, if the soldiers have mutinied as you suppose, they
could be going after officers."

Even though he knew this was the sensible thing to do, he
couldn't countenance taking off his uniform out of fear of the
soldiers.

"I'm going to headquarters, Dilara Hanım, should I make a
mockery of myself by wearing civilian clothes?"

Using the distant, mocking tone that she knew from experience was always very effective in taming Ragıp Bey, Dilara
Hanım said:

"I don't think anyone's going to be in the mood to laugh
during a mutiny."

Then she added in a feminine, almost pleading manner:

"Please, I beg you . . . For my sake . . . "

Ragıp Bey started to undress with a slight smile, and Dilara
Hanım brought out the civilian clothes he'd left there in case
he needed them and spread them on the bed one by one, she
helped her man, who might never return, to get dressed and to
tie his necktie. She left the room to tell the servants to get the
carriage ready and prepare breakfast as quickly as they could,

then when she returned and saw that Ragıp Bey had put on his bandolier and was wearing his gun she objected again.

"Please don't wear your bandolier, put your gun in your pocket, God forbid, if something should happen, if they see your bandolier they'll know you're an officer."

Ragıp Bey nodded and put his gun in his pocket.

Breakfast was ready when they went down, Ragıp Bey wanted to set out at once, but Dilara Hanım insisted he eat something and have some tea.

Ragıp Bey had never seen Dilara Hanım behave like this, it wasn't like her to insist on anything, but it also pleased him that a woman dared to insist he do anything.

"You remind me of my mother," he said.

Dilara Hanım tossed back her hair, which she hadn't had time to tie up, and as she looked at her man, who was on his way to the center of a mutiny, who was going to face death, sorrow darkened and enlarged her pupils.

As the time to part approached, the possibility that they would never see each other again sparked a divine fire, like a spark that ignited dry leaves in the depths of a deep forest, a fiery sorrow that was not created by humans but by God, which shared its glory as it burned in the deepest and most inner places and which we carry as part of our existence and conceal even when we are the most cheerful because we are mortal and surrounded by mortals. The sorrow grew and spread through their entire souls, touched each feeling in the places where it found them, and pulled them into the fire, all of these feelings tried to rise as fiery flames, they all became intermingled with the same sorrow and burned hotter than usual; love, compassion, worry, longing, pain, and even lust burned explosively like large-trunked, moss-covered trees, they were confused by a red pain and time lost its integrity and disappeared. The sorrow was so heavy it was as if they didn't live the moment they were experiencing because they couldn't carry it, they began to depart the future that had not yet arrived, the disappearance of the face they saw, already missing the face they saw.

With the bumbling haste of someone who had to leave but didn't want to, Ragıp Bey rushed to the door, knowing that later he would regret his haste.

"I have to go now, Dilara Hanım."

"Of course . . . "

She reached out and touched his shoulder as if she was removing a thread that wasn't there, then as she pushed him towards the waiting carriage she whispered softly, "Come back to me, Ragıp Bey . . . Spare me yet another sorrow."

Ragıp Bey hurried to the carriage and got in, he heard the driver shout at the horses and wheels clattering over the stones.

Before they turned into the street, he turned to look out the back window to wave for the last time. Dilara Hanım had gone inside, the door was closed; for a long time the image of the empty steps in front of the house remained in his mind like a painful wound.

The streets were deserted and the driver proceeded slowly, as Dilara Hanım had advised, so as not to attract attention. The doors and shutters of the mansions were closed; the trunks of the trees in the gardens, wet from days of rain, were a glistening brown like dark, sweating faces; he saw that there were buds on some of the tree branches, an early white flower had bloomed, hanging its head like a shy little girl. "Spring is coming," he thought in surprise, as if he'd forgotten about the existence and the changing of the seasons as he dragged himself from one day to the next.

As usual, Ragıp Bey was uncomfortable in civilian clothes, as he pulled at his jacket collar, which felt as if it might come off, he thought about what he had to do and what might have already happened, a few blocks from the barracks he decided to leave the carriage, proceed on foot, and observe the situation from a distance.

As they neared the headquarters he stopped the carriage and got out, and after telling the driver again to get back to the mansion as quickly as he could and not to leave, and that they should close the garden gates tightly, he set out along the muddy streets, scanning his surroundings, and as his thin shoes and his trouser cuffs became muddy he got angry at the mutineers as if this was their fault; everything seemed quiet as he approached headquarters, it was silent, the only strange thing was that there was no sentry at the gate.

Then, suddenly, a few soldiers appeared at the gate, they were pushing each other, when he looked closely he saw that they weren't pushing each other, they were beating someone they'd encircled. When the soldiers moved apart slightly, he saw that the man they were beating was naked from the waist up, and the blood that flowed over his chest from his face was like a red wound. The man didn't even raise his hand to protect himself, even from a distance you could see he no longer had the strength to move. Whatever happened, he moved at that moment, or he turned his head toward Ragıp Bey, something happened and Ragıp Bey realized this was the handsome lieutenant from the second unit, the soldiers had called him "Gorgeous Ihsan Bey" because he was so handsome.

One of the soldiers leaned the lieutenant against the wall, when he saw two of the soldiers point their guns at him with a smile, only then did he realize, the mutiny had been discussed for days and it had been said that "it might be a catastrophe," you could realize that a catastrophe was coming, you could describe it, say it, but nothing you said or described was enough to convey the frightful plainness of reality. You could talk about chaos, catastrophe, horror with great, broad statements, in this broad narrative there was a place for each person, each move, each feeling, but catastrophe itself was simple, very narrow, very tight, impossible to enter or exit. This moment, for instance, these soldiers who a few days ago had stood at attention before him, who listened to all his commands, who always obeyed, who he'd thought would fight shoulder to shoulder with in a war, were leaning the young lieutenant against the wall and getting ready to kill him with a smile, perhaps without even feeling any anger toward him.

There was no sound, no shouting, no sharp movement that would remain in the memory, everything was simple and plain, it was almost like a joke, Ragıp Bey realized that the mutiny meant the disappearance of the sense of catastrophe, people losing their sense of terror, everything including death seemed ordinary.

The sun was rising, the square in front of the barracks was filled with rainwater, and the mud was crisscrossed with the tracks of carriage wheels and the prints of soldiers' boots; as the sunlight struck the puddles, an ashy color was reflected on the undulating mud, the square seemed to be surging like an undulating brown sea in which millions of fish swam. For a moment, grasping the handle of his gun, Ragıp Bey considered diving into this sea of mud and rushing toward the soldiers, but he figured they would notice him and shoot him before he got there; he waited in desperation for the rifles to explode and for the lieutenant to fall into the mud.

As he waited for the moment of the lieutenant's death, he sensed that the soldiers who were about to kill him would not do so out of anger, rage, or resentment but simply from the desire to satisfy the sense of infinite freedom a mutiny gave to those who took part in it. This mutiny dragged them far from their pasts and their identities like branches that had been broken in a storm and swept into a river and abandoned themselves to the current believing that all responsibility lay with the river that was dragging them away with a pleasure that could be called childish; it was as if they were in the ecstasy of the fervor that grips those who are swept up in momentous events; there was no boundary to impede them, and they rushed headlong toward the last point to which this boundary could extend, toward death.

As he waited for the sound of the rifles, he heard a sergeant who'd come out the door shout at them; the soldiers left the lieutenant they'd just leaned against the wall to shoot, making crude, lower-class jokes as they made their way inside, they hadn't cared about the lieutenant's death, and now they didn't care if he was alive. The lieutenant remained like a red dot at the foot of the wall across the vast square. Even though Ragıp Bey knew he should get out of there, he couldn't, and he continued to look at the man; the lieutenant started to bend forward slowly, when his body was almost parallel to the ground he fell facedown into the mud.

Ragıp Bey walked away, toward the narrow streets behind Pera. He'd decided to go to the Ministry of War in Beyazıt, there was no other place he could follow what was going on. A deep roaring, a frightening sound, was coming from the city, but the streets were deserted, it was as if the sound was coming from underground. Keeping to backstreets and avoiding main streets as much as possible, he made his way down from Tepebaşı and reached Karaköy square; the roaring seemed nearer, but the square and the bridge leading to Eminönü were deserted, there wasn't a soul to be seen. The Golden Horn flowed green under the bridge like an emerald dagger God had thrust into the city, dividing it in two, one side cheerful, amusing, playful, and wealthy and the other resigned, quiet, solemn, and poor, two ways of life, two religions, two styles.

There were large stains on the bridge, and as he approached he saw that they were the bodies of officers who had been torn apart with bayonets, the blood in which they were covered had dried and darkened; they'd been killed and left there. Even though he knew the mutineers would kill him if they saw him, he dragged them one by one from the middle of the bridge to the side. There was a strange, bitter taste like well water in his nasal passage; he had clenched his teeth and made a face in disgust at the mutineers; not long ago he and these mutineers had fought the enemy together and trusted each other with their lives in the mountains, they'd broken the sacred oath they'd made in the face of death and had killed their officers. He felt belittled by this betrayal, they had to kill the men who'd killed those officers, they had to take revenge in order to overcome this sense of disparagement, he knew that they would kill them, they would make these soldiers pay for what they'd done, and the two sides would never have the same trust in each other.

When he reached the other side of the bridge, the ground was trembling from the roaring, but the square in front of Yeni Camii was also deserted, only at the very end of the bridge there was a military guard hut and a machine gun. When he looked inside the hut he saw the body of a captain who'd been shot in the neck, the mutineers had left after killing the captain without even taking the machine gun. He grew angry at them once again for leaving the guns behind, for years they'd been told not to leave guns behind but they still did it.

After he'd made his way around the mosque and started up Babiali Hill he encountered a group of mutineers, they were making their way down the street in a disorderly manner, shouting "Long live the Sultan! We want sharia!" and some of the riffraff of the city watched them as they walked along beside them; a few of them were wearing turbans and could have been mullahs. The crowd moved like a drunk on the verge of falling, staggering from side to side, trying to force open the doors of some of the newspaper buildings, but not trying too hard and moving on when they failed, occasionally they shouted, "Long live constitutional monarchy!" unaware that they were shouting contradictory slogans. They seemed indecisive. Ragıp thought he could scatter them like a flock of birds if he had a squad of good soldiers.

He followed the mutineers as far as Hagia Sophia square, which roared like a deep well that had been carved out under the city, and there he saw the real crowd. The majority of the crowd, which was like a colorless slurry with a heavy human smell, were vagrants and ne'er-do-wells who'd come to see what was going to happen. There were no more than a few thousand mutineering soldiers. Nor was there the excitement he'd expected from a major uprising, it was as if they were bored because the show they'd been expecting hadn't started yet.

From the rows of glistening bayonets, he realized that the parliament building was surrounded by soldiers. An experienced officer could see from the alignment of the bayonets that the soldiers were disorganized. The soldiers lined up by the side of the road were better organized. There didn't seem to be any officers around, sergeants were in command of the units. He made his way through the crowd toward the parliament building, keeping away from the soldiers to avoid being seen by anyone who knew him; people with hungry faces and frozen expressions didn't object when someone pushed past them, they made way with a gesture of indifference.

As he neared the parliament building, he saw a carriage approaching from Çemberlitaş, parting the crowd; the crowd surrounded the carriage before it could reach the parliament building; soldiers opened the carriage door, a pasha appeared and the crowd looked at him.

Then he heard someone shout,

"That's the minister of war! Shoot him!"

The crowd swirled around the carriage like a whirlpool, it pulled the pasha in and swallowed him; he could see the row of bayonets moving up and down; when the crowd retreated, the pasha's bloody body lay on the pavement. When Ragıp Bey looked at the body, whose white beard was stained with blood, he saw that it wasn't the minister of war but the minister of justice. They'd killed the wrong man.

After killing the pasha, the crowd once again became calm, it was as if they hadn't just murdered someone; people moved slowly as if they were drugged, but, as had just happened, they could suddenly become inflamed, then, after killing someone, return to a state of calm, it was as if they weren't aware of what had just happened, it was as if they were all having the same nightmare together.

The trembling crowd didn't shout, but as they murmured among themselves they created a frightening roar, there was no leader to make them move or stop, if someone had shouted for them to disperse, they would have dispersed, if someone had shouted for them to attack they would have attacked, but there was no one giving orders. Mullahs in dirty turbans could be seen in the crowd, but there was no one from the ulema who people knew and respected. From time to time one of the mullahs shouted, "We want sharia!" and the crowd would pick up the refrain.

Ragıp Bey wanted to get to the ministry of war and warn them to act at once so once again he took backstreets, a determined unit with a machine gun could put down this uprising in a quarter of an hour, he realized that if he needed to he could find Mahmut Muhtar Pasha, Commander of the First Army, and volunteer to put down the mutiny if they gave him a unit.

The entrance to the Grand Bazaar, which was usually an array of colors and nationalities including Ethiopians, Arabs, Kurds, Gypsies, Jews, Armenians, Greeks, and Albanians, moving up and down like colorful clouds emerging from a rainbow, was deserted; scarf-makers, wicker-weavers and jewelers had pulled down their shutters and closed their shops and the peddlers of sherbet, halva, and fruit had disappeared.

Even the stray dogs that were usually seen everywhere all the time were gone. He made his way through the deserted streets until he reached Çemberlitaş, where he noticed that the crowd had thinned out a bit, and soldiers were standing around in disorganized groups. Then he saw a reconnaissance unit, under the command of Colonel Spathari Efendi from the First Hassa Regiment, marching in lockstep toward the mutineers; he could recognize the sound of boots hitting the ground in unison even through the nebulous roar.

When the reconnaissance unit came face to face with the mutineers, both sides hesitated. Either because he had so few soldiers with him or because he had strict orders not to engage, the Greek colonel made a mistake that would cost him his life within a few minutes; instead of ordering the mutineers to disperse in a determined voice, he tried to admonish them in a friendly manner:

"Disperse, don't rebel against the state, return to your units, you're soldiers, behave like soldiers."

The soldiers looked at the captain with mocking smiles, their brief surprise at coming across a disciplined unit disappeared when Spathari Efendi took a friendly approach. They hated the officers so much that they weren't going to be appeased by a few friendly words; on the contrary they saw this approach as a sign of weakness and they became more arrogant and angry; for years they'd experienced the oppression of having to take orders and submit, and the fantastic freedom of the mutiny erased all emotions, only hatred and fear remained; any voice that didn't frighten them only increased their hatred.

The soldiers started to mock him in a crude and impudent manner.

"Look at him, look at how much the infidel knows."

"Have you been circumcised, Captain Efendi?"

"Come on, let's circumcise him."

Spathari Efendi's handsome Greek face froze and paled like

a wax mask; he realized death was approaching in the manner officers most feared, destroying his honor.

All he could say was, "Friends."

That was the last word he spoke, one of the privates raised his rifle and shot him, shouting, "Shut up, infidel," they fired their guns joyfully, as if they were at a festival; after each explosion, the bullet penetrated the already dead captain's body with a sound like a stick hitting wet laundry, the impact of the bullets made the dead body quiver and twitch like a large fish washed up on the shore.

When they saw that their commander had been killed, the reconnaissance unit under the captain's command threw down their rifles and disappeared into the crowd.

Ragıp Bey was disgusted by the cowardice of the privates in the reconnaissance unit and by the way the mutineers had turned soldiering into brutality, his face darkened with hatred; for a moment he considered pulling out his gun and shooting the soldiers who'd killed Spathari Efendi, but he feared being caught himself. This wasn't fear of death, he wasn't afraid of death, he'd always lived with death, he'd never considered it something separate from himself, it was not an enemy but a part of his being; his relationship with death was like the relationship of a truly religious person with God, he didn't flee it but rather took shelter in it; what frightened him was the prospect of being killed in a mocking manner by someone he didn't respect.

He walked quickly toward the ministry of war, when he reached Beyazıt Square he saw the main crowd; the mutineers had surrounded the ministry, a large crowd, many of them wearing turbans, were lined up behind them. They were pulling at the iron fence that surrounded the ministry, bending the bars down to the point where it seemed as if the fence would collapse. The crowd was livelier and more enthusiastic now that they were facing a target, they were blowing horns and shouting, "God is great," and, "We want sharia." Here too a heavy human smell rose above the square. Soldiers were lined up in two rows behind the ministry fence, they remained orderly under the command of their officers and faced the crowd. Ragıp Bey felt that if this continued the soldiers in the garden might join the mutineers. They were impressed by the crowd, the turbaned mullahs, the shouts of "God is great," the black flags with Koranic verses emblazoned on them.

He started to think about how he could get into the garden; it wouldn't be possible to push his way through the crowd, they would have torn him apart and scattered his limbs before he got there.

Then he became aware of a commotion over toward Vefa, a maxim unit with machine guns was coming to support the forces in the ministry of war. Ragıp Bey began moving in that direction. He was able to catch up to the unit before it entered the ministry garden, when he saw that the commander was Major Şükrü Bey, who'd been his classmate, he shouted his name at the top of his voice to be heard over all the noise, at first Şükrü Bey didn't recognize the man in civilian clothes and muddy shoes and wrinkled jacket, but when he drew closer he realized who he was.

"What happened to you, Ragıp?"

"I'm trying to get into the ministry."

"Come with me."

They all went into the ministry together and closed the iron gate behind them. Şükrü Bey placed his units under the trees and said to the sergeant, "I'll be back, let the soldiers rest until I get here," then turned to Ragıp Bey.

"What are you going to do?"

"If I could find a decent uniform first . . . I feel strange in these civilian clothes."

"I'll find Muhtar Pasha and let him know I'm here, our classmate Rıfkı from intelligence is here, go see him in the meantime, you're about the same size, he'll find a uniform that fits you."

"O.K., tell Muhtar Pasha that I can scatter these jackals with a cannon battery and a maxim unit, I've just come from Hagia Sophia, this is an ignorant crowd, they have no commanders, a determined sortie would scatter them like partridges."

"Let me get the Pasha's orders first."

As he was leaving he turned back to Ragıp Bey. "Do you know Muhtar Pasha, have you ever served together?"

"I know him from Germany, we were on maneuvers together there."

"O.K., I'll mention you to him."

Ragıp Bey went into the ministry building to look for Major Rıfkı Bey. Long stone corridors echoed with the sound of officers' boots as they ran from one office to another, telephones rang, orders were barked out in loud voices, weary-looking privates stood guard outside doors. Ragıp Bey excitedly asked one of the young officers who was passing by where the intelligence department was, and the officer answered without looking at him.

"Take the stairs at the end of the corridor and climb to the second floor."

All hell was breaking loose in the intelligence department, officers were turning the rotating armatures of their magneto telephones, trying to reach military units in various districts of the city, privates brought notes and left them on the desks, spies disguised as mullahs, beggars, or peddlers walked with a briskness that differed from their torpor in the street, whispered something to one of the officers, and then went back out into the square. When he asked one of the privates for Rıfkı Bey, he pointed to an officer sitting at a desk by the window shouting into a telephone.

When he went over to Rıfkı Bey, he slammed down the telephone and swore colorfully.

In spite of the difficult situation, Ragıp Bey smiled because he remembered how irritable Rıfkı had been at school.

"How's it going?"

Rıfkı Bey raised his head, looked at him for a moment, then grumbled, "Who are you?"

"I guess things aren't going well."

"What are you saying, man, who are you?"

"If you're confused enough not to recognize me, the situation must be really bad."

This time Rıfkı Bey looked at him carefully, then slapped him on the shoulder.

"Shame on you. What's with the getup, did you join intelligence too?"

"You can't see it in here, but the people outside don't like officers' uniforms, on the way here I counted seven who'd been killed, they shot Spathari right in front of me. If I'd come here from Nişantaşı in uniform I'd be with them now."

"You came from Nişantaşı?"

"Yes, I took the long way around. Don't pay attention to the crowd outside, an artillery battery and a maxim detachment could disperse them, they don't have any commanders."

"What are you saying, their numbers are growing every minute, look, I just heard that the Fifth Regiment in Zincirlikuyu and the second battalion of the Seventh Regiment are going to join the mutineers."

"Rıfkı, I'm telling you what I saw with my own eyes, they're indecisive, tell Muhtar Pasha, I'm volunteering, give me an artillery battery and two battalions with heavy machine guns, I'll have Istanbul quiet again in two hours."

"Do you know they've besieged the parliament building?"

"I told you I just came from there, aren't you listening to me?"

"It would be best if I take you to the Pasha, you can tell him in person."

"Find me a uniform first so I can get out of these civilian clothes."

"I have a spare uniform, put it on if it fits."

"Where?"

They went into a small room to the side, Rıfkı Bey took out his major's uniform and gave it to him, then went back to the office so he could change in private. After Ragıp Bey had put on the uniform he sighed deeply, he no longer felt half naked.

When he went back, he saw everyone in the office shouting cheerfully and slapping each other on the back.

"What's going on?"

"The First Cavalry Brigade is on the way, they're about to enter the square. Come, let's go upstairs and watch."

When they reached the windows on the top floor, the cavalry brigade was galloping into the square with the pennants on their long lances waving in the wind as they attacked the crowd. From above, they could see that as the cavalry charged through the crowd they left a corridor empty of people behind them, like a child drawing a line in the sand with his finger. The cavalrymen galloped in circles around the square, creating more lines empty of people. Then the square was completely empty. Just a moment ago there'd been thousands of people there, but they'd vanished, as if those who'd been watching them had imagined them, there was no sound in the square but that of the galloping horses. There was no sign of the thousands of people who'd been there just a moment ago.

Rıfkı Bey slapped Ragıp Bey on the back. "Good for the cavalry, see, sometimes they come in handy too."

After the cavalry brigade charged through the square one more time, they started entering the ministry garden through the large gate at an arrogant trot. Ragıp Bey didn't pay attention to the cavalry coming in but looked at the narrow streets that led into the square, as the cavalry came in through the gate, the crowds were starting to appear at the ends of these streets.

Ragıp Bey made a face.

"Don't get all excited for nothing, Rıfkı, this isn't something that can be taken care of with circus acts, the square will be full again in less than five minutes."

As soon as he'd finished speaking, the square started to fill up again; the skirmishers were in front with their rifles, and the growing crowd of civilians was behind them, they were approaching the iron fence.

"Rıfkı, take me to the pasha, the only solution is the one I'm proposing, we really have to make a sortie and disperse this crowd, I'm telling you, every minute we wait will work against us."

"Let's go, you've convinced me, let's see if you can convince the pasha."

They hurried downstairs and went to Muhtar Pasha's waiting room, the room was full of officers, informants, clerks, they all wanted to see the pasha as soon as possible and tell him whatever news they had. Rıfkı found the chief clerk and pulled him aside.

"Ragıp Bey just came from the parliament building, he saw the skirmishers' positions, he saw their guns, he has something very important to tell the pasha, the pasha knows him from Germany too and likes him, I beg you, we don't have any time to lose."

The chief clerk and Rıfkı Bey had worked together before, they went way back, he knew he wasn't asking to see the pasha for nothing.

"I'll take you in, but you have five minutes, the major needs to say whatever he has to say quickly."

When they went in, Muhtar Pasha was standing straight in front of his desk, listening to what the staff officers around him were saying. He was a handsome man and was known as a good soldier, officers respected him, he'd spent many years in Germany, there he'd been known not just as a good soldier but for his skill at fencing and with beautiful women, he earned the friendship of the German military aristocracy. Now he didn't know what to do, he didn't know how to put down this mutiny, which he thought was idiotic; it was difficult for him to shed the blood of soldiers who had served under him, but it was also an affront to his honor to be attacked and besieged by his own men.

When he saw two majors waiting for him at attention, he spoke in a slightly irritated tone.

"What is it?"

"Sir, Ragıp Bey has just come from the parliament building, he got a look at the mutineers, if you'll allow him, he has something to say."

Muhtar Pasha just looked at him.

"Ragıp, aren't you the Ragıp who got a medal for the maneuvers in Germany?"

"Yes, commander."

"Have you been reassigned to headquarters?"

"No, pasha, I came here because my units have joined the mutiny."

The pasha nodded his head.

"O.K., Ragıp, tell me, what is it."

"Pasha, this morning I walked here from Nişantaşı in civilian clothes, I walked among the mutineers. The people outside are just riffraff, there are more vagrants than soldiers, there's no commander in charge. They're just roaming around in a disorderly way, killing any officers they come across. We could disperse them in half an hour with an artillery battery and a machine gun unit, with your permission I would like to volunteer to do this."

"You think you can scatter them in just half an hour?"

"I can, pasha, I'm sure they'll scatter when they see a

determined unit and heavy guns, in any case they're not from Istanbul, they have nowhere to go, they'll all go back to their barracks, we can catch the ringleaders in the evening"

Muhtar Pasha took a pointer from his desk and started tapping his boots with it.

"Yes, I know you and I believe what you say, but the Grand Vizier gave strict orders, we're not to open fire on the mutineers, the minister of war has resigned. He even wants us not to shoot even if they do, but I informed them that we will shoot if they attack."

"Pasha, you yourself know better than I do, but we have to strike while the iron is hot, more soldiers will join the mutiny if we delay, at the moment most of the units in Istanbul have yet to make a decision, but every passing hour works in favor of the mutineers and against us."

The pasha couldn't decide. He hesitated to attack his own soldiers, but the real reason for his indecisiveness was that he didn't understand the real reason for the mutiny, he didn't know who was behind it. When the mutineering units fired, who would he be shooting at; what made him think was that there might be some power behind the mutineers that he didn't know about, in the end he could get into trouble, he could end up being seen as a traitor who'd killed his own troops.

Then a clerk came in and handed the pasha a telegram. Once the pasha had read the telegram, he looked at Ragıp Bey.

"A group from parliament is going to the palace to speak with His Majesty the Sultan, we've been ordered to wait until this meeting is over."

Ragıp Bey didn't know what the pasha was thinking, he'd never given a thought to the political aspects of this mutiny, all he wanted was to teach the soldiers who'd killed an officer before his eyes a lesson. The thought of surrendering the capital to them made him crazy with anger, for a moment he couldn't control himself.

"You're making a mistake, pasha!"

When Muhtar Pasha turned and looked at Ragıp Bey, he had the rage of a real soldier in his eyes.

"I don't understand, Major."

Ragıp Bey realized he'd gone too far, he was being disrespectful.

"Pasha, if we delay putting down the mutiny until evening, the mutineers will control the capital tomorrow, all of the units will join them, every second that passes will make them bolder and stronger."

Muhtar Pasha was no longer listening to Ragıp Bey.

"You're dismissed, Major, we're going to wait and see what the outcome of the meeting at the palace is."

As Ragıp Bey left the room grumbling, "We lost Istanbul today, Rıfkı, just now," the elderly Sultan, to whom a delegation from parliament had been sent, looked like an anxious fortune-teller through the smoke from the cigarette stuck in the corner of his mouth, the large nose and the hennaed beard that had once given his face a look of grandeur now gave him the comic and feeble appearance of a carnival mask and made him seem comical and weak. He glanced at the note the young clerk had brought and then put it on the coffee table next to him. Doctor Reşit Pasha thought that the Sultan had forgotten the cigarette in his mouth and that it would burn his lips, but he took the cigarette, stubbed it out in the ashtray, and sighed deeply as he lit another one.

"Just look at the state of things, doctor, the worst disgrace of our life occurs in our old age as we're preparing to leave the world, soldiers are killing our officers in the capital, two groups of soldiers are facing off against each other."

"Why are you complaining, my Sultan, your soldier slaves are shouting 'Long live the Sultan' everywhere, they're shouting out their loyalty to you."

The Sultan looked at Reşit Pasha with a smile that mixed

understanding and mockery, as if, despite his great dismay, he was looking at someone even more desperate than he himself was.

"Doctor, you've been with me for years, in this very room you've heard me say so many things about the state of the nation, but you've learned nothing, you're a good doctor but you don't understand politics."

The doctor, who was accustomed to this self-satisfied attitude that denigrated everyone around him, simply bowed his head and said nothing.

"Who wouldn't seem incapable in comparison to you, Your Majesty."

"Don't say that, doctor, at the moment I'm the one who's desperate and helpless, I've been ensnared in such an intricate conspiracy that there's no way out."

"Why do you say that, Your Majesty, your soldiers are shouting your name."

"Oh doctor, don't you see that the people who are shouting my name are the ones who are going to lose this battle, do you know what happens to the man whose name the losing side shouts?"

Reşit Pasha didn't dare ask what would happen, in any case the Sultan didn't expect him to say anything and continued.

"This will end in our losing the throne, or even, God forbid, losing our head, I'm not upset at the prospect of our own death, but they'd crush our children, our family, this is what I'm worried about."

Reşit Pasha, who'd thought from the beginning that the Sultan had a part in this mutiny and that the old man hadn't told him because it was his nature not to trust anyone, lowered his head so the Sultan wouldn't see disbelief in his eyes. The Sultan, who for his entire life had done everything he could to understand whoever was in his presence, who combined the instincts of both hunter and prey because he'd lived both as a hunter who pursued people and tried to capture them and as prey who feared being killed by others, and who had sharpened his skills to the point that he was like a lightning rod that gathered clouds of emotion around it, immediately sensed what the doctor was thinking.

"You don't believe me, Pasha?"

"I beg your pardon, Your Majesty, is it a slave's place not to believe?"

The Sultan laughed abruptly, it cheered him up to put someone in a difficult position.

"Of course no one tells a sultan they don't believe him, they can't, but they all make the same gesture to conceal their disbelief, I sense their disbelief from what they do to conceal what they think, for example the way you bowed your head and averted your eyes just now . . . "

Then he returned to his former mood and made a face.

"I always tell you to read murder mysteries, those books contain the secret of life and of power . . . You get better at analyzing what's going on. Don't you see that there's something peculiar about what's happening, you'd see if you were accustomed looking at things carefully. The skirmisher brigades the Committee brought in are rebelling, who were they brought in to oppose, they were brought in to oppose me, now they're rebelling against the people who brought them. If Muhtar Pasha, Commander of the First Army, were to make the slightest move with the First Army, he could crush them, besides, the skirmisher battalions aren't being led by officers, the soldiers either killed them or they fled to save their lives. But the First Army isn't making a move. Why, doctor? Why hasn't the First Army made a move? This is what makes me think."

He lit another cigarette.

"Intelligence has been coming in since morning, of course I know what's going on everywhere, but there's no one I can give orders to. The First Army doesn't move, the Grand Vizier doesn't move. It looks as if the mutineers are against the Committee, but the Committee doesn't move. If the Committee pressured the Grand Vizier a bit, if they told Muhtar Pasha that they supported him, they could put the mutiny down. But they don't. They know Muhtar Pasha won't make a move, that he won't attack unless he gets a direct order, that he'll fear for his own head. Tell me, doctor, why doesn't the Committee do anything, what happened to the heroes of constitutional monarchy, why are they so quiet? My enemy is their silence, doctor."

This time Reşit Pasha was truly confused.

"So, who incited them to mutiny, Your Majesty?"

"The people who had Hasan Fehmi Bey killed are behind the mutiny, doctor."

The doctor was unable to contain himself and shouted out:

"The Committee!"

The Sultan looked silently out the window at the vibrantly sparkling, phosphorescent blue of the Bosphorus, nothing about his manner seemed to confirm what Reşit Pasha had said. When the silence continued for longer than he could bear, Reşit Pasha asked:

"Wasn't it the Committee?"

"I doubt they're that intelligent, doctor, if they were capable of this they would long since have been able to seize the reins of the empire, but they weren't able to . . . They haven't been able to take control of Istanbul. Why Salonika, that's what you should ask, doctor. Because the Third Army, which the Committee controls, is in Salonika. They couldn't be the masters of Istanbul without bringing the Third Army here, they knew this. But how could they bring this army here?"

Even though the situation was so uncertain, it pleased him to see that Reşit Pasha was listening to him admiringly, it always pleased him to see his mind and his superiority reflected in other people.

"The troops of the Third Army will come to the capital soon, doctor, they set up supply depots a long time ago, I was curious about why they were stocking supplies, even though it occurred to me I wondered how they could do that when the First Army was here. It didn't occur to me that the First Army could be rendered ineffective."

Reşit Pasha shook his head and murmured to himself:

"So it is the Committee . . . "

"I doubt the Committee organized all of these things, doctor."

If Reşit Pasha hadn't been able to control himself he would have lost his temper and shouted, "So, who then?" but he contained himself and looked at the Sultan like a curious child.

"You need to be intelligent to pull something like this off, and the Committee isn't intelligent, though Talat might be a bit smarter than the others. Second, you need a lot of money . . . Who has money, doctor?"

Reşit Pasha almost said, "You do, Your Majesty," but he managed to stop himself at the last moment.

The Sultan suddenly asked him a seemingly unrelated question.

"Where is Enver now?"

Reşit Pasha replied innocently:

"In Berlin."

Then he was astounded by his own answer.

"The Germans . . . Do you suspect the Germans, Your Majesty?"

"It's very possible, Reşit Pasha. It's very possible."

"What about summoning the German ambassador and discussing it?"

"They would laugh at me, doctor, what would the man say, would he admit it? You said it too, the mutineers are shouting my name, what evidence do I have for blaming the Germans?"

The Pasha was now very confused.

"Could the Committee take their treachery to that level, Your Majesty?"

"Most of them probably don't know, they'll be thinking that the reactionaries' mutiny was organized by the Sultan. Only a few people at the top would know, and they will have convinced themselves that this is for the good of the empire."

Just then one of the Sultan's aides came in, leaned down, and whispered something into the Sultan's ear, Reşit Pasha thought he heard the word "sergeant" being whispered, but he wasn't sure. The Sultan quickly rose to his feet, smiling politely at the doctor, who stood when he did.

"Doctor, it's chaotic out there, you can ride in one of the palace carriages, your own carriage can follow behind."

He turned to his aide.

"Arrange for four cavalrymen to escort the doctor to make sure nothing happens to him on the way. Let me know when he's safely home."

As the doctor made his way toward the door, the Sultan started moving toward the secret door that led to his office, then suddenly stopped.

"Doctor, you live on the Asian side, don't cross to the other side tonight, I may need you at any time and you'll be too far away. I heard your son has moved to Nişantaşı."

"Yes, Your Majesty."

"Stay with your son tonight."

"As you wish, Your Majesty."

As they made their way down Yıldız Hill, he saw the Hassa Regiment lined up in two columns, precautions had been taken against a possible attack; the soldiers and the officers commanding them had the swaggering seriousness that came from the idea that they were part of a momentous event. In a land where history was often shredded and rewritten, in the middle of a disaster during which history was being rewritten, these poor souls were only a hundred yards from the Sultan for whom they were prepared to sacrifice their lives, but they would never learn what was really going on, they would never learn the truth. "Even I didn't know," Reşit Pasha told Osman later, "I still don't know, I found what the Sultan said logical, but I'm sure he was up to something, that he hadn't been sitting still, but he hadn't told anyone what he thought, he didn't trust anyone, but now, talking to you, I realize I didn't trust him either, what do I know, perhaps it doesn't make sense to look for trust in a relationship with a sultan."

Evening was approaching, shadows were lengthening, a tranquil coolness descended onto the streets, and in the houses of Akaretler, lined up like meek, yellow cats, in the budding horse-chestnut trees, in the smell of grass that wafted from the vegetable gardens in the back, in the cobblestones that seemed to be fleeing before the carriage, and in the rattling of the wheels there was a wittiness, a lightness, a flirtatiousness peculiar to spring that pleased Reşit Pasha.

The Pasha wasn't naïve enough to not realize that the dangers the Sultan spoke of also targeted him. If the Sultan lost his head, everyone closely associated with him would lose their heads too, this was a tradition, and even though there wasn't absolute trust between them, he was known as one of the people closest to the Sultan, but he wasn't overly worried about this deadly possibility.

Ever since he'd started to believe that he was getting old, he'd secretly become weary of life, he'd detached himself from his passions, he'd begun waiting for the time of his departure with resignation; in spite of the grandeur and wealth in which he lived, he was a man who measured his life with women, since he'd decided he was no longer as powerful and impressive as he'd once been, life had also lost the charm it had once had, this was the secret he didn't share with anyone, it was his simple but defining secret; he wasn't interested in what was going to happen from now on, it was like listening to gossip about a distant relative, he listened with momentary curiosity, but he was less interested.

When they arrived at Hikmet Bey's mansion, the gardener came running when he saw the carriage bearing the palace crest and the mounted escort, opened the large iron gate, and the carriages raced through the garden and stopped in front of the mansion. Hikmet Bey, who had been informed that a carriage from the palace escorted by four cavalry men had arrived, went to the door worrying that something had happened to his father, he was relieved when he saw Reşit Pasha step out of the carriage.

"Welcome, father, welcome . . . "

"The Sultan has decreed that I will be your guest, Hikmet, I've been ordered to stay at your house tonight."

They dismissed the carriage and the escort and went inside.

"Have you heard about what's been going on?"

"I know as much as anyone, we heard that the troops have mutinied and are demanding sharia, this morning we heard some gunfire coming from the direction of Taşkışla. But I don't know what happened after that, friends sent me word that I shouldn't leave the house because the situation is chaotic, so I stayed home."

"You did the right thing . . . The soldiers have surrounded parliament and the ministry of war and are waiting, the minister of war has resigned. A delegation from parliament was going to meet the Sultan, I think there's going to be a general amnesty. This evening it will be clearer where all this is heading."

Hikmet Bey brought his father to his study. There was a soft peace there, like a fur you would want to caress, and the light that filtered in the window through the half-closed shutters liberated everyone who entered from their sense of alienation. There was a fragrance that combined the English soap Hikmet Bey had used since childhood, tobacco, and books, and which, even though it was masculine, sheltered the loneliness of fragility. A fire was burning in the fireplace and an orange light with a slick shadow emanated from the small lamps in the corners.

"Would you like some coffee?"

"I would, that would be nice."

Hikmet Bey ordered coffee. He returned to his place and sat, and his father looked carefully at him to determine how his health was.

"You look well."

"I'm fine."

The pallor was gone from Hikmet Bey's face, and had been replaced by a healthy, rested expression, the purple rings that had made his face look like a pansy were also gone. His eyes still appeared grave, but they were livelier, and his handsomeness had changed form, he was now a bit more ordinary, less noticeable. He no longer had the creases of sacred silence seen on the faces of melancholy people who have suffered great agony, and which attracts others with an irresistible charm, or he'd hidden them in a deeper place; that sorrow definitely revealed its presence in some movement, in a glance or a gesture. In his new house, with Hediye, he felt a peace that resembled happiness, even though he couldn't call it that; his soul was like his office, comfortable, quiet, but introverted and distant from life.

From time to time he visited his mother, got together with friends, talked politics, criticized the Committee, but even his criticism had become more mature, he used fewer rash and destructive words than he used to, he simply told what he believed to be the truth, and saying that was enough for him. When he settled into his armchair in his office at night, Hediye sat next to him, silently watching him read books, she waited carefully to sense if Hikmet Bey wanted anything before he had the chance to ask for it, she could always sense Hikmet Bey's wants before they even came to his mind.

At that time his life was like a pause after a strong, sharp ascent in a song, an interval during which he could catch his breath, but although Hikmet Bey didn't tell anyone, he thought his song had come to an end. He didn't know that this silence was a pause between two ascents, that he was on the verge of a strong, new note.

Father and son had dinner alone together. Hediye didn't appear at all. Hediye always ate with Hikmet Bey, and she'd freed him from the embarrassment of not being able to invite her to the table, and once again she'd earned the tenderness and gratitude of the man she loved. She was bound to Hikmet Bey by an unconditional love, her every thought, feeling, and instinct aimed to lessen his load and open space for him, there was no room left in her soul for her, for her own self. She'd given up her own desires, pleasures, and will and attached her own happiness completely to Hikmet Bey's; this terrifying abnegation that might seem sad to someone else was the only mode of existence that could make Hediye happy, she held on to life with Hikmet Bey's hands and she'd left herself no choice but to cling more tightly to Hikmet Bey. This terrifying attachment made her capable of sensing whether her presence or absence would please Hikmet Bey, even before he himself knew.

At dinner, Hikmet Bey said, "A very good year," as he poured his father some expensive French wine, just as it is permissible for a former coquette who'd settled into marriage to be slightly coquettish from time to time, Hikmet Bey also derived pleasure as much from his memory as from his palate as he held on to some of his expensive pleasures.

In this city that was preparing to experience its own Armageddon, father and son, both somewhat detached from life for different reasons, talked about events that would determine their future with a lack of concern that was almost comical.

"What do you think is going to happen, father?"

"I don't know, Hikmet, but it's no secret that nothing good will come of it, we have to be prepared for anything . . . My position connects my future to the Sultan, and after what I saw today, I'm not very hopeful about his future either. It seems the end is near for old people like us; I've lived what I had to live, to tell the truth, destiny was generous to me, if it's more miserly from now on it wouldn't be fair to complain. Now I'm worried about you, what will your future be, what kind of country will you live in, with all this turmoil, how can this country avoid bloodshed? I don't see any will that suggests security and decisiveness, for a long time the empire is going to be dragged from one hand to another, God forbid, it might even break up. Then what are you going to do, what will you do, what are your children going to do? Maybe the time has come for you to move to Paris, you've always loved it there and you've always wanted to go back."

Hikmet Bey didn't get into the subject of Paris, he thought he was never going to move anywhere again, he no longer had the strength to establish a new life somewhere else.

"Are clashes going to break out between the mutineers and the army?"

"They certainly will, if not today, then tomorrow. If you look at history you can see, once momentous events begin, they don't stop without bloodshed. Fighting is inevitable. But when and how, I don't know. It's not that I'm frightened, if there's fighting, one side will win, then there'll be calm again; what concerns me is that there's no authority in the city, no one knows who's going to win, then looting could begin at any time then, they might start attacking wealthy mansions and women. Do you have a gun?"

Hikmet Bey tried to hide his smile, it had been a long time since anyone had mentioned a gun to him out of fear of reminding him of his past.

"I have a gun."

"Good . . . Keep it within reach. There are military barracks on either side of you, unruly soldiers could come this way."

"I had the doors locked. In any event there's not much we can do, father . . . We just have to wait and see what destiny has in store for us."

Reşit Pasha found his own lack of concern natural, but it disquieted him to see that his son was so unconcerned about what was happening, that he gave so little thought to his future, worst of all that he had no interest in the future of the country that he'd joined secret organizations in order to change.

Suddenly he changed the subject and asked, "What are you up to these days?"

Once he himself had become a father, Hikmet realized that this question also contained the questions, "Are you happy, have you come to terms with the past, do you miss Mehpare?", he'd long since learned that fathers never cease to worry about their children, that this was a curse passed down from generation to generation, he began looking for answers that would put his father at ease.

"I'm fine, father, I really am. I have a peaceful life, I've come to terms with the past, it's just that I no longer think that a person can control his destiny or change his future, I think my frustration changed the way I think. I once had a great deal of trust in the Committee. But later I realized that anyone who enters politics has a bit of Sultan in them, to me it makes no difference whether it's Enver or the Sultan in the palace. I don't see any difference between them. And I've begun to think that our traditions aren't compatible with true freedom. I suppose the reason I'm not excited about what's going on is that I was dreaming of an Ottoman Revolution like the French Revolution. I haven't read history carefully, this is not a land of revolutions but of rebellions. Whatever you do, whatever you call your form of government, you end up with a sultan at the top."

He picked up his wine glass and sniffed at it before drinking.

"What a lovely aroma it has, doesn't it? It seems that if you can't make a country's wines you can't make its revolution."

He took a sip of wine and, before swallowing it, held it between his tongue and palate and waited for the fruity perfume beneath the acrid taste to spread to his nasal cavity.

"But I imagine you were asking about my personal life. My answer regarding this is the same, I'm fine. I've forgotten about what happened. As my mother would say, it's just that I'm a bit weary of life. You could say that I've retired in a sense, but don't worry about that, it's a nice life, and at least it's not dangerous. I no longer ask myself every day what I expect from life, it's shown me what it's capable of giving and I saw what I'm capable of taking. I no longer meddle with life, and I don't want it to meddle with me. I've created different, more pleasurable troubles for myself, I read Cervantes and Rabelais, I read Fuzuli and Baki, who lived in the same century, I'm curious about why they're so cheerful and critical when everyone here, now, is so melancholy and hopeless, I find this interesting."

Before he was able to finish this comment, they heard gunfire and shouting, it didn't seem as if there was fighting, they realized that soldiers were firing into the air.

"They must be mutineers," said Reşit Pasha, "normally soldiers would never shoot around here, I wonder if they're returning to their units in Zincirlikuyu."

"If they're shooting in such an unconstrained manner, the mutineers must have forced the loyal units out of the city."

Even though they didn't think they had a strong relationship with life and the future, when the truth confronted them in the form of gunshots and shouting soldiers, both of them realized that the poverty, denigration, and death that were easily dismissed from a distance could be more scorching when they drew nearer. For a moment, the same image passed through both their minds, the image of them being dragged and humiliated by soldiers who'd broken down the door, of the furniture being looted, of the women becoming victims to boorish lust; they also remembered that there were worse things than death.

Reşit Pasha asked his son to turn off the lights. After Hikmet Bey had doused the lamps in his study, he ordered the servants to douse all the lamps in the house, to close the shutters and bolt the doors. For a moment he considered getting his gun, then dismissed the idea because he thought it might be too dramatic.

They stood before the window together in the darkness; because neither of them knew the aims of either side in this conflict, neither was certain which side they would choose. While Reşit Pasha wanted the mutineers who supported the Sultan to win, Hikmet Bey thought it would be better if the army and the Committee won.

They stood and waited in silence.

The sound of gunfire receded. Reşit Pasha said, "I think that's enough for today, we'll see what tomorrow brings." Then he said, "I'm going to bed now, I'll be getting up early and going to the palace in the morning."

As Hikmet Bey escorted his father to his bedroom he realized how strange it was that he hadn't asked anything about Mihrişah Sultan; even with the city was in such turmoil, he hadn't wondered how his former wife was.

When Hikmet Bey returned to his study and continued drinking wine, he didn't know that as soon as the mutiny broke out his father had sent someone to Kanlica at once to see how things were there, once he'd learned that there were no mutineers on the Asian side and once he'd learned that guards had been assigned to protect those close to the Sultan, he felt reassured. Of course fathers don't tell their sons everything, just as sons don't tell their fathers everything; even though they were father and son, there were dark gardens that men didn't speak of to each other, where another man's light should never shine, the ghosts of women wandered there, poisonous fruit that no one else should know about grew in these gardens.

As he wondered why his father had behaved this way, he thought back to his own past, to his former wife, even though he didn't mention her name, to this garden in which he attempted to hide from everyone, even from himself, and the memories he'd buried in the tunnels of forgetfulness came pouring out. Even though he knew how much pain they would leave behind when they went, Hikmet Bey welcomed them with an almost pathetic delight. Hikmet Bey, absorbed in his memories, had forgotten about what was happening on the streets of the city in which he lived and what kind of morning was awaiting them, but Reşit Pasha's prediction had proven correct; at the end of the day the mutineers had been the victors because of the commander of the First Army Muhtar Pasha's indecision and had seized the capital for what would prove to be a short time.

The following morning Hikmet Bey would be very surprised, he would be deeply shaken to realize that his soul was still receptive not just to memories but also to dreams about the future.

12

Ragıp Bey realized that the city would surrender to the mutineers three or four hours before Hikmet Bey and Reşit Pasha heard the gunfire.

He sat next to Rıfkı Bey all day, waiting for the order to attack, when he got bored, he toured the units that were posted in various parts of the garden, which was as large as a neighborhood, and watched the mutineers pressing against the garden fence.

Twice the mutineering soldiers attacked and tried to seize the ministry, the first time they were repelled with pressurized water and the second time Mahmut Muhtar Pasha came out and commanded the units to fire into the air, but Ragıp Bey could see how unwilling the units in the ministry garden were.

In the evening, as darkness was falling, officers from the ministry's band and civil servants wandered in groups through the garden trying to convince the soldiers to join the mutiny. Ragıp Bey heard with his own ears that soldiers were grumbling that they wanted to leave the ministry garden and join the mutineers; just as he'd surmised, with every passing moment the morale of the loyal units was weakening and the mutineers were gaining confidence.

When it grew dark he went back into the ministry building, where all the lights had been lit, and went to see Rıfkı Bey; the commotion of that morning had subsided and everyone looked glum.

He asked Rıfkı Bey if there was any hope.

Rıfkı Bey shook his head.

"I heard that Muhtar Pasha begged the prime minister, the Grand Vizier, and the minister of war to give the order to attack, but they all insisted that he was not to attack under any circumstances."

"Rıfkı, the ministry is under siege, the soldiers have mutinied, why is your pasha still waiting for orders?"

"Ragıp, you have no idea about these things, they're hazardous, tomorrow he could be court-martialed for disobeying an order. He could even be handed over to the mutineers as a traitor. It's not clear who's doing what and which side anyone is on, what can Muhtar Pasha do."

Meanwhile they'd learned that the Sultan, who'd met with a delegation from parliament, had issued an imperial decree forgiving the mutineers. Toward seven o'clock, a lieutenant rushed in to speak to Rıfkı Bey.

"Our soldiers are trying to move closer to the gate, they're getting ready to join the mutineers, commander."

Rıfkı Bey made a face and said he would inform the commander, if this news had arrived that morning everyone would have sprung into action and started planning how to prevent this, but now everyone was losing hope.

When Rıfkı Bey returned a little later his face was ashen.

"Muhtar Pasha has decided that the First Army is no longer viable from a military point of view, he has tendered his resignation and will be leaving the ministry soon."

Ragıp Bey jumped to his feet.

"Is that Pasha mad, he's destroying his entire career in a single day, is this any time to be such a coward?"

Even though Rıfkı Bey disapproved of Muhtar Pasha's action, he'd served under him for many years and was reluctant to accuse him of cowardice.

"Don't say that, Ragıp, if this was simply a military issue the pasha would do whatever had to be done, he's a courageous man, I've seen proof of this on many occasions, but this time there's politics involved, the Grand Vizier has resigned, the minister of war has resigned, the chief of general staff has ordered soldiers to be sent to Hagia Sophia square to take the mutineers' guns and then join them, even the speaker of parliament, the Committee's darling, says we shouldn't resort to arms. What should Muhtar Pasha do? If you show him the enemy he'll attack, but the Pasha doesn't know who's an enemy and who's a friend."

Just then Şükrü Bey, who'd helped Ragıp Bey get into the ministry garden, arrived out of breath.

"What's going on, they say the Pasha has resigned, we've been ordered to return to barracks."

Rıfkı Bey nodded his head.

"The Pasha has resigned, that's correct."

The three officers looked at each other. Ragıp Bey asked the question that had passed through all of their minds.

"What are we going to do?"

Şükrü Bey sat down and lit a cigarette.

"There's nothing we can do here, if we waste time here the mutineers will wipe us out along with the rest of the officers, even if they don't kill us we'll be humiliated. I think we should leave the city right away, we can try to find a couple of horses at Edirnekapı and hold out in Çatalca. Salonika will make Istanbul pay; the Third Army will move soon, and we can join them."

Ragıp Bey didn't even have to think about this.

"Fine, let's go."

Rıfkı Bey shook his head.

"You go, I'll stay, someone needs to keep our friends informed about what's going on here, we can't completely abandon this place."

Şükrü Bey tried to persuade his friend.

"They'll kill you."

"I'll change out of my uniform, I'll wear the civilian clothes Ragıp wore this morning before he changed into my uniform. In the morning we needed a uniform, uniforms were precious then, but now I need civilian clothes because the uniform has lost its value. It only took a day to leave behind the uniform we've always worn."

Ragıp Bey wasn't in the mood to mourn the uniform.

"Come on, let's go then. There's no time to lose and there's much for us to do. When we return with the Third Army we'll settle accounts with the people who cheapened the uniform."

Rıfkı Bey put on the civilian clothes and as the three officers were leaving the building, Muhtar Pasha exited the side gate in his carriage; when the mutineers besieged his house the following day, he escaped disguised as a Greek fisherman and took refuge with the Germans, and, like all those who destroy their careers in a single day, he would wonder what the mistake he made "that day" was, but he would never quite be able to figure out what it was.

In the ministry garden there was the profound disarray seen in defeated armies. In the darkness of the night that descended like purple velvet, sergeants with trembling oil lamps, whose light turned the shadows of everything it touched into monsters preparing to attack, looked for their soldiers under the trees, the cavalry battalion's horses became agitated by the noise and reared and neighed, the sound of horseshoes on the paving stones made the soldiers load their rifles, units that had lost their officers tried to move out the gate at the same time and ended up trampling one another, the soldiers cursed and exchanged blows to suppress their fear.

Most of the officers had snuck out of the garden in order to leave the city, those who hadn't would either be beaten by the soldiers on the streets or, if they were less fortunate, shot, no one knew exactly how many officers were killed, but it was said to be about forty

With its darkened windows and the large, open door that looked like the mouth of a giant who was about to scream, the magnificent war ministry building looked like a deserted, pitiful, burned-out ruin.

Using the darkness to their advantage, the three officers went out through the gate on the Mercan side; Şükrü Bey and Ragıp Bey bade farewell to Rıfkı Bey, who looked like a rural shepherd in his civilian clothes.

Şükrü Bey said, "I know some people at the stables in Edirnekapı, let's go and get some horses."

"You go to Edirnekapı and arrange for the horses, there's something I have to do, I'll take care of it and be back in an hour. If I'm not back in an hour, something has happened to me and you need to get going."

After he left Şükrü Bey, Ragıp Bey headed for the *tekke*, before he left the city he wanted to kiss his mother's hand, say farewell to his wife and find out what the Sheikh thought about the mutiny.

For the first time, he found the *tekke*'s large gate closed, he knocked with the brass knocker and waited for the door to be opened, there were sounds of gunfire in the city.

He found the Sheikh with a foreign woman who spoke with a strange accent and her two sons, who were about thirteen or fourteen; the woman was weeping but she continued to speak without sobbing or raising her voice.

Sheikh Efendi calmed her with the tranquility he always possessed.

"Don't worry, Emily Hanım, in fact you're not in any danger, but since you're hesitant we'll find a solution."

Then he turned to one of his followers who was waiting by the door with his hands clasped over his belly.

"Our ladies can find an abiya for Emily Hanım and she can

wear that, bring her sons some of our clothes to wear. Then find one of our boatmen, have two of our followers accompany them and bring them to the lodge in Üsküdar."

Then he turned back to the woman.

"In the morning you can go to your friends in Beylerbeyi. Don't worry, no one will touch a hair on your head as long as our followers are with you. Now go change your clothes and get going. Go in peace."

The woman kissed the sheikh's hand, her sons imitated her and kissed his hand in an awkward and unpracticed manner. When the woman and her children had gone, he gestured for Ragıp Bey to join him.

"Welcome, Ragıp Bey, how are you, I was worried about you."

"Thank you, your excellency, on account of your prayers I'm well."

When he saw Ragıp Bey looking at the woman who was going out the door with her sons, the sheikh explained briefly.

"Emily Hanım visits the *tekke* often, her husband used to work at an embassy, she remained here after he died. Soldiers were shooting in front of her house, she was frightened and wanted to go to her friends and asked for our help."

Ragıp Bey believed once again that he would never fully grasp the secret of this *tekke*, he would always encounter something that surprised him. Then he got to the point.

"You know what's going on, of course . . . "

"I've heard. The Ulema doesn't approve of what's going on, the Sheikhs of the *tekkes* are strongly opposed to this mutiny. Men of religion are not involved in what's going on, the only people participating in the name of religion are a few religious fanatics from the madrassas. There's a fool-saint called Derviş Vahdeti, and there's Said-i Kürdi, who wears a dagger in his cummerbund, he's another story. Let me tell you straight, Ragıp Bey, God and religion are being mentioned a lot, but what's going on has no connection to either God or religion. Anyone seeking the cause shouldn't look to religion, he should look in places that bear no relationship to religion."

For the first time Ragıp Bey sensed anger in Sheikh Efendi's voice, in whose echo there was always a faint and penetrating melancholy and a fragile resignation that made any mortal he spoke to identify with him.

"The damned Sultan is stirring them up," he said.

"The truth is usually not in the place we think we'll find it, Ragıp Bey, I've always doubted truth that's found too easily. I believe that it always requires effort to capture the truth, truths we think we've arrived at too easily are lies that have been spread so that they can be grasped as truths."

The Sheikh's voice had become calmer, had returned to its usual tone, but Ragıp Bey could feel the concealed reproach in his words, he sensed he was being put in his place for being so insolent as to speak rashly in his presence and he was ashamed, and he tried to conceal his shame beneath an indifferent arrogance.

"If it wasn't the ulema or the Sultan who stirred up these mullahs, then who was it, Your Excellency, who brought these soldiers out of their barracks? What is the truth?"

"People always say they want the truth, but sometimes I think they're after what they've already decided is the truth, they don't want the truth, but they want what they believe to be the truth to be proven. This weakness makes people blind, Ragıp Bey, they can't even see what's right in front of them. And perhaps you don't want to see the truth. I can never decide if the truth is God's blessing or a curse, I always sense a fire in it, not every eye can see it, not every hand can touch it, the truth burns, Ragıp Bey, not everyone has it in them to grasp it."

Then he added in sorrow, as if for himself and not for Ragıp Bey:

"God help those who seek the truth."

Like everyone who carries a sorrow that cannot be explained to others, like everyone tortured by the fire of a secret that can not be revealed, Sheikh Efendi turned every conversation, every discussion into an inner reckoning without letting the other sense it, whoever that other might be, the secret he carried was such a human secret, the sorrow that burned his soul was such a human weakness, anyone listening to him could find something about themselves in his words, in his inner reckoning, and illuminated themselves with the sparks that his words became.

He suddenly changed the subject, unconcerned that Ragıp Bey was waiting to learn the truth from him.

"What are you planning to do now? It's not quite safe to wander around the city in the current situation, would you consider staying at the *tekke* for a while, it's still the safest place in the capital."

"This is not a time to hide, Your Excellency, with your permission I want to leave to join the army that will be coming from Salonika, my friends are waiting for me at Edirnekapı. We'll get horses from the stable there and set off immediately."

Sheikh Efendi smiled as if he was demonstrating that he was pleased.

"That's a good plan . . . Has the army from Salonika begun to move?"

"I don't think they've started to move yet, but I'm sure they won't allow these vagabonds to get away with it, they'll definitely do something. Whatever they do, there'll be a part for us to play in it."

After Ragıp Bey married the Sheikh's daughter and became his son-in-law, their relationship didn't change, their undeclared friendship continued as before, they trusted each other and were each proud of the other's achievements.

Even though Sheikh Efendi had heard about Dilara Hanım

he never brought the subject up, and indeed didn't even allude to it. He knew that his son-in-law loved a woman other than his daughter, but he accepted this fact, which went against his beliefs and his moral code, because his friend found it did not go against his own beliefs and moral code, and he respected this silently. Later he said to Osman, "Never judge anyone by your own criteria, but judge them by their own criteria, an immoral man is not one who doesn't obey my moral code, an immoral man is one who does not obey his own moral code."

Sheikh Efendi pulled at the hem of his robe as he prepared to stand.

"I suppose you're going to see your mother before you leave . . . "

"With your permission, I would like to receive her blessing."

"I'm sure they've already heard you've come and are waiting for you."

They stood together, and the Sheikh looked at Ragıp Bey as if he envied him for being able to leave, or at least that's how it seemed.

"Let me know if you need anything."

Ragıp Bey responded to Sheikh Efendi's usual farewell with the same answer he always gave.

"Keeping us in your prayers will be more than enough."

His mother waited for him in the simple room that had been set aside for her in the *tekke*'s harem with a white muslin scarf on her head, her face was sour, she was against smiling because it seemed a betrayal of the pain she'd suffered at a young age from the blows of war, migration, raids, and death, the web of lines on her face would not have known how to express joy, her small black eyes forever seemed to be looking to see the disaster approaching her sons before anyone else did, and she had a terrifying and almost unnatural love for her children which they sensed when they were with her, though this was never revealed in her manner or in the way she spoke.

As Ragıp Bey kissed her hand, she asked the same questions she unfailingly asked regardless of the circumstances.

"Are you hungry? Have you eaten?"

Ragıp Bey suddenly realized how long it had been since breakfast, since Dilara Hanım had made him eat something, but he lied.

"I've eaten . . . How are you? Are you comfortable here?"

"Thanks to God I'm well, I'm comfortable, don't worry about me. They say the soldiers have mutinied."

"Yes, a few reprobates have mutinied."

"I've heard they're taunting the officers."

When he heard his mother talk about the mutineers as if they were neighborhood bullies, he couldn't contain himself and laughed; he realized what his mother really wanted to ask.

"Nobody has taunted me, mother."

"Good. Have you heard from your brother?"

"Last I heard he was in Berlin, I imagine he's in Salonika by now, don't worry about him either. I'll be leaving the city soon and heading for Salonika."

"Aren't you staying tonight?"

"I have to go, my friends are waiting for me, I came to kiss your hand and get your blessing before I leave."

"Are you leaving right away?"

"I must, mother."

There was a long silence, in the end his mother stood.

"Fine. Do what you're bound to do. May God be with you."

"Is there anything you'd like me to do, is there anything you need?"

"I don't need anything, don't think about me."

As Ragıp Bey kissed his mother's hand and left the room, the old woman gestured to the room next door.

"That's Hatice Hanım's room."

"Let me say farewell to her too."

"Don't waste too much time, you need to be on your way, don't be late."

"Yes, mother."

The old woman, who never spoke of her hatred for her daughter-in-law and had never once complained about her to her son, went back into her room and closed the door before Hatice Hanım's door opened.

Hatice Hanım was in the last days of her pregnancy, her hands were swollen like well-fried puff pastries and her feet had rounded like knobs; her belly protruded like a large boiler. When Ragıp Bey entered she was reading the Koran by the dim and dispiriting oil lamp next to her, after looking up and seeing her husband, she put the book on her lap but didn't move. She didn't forgive her husband for loving another woman, anyone who did forgive him, even her own father, was an enemy; she didn't utter a word of welcome but simply glared at him scornfully as if he was a servant who'd entered without permission.

"How are you, Hatice Hanım?"

"I'm well, praise God."

Her tone had the cold and suffocating resentment of a woman who's been betrayed, who felt completely alone because in her eyes it was not just her man who'd betrayed her but everyone, and indeed even life itself, and which combined a pleading for some hope of emerging from this desperation with hatred for having been dragged into this desperation in the first place.

For her this betrayal was like a ring of fire around a scorpion, it set her apart from anyone who had not experienced betrayal and left her alienated. This was a desolate solitude that no other living creature could enter, that no one could know except those who had been betrayed. The jealousy she felt toward the other woman didn't suffice to fill the volume of the desolation in which she lived her life, she nourished a jealousy toward anyone who hadn't been betrayed, they all possessed the same wickedness and treachery, and this made her selfish and malevolent. Because she felt that she wanted to beg to be rid of this desolation and enmity that wrapped her body and soul like gigantic strips of seaweed that did not allow her to surface and breathe, she had to remain cold and distant to avoid doing so.

Ragıp Bey saw that his wife wasn't even going to ask how he was, she was denying him even a simple greeting, she remained motionless as if she wanted him to leave right away; fate had brought them together in such a way that for one of them to be happy, the other definitely had to be unhappy.

When these two people whose emotions, wants, and loves were very reasonable and right came together, they turned into two murderers who met in a misty darkness, the one who wanted to keep his happiness alive had to kill the other's happiness.

"I'm going to Salonika, I'll be leaving soon, I came to say goodbye."

"Goodbye."

For those who betray, betrayal itself is not enough, they become selfish enough to ask the person they betrayed not to be upset about this, not to suffer, not to allow their pain to cast a shadow on the pleasure they're experiencing with someone else they love. They want the person they've betrayed to clean up the mournful shadow that betrayal created and that has seeped into the lives of both the betrayed and the betrayer, that they spare the betrayer from guilt and pangs of conscience, the shame of unjustly having upset someone; they consider it permissible to debase themselves before the person they betrayed, to make this person pity them, to try to get a kiss by being laughably frivolous, but the person they betrayed will never give them this gift; the person who was betrayed never voluntarily surrenders this last weapon to the person who betrayed them. When Ragıp Bey set out on a journey into the unknown on the night the city was shaken by the mutiny, he tried to make her pity him to get the gift he wanted without realizing he was doing so; if he had realized what he was doing he would never have done it, but at that moment he was so in need of a smile from this woman who had grown cold in her own sorrow, wanted so much for his conscience to be eased by this woman who read the Koran alone in a cold room, that he could not contain himself.

"Fighting seems inevitable, I might never come back, give me your blessing."

He never forgot Hatice Hanım's answer.

"I have no claim to you."

Ragıp Bey looked at his wife's belly, but he realized it would be inappropriate to say anything about the baby that was about to be born.

"I won't disturb you any further, goodbye."

Hatice Hanım had already picked up her Koran and begun reading again, she didn't find it necessary to raise her head.

"Good luck."

When he left the *tekke*, the mutineers' celebratory gunfire flashed like deadly fireflies with a ceaseless booming over the city that had turned its lights out, and thousands of bullets left red lines streaking behind them. The soldiers could find no other way to celebrate their temporary victory than to create an alarming cacophony, to frighten those who didn't share their enthusiasm.

He walked along the shore of the Golden Horn as it murmured and gurgled occasionally as if it was telling a fairy tale thousands of years old that no one was listening to; as he passed the darkened houses on his way to Edirnekapı, the image of Hatice Hanım reciting the Koran in her deep and bitter voice in that dim room made him want to go to her, throw himself at her feet, and beg for forgiveness. He sensed this was a temporary feeling, that there was another image beneath the deaths he'd seen all day, beneath the sense of having been defeated by the mutineers and all the sadness that encircled his neck like a noose as he walked those pitch-dark streets, and that this image made everything feel more bitter than it actually was; if that morning when he'd looked out the carriage to wave for the last time he'd seen Dilara Hanım instead of empty steps, he would still have been upset about what he'd experienced, but he would not have felt so lost, disappointed, and alone.

When he arrived at the stable in Edirnekapı he was perspiring despite the coolness of the night; in the stable, where saddles, stirrups, and crops hung from the wall, there was a heavy warmth that smelled of animals and dung; the wet sounds the horses made as they crunched the straw in front of them was mixed from time to time with the sound of horses rubbing themselves against wooden posts and the brief, irritable neighing of a stallion.

Şükrü Bey was leaning against the wall of the ostlers' room near the entrance, smoking a cigarette and waiting for Ragıp Bey, when he saw him coming he tossed his cigarette impatiently on the ground and crushed it with the toe of his boot.

"You're late."

"I had to walk, are the horses ready?"

"Yes."

Şükrü Bey called into the ostlers' room.

"İsmail. My friend is here, bring the horses."

A short man with a heavily wrinkled face emerged from the ostlers' room, glanced at Ragıp Bey as if to decide whether he deserved a horse, walked into the darkness in the back of the stable, returned a while later with two horses, and held the horses' heads tightly so they could mount.

After they mounted their horses, Şükrü Bey gave something to İsmail.

"Thanks, İsmail, take care."

"Good luck, sir."

Without saying anything to each other as they left the stable, they both galloped their horses, they wanted to be part of an army, to receive orders, to command soldiers who would immediately obey their orders and to overcome the shame of this defeat. As they moved away from the walls of the city, Ragıp Bey thought he'd left Dilara Hanım all alone in this chaotic city without even being able to tell her he was leaving.

The gunfire continued all night in the city, and thousands of bullets rained down on the rooftops, rattling like dead birds, these were the cartridges of the soldiers who were frightened by their victory and who fired to encourage themselves and celebrate the pleasure of freedom, but all night Dilara Hanım heard the sound of death in those gunshots; she thought that Ragıp Bey was in the middle of this conflict, that he was in danger, and she was worried.

She was unaccustomed to worrying about men, and these ambiguous feelings that wandered through her like seabirds without ever landing, with quick jabs like those of a sharp trowel making a statue out of a sand dune, turned into a deep longing and a love she believed she must hold on to; the places in her soul that his presence could not fill were filled more powerfully by his absence.

She remembered with deep longing all of the things about Ragıp Bey that she liked, his honesty, his boldness, the silence that did not seek a response to his feelings, the kindness this silence expressed and that asked no questions, his body, which knew when to be brutal and when to be tender in bed, and remembered with compassion the things about him she didn't like, his deep ignorance about literature, his terse, harsh manner of speaking that made it seem he was afraid to use big words, the lack of flexibility seen in those raised with strict discipline. In life, when time was divided into slices and each slice had a different light, Ragıp Bey was flawless in some slices of time and lacking in others, but now she saw him by the unquenchable light of death and saw only a brave, honorable person. This eternal light shone on his admirable traits, his faults turned into lovable transgressions that deserved to be forgiven, that even gave him a naivete, an innocence, that enhanced his charm.

At another time, she would have realized where she would be carried by the marvelous combination of longing and compassion for a man, she would either have distanced herself from it because it would inevitably have led her to fall in love or she would have taken the time to examine whether these feelings were as real as they seemed, but that night, when the city was as frightened as a child, she arduously abandoned herself to these feelings. She allowed her feelings to mingle and grow, she nourished them like a mother's womb; perhaps she missed having feelings for a man, perhaps she felt it would be a mean betrayal to quench the growing love she felt for someone she worried might die; she would never know.

She woke the next morning to screams and coarse shouting. She rushed out of bed, ran to the window, and saw that three marines from the marine unit stationed at the shipyards had cornered the Greek servant, they'd pushed her against the iron bars of the fence and were trying to lift her skirts. She put her abiya on over her nightgown, rushed outside barefoot, her anger gave her the strength to push open the heavy iron gate by herself, and she shouted at the top of her lungs, "Leave that girl alone!"

The three inebriated marines had been drinking all night, when they were confronted by a Muslim woman shouting at them they stopped for a moment, they couldn't decide whether to withdraw or to carry on with this despicable act. The seven-

hundred-strong unit of marines from the shipyards were notorious for their depravity and hooliganism; they smoked
hashish, were entertained by belly dancers and slept with boys
in their barracks, frightened the tradesmen and collected protection money. None of the other soldiers taking part in the
mutiny molested any women, it was only these marines from
the shipyards, who drank wine laced with opium as they
walked the streets shouting, "We want sharia," who harassed
women who hadn't covered their heads. Now they were being
confronted by a Muslim woman, and harassing a Muslim
woman, especially during a mutiny that was calling for "sharia,"
could be problematic.

Dilara Hanım saw that the marines were indecisive and
continued to shout at them, as she shouted she expected people in the vicinity to hear her and come to her aid.

"Get the hell out of here, is it sharia to attack women?"

Dilara Hanım's gardener and servants came rushing out,
and the angry faces of servants appeared in the doorways of
neighboring mansions.

Hikmet Bey heard the commotion and went to the window,
and when he saw the three mutineers, the shouting woman in
her abiya, and the crying Greek servant, he flew into a rage as
if his own family was being attacked.

The silent anger that had lain dormant under his meekness
and his settled tranquility rose from within him, unthinkingly
he took his gun, which he had not used for a long time, from
the drawer, put it in his belt, and, shouting, "Come with me,"
rushed downstairs and out to the neighboring mansion's gate;
his servants and workers followed him, sharing his anger.

"What's going on here, are these men harassing you,
madam?"

The marines gripped their rifles tightly, and, their eyes red
from sleeplessness and drink, they looked around at the crowd
gathering around them, the elegantly dressed Hikmet Bey,

Dilara Hanım in her stylish abiya, and tried to decide what to do. They felt that if they beat one person in the crowd, the rest would flee, but there was a Muslim woman in an abiya present, if word spread that the marines from the shipyard harassed a Muslim woman they might be in a world of trouble, in these days when officers were being hunted like birds, the entire city had become a hunting ground, they could be killed for nothing, no one was going to care about three hooligans.

Hikmet Bey turned suddenly and scolded the marines.

"How dare you disturb one of the Caliph's slaves in his own capital, do you know the penalty for harassing a Muslim woman?"

When the marines heard precisely what they'd feared hearing, one of them objected half-heartedly.

"We didn't say anything to the Muslim woman, we were just covering the head of the other woman who wasn't wearing a scarf."

"The woman without a scarf, the Greek servant, is also His Majesty the Caliph's slave, get out of here and don't come back, this is a respectable and honorable neighborhood, there's no place for hooligans here."

When the marines realized that the fun was over and things were starting to get ugly, they grumbled that the woman shouldn't have gone out with her head uncovered, swaggered to the end of the street, raised their rifles and fired a few bullets into the air, and disappeared from view shouting, "We want sharia."

When they heard the gunfire, the servants retreated to the mansions and closed the doors.

Dilara Hanım turned to Hikmet Bey.

"Thank you, sir, thanks to you we escaped being harmed by these hooligans."

"Don't mention it, ma'am, I did nothing, they would have left in any event, they wouldn't have dared to harass a Muslim woman. Are you all right?"

"I'm fine, thank you. You must be Reşit Pasha's son Hikmet Bey, I'd heard you moved in but haven't had the opportunity to meet you. Would you like some coffee?"

"I don't want to impose."

"Please, it's no imposition at all."

Dilara Hanım sent her servants back inside and scolded the Greek servant girl.

"Why did you go out with your head uncovered?"

"When the cook said we were out of salt, I ran to the grocery store on the corner . . . "

"Until I say otherwise, none of the women are to leave the house, the men can do anything that needs to be done outside the house."

When they went into the living room together, both of them were pale from what had just happened and took occasional deep breaths. Now that it was over, they could better see how dire the situation had been, only now could they think about what would have happened if one of the marines had pointed a gun at them; while it was happening, they'd experienced everything at a fast pace without noticing the details, as if they were looking out a train window. Their emotions had flowed chaotically like a changing landscape, fear and agitation had not taken on a distinct form, but now they paused and looked more carefully at what had just happened.

"Our girl's thoughtlessness placed you in danger. You put yourself at risk for us."

"Not at all, they were frightened when they saw you and realized what they were doing. You could have handled the situation without me, but when I saw them at your gate with their guns I couldn't hold myself back. I have to admit that your presence encouraged me, to tell the truth, if I hadn't seen you there I might have hesitated to go out, but I felt you were more intimidating to them than I was."

Dilara Hanım involuntarily compared Ragıp Bey when he'd

rescued her from those two hoodlums and Hikmet Bey's behavior when he'd defended her against the marines. Once Hikmet Bey said to Osman, "They always compare, women always compare men to each other." Of course she appreciated the kindness of what he said, how he'd played down his role and his courage and how he'd stressed that her own response in the face of grave danger was equal to his, but she'd been more impressed by Ragıp Bey's wildness, the way he was prepared to test his courage and manhood at any moment and the way he'd challenged not only the hoodlums he'd beaten up but the woman he'd rescued, she liked the man's wildness.

The servants tried to overcome the effects of the incident, struggled to keep their hands from trembling as they brought the coffee. Dilara Hanım uncovered her head and combed her unruly hair back with her fingers.

"Excuse the state I'm in, I don't know how I went out like that, with my hair a mess, when I heard the screams . . . "

"Please, ma'am, I shouldn't have imposed on you like this, I was just going to stay a moment."

"Please, drink your coffee."

Dilara Hanım rose to her feet as she spoke, glanced surreptitiously in the gilded mirror, and tidied her hair without letting Hikmet Bey notice.

"With your permission, I'll go change, I'll be right back, please feel at home."

When Dilara Hanım left, Hikmet Bey picked up his cup, went to the large window, and looked out at the garden as he drank his coffee, it seemed so quiet, as if nothing had just happened there. When he heard the door open he turned and said, "What a lovely garden you have," but it was not Dilara Hanım standing in the doorway.

From time to time when Hikmet Bey looked at someone or something, he didn't see the whole but only a part and, strangely, formed a bond more quickly when he saw a part rather than the whole; now he saw a pair of hands holding a book; the ends of the index fingers curled slightly toward the middle fingers, the knuckles bulged slightly, they were long and white, and the most innocent hands he'd ever seen. He raised his eyes from the hands to the face to the long, curly brown hair draped over one shoulder and falling over her chest, her chin was slightly pointed, she had an oval face with a large forehead, thick eyebrows that reached her temples, crystal clear, black eyes with a direct gaze: a young girl's face. Standing in the doorway was young girl with the boldness and purity of those who don't have a relationship with life, whose strong upbringing led her to conceal her arrogance and whose indifference and untouchability were more impressive than her beauty.

The two of them looked at each other with the same surprise, neither of them had expected to meet anyone in that living room.

"Are you waiting for my mother?"

"Yes. ma'am. You must be Dilara Hanım's daughter?"

"Yes . . ."

Dilevser didn't ask, "You?" but the sentence she didn't complete asked this question.

"I'm your neighbor, Hüseyin Hikmet, your mother asked me to wait here."

"Does my mother know you're here?"

Dilevser asked this question in such a way that it implied, "Isn't this a peculiar hour to pay a visit?" Hikmet Bey smiled.

"I'm aware that this is not a proper hour to call, ma'am, it happened this way because we had a somewhat extraordinary morning. I hope I'm not disturbing you."

"Please, I was just surprised. There's usually no one here in the morning . . . "

Hikmet Bey looked at the book she was holding and tried to read the title, but he couldn't because her fingers were obscuring it. He was curious about what she was reading but was hesitant to ask.

"You start reading early."

Dilevser looked at the book as if she'd forgotten she was holding it.

"Habit, I don't go anywhere without a book, I always want to have a book within reach, my mother says I read morbidly."

"What kinds of books do you most like to read?"

"In fact my mother is right, I'm morbidly greedy about reading. I read almost everything, but I like novels and poetry best."

For a moment he forgot the mutiny in the city, what had happened a short while ago, even almost forgot Dilara Hanım. For a man like Hikmet Bey, it was a great boon to encounter a woman in the Ottoman capital who could talk about literature.

"If you don't consider it too forward of me, might I ask who your favorite writer is?"

"There are many writers I like, but I suppose lately I've been taken by a Russian writer named Tolstoy, I read a book of his called *Anna Karenina*."

"I loved that book too."

Dilevser looked at Hikmet Bey carefully for the first time, and with slight surprise.

"Have you read it?"

"Yes, recently, a friend of mine gave it to me, I like all Tolstoy's books, when I think of Tolstoy, the image of two palms comes to mind, two hands between which all of life flows, it's as if the man carries every aspect of life in his hands."

"I've never thought about it like that. I think I was moved by the pain she suffered. How selfishly men behave toward women . . . How distant they are from the world in which women live."

"Do you really think the world in which women live is so foreign to us?"

When Dilara Hanım came in they both fell silent, as if they'd been caught telling each other secrets; this sudden silence was not the cold, tedious silence of two strangers, on the contrary, it was the living, breathing silence of two people who knew each other well and tried to conceal their connection, it spoke almost in its own language, attracting more attention than words would have, a silence written by partners in crime.

Dilara Hanım broke this strange and unaccountable silence.

"So, you've met Dilevser."

Hikmet Bey smiled as he answered.

"We talked a little about books, but I can't really say we've met, I've only just learned that this lady's name is Dilevser, I think I surprised and unsettled her by being here at this hour."

With the sensitivity that enables young girls to find meanings that others miss in every word, when she heard herself referred to as a lady rather than as a young lady in that living room for the first time, she felt an excitement that no other word could have given her and the joy of opening a door to the world of adults that had always been closed to her.

Dilara Hanım felt the need to explain to Dilevser why there was a strange man in their living room.

"If not for Hikmet Bey something terrible could have happened to us this morning."

"What kind of terrible thing, mother?"

"Oh, Dilevser, it's time to take your head out of your books and look around. Didn't you hear what happened this morning?"

She related what happened, how Hikmet Bey had arrived in the nick of time, how he'd rescued them from the marines, heaping praise that embarrassed him. Hikmet Bey felt obliged to stop her.

"Your mother is being polite and giving me too much credit, even if I hadn't been there . . . "

He was unable to finish his sentence, there was a terrific commotion accompanied by gunfire coming from the vicinity of Yıldız Palace, reminding them of another reality that was not theirs but that besieged their lives, that they were defenseless in an ungoverned city in the hands of mutineers, and that their fragile lives were under yet another threat of being torn apart.

As Dilara Hanım walked to the window as if she would have been able to see anything, she asked with an excitement she tried to suppress:

"I wonder what's going on."

"I don't know," said Hikmet Bey, "I'll send one of my footmen to the palace at once to find out. My father went to the palace this morning, I hope it's nothing bad. But you can't remain here alone, the marines who were here this morning found a mansion with no man present, there's no telling what they might do, please stay in our mansion for a time, until things calm down. We have a separate apartment for guests, you can bring your servants if you wish, I don't know if we can provide you with the same comfort you have at home, but we'll do our best."

Dilara Hanım declined, thinking there might be gossip if a mother and her daughter stayed in a single man's house, and also because Ragıp Bey wouldn't like it.

"Thank you, but we don't want to impose, besides, I don't think they're going to start attacking houses."

Hikmet Bey immediately understood the reason for Dilara Hanım's hesitation.

"Dilara Hanım, at any other time I would never dream of suggesting such a thing, but these are extraordinary times, now your safety, your life, comes before any other concerns, you won't even see me if you don't want to while you're in our mansion, you'll have your own apartment . . . We don't know what's going to happen, but if your servants join mine we could set up a force to protect the house."

When she declined for the last time, making it clear she was in fact accepting rather than declining, she was thinking more of Dilevser than herself, of what could happen to her if there was an attack.

"But we'll be a great imposition . . ."

"Please, ma'am. It's no imposition, indeed it's an honor. With your permission I'll go make all the arrangements, meanwhile I'll send someone to Yıldız to find out what's happening there."

Before leaving, Hikmet Bey turned to Dilevser.

"Don't worry about your books, I think my humble library will satisfy your desire to read during your stay."

As he walked quickly through the mansion garden, worried about his father, he felt an agitated cheerfulness that reminded him of his youth, something that was easily moved, that leapt from mood to mood depending on what he saw, that was contained within a small cocoon that vibrated with feelings that were completely cut off from the effects of the world and which emerged from the bottom of his heart in the very depths of the irresistible and unsheltered human soul. There was no clear, obvious reason for it, it was rooted in a vague satisfaction created by a vague intuition, in an image whose existence was doubtful, like a star seen faintly through a telescope. Hikmet Bey believed suddenly that destiny would once again grant him the chance to dream. Being able to dream . . . This was the gift he'd longed for most in recent years, and he'd grown bitter toward life because he'd been deprived of it.

As soon as he entered the mansion, and under Hediye's watchful gaze, he ordered the servants to make the necessary preparations for the guests and sent one of his footmen to the palace for news about his father and another to Mihrişah

Sultan with a letter inviting her and Rukiye to stay with him for
a while.

When the footman he'd sent to the palace arrived at the
gates of Yıldız, he saw that thousands of soldiers, with the
marines from the shipyard in the lead, had gathered there, they
were shouting, "We want sharia," as they attacked a carriage
that had been approaching the palace. They'd climbed onto
the carriage steps and were leaning through the windows to
beat the passengers.

The driver realized he couldn't approach the main gate so
he executed a deft maneuver to avoid the crowd and made his
way toward a smaller side gate that was used by the palace jan-
itors, the footman made his way toward the gate that had been
opened for the carriage, and the guards recognized him and let
him in.

Two pashas with blood-covered faces emerged from the
carriage, their epaulettes had been torn and hung from their
shoulders like gaudy ornaments, their disheveled and bloody
beards making them look as if they'd just come from a battle.

The footman made it known that he wanted to see Reit
Pasha, that his son was worried and had sent him to learn what
was happening, a short while later a guard came back and said,
"His Excellency the Pasha is with the Sultan at the moment, he
can't see you now but he's fine, he says that his son need not
worry."

Reşit Pasha was sitting with the Sultan in the middle hall of
the large chamber, waiting for a reply from Tevfik Pasha, to
whom a man had been sent to offer him the position of Grand
Vizier, the Sultan smoked in distress, from time to time glanc-
ing in the direction of the roaring crowd outside.

"Look. There's still no reply, I've appointed him Foreign
Minister before, I've appointed him Grand Vizier before, he
couldn't decide then either, now he's asking all manner of
questions, thinking all manner of things as he tries to decide.

To tell the truth his indecisiveness is the reason I'm appointing him Grand Vizier . . . What a strange world this is, a man is going to climb to the highest position a slave can reach simply because he can't decide. If you ask why, at the moment we need a man who won't make decisions, who won't move, a man who'll wait and see how events unfold. Because no one knows what will happen if someone makes the wrong decision."

Just then the sound of the crowd grew louder.

"What's going on, doctor, something's happening . . . "

When they looked carefully into the crowd, they saw that soldiers had surrounded a marine officer and were beating him. The Sultan stood hurriedly.

"They're going to kill that officer, doctor, we must stop this at once."

Just as the Sultan was opening his mouth to call his aide, a clerk walked in.

"The Chief Clerk Ali Cevat Bey has returned, Your Majesty, he requests an audience with you."

When he heard that the man he'd sent to Tevfik Pasha had returned, the Sultan glanced at the crowd for a moment, then turned back toward the door.

"Send him in at once."

The chief clerk was struggling to catch his breath as he entered.

"What happened, Ali Cevat Bey, what did Tevfik Pasha say?"

"He accepts, Your Majesty."

The Sultan let all the air out of his lungs with a single breath and sat in his armchair.

"Good . . . "

The commotion outside grew louder, when he turned to the window again he saw that the officer's face was stained red, sometimes the soldiers threw him to the ground and kicked him and at other times they lifted him to his feet to punch him.

The officer shouted at the top of his lungs to be heard in the palace, from which he guessed the Sultan was watching the crowd.

"I am an honorable officer who has performed his duty. If I am at fault let His Majesty punish me, I am prepared to pay the penalty!"

The chief clerk recognized the marine officer surrounded by soldiers.

"That's Lieutenant Ali Kabuli Bey, he's a good captain, I know him personally too, sir, he has a very good reputation in the navy."

The Sultan suddenly stamped his foot.

"Where is Şakir Pasha, they're killing a man in front of our gates and the chamberlain is nowhere to be found, is there no one in our palace, not a single officer or pasha, who can prevent a murder, Ali Cevat Bey? Go find Şakir Pasha at once, tell him to put an end to this, he needs to get that officer away from those soldiers."

Ali Cevat Bey, with an agility not to be expected from someone his age, almost ran out of the room, he forgot to knock on the door as he rushed into Şakir Pasha's office and he caught Şakir Pasha hiding behind the curtains as he watched what was happening outside.

"Pasha . . . Pasha . . . Don't you see what's going on, an innocent person is being killed before the Sultan's eyes. I am relaying His Majesty the Sultan's command, you are to go out at once as chamberlain and rescue this innocent officer from the crowd."

Şakir Pasha hurried past Ali Cevat Bey, descended the stairs, and went to the front of the palace; his stentorian voice could be heard in the Sultan's hall as well.

"My sons, calm down. This is the Sultan's decree. If this officer is guilty he will be punished, he will be tried at once. Surrender that officer to me, to your commander!"

The crowd seemed to pause for a moment, but one of the marines from the shipyard shouted angrily.

"Do you know what he did to us, Pasha?"

Another marine piped up, "Do you have any idea how much the officers beat us, Pasha Efendi?"

Rather than calming down, the crowd seemed to become more agitated, as if they realized they had an illustrious audience, the power that governed the empire was watching them, and they wanted to put on a show befitting their audience.

Ashen-faced, looking like a statue made of wet ash, the Sultan watched thousands of soldiers tear the officer apart with their bare hands, they tore his head from his body, dragged his headless body on the ground, and raised his head aloft so their audience could see it.

"What did I do to deserve this, what sin did I commit, doctor? They tear my officers apart before my eyes. May God punish those who dragged this nation to this point. They've always complained about me, but in the more than thirty years of my reign there's never been a disgrace like this, then the others came and look what's happening."

It was as if Reşit Pasha had collapsed in his seat, he didn't hear what the Sultan was saying, he saw nothing. The constant roaring of the crowd filled his ears, and before his eyes was the disembodied head, with its bloody eyelids open and severed veins hanging from it like purple threads.

He'd learned an unforgettable lesson about what an uprising was.

13

When Constantine held her finely curved chin tightly in his left hand and turned her face and brushed the hair that had fallen over her temple with his right hand and began to run his tongue over her, Mehpare Hanım realized what was going to happen, and excitement and fear spread from her loins throughout her body, dazzling her.

She held the man's left hand and brought it to her lips and licked his palm like a cat with her little, pink tongue; this was a special code between them that they never spoke of openly, Constantine showed her what he wanted to do by licking her cheek, and she touched his palm with her tongue for him to sense that she was ready; now she waited for the slap that would land on her face, for the burning on her cheek that would send a fire spreading throughout her bloodstream, but the slap didn't come.

Mehpare Hanım waited, her fear increasing by the moment; a tense fear that spread to a larger area like a thick, rough, black broadcloth rubbing against the folds of her brain and brought her to the verge of a peculiar unconsciousness. As this black cloth spread over her and pulled her into the darkness, sharp and pointed flashes of pleasure like knife tips sparked on and off, making her brain tingle.

Constantine had taught her to derive pleasure from fear, to use fear to sharpen and nourish the lust that touched every part of her body with its claws like a black tiger. When he moved his hand to her cheek Mehpare Hanım kept her fear at the right level, the fear was never enough to make her panic and recoil from desire, but it never lessened to the point where she could submit herself to pleasure comfortably.

She waited for the slap to land with a fear that touched her skin like a razor's edge, but what she was expecting didn't happen every time, she didn't know when it would happen either, in any event what made their lovemaking so unforgettable was an unknown large enough to accommodate every feeling. Mehpare Hanım could never sense what was going to happen, as she waited in this uncertainty she created what would and wouldn't happen in her imagination, it was so real she could feel it.

Constantine moved his hips back a bit, they continued touching each other lightly, these light touches were a sign that a big blow was coming; Mehpare Hanım waited for it, every touch heightened her anticipation and desire, she begged, shouted, swore in Greek, but the maddening light touches continued, sometimes he drew circles with his fingers, sometimes lines, then at the most unexpected moment Constantine pushed his entire body against her and their genitals were pressed together; then Mehpare Hanım screamed as if she'd been thrown into a chasm from the top of a mountain, the blows came one after the other, she started to rise to the sky, but just when she thought she was going to touch the clouds Constantine suddenly pulled back, began touching her lightly again and licked her cheek, and the sound of the sudden slap echoed throughout the universe, with this sound a red fire rose from Mehpare Hanım's loins to her brain. As he did all these things, Constantine whispered in her ear, telling her what he was doing in both Turkish and Greek.

First he asked slowly:

"What am I doing?"

When Mehpare Hanım was late to answer, Constantine shouted at her with a startling impatience.

"Say it!"

Mehpare Hanım narrated what he was doing, her voice struck the walls violently like a wrecking ball at the end of a chain, the walls collapsed one after the other with a painful pleasure, she was liberated from all colors and images by an endless white brightness that embraced her.

Constantine suddenly went slack and calmed like an evening sea, their genitals melted into each other, Mehpare Hanım felt as if she was being filled, as if she had found a missing body part and become whole; they remained like this, Constantine took parts of her lips between his, the corner, the middle, sucked on them as if they were grapes and then released them, Mehpare Hanım wanted to move but he held her fast in his arms and said, "Don't move now, just think about what we're doing, think without moving." Mehpare Hanım thought about what they were doing, thinking about her awareness of everything they were doing enhanced her body's pleasure, which was already on the point of losing control.

As a trembling began in her heels and rose through her body as small contractions, Constantine pulled away, they felt the warmth of each other's genitals, when only this small sensation of touch remained it was like hanging over a void by a thread.

Mehpare Hanım shouted almost angrily.

"No!"

Constantine's face was strained with pleasure, and an animalistic smile appeared that Mehpare Hanım only saw when they were making love.

"Yes, stay like that."

"You're an animal!"

"Stay like that, don't rush, feel, just feel."

As Mehpare Hanım's body was wracked by contractions, she wrapped her hands around Constantine's waist and pulled him toward her, but Constantine didn't move. Mehpare Hanım was on the verge of the greatest pleasure human flesh can experience; the desire rose violently, but because it somehow didn't end it included pain. She felt as if her body would explode and shatter into pieces with a horrific pain that her body couldn't endure, but she couldn't give up.

Constantine suddenly pulled her toward him and pressed their genitals together, a blinding bolt of lightning struck within her, her brain felt numbed, the numbness spread from her arms to her hands, to her fingers, she thought she was going to faint; now two bodies were slamming against each other without stopping, the pace never slacking.

The screams rose intermittently at first, then flowed freely like wild water tumbling over a waterfall, then after continuing for a time they slowed and finally stopped.

They both fell still, their bodies covered in perspiration and they felt the evaporating warmth of each other's wetness on their bodies; Constantine kissed her softly on the cheek, caressed her hair, which was wet at the ends, stroked her face with his fingers, tenderly following the lines of her face as if he wanted to get to know her.

This tenderness, these soft touches, made the fear, violence, and pain she'd felt while making love, and would feel again the next time, almost sacred.

They were different in many respects from other couples in the world, one of these differences was that after making love like this, Constantine was the one who surrendered his body, which still bore the pain of the recent lovemaking, to an unhurried lethargy, to a sleeplike reverie among the disordered bedsheets that still carried the warmth of what they'd just experienced there. Like a man, Mehpare Hanım was always the first to get out of bed.

She kissed Constantine softly on the cheek, got up, went to the adjoining bathroom, and got into the white porcelain clawfoot bathtub that Constantine had brought from Austria. She washed her body with a large-holed Aegean sea sponge that still retained the magical form of a sea creature; each time she scrubbed her entire body with the sponge, as if she wanted to expunge the traces not just of the most recent love-making but of all the lovemaking she'd ever experienced in order to become a virgin again to begin making love afresh.

She returned to the bedroom wrapped in thick towels, since she'd started living with Constantine she'd adopted a new style because this style was more comfortable for her; she was no longer ashamed to be naked in her man's presence, this aroused her because she saw it as an exciting sign of intimacy. She lowered her head in front of the mirrored console, let her wet hair fall forward, and began to dry it with a towel; Constantine, like a woman who was hurt because she felt that a man leaving the bed too soon showed a lack of sensitivity, tenderness, and love, had always been disturbed by the way Mehpare Hanım abruptly got out of bed like this, but he never said anything.

He sat up in bed, propped himself up on his elbow, and watched Mehpare Hanım dry her hair.

"Do you know, I think you have some man in you."

Mehpare Hanım tossed her head back to fling her hair out of her face.

"You see me that way because there's a woman in you too."

Constantine smiled the roguish smile that suited him so well.

"Fine, so when we're in bed does your man make love to my woman or does my man make love to your woman?"

Mehpare Hanım didn't turn her head, she just gave him a seductive glance from the corner of her eyes.

"All of them at the same time . . . We have so much fun because there are so many of us."

Even though Constantine said nothing, she sensed he was

hurt because she'd left the bed too soon, she sensed this every time, she went over to him and kissed him on the cheek.

"But I'm very pleased with your man . . . He's wonderful."

She dressed quickly, tied her wet hair in a scarf, told Constantine to sleep for a while, and went downstairs to the kitchen to have tea; she liked having tea while she chatted with the cook and watched her prepare the food.

Sula was the only servant she'd ever liked, who she enjoyed talking to, and who she saw almost as an equal. She was the most famous cook in Salonika, all the rich families tried to entice her and offered her large salaries, but they couldn't get her to leave Constantine.

At first Mehpare Hanım was cold and distant as she was with other servants, she concealed her hatred toward and fear of the poor behind this distance. But this tall, fat woman, who was a composition of incredible curved lines, was so indifferent to life, looked down on the rules and values that people accepted without question like the monks who wandered alone at night in Ancient Egypt, she was very pleased with the work she did, she governed her kitchen with a powerful authority as if she was governing an empire, she slid about like a dancing seal with an agility that was surprising for someone with such a large body, singing songs as she did so, people wanted to be friends with her, indeed wanted to be servile to her. She didn't accept anyone's friendship, not even Constantine's, she was caustic and scornful to anyone who entered the kitchen, or else scolded them and threw them out. She never talked about herself, and because of this people made up more stories about her every day; some said this old woman had been a pasha's mistress when she was young, some said she'd once had a passionate love affair with a pirate, some said she'd worked at a very expensive brothel, some said she'd been Constantine's father's mistress, and once there was even a story that she'd been in the imperial harem.

Mehpare Hanım soon noticed her aura of untouchability and the provocative indifference that disturbed wealthy masters when it appeared in poor people, she wanted to put this woman, who was able to get people to love her without being nice to them, in her place. Mehpare Hanım started going into the kitchen more often. Sula, who was caustic with others, didn't say anything to Mehpare Hanım for some time, she acted as if she wasn't aware she'd entered the kitchen. One day when Mehpare Hanım was prowling around the kitchen her hip knocked a pot full of food off the counter.

Sula turned, glanced in the direction of the sound, then went back to what she'd been doing and said calmly:

"You're a beautiful woman, but you walk like an elephant."

Mehpare Hanım froze when she heard this. She couldn't believe a servant could talk to her like this, she couldn't comprehend it, she would have been just as surprised if Constantine's splendidly beautiful horse spoke to her one morning in the stable. She was too amazed to come up with an answer, and just as she was about to explode in fury she noticed that the woman who'd told her she walked like an elephant had large hips under her dress that gyrated like millstones and she laughed in a way that surprised even herself and left the kitchen without saying anything.

Over time, though she couldn't quite grasp how, they became friends. Sula accepted life without any expectations or complaints and behaved so naturally that Mehpare Hanım too fell under her spell. It was not Sula but Mehpare Hanım who benefitted from this, she was secretly proud to have become friends with a woman who didn't make friends with anyone. They often had the sherbets of various colors, lemonade with grated lemon peel in it, tea and the nice-smelling coffee that Sula made in the kitchen, and talked about men; the old woman's ideas about men made Mehpare Hanım think, but also made her laugh, once she said something that stayed in her mind for a long time.

"You have to leave the bed without satisfying a man completely, you should leave him a little hungry so he comes back quickly and enthusiastically."

That day, after the morning lovemaking, the need for silence rose in her soul and she took refuge with Sula in the kitchen.

Some feelings follow you like a shadow, but you can't grasp them, and every move you make to catch them drives them further away; Mehpare Hanım sensed that there was an elusive feeling like this behind what she experienced with Constantine.

In fact it wasn't a single feeling, it was a complex of feelings, and their lovemaking made these feelings more apparent, more visible. At times she became disquieted and irritable because of the shadows of these feelings, the weariness of betrayal that penetrated her soul the way damp penetrates wood, the suspicion that the perfect harmony and the splendid flashes of lust during their lovemaking were nourished by a lack of love, the occasional longing for a simpler, more tranquil love that was more real and believable, and the conflict of knowing that in fact she didn't want a life free of doubt that would allow her to find a safe love.

Perhaps it was because this twilight of complex feelings gripped her more forcefully after making love that she got out of bed quickly and fled, and Sula's naturalness, which tamed all feelings and made them seem insignificant, and her indifference to winds other than her own, like a forest living by itself, soothed Mehpare Hanım with a glass of tea.

When Sula saw her wet hair and flushed face she understood what had happened, she poured tea with a smile that she confined to the corner of her lips, and gave it to Mehpare Hanım, then continued plucking the pheasant that the hunters had brought for lunch; the counter was covered with shiny golden, red, purple, and dark blue feathers.

Before she could say anything one of the Greek servants

came in, he was about to say something but stopped when he saw Mehpare Hanım, he just stood there with a look of excitement frozen on his face and Sula asked him in her usual reproachful tone what he wanted:

"What happened, did you catch your ugly sister with your father, why is your face like that?"

The man looked at Mehpare Hanım and didn't say anything.

"Talk, son, did you forget what you wanted to say, you're enough of an idiot to forget . . . "

The man finally spoke.

"They say there's a great uprising in Istanbul, there's blood in the streets, the mullahs are cutting everyone down, the whole city is shaken by the news."

"There's an uprising in Istanbul?"

Mehpare Hanım jumped up from her stool but then she felt dizzy and leaned on the table, she glazed over, her hands felt cold, she was about to faint, the word "uprising" evoked horrible and bloody images. Sula almost embraced her, sat her back in her stool, and brought her a glass of water. After she sat down, Mehpare Hanım tried to calm herself by taking deep breaths; her body, which had reacted to the news before her feelings, was losing its strength and was on the point of collapse. She rocked back and forth in her seat, feeling almost nothing, her face was pale and a lock of wet hair fell across her forehead. For the first time, the pallor of old age appeared on her young and sultry face.

It was as if the air around her had been sucked away, as if she'd been wrapped in a sheath that kept out all sounds and feelings; she sensed there was a great anguish waiting for her just outside the void that surrounded her, she was so afraid she wouldn't be able to withstand this approaching anguish that she was exhausted before she even felt it.

"Get the carriage ready," she said with difficulty.

Sula gestured for the servant to get the carriage ready and asked Mehpare Hanım tenderly:

"Where are you going?"

"To the post office."

"Let me tell Constantine, don't go alone in this condition."

Mehpare Hanım shook her head.

"No, don't wake him, tell him after I'm gone, I have to send a telegram at once."

Sula was going to offer to accompany her but realized Mehpare Hanım didn't want anyone from the household with her, she couldn't bear seeing anyone who reminded her of the life she was living.

She escorted Mehpare Hanım to the carriage and helped her climb in. Mehpare Hanım went to the city in fear that the strange void surrounding her would be torn away, that the sheath in which she was wrapped would be pierced, and praying that nothing would happen to Rukiye. The streets were crowded, people were rushing from place to place, when she saw the crowds she lost her faint hope that the news the servant had brought wasn't true. As the carriage approached the city center, she saw that the band on the café terrace by the White Tower was playing the *Marseillaise*, she remembered that the same band had played the *Marseillaise* in the same place when constitutional monarchy had been proclaimed, it was as if they'd been playing the same song in the same place for a year.

When she got out of the carriage in front of the post office she saw a large crowd trying to get in, the doors were cracked and the windows were broken, an old woman fell and was unable to get up, men were punching and cursing each other.

When she couldn't get into the telegraph office she started walking toward the harbor. It was as if she couldn't decide what to do and someone was telling her; the nape of her neck was numb, her eyes were throbbing as if they were about to jump out of their sockets. Soldiers were marching past constantly, the sound of their boots echoed in her brain, people gathered in groups and talked excitedly, there was a sense of anger in the air and people were demanding revenge.

Mehpare Hanım watched everything as if through frosted glass; she saw and heard everything, but the great commotion around her wasn't enough to evoke a sense of reality. It was as if life had lost its authenticity.

The harbor was very crowded as always, the Istanbul ferry lay at anchor off the shore, but that day the *caiques* that brought the passengers out were empty. Mehpare Hanım made her way through the crowd and started to look for someone who was bound for Istanbul, just at that moment she caught sight of an aging dervish. She went over to him at once.

"Are you going to Istanbul?"

"Yes."

"Do you know Sheikh Yusuf Efendi in Unkapanı?"

"I do."

"For the love of God, will you take a message to him?"

"Certainly."

"Can you say that Mehpare Hanım is concerned about Rukiye's well-being, she's waiting for news."

"I will, of course."

"Will you be able to remember the names?"

The dervish smiled.

"Don't worry, I still have enough of my wits about me."

The dervish gathered his robes and got into a *caique*, and she watched it move out toward the ferry, leaving a wake behind it. Frightening possibilities wandered through her mind, which had been shaken by this terrifying news. Her only connection to the daughter she worried might have died was the man in the *caique* on its way to the ferry, and she didn't even know him. The route the dervish was taking would bring her either good news or news of death, and the dervish in the *caique* didn't look like someone who would receive news that would determine a woman's entire future.

She left the harbor and started walking. When she looked up she realized she'd reached the city's outer neighborhoods. She leaned against a tree just beyond the Alatinis' large, three-story mansion; she found herself absorbed in a frightening and morbid dream and she didn't know how it had begun. She was dreaming about her daughter Rukiye's funeral. The mutineers had raped and killed her. Sheikh Efendi, his face white and transparent, recited the Koran, Hikmet Bey was weeping quietly, she shaped the minutest details of the funeral in her imagination, how they placed Rukiye in a coffin, how they placed a green cloth over the coffin and tied a white scarf to its head, how she was carried on the shoulders of the mourners, how they dug a hole in the ground, how the coffin was lowered into the grave . . . She experienced the pain she would have experienced if the funeral was real, she sobbed as if her dream was true; one part of her wanted to end this dream, she wanted to be free of these images and this pain, but another part of her couldn't give up this dream; with an almost pathological passion, she wanted to cling to this fantasy and suck all of the pain out of it until her soul bled and nothing was left, like an animal sucking milk out of a teat until in bled, she stood by the shore and watched the daughter who had not died being buried.

The poison that had accumulated with her betrayal of her husband and her abandonment of her children and that she'd kept in the hidden compartments of the soul where people hide their treasures and their poisons had emerged suddenly, at a moment when her body was defenseless in the numbness after lovemaking, when she'd heard the news that there was an uprising in Istanbul, the side of her that didn't approve of most of the things she did was getting revenge on the side of her that was content with what she did. She suddenly began to believe that Rukiye had been killed when she was making love to Constantine and that this was a punishment for her betrayal; at that moment she was disgusted by her own body, by Constantine's body, and by their lovemaking. She wanted to leave Salonika, to leave Constantine, to go far away, to be alone.

As she thought about leaving, she wondered how she was going to get back to the mansion, she was on the outskirts of the city where it was impossible to find a carriage; she looked around anxiously and saw that there was a carriage waiting behind her, as if she were in a fairy tale in which a pumpkin had turned into a carriage, it took her quite some time to realize it was the carriage in which she'd come, it had been following her the whole way.

When she got into the carriage and slumped exhausted in the seat, she was still wracked with trembling and contractions, all that was left of the terrifying dream was the fearsome weariness and the trembling. As they made their way toward the house she felt that she didn't in fact want to return to the mansion and to Constantine, but she also realized that there was nowhere else she wanted to go, that there was no place where she could be happy; she didn't even want to be with Rukiye, and she suddenly doubted the source of her terrifying fears about her daughter's well-being. Was she anxious that something bad had happened to someone she loved or had she felt all these fears because she felt she had to be sad for someone it was her duty to love?

At that moment of exhaustion, she was no longer certain about the feelings she had for anyone, did she love her children, her paramour, her first husband, her second husband, had she ever loved them, could she love anyone, she didn't know if she carried feelings for anyone at all. It seemed to her as if she was nothing but a body, and that in order for this body not to be a zombie she had to spend her life filling it with false feelings. She couldn't decide if her doubts about her feelings had emerged because of the catharsis and exhaustion that occurs after a great convulsion or whether the truth had appeared behind the false feelings that had been shaken by a tragic anxiety. She had lost her sense of her own authenticity just as she'd lost all sense of the authenticity of the world around her, from now on everything would be vague and doubtful, she feared it would always be like this.

The only feeling that was real for her was fear, she didn't know the real reason for this great fear, she was afraid of loneliness, of desolation, of being unable to discover the feelings that would allow her to be among people and live with them, of the uncertainty that enveloped her.

She feared she would not be able to reach the people everyone needed in order to be able to relate to themselves, that they needed to use as a mirror to see their own reflections, their feelings and thoughts, and that she would lose her relationship to herself, she felt this not with intelligible words but with a confusion of vague feelings, she wasn't just frightened that she would lose her lover and her children, but also that she herself would slip through her own fingers.

She went all the way to the mansion with known fears and doubts and unknown fears and doubts that wore out her already weary body. When she arrived home there was nothing left in her but exhaustion and a desire to sleep, her head was getting heavier and her eyes were closing.

She never told anyone, not even Osman, what she felt in the carriage that day, in any event Mehpare Hanım was the most reticent of Osman's dead, hers was not the usual reticence of someone who wanted to hide an incident and their feelings, hers was the unshakeable reticence of someone who suspected that her body carried no soul.

The only thing she said about this to Osman was, "If it's true that nothing is real, then shouldn't we choose the fake?" Osman understood neither the question nor the reason for it and put it down to Mehpare Hanım's oddness. It didn't occur to him that this was the only serious question Mehpare Hanım had ever asked, but even if this possibility had occurred to him, he would have been certain to remember that Mehpare Hanım was clever enough not to ask this question often.

After Mehpare Hanım arrived home and Sula helped her to bed and she plunged into a sleep that was as dark and sticky as mud, Cevat Bey left the train from Berlin at Salonika Station and immediately rushed to the Committee headquarters, where messengers were coming and going constantly, telegrams were brought from the military telegraph office, officers and civilians held one meeting after another, plans were being made, orders were being issued, and representatives were being sent to the four corners of the Empire. He was welcomed at the center with false anger and concealed joy. There was an air of decisiveness and a satisfaction with this decisiveness in the groups that gathered at the bottom of the stairs, in the corridors, and in front of doors.

Cevat Bey greeted old friends as he made his way to Talat Bey's office, he met Major Necip Bey, with whom he'd joined the organization in Istanbul; after the two comrades embraced, he asked the question he'd wanted to ask someone since he got off the train.

"What's going on?"

"What do you think, the mullahs stirred the soldiers up and got them to mutiny."

"What's the situation in Istanbul?"

"The mutineers are in control."

"What is the Sultan doing?"

"He's acting as if he's not involved, but he's the one behind this wickedness. This time we'll finish him."

"What have you decided to do?"

"We've put together a force consisting of twenty battalions from the Third Army, the Second Army, and those units of the

First Army that were stationed outside Istanbul, there are also ten cavalry units and nine cannon batteries. For now, Hüsnü Pasha, commander of the Salonika Reserve Division, has been placed in command of this army and Mustafa Kemal Bey has been appointed chief of general staff. We're also registering civilian volunteers, that is, it won't just be military units, there'll be a people's army made up of civilians. For now this is between the two of us, but when the army arrives in Istanbul we'll put Mahmut Şevket Pasha in command, he's more severe, we thought he'd do a better job of putting down the mutiny, but we don't want the Sultan to get wind of our intentions . . . "

Cevat Bey was pleased by how quickly and decisively the organization was acting.

"To tell the truth, you've pulled everything together quite quickly, good for you . . . I was a bit worried on the way here but now I feel at ease. Have you been in contact with Enver Bey?"

"Of course. Talat Bey is exchanging frequent telegrams with him. In fact he's already on his way, but he probably won't catch up to the army until it reaches Istanbul. Everything is ready now, headquarters foresaw what was going to happen and made arrangements in advance."

Cevat Bey asked a question as if he already knew the answer.

"What did Enver Bey say about Mustafa Kemal Bey being appointed chief of general staff?"

Like all of the Committee members who knew that Enver Bey was secretly jealous of Mustafa Kemal Bey, Necip Bey answered with a mocking smile.

"He didn't say anything but he'll come up with a plan when the time comes."

Cevat Bey became serious again.

"Anyway, I'll go see Talat Bey, meanwhile sign me up for the army, I'll go with them too. And what do you call this army, you've gathered units and volunteers from all over the place, is it called the people's army?"

"No, Mustafa Kemal Bey came up with a good name, he dubbed it the Movement Army."

"That is a good name . . ."

"Come see me after you've seen Talat Bey, I'm in that office there, don't make promises to anyone for this evening, you'll be staying with us."

Before he left, Cevat Bey asked the question he'd been distressed about and had wanted to ask from the beginning, trying not to seem too worried about his brother at a time when everyone's life was in danger.

"Have you heard anything from Ragıp?"

Necip Bey slapped his forehead.

"Sorry, I forgot what I wanted to say first and started talking about army business. Ragıp managed to get out of Istanbul, a friend brought news yesterday that he'd reached Çatalca, he's waiting for the army there."

Cevat Bey took a deep breath and said, "Thanks, I'll see you soon."

Talat Bey's office was crowded, everyone was coming in to ask him questions, they expected him to solve every problem and he was doing his best to do so. Even though he was buried in work, he stood when he saw Cevat Bey and embraced him and kissed him on both cheeks in his usual unpretentious and indeed almost rakish manner. Even though he regarded the Committee's military members with a sneaking suspicion, especially those like Cevat Bey who were close to Enver Bey, he was careful to maintain good relations with them, he always protected the party's balance.

"Welcome, how are you? How was your trip?"

"Thank you, the trip was fine. More importantly, how are you? We've lost Istanbul to the reactionaries."

Talat Bey slapped Cevat Bey on the shoulder and smiled.

"Every cloud has a silver lining, Cevat Bey. Soon they'll all regret what they've done. God willing, we'll finish what we weren't able to finish last time."

He gave a note on his desk that he'd just written to an officer who came in.

"I wrote a telegram to the Sultan, but I want Mahmut Şevket Pasha to look it over and make any changes he wants before sending it to Yıldız in his name, let's let the Sultan know about our preparations and that the army is almost ready to get moving."

Cevat Bey looked at Talat Bey carefully to see whether or not he was serious.

"You're informing the Sultan that the army is getting ready to move?"

Talat Bey pretended he didn't understand Cevat Bey's confusion, he was accustomed to officers being childishly inept at politics, their inflexibility in valuing bravery over intelligence, someone like Cevat Bey, who was one of the most brilliant and intelligent of the organization's military members, couldn't grasp the move's significance, he explained what he wanted to do slowly and clearly like an understanding teacher.

"The Sultan will learn that the army has started moving anyway, he may already know, if we don't inform him about it he'll think we're moving to dethrone him, then he'll use all his power, money, and pashas to support the mutineers openly, and this would make it difficult if not impossible to take Istanbul back. But if he hears from us that the army has set out he'll believe we can come to terms, to protect his throne he won't support the mutineers, at least not openly, the government will try to remain neutral."

"O.K., so we're not going to dethrone him?"

"Of course we are, but we're not obliged to tell him now. In war, isn't it essential to surprise the enemy and catch him off guard?"

Cevat Bey realized that Talat Bey was right and felt like a fool, but even though he was ashamed of what he was going to do he objected.

"In the army it's also essential not to keep the enemy informed."

Talat Bey ignored this objection, he sensed that Cevat Bey understood the situation.

"This information will destroy the enemy, Cevat Bey . . . I'll give him information that he'll use to destroy his future. Of course, he's not stupid, he'll be suspicious, but suspicion will make him indecisive, we'll be in Istanbul before he makes that decision."

Then he changed the subject.

"What are you planning to do?"

"I'll go to Istanbul with the army."

"Good . . . Your being in Istanbul will be good. It's time for you to learn a few things about politics, and Istanbul is the best place for that."

After he left Talat Bey, he told Necip Bey he would return in the late afternoon and left headquarters to join the excited crowds in the streets; it seemed as if all of Salonika had mobilized, the city had abandoned itself to the enthusiasm of a common struggle, just as it had when constitutional monarchy was declared.

Perhaps for the first time, Cevat Bey looked down on and even slightly pitied crowds that were supporting his own struggle, trying to find hope in anything that happened, enjoying being heroes, even minor heroes, in a great event; none of them knew the truth or ever would, they would make the mistake of thinking that decisions others had made without their knowledge were expressions of their own free will, and they would reap a small share of joy from this pathetic delusion.

With this latest incident, Cevat Bey felt he was in the same position as the people he pitied; now he guessed there were

302 · AHMET ALTAN

realities he hadn't been told about, that each move had been planned well in advance. As he worried that things might turn ugly, his closest friends, with whom he thought he was sharing a great struggle, might be mocking him behind his back.

He sat in a beer hall on the waterfront and ordered a beer, was it possible that they would conceal the truth from him, why would they do this, it couldn't be because they feared he might betray them, he was certain about that, then what, why did he feel imprisoned behind a wall of secrets? It could be that they thought he might object, but there was no reason for them to think this. Many times they'd seen Cevat Bey support every move, every initiative, for the success of the struggle he believed was sacred; then what was the secret that everyone but him knew, why had they excluded him and thrown him out among the crowds that moved past him unaware of what was going on? After finishing his beer he decided to talk about this with Necip Bey that evening.

He spent the rest of the afternoon strolling idly through the streets. He didn't want to go to the headquarters of the organization he loved so much, of which he saw himself to be an inseparable part. He wandered down unfamiliar streets, went into shops he'd never entered, sat in coffeehouses he didn't know, he saw another side of Salonika, he felt its millennia of secrets in the eyes of the women walking down the streets, in the gestures of shopkeepers' customers in little shops, in the way wealthy businessmen walked, in the Jewishness that was stamped on the city.

It was if the city too had become alien to him, as if it had been taken over by another life he didn't know; he realized he had never known this city, that was the day he understood that even if they recaptured Istanbul they would lose Salonika one day; later he told Osman, "I suddenly saw that we'd never really known the city in which we felt most secure, if we'd raised our heads and looked around a bit, if we'd known

Salonika, if we'd mingled with these people instead of saving them, perhaps the empire wouldn't have collapsed the way it did."

In the late afternoon he went to headquarters to pick Necip Bey up. He couldn't wait until they got to the house and brought the subject up while they were on their way.

"When did you find out that something was going on in Istanbul?"

Necip thought about this.

"If I'm not mistaken, the first news came from İsmail Canbolat Bey, I think we heard about two hours after the soldiers mutinied."

"Then how could everything be made ready so quickly, how were decisions made about which units would be taken from which armies, where the soldiers would stop and put up for the night, when were the supply depots for a campaign like this set up?"

Necip Bey spread his hands.

"How should I know, brother, I never thought about it, everything happened so quickly, it was as if everything was ready."

Necip Bey suddenly stopped in the middle of the street, he'd only just understood what Cevat Bey was asking.

"What do you mean?"

"I'm not saying anything, I'm just curious . . . How could our unwieldy army shake itself off like a colt and move so quickly?"

They walked along without speaking for a while. Necip Bey started to speak in a low voice.

"Maybe they received intelligence from Istanbul in advance and started to get ready."

"Who?"

"The Committee headquarters, of course . . . "

"Weren't you at headquarters, didn't you hear anything?"

"I was at headquarters, there were some rumors, of course, but there was no solid information."

"O.K. then, who made these preparations without you knowing about them?"

Necip Bey sighed.

"Probably Enver Bey and Talat Bey. Maybe they knew. They might also have let Mahmut Şevket Pasha in on it."

"I was with Enver Bey two days ago, he didn't say anything to me."

"Cevat Bey, you know that secrecy is essential in these matters . . . Isn't this the way we've been living for years?"

Cevat Bey shook his head.

"Secret from us? Don't they trust us anymore?"

Necip Bey tried to put Cevat Bey at ease.

"This isn't an issue of trust, of course they trust you, why wouldn't they, aren't we all in this together, don't we do everything together? Perhaps they didn't trust the information that was coming from their own soldiers, they didn't want it to spread, they didn't want everyone getting worked up over nothing."

"Enver Bey wasn't concerned when I told him that the soldiers in Istanbul were getting restless, he wasn't concerned when he heard that Hasan Fehmi had been killed. What's going on, Necip Bey, who's managing us? If they don't trust us, who do they trust?"

The evening was unpleasant, they were eaten by the suspicion that the people they trusted most no longer trusted them, that they were doing things without informing them, but in fact neither of them was prepared to accept the weight of such a suspicion, that the struggle that gave their lives meaning, that had almost become the reason for their existence, was treating them like strangers. As they tried to assuage each other by telling each other not to exaggerate, they were in fact trying to assuage themselves in order to gain time to build up the strength to carry the suspicion they knew was going to remain with them.

Cevat Bey woke up relaxed after a restless night, at least he wasn't the only one who'd been excluded from the secret labyrinth, an object of ridicule, set apart from the few, everyone was being treated the same way; he found excuses for what Enver Bey and Talat Bey had done, he convinced himself that they'd done the right thing, but in fact inwardly he knew he didn't believe this. At that time he didn't have the strength to be honest with himself, he knowingly chose a lie and accepted it with gratitude.

They went to headquarters without talking and performed the duties they were assigned eagerly as if they'd made a decision together based on what they'd talked about the previous night. The military preparations were completed at an incredible speed.

The first units moved by train two days later. Cevat Bey took his place on the first train. He experienced the joy of going to war, of going to fight on a front where it was clear who was friend and who was foe.

On the day when Cevat Bey set out enveloping his disquiet and doubt with a peace constructed from false excuses, a man who looked like a Bulgarian came by Mehpare Hanım's mansion in the evening to bring her a brief message.

"Rukiye Hanım is well, there's no need to worry."

That was all, there were no greetings, expressions of affection, nor was there any signature, though it was clear who had sent it. Someone who didn't want Mehpare Hanım to be upset, to worry, who'd managed to get the message to Salonika in two days despite the turmoil on the roads, but who hadn't even included a greeting.

After receiving this brief message consisting of a single sentence, Mehpare Hanım experienced three feelings, one was definitely related to the information, she didn't know when or how the other two had formed; first she was going to leave Constantine but she knew she wasn't going to do this in a hurry; second, she truly missed her children, she felt the need for their bodies to touch her body, to touch their faces, their hair, to look into their eyes, and she grasped that this was a real feeling and experienced firsthand how a person could know that a feeling was real.

Third, she was pleased to believe that the Sheikh still loved her.

That the message had not contained a single expression of love, that it hadn't even contained a greeting, was enough to make Mehpare Hanım believe that the Sheikh still loved her.

If she'd seen the expression of love that was usually written at the end of every letter, she would probably have been saddened by the thought that she'd been forgotten.

14

The only thing Mihrişah Sultan was curious about was whether or not "that geezer" would be able to regain his former power. She'd never forgotten that the Sultan had once exiled her from the city, she only ever referred to him as "that geezer." Every day when Tevfik Bey, the son of the residents of the neighboring waterfront mansion, a clerk at the chamber, returned from Babıali, Mihrişah Sultan greeted him excitedly and asked him to tell her everything that was going on and made assessments as if she was directing a war, depending on the news she would either fall into despair, get angry, or be pleased. Anyone might think that the mutiny in the city had broken out because of the dispute between the Sultan and Mihrişah Sultan.

She stopped giving the large parties that had terrified the neighborhood since the mutiny began and took a break from the concerts that all the ambassadors, diplomats, and Ottoman intellectuals attended as well as the balls from which the sounds of music and laughter spread almost throughout the neighborhood. At those balls, her deep eyes, overflowing beauty, and silent splendor left everyone else in the shade of ordinariness, then she illuminated those she chose with her own light. Even the most beautiful women could only reveal their beauty when they reflected her smile, and the most intelligent men only felt themselves to be intelligent when she appreciated their wits. She used everyone, indeed the whole world, like a mirror, she only saw and watched herself, the world around her only came to life when it reflected her image.

Her arrogance, which was as magnificent as her beauty, never begged to be satisfied like that of others, she was never sated by the miserable banquets composed of compliments and never boasted the way they did, she just smiled at the compliments and never stooped to boasting. Her arrogance could only be satisfied if the whole world was laid at her feet, and "that geezer," who seemed to be growing more powerful again, breached her arrogance simply by existing.

It was this breach of her arrogance, which she'd believed nothing could limit, that led her to become interested in politics, which she'd viewed as male folly, and even military matters, which she'd described as "an even greater display of folly"; now she wanted to hear about everything that was happening, she wanted to hear about changes in the cabinet, about the Grand Vizier's statements, about what the mutineers were doing, about the Sultan's attitude, about the preparations the Committee was making in Salonika, she listened attentively to even the most insignificant details.

Every evening, Tevfik Bey, with his sandy hair flowing in waves from under his fez, his soft sandy moustache, eyes that were sometimes like those of a tired old man and sometimes like those of a naughty child, his unassuming nobility, which relied on a past that stretched back centuries, the deep knowledge of literature and music that he possessed despite his youth, the hidden sadness in his voice, which was full of tenderness, as if he was caressing a child, sat across from Mihrişah Sultan in the waterfront mansion's large hall, which looked out over the Bosphorus, and told her all of the latest developments; there was a surprising richness in his talk, decorated with the amusing anecdotes caught by the fish hook of a sardonic wit that had been cast into daily life, important information known only to senior government officials, serious comments, descriptions of conflicts among the pashas, and comic gossip about misunderstandings. Perhaps because of the English governesses his father had brought from England when he was a child, he had a peculiarly English sense of humor as well as a coldness unusual among Ottomans, he didn't panic when he was pressed, he related everything with a slight smile.

It was also Tevfik Bey who informed Mihrişah Sultan that the Movement Army had set out.

"When will they reach Istanbul?" Mihrişah Sultan asked excitedly.

"I think we'll see them on the outskirts of Istanbul within a week, I've heard they're moving quickly."

"What do you think is going to happen when the Committee's army arrives?"

"I think that more blood will be shed, my lady."

"Do you think there'll be war?"

"The mutineers are preparing to stand against the Movement Army, they're bringing all the units in the area into Istanbul, it looks as if there will be fighting, even if only on a small scale."

"So what is that geezer doing?"

"He's not doing anything, he'll support whoever wins, but there's not much of a chance that the mutineers will win."

"What are you saying, Tevfik Bey, do you mean that the geezer will cooperate with the Committee?"

"The Sultan would cooperate with them if it meant he could keep his throne, but the Committee isn't prepared to cooperate with him anymore, they won't miss this opportunity to dethrone him. They would have to be stupid to miss this opportunity that the mutineers have given them, and even though I've never encountered anyone who considers them intelligent, I doubt if they're that stupid."

"What does Tevfik Pasha have to say about this?"

"That Grand Vizier, my lady?"

"Yes, Grand Vizier Tevfik Pasha."

"He hasn't decided what to say yet, ma'am. You know, making decisions always tires the Grand Vizier, that's why he always waits for others to make decisions for him before he decides himself. I think that this time, once again, whoever wins will decide what the Grand Vizier decides."

From that day onwards, Mihrişah Sultan followed the Movement Army's every step, as Tevfik Bey told Osman, "Mihrişah Sultan, whose grasp of geography was limited to the fact the world was round and that Paris was at one point and Istanbul was at another," learned the locations not only of all the cities between Salonika and Istanbul but of all the towns as well. She waited excitedly for Tevfik Bey every evening, she was as pleased as a victorious general to hear that the Movement Army had advanced past a town or two.

Mihrişah Sultan wasn't the only one who waited excitedly for Tevfik Bey, every evening, for other reasons, Rukiye waited for this Ottoman prince who didn't like the Sultan to return from Babıali. It would have been easy to surmise that this young girl was on the verge of falling in love with Tevfik Bey, but it would not have been easy to deduce her reason for falling in love.

Because Hikmet Bey visited the waterfront mansion often ever since Mihrişah Sultan moved there, Tevfik Bey often came with Selim Bey and Ahmed Samim Bey, who was known for the fiery articles he wrote, and had become friendly with Hikmet Bey and Mihrişah Sultan; in time he began visiting even when Hikmet Bey wasn't there; he amused both Mihrişah Sultan and her French ladies in waiting. It couldn't be said that he paid too much attention to Rukiye.

Although there was no apparent reason, perhaps because of Tevfik Bey's studied lack of interest in Rukiye, or a woman's extraordinary instincts, or just to make conversation, Mihrişah

Sultan said to Rukiye, "Is this young man in love with you, he comes so often."

Sometimes all the doors of a person's soul open up to life like a cheap tavern that's ready to accept anyone who passes by, on such days, someone who until then had been unimportant, or a sentence that would not previously have made sense, enters the door of a person's soul and finds an important place for themselves, when the doors close again, that person or that sentence settles in and stays. Perhaps it was on such an occasion that a sentence Mihrişah soon forgot found a place for itself in Rukiye's soul, she began to watch Tevfik Bey's every move to see if he was in love with her; she enjoyed watching him more and more, enjoyed listening to him more and more, and she decided this young man was in love with her, but when she made this decision, she was in fact passionately attached to the idea that Tevfik Bey was in love with her.

At that time, even if she'd given up on Tevfik Bey, she would have been unable to give up that idea, she was unable to carry on with her life without that idea, but she was not aware of this. She asked herself what would happen if she returned his love, even the question itself excited her, she wanted to see what would happen when she fell in love, the magic of the words "loving" and "being loved" stood in front of the feelings that had not yet appeared, they paved the way for these feelings, the words even gave birth to the feelings they described; in fact it was a peculiar and reverse birth, no names were given to the feelings, the names gave birth to the feelings.

From then on she looked for a sign in Tevfik Bey's every word, every deed, every smile, and she found the sign she was seeking each time; even today, none of Osman's dead knew whether these signs had really existed; for Rukiye, however, believing that they existed changed her feelings in a real way.

Once she'd decided that Tevfik Bey was in love with her, she was seized by a sudden impatience, she began to have an unbearable desire for the feelings that had appeared in the signs to be proven to her with words. She sidled up to Tevfik Bey more than usual to provoke him into speaking and expressing his feelings, she spoke in an insinuating manner, but she couldn't bring about the closeness she wanted and didn't hear the words she longed to hear.

Before the mutiny began she decided, without realizing that what she was doing would change the entire course of her life, to write Tevfik Bey a letter; when the mutiny erupted suddenly and Tevfik Bey became more interested in Mihrişah Sultan and the mutiny in the city she decided to put it off, but the reason she put it off wasn't that she thought a love letter would be insignificant in the midst of a great battle—as Tevfik Bey, who didn't yet know he would die young, told Osman later with his distinctive smile, "What woman believes that war is more important than love, it was male stupidity to believe this"—it was only because she dreamed about what they would do after Tevfik Bey answered and she was worried they wouldn't find time for this.

Like Mihrişah Sultan, she too listened to news of the war with excitement every evening, growing impatient for what was to come, she waited for this mutiny, which seemed to be blocking the path to love, to come to an end and make way for her to experience what she wanted to experience. Because politics was foreign to her it took her some time to decide which side to choose, when she finally realized the Committee had a better chance of winning, and because she wanted this victory to happen at once, she started to support the Committee inwardly and, like Mihrişah Sultan, she began to be pleased by their every advance.

She didn't know that the Committee she awaited with such longing would shoot and kill the man she loved some years later in a raid, she had a fierce desire for what she wanted to come true, and she waited for the people who would execute

the man she loved to arrive in the city and be victorious with
the terrifying helplessness of a person who didn't and couldn't
know the outcome of what she wanted. If during these days
Rukiye had been given control of destiny, she would without
realizing it have drawn it just as God did, she would bring the
Committee to Istanbul quickly and set the stage for the disaster that would befall her and the man she loved.

Not just Mihrişah Sultan and Rukiye but everyone, the
entire city, waited for events to unfold, some anxiously, some
hopefully, but all excitedly, every day new information, new
rumors, and new gossip spread, and everyone reached their
own conclusions from what they heard.

The Ottoman Association of Education, an Islamic education association composed of high-level religious teachers, and
of which Sheikh Yusuf Efendi was a member, gathered and
released a statement denouncing the mutiny and supporting
constitutional monarchy, demonstrating that the men who
appeared to be mullahs and who had stirred up the mutineers
were not associated with the prominent religious ulema of
Istanbul. During the meeting at which they composed this
statement, Hoca Rıza Efendi asked openly:

"Do any of you know any of these so-called mullahs wandering around with green flags?"

No one spoke, only Sheikh Sadullah Efendi, who always
spoke with a melodic undulation as if he was singing a hymn,
answered.

"I met one of them once, a man called Derviş Vahdeti. I
entreat God that I not be unfair to anyone, but the man
seemed to me to be completely ignorant. He seemed to have
memorized a few hadiths so he could pretend to be a hodja."

In a dramatic voice that suited his inborn anger, Necmi
Efendi, a teacher of Islamic jurisprudence, stated what was on
everyone's mind.

"How can this ignorant mob use our name so crassly, how

dare they come out in our name and equate themselves with sheikhs and hodjas who spent years putting their noses to the grindstone in madrasas. How could they presume to lead the soldiers without consulting anyone, without bothering to seek the opinion of the ulema, with such impious bravado? If they're this audacious today, who knows if they won't knock down the doors of our mosques, madrasas, and *tekkes* and try to teach us our own religion, that they won't interfere in our worship?"

As everyone nodded their heads in agreement with Necmi Efendi, Sheikh Yusuf Efendi took the floor and began to speak in his usual manner.

"Of course you know better than I do, but it has to be said, sharia has soldiers, but soldiers can't have sharia. In a land where a Muslim community lives according to sharia law, for one group to pick up guns and demand sharia as if it wasn't already being practiced constitutes the tyranny of Muslims by Muslims. Muslims with guns oppress those without guns. I think it would be prudent to warn everyone before things go too far, I think that we should make a statement that our association does not approve of this movement."

No one present objected to this idea, they decided to write the statement together; in fact even this statement was a sign that the mutineers would lose; if these hodjas, who had connections in the four corners of the empire and who heard even the least significant details, thought that the mutineers would win, at least some of them would have declined to be part of this unified stance, but they all sensed how things were going to go; some agreed to openly oppose the mutiny because they realized what was going to happen, while others, like Sheikh Yusuf Efendi, sincerely believed that this was the right thing to do.

Whatever their reasons, whatever reckoning led them to participate in writing that statement, it was a significant undertaking for a nation on the verge of a religious war, but the Committee ignored the ulema's initiative. They even stated that they suspected hostility by saying that "they opposed the mutiny, but their statement didn't support the Committee."

This statement was erased from the history books, ignored, reduced to footnotes in fine print, the voice of the sheikhs, hodjas, and mudarris melted and vanished into the void.

Later, Sheikh Efendi told Osman in a tone that was devoid of anger and bitterness, "To kill someone you first have to kill their voice, you have to destroy the voice that proclaims beliefs, the owner of the voice disappears on his own, they killed our voice, the voice that was protecting religion, if you look carefully you can see that by killing our voice, they kept Derviş Vahdeti's voice alive, and that was the voice that was most hostile to them. So many years have passed since then, I'm dead now, those who killed my voice are also dead, but now if you listen carefully you can still hear Derviş Vahdeti's voice, he's still alive, they kept his voice alive and therefore they also kept him alive. Like everyone who owes their existence to their enemies, they most loved the voice of the man they dragged to the gallows."

During those tumultuous days, Sheikh Yusuf Efendi did not know his voice was going to be killed, he still closed his eyes in apprehension as he listened to news that came from every direction, he withdrew into the reddish shade of the candlelit hall and prayed that "the believers not be slaughtered." Hasan Efendi, who wandered through the city all day and chatted with the rebellious sergeants, soldiers, and the officers who'd risen through the ranks and bore a grudge against the officers from the academy, brought the most accurate news every evening.

As the Movement Army approached the city, he asked Hasan Efendi:

"Will the mutineers fight the Movement Army or will they lay down their arms at the last minute?"

"They're determined to fight, my Sheikh, yesterday units who support the mutiny moved from Çatalca to Istanbul."

"The Caliph doesn't support this mutiny, I know the ulema opposes it, the people don't seem to have any great appreciation for them, the army that's coming is powerful, then who do the mutineers trust?"

Hasan Efendi answered quickly because he hadn't ever thought about this.

"They trust in their faith and in God."

"The army that's coming has faith and God as well, Hasan Efendi, and this is war, not worship, weapons are as important as faith."

The next morning Hasan Efendi set out with these questions in mind, and when, in front of the Taşkışla barracks, he met a sergeant from Yozgat who he'd befriended a few days earlier and began chatting with him, he asked the question Sheikh Efendi had asked him.

The sergeant put his hand in his uniform and scratched his chest, then explained as if he was a general.

"Look, my dear Hasan Efendi, you shouldn't be deceived by appearances, if you do you'll be finished, why isn't His Excellency the Caliph saying anything, so he can catch the infidel Committee napping, we received the news from a solid source, when the Movement Army arrives at the gates of the city, His Majesty the Sultan will come out and say to the soldiers of the Movement Army, my sons, come and gather under the flag of sharia, join those who are fighting for God's will. Now tell me, will these Muslims listen to the infidel Committee or to the Caliph? When those soldiers join us, we'll cut the infidels' throats with a dull saw as if we were sacrificing sheep at the foot of the walls. Those Committee officers are coming to their own deaths, but they don't know this . . . "

Unlike the Sheikh, Hasan Efendi wanted with all his heart for the mutineers to win, he wished that the corrupt, the whores, and the lechers would tremble beneath the sword of sharia, that they too would be imprisoned in a world without sin; it was as if this was his revenge on life, but because he didn't know that he had this anger and desire for revenge in him, he thought it was because of his love for his religion.

He had difficulty explaining the Sheikh's opposition to the mutiny. In the rare moments when he thought to himself, he decided that "the Sheikh is sometimes blinded by his love for that whore," it was strange that he thought the Sheikh had a weakness like this, but even though this battered his admiration somewhat, it increased his love.

He persisted in order to make sure that what the sergeant said was true.

"What if the Caliph doesn't say anything like this?"

"Don't be a child, Hasan Efendi, is that possible, if it was your throne they were after, if they were rebelling against your caliphate, wouldn't that be what you said?"

"I suppose I would . . . The soldiers will listen to him, there won't be any opposing voices, will there?"

"Is it possible that he wouldn't listen to the Caliph but to an officer who beats him three times a day . . . You'll see, the officers' blood will flow like water, they won't have time to profess their faith before they die, they'll go to the next world without being purified."

"Do the soldiers have brave hearts, that is, when they see the huge army before the city, the pashas with big beards, the cannon . . . "

The sergeants moved back and tensed.

"What are you saying, Hasan Efendi, these are the Prophet's soldiers, their hearts don't quail in the slightest, what is a pasha next to the great Caliph? Don't worry about us, the soldiers also know that they're fighting for the Caliph, that this is jihad in the name of God."

Hasan Efendi left the sergeant, he'd found the answer to

the Sheikh's question, which had been nagging at him. He understood why the soldiers weren't tense and panicked by the army that was on its way. It was possible that the officers of the Movement Army would fall into a deadly and bloody trap outside the city walls, everything depended on the Sultan uttering two words, the Sultan would decide who was to die in the coming battle.

On that spring day, which was warmed by a pale blue light, Hasan Efendi left Taşkışla feeling pleased about several things. What pleased him more than anything was that he would be able to bring Sheikh Efendi an answer to the question he'd asked. The feeling of animallike loyalty that he nourished within himself determined who he was more than his ideas, beliefs, and emotions, it was as if God had created him to be faithful to someone and had chosen Sheikh Efendi as a focus for his loyalty.

Hasan Efendi's thoughts played among themselves like children playing in a courtyard surrounded by thick walls, but they never climbed over the high walls of loyalty, they didn't even allow it to cross their minds. He satisfied the desire to betray that lay in the depths of a feeling of intense loyalty that was almost unbearable in small ways by bringing information the Sheikh couldn't find on his own, thereby inwardly allowing himself to feel he was superior to and more talented than the Sheikh; even his desire to betray was of more service to the person to whom he was loyal.

When he got to the avenue in Beyoğlu, which seemed buried in the infinite shadow of centuries of intrigues, loves, and murders, he saw that all the embassies in Pera were flying their flags as protection against attack; flags of various colors with eagles, crosses, and stars were waving coyly in the breeze, the sacred color red was in each of them as a line, a star, or a cross. This red was there so that people would believe that people who had died in wars throughout history only to be forgotten by the next generation had not shed their blood in vain and strangely, this bright red on pieces of cloth that surrendered to the wind at the end of long poles was enough to convince people of the necessity and sanctity of having their blood shed, as Hikmet Bey said, "Even this was enough to raise suspicion of the pathetic nature of mankind to give their lives without questioning."

When he went into the back streets, Hasan Efendi encountered a group of drunken marines, he followed the men, who were shouting, "We want sharia, long live the Sultan," in voices slurred by drink; in the empty streets, a few vagabonds walked along with them and watched them with a mixture of fear and curiosity, as if they were watching animals that had escaped from the circus.

The marines stopped in front of a butcher whose shutter was half closed and started bargaining; three of them exchanged their rifles for a whole, skinned lamb, they shouldered the lamb and sang as they continued on their way. It was clear they had no aim, they had no place to go, they were just trying to scrounge food for their dinner. They frightened a Greek grocer and filled a basket with the wine they took from him.

The marines didn't look like the soldiers the sergeant had been describing, and this made Hasan Efendi angry, because it destroyed his hopes and expectations about the future of the mutiny.

He forgot how many of them there were and that they were armed, and grabbed the arm of the man in the lead.

"Brother, look at the state you're in, have you no shame or fear of God, you call for sharia with your drunken mouth, you pollute our Caliph's name with your stinking breath!"

The leader of the marines replied in a blatantly threatening manner as he tried to figure out if there was anyone else nearby.

"What's the matter, mullah, why are you angry, we're risking our lives for sharia . . . "

"Save you stinking life for yourself, get off these streets, has Islam become so debased that it falls to you to protect it?"

House windows began to open, more and more people were becoming curious about the commotion, many of the residents of the neighborhood were not Muslim, but like everyone in Istanbul they were fed up with the marines and were waiting for someone to shut them up.

"What's it to you, mullah, just because you have a robe you think you're the Shaykh-al Islam?"

Hasan Efendi had already decided what he was going to do even if the marines didn't say anything, but the man's arrogance made him even angrier; when he brought his strong fist, which was as big as a rock, down on the marine's head, the marine fell with blood streaming from his mouth and nose. Some of the marines, frightened by Hasan Efendi's size and strength, tried to point their rifles at him, but they couldn't, they were so drunk they couldn't point the rifles they were dragging along by their barrels; Hasan Efendi, who used this to his advantage, suddenly forgot he was a mullah and suddenly became "Hasan the Marine" of old.

He hit those he could reach over the head with his large fist and knocked them out, shouting, "Get out of here, you cuckolds, or I'll knock all of you out." In the blink of an eye, four of them fell next to the lamb they'd dropped, their noses broken, their cheekbones caved in, and their temples burst; when those who were still standing grabbed their rifles and started to flee, the sound of applause came from the windows; half-naked Greek women, most of whom worked in the brothels of Beyoğlu, shouted, "Long live the mullah," gestured for him to come to their houses, and laughed.

The street, which had been temporarily liberated from the terrifying crisis that had besieged the city, came to life with the women's cheerful cries and salacious jokes, then the windows were closed again and the street was once again as silent and deserted as all the others.

Hasan Efendi straightened his conical felt hat and continued on his way, but when he realized that the image of the plump, white bodies he'd glanced at the windows had become stuck in his mind, he feared he would be tempted into sin and recited three verses of the Koran and swore to God that he repented, he tried to forget what he'd seen, but the complicated and pleasure-filled dreams about which he could speak to no one would remind him for years of what he'd briefly glimpsed in those windows.

Even though he'd been on his way to the ministry of war in Beyazıt, he gave up that idea and headed toward the *tekke* to tell his Sheikh as soon as possible about what he'd seen and talked about, in the end, the only person who could save him from the dark fires of his secret sins was Sheikh Efendi, who always waited in the same place.

15

Friendships and loves grow and develop quickly under severe pressure, just like the strange and magical plants that grow when they're stepped on; in times of great and widespread threats, dangers, and fears, these terrifying events surround people like a warm greenhouse they can't leave, they create a climate in which the feelings that wrap around other people grow quickly like vines; in those anxious days, as the city waited for a bloody battle whose outcome was uncertain, the emotional relationship between Hikmet Bey, Dilara Hanım, and Dilevser developed at an unexpected pace.

Hikmet Bey's educated politeness was such that when necessary, his presence was not felt; this politeness created a large, safe place in which both of his guests could move comfortably; that he never insisted, invited or made a show of being a good host, the sense of trust provided by manners that had been distilled in a centuries-old still, allowed Dilara Hanım and Dilevser to approach him without hesitation, and anxieties they might have felt in a situation like this disappeared within a few hours.

In this neighbor with whom she'd just become acquainted, Dilara Hanım found something that was rarely encountered in life, the kind of male friend she'd thought didn't exist, from the first moment they'd both sensed that there would be no emotional connections between them that could shelter lust, love, or small flirtations. Dilara Hanım liked rough, lower-class men who tended toward wildness and bullying; what excited

her was an animallike violence in a male body, she derived
pleasure from training and taming this violence with her own
body, she got tired of those she was able to tame and was smit-
ten by those she wasn't, but Hikmet Bey didn't have that kind
of roughness or violence.

The spoiled son of a very beautiful woman, Hikmet Bey
wanted extraordinary beauty in the women with whom he'd
fall in love; he was also attracted to purity and innocence. The
only thing he had in common with Dilara Hanım was that he
too liked being with lower-class women when he wasn't in
love, women who surrendered to their bodies' desires unques-
tioningly, and this carnal desire for the lower classes was like a
distinguishing characteristic of the nobility.

On the first day, mother and daughter ate lunch in their
apartment; at dinnertime, when a servant asked whether they
would prefer to eat in the apartment or in the dining room,
Dilara Hanım realized they were being invited to dinner, she
said they would eat in the dining room, and they dressed and
joined Hikmet Bey.

After Hikmet Bey asked them if they were content with
their apartment and if they needed anything, they talked about
the mutiny, what had happened that morning and what might
happen in the future.

As they talked about what the entire city was talking about,
it was as if they whispered the codes which helped those who'd
left the main roads of accepted rules and morality and took
their own paths to explore other aspects of life to recognize
each other very quickly; this was a secret language, it was less
in the sentences than in the choice of words, emphasis, pauses,
smiles, and glances. It was a special language that those who
lived their lives bound to the masses could never speak, and
those who had distanced themselves from them adopted it
without realizing, those who spoke this language soon got
along with each other regardless of what they thought.

When the subject of the marines who'd attacked the maid came up, Dilara Hanım made a face and said:

"This is a weakness particular to men, and like all male weakness it comes out as roughness and aggression, women never attack men like this."

Then she added with a mocking smile.

"At least not in the street."

Hikmet Bey realized that she'd uttered this last sentence because she trusted him and that Dilara Hanım didn't speak with all men like this, and he was pleased by this privilege that had been granted him.

He leaned back in his chair and asked with an emphasis that made the joking in his tone clearer:

"I think you're disparaging all men rather than just those marines."

"I don't know," said Dilara Hanım.

Then she continued as if she was talking to herself.

"Was I being disparaging? I didn't think so, but even if I was, I can't say that men don't deserve it."

"Why do you say that?"

Dilara Hanım thought for a moment.

"I think they're unable to show their feelings, more accurately they're unable to show their feelings at the right moment; it's as if they're afraid women might realize they're human too. No woman is frightened of having human weaknesses, but men are. Don't you disparage someone who talks about courage all the time and who you see is a coward?"

Hikmet Bey turned to Dilevser, who was toying with the crystal glass in front of her.

"Do you disparage men the way your mother does?"

"I don't know enough men to be able to make a generalization, but what I've read about in novels demonstrates that my mother is right."

"Don't you find it odd that the male writers who wrote those novels disparage their own gender like that?"

"It never occurred to me to categorize writers as men or women."

Dilara Hanım jumped in:

"When writers seek truths about women they of course discover truths about men as well."

Hikmet Bey asked in a somewhat melancholy tone:

"Is there a truth about women, Dilara Hanım?"

"There are so many."

"I would like to learn them."

"What you would do if you did learn, if I told you all the truths and you learned them, what would happen, in time you would get bored. I would pity any man I saw who knew all the truths about women. It would be like a cat unravelling a ball of yarn, once it's unraveled there's nothing left to play with."

"Do you think we have no other amusement except women?"

Dilara Hanım said, "As if," in her derogatory manner.

"Politics, war, money . . . Will you amuse yourself with those, will you be content with those? Napoleon won all his battles, he knew politics, he had a lot of money too, the empire's treasury was his, was he happy? Maybe this is the difference between men and women. A man can't be happy with any of these things. You absolutely have to have a woman in order to be happy, but a woman, yes, if a woman got involved in politics, war, intrigues, money, any one of these things would be enough to make her happy."

"Then why aren't you involved in them?"

"There are women who are involved, but men have worked hard to keep us out of these areas, because even if you don't know, you sense that if we took over in these areas we could have so much fun without men, that we could even be happy;

326 · AHMET ALTAN

I think men are afraid of this, they took all the amusements for themselves and they can't enjoy them. You can't find happiness without women, I think that a man without a woman is a lost man."

With the melancholy smile that women couldn't resist when they saw it, Hikmet Bey replied as if he was mocking himself as well.

"There are men with women who are lost as well, I've heard a lot about men who have become lost because of a woman."

Dilara Hanım gave an answer that could be considered cruel.

"They're the ones who like being lost."

Hikmet Bey told Osman, "I thought about these words a lot, but I decided it wasn't true, no, they don't like being lost, it's just that they're not protected against their own feelings, they don't struggle to free themselves from the temptation to experience these feelings as far as possible." He paused and added, "I don't know, in fact I wasn't able to make a clear decision, is it possible to like being lost, did we love being lost in a woman more than we loved the woman herself, was this a weakness or a strength, my opinion about this changes every time I think about it."

After dinner they retired to Hikmet Bey's study and continued their conversation in front of the fire, Hikmet Bey liked Dilara Hanım's talk, she could occasionally be stern and cruel; when her intelligence was mixed with her merciless words there was a burning yet delicious taste, and she managed to present this in an elegant way.

Hikmet Bey enjoyed listening to her, sometimes his mouth burned as if he'd eaten spicy food, but what caught his attention more than Dilara Hanım's talk was Dilevser's silence. Dilevser was able to use her silence effectively; in some, silence might seem like a fault, a void, ignorance, but in Dilevser it was like a plain jewelry pouch of unadorned but valuable leather, you wanted to open it to see the jewelry inside. As Hikmet Bey told Osman, "The power to create this effect isn't something learned later in life, it just comes to some people naturally, the desire to open the pouch made one uneasy, anyone who spoke in the face of that silence felt a fear of being demeaned."

Hikmet Bey kept trying to draw Dilevser into the conversation, hoped to hear a few words signaling that the young girl admired his talk, but it couldn't be said that he succeeded at this; every time Hikmet Bey asked her a question, Dilevser looked at her mother with a smile as pure and innocent as her hands and waited for her to answer.

Hikmet Bey liked Dilara Hanım's talk, her intelligence, and the breadth of her knowledge, but he was attached to Dilevser's silence. At first glance, it was as if uneasiness and curiosity attracted him to the silence, but these weren't the only reasons. There was something else that was inexplicable, even though they hadn't known each other long, their only conversation had been the one about literature that morning, but when he looked at this young girl, Hikmet Bey felt a strange closeness that was difficult to explain, as if they'd spent many years alone together on a deserted island, as he confessed with slight surprise later, "A closeness like love, but completely without any reason."

As is always the case when this happens, the inevitable desire to form a bond appeared immediately, he opened his wings like a peacock showing off to his mate, relating a narrative adorned with his memories, thoughts, poems, anecdotes as if he was throwing a spear to pierce the silence that faced him. When he talked he implied that he'd had adventures in his youth that would shock and agitate a woman, especially a young girl, but what was actually seen when he opened his colorful wings was the purity and innocence he'd never lost despite everything he'd lived through; some people brought the scent of sin to even the most innocent subjects they

brought up, but Hikmet Bey added childishness and innocence even when he touched on the greatest sins. Both mother
and daughter sensed this, Dilara Hanım found in it a sugges-
tion of a friendship she could trust, and Dilevser found a sheltered attraction that she felt only when she read novels, when
she was absorbed by the lives of the people who wandered
amid the rustling of pages and the smell of paper.

Dilara Hanım felt the bitterness felt by women accustomed
to being admired everywhere all the time, when they see that
someone else, even if it was their daughter, had been chosen;
when she realized the man was interested in her daughter she
felt a sudden ache, but this passed so quickly it surprised her,
and it was replaced by a motherly curiosity as she started to
size Hikmet Bey up to see if he was suitable for her daughter.
He was a wealthy man, he was the son of the palace physician,
he had a very good education, he was elegant, he was well-
intentioned without being boring, these were his good sides,
but he'd suffered a heavy blow in the past, she was certain it
would not be easy for them to see the scars left behind by this,
but they were hidden somewhere. How would such a wound
impact their future, would he forget his former wife, could a
young girl who knew nothing except books heal a wound left
by a cunning and seductive woman whose beauty was legendary; she weighed all of this quickly with the cold-blooded
impartiality peculiar to women and decided not to stand in
their way but to watch how things unfolded.

They spent that anxious night like three people who liked
each other and found each other's presence reassuring, who
had gathered around a fire on a remote mountain, Hikmet Bey
parried Dilara Hanım's sardonic attacks with understanding
smiles and little jokes, once Dilevser laughed aloud at one of
his jokes, surprising both her mother and Hikmet Bey, and also
pleasing him. She didn't know that night, or indeed ever, that
this little laugh created a tremor in Hikmet Bey's soul, that she

had unwittingly pointed out a harbor to a lost soul who was seeking shelter.

In this laugh there was an unexpected bubbling of joy seen in somber young girls who are mature for their age and in unhappy women, the glittering, crystal melodiousness of a happiness that had been suppressed for a long time, that had become accustomed to being concealed, that searched for a way out and the grateful pleasure of finally being able to laugh. This laugh was so effective, it evoked the same pleasure and joy in those who heard it, and the thought of having caused this laugh's glittering reflections led Hikmet Bey to consider it a great success. For a face that had regarded life from a far and distant place, a face that had become so accustomed to unhappiness and hopelessness that it couldn't express its unhappiness, to be illuminated by a sudden cheer and participate in life, the sparks created by the abrasion of an excitement that had been closed for ages against the unhappinesses as it gushed to life was surprising and joyful, like fireworks suddenly exploding on a deserted and gloomy shore.

That night Hikmet Bey didn't go to his room as before, with the heavy silence that besieged the city and the frightening echoes of gunshots, but rather with the chiming of a laugh; he couldn't see the pathetic helplessness of the joy of having been able to make a little girl laugh; he couldn't decide if he missed a laughing woman or being able to make a woman laugh.

When he entered his room he saw that Hediye was waiting for him. As usual, she was silent; she helped Hikmet Bey undress without a word, without raising her head, laid him in the bed she'd warmed with hot-water bottles, took the bottles and went to her room without saying anything. With the frightful selfishness of happy people, it was only in the morning that he noticed Hediye hadn't stayed the night with him.

Dilara Hanım sensed that Dilevser had a dreaminess about her that resembled happiness, that this time her usual

330 - AHMET ALTAN

indifference to what was going on around her was because she was weighing many of the sentences that had been uttered that night and trying to reach conclusions from them, but unlike her daughter and Hikmet Bey she wasn't someone who could easily detach herself from life and close herself up in her feelings to be happy or distressed about them. At every moment she was also aware of the truths that floated around all of these feelings; she also wondered about what was going to become of them, about what was going to happen, about how and where Ragıp Bey was.

Life, which is a master at converting simple truths into endless worries, traps people in a web of vague and complex questions like a spider whose legs are all made of the unknown, it enjoys watching them struggle to free themselves from the web and answer the questions, it brings its cruelty to the point of believing that people are excited by this and would get bored without it; among the many people who were worried about someone, Dilara Hanım and Ragıp Bey worried without knowing they were only three hours away from each other, without knowing that simple truth.

As Dilara Hanım thought about Ragıp Bey in the mansion in Nişantaşı, Ragıp Bey, in a churchyard in Yeşilköy, looking out over the white tents illuminated by torches that stretched as far as the countryside, the lights in the windows of the mansions that the pashas were using as headquarters, and the cold night that adorned the dark shadows of this little fishing village with a leaden, snowy brightness, was also thinking about Dilara Hanım and the attempt that would be made the following day to capture the capital of the empire.

In Çatalca he'd managed to catch the train from Salonika that had set out with the vanguard units, he was assigned to an infantry unit at once, and found his brother Cevat Bey as he was getting off the train at Yeşilköy. They embraced happily, spoke briefly, concealing their long-held suspicions about the

Committee beneath the excitement of preparing for battle, then parted, one to join his unit and the other to join his comrades from the Committee. The officers and parliamentarians who'd managed to flee Istanbul were coming to Yeşilköy, sometimes in groups and sometimes alone. Parliament met unofficially in Yeşilköy.

Day and night, smoke-spewing trains came and went, they were carrying soldiers, munitions, and provisions from Salonika to Yeşilköy. It was as if the sound of marching military units had become part of the ground, it echoed in the villagers' ears even when there were no soldiers marching.

The Committee made a sudden decision to appoint Third Army Commander Mahmut Şevket Pasha to command what Mustafa Kemal had named the "Movement Army," and Enver Bey rushed to Yeşilköy from Berlin. As Cevat Bey explained to Osman later, the Movement Army's general staff had placed the nation's future in the hands of three people, but at the time no one, not even those people themselves, was aware of this. Later Enver Bey, Mustafa Kemal Bey, and İsmet Bey would come to power in succession; these three men, who had such different temperaments and didn't resemble each other in any way, tied the nation's destiny to themselves like a military chain. Enver was the bravest and most intrepid of the three, Mustafa Kemal was the best organizer and the most passionate, and İsmet was the most cautious and the best soldier; how strange that of these three men who used military force to come to power, the best soldier was the last to do so.

As Ragıp Bey smoked in the churchyard that night, no one knew what was going to happen yet, or if they were going to be alive the following day.

He'd found the churchyard while he was looking for a quiet place to conduct the brief and secret ritual that every soldier conducts before engaging in battle. This stone courtyard, paled by the night, seemed the most appropriate place to conduct this ritual. He would order all of his emotions again before facing death, bid farewell to his life as he had done many times before, strip whatever belonged to life from his soul, bury all feelings about life and expectations for the future in a deep place where he could find them if he survived the battle, see the following day as the only future that awaited him, distinguish everyone as either friend or foe, and devote his daylong life to hating his foes. He voluntarily relinquished his hopes and dreams. War had to be the only thing on his mind, any dreams or yearning he clung to would lead him to fear and avoid death.

As he finished his cigarette, he was prepared to enter death's presence, to submit himself to it the following morning along with thousands of others. As he crushed his cigarette butt with his boot he looked up at the sky, smiled as he did every time, and whispered in an almost mocking tone:

"Only you know what comes next."

As was his custom, he washed life off and prepared for death, but he was unable to erase Dilara Hanım's face from his mind. He was at ease about his mother because he had entrusted her to Sheikh Efendi and to his brother, but there was no one to whom he could entrust Dilara Hanım. Like many men in love, he worried that without him, the woman he loved would be subjected to evil, be insulted by other men, and be polluted, and he couldn't shake this feeling; like all feelings he couldn't shake, this made him angry, he wasn't even able to realize that this feeling wasn't worry but yearning. He ran into his brother as he was leaving the churchyard.

"I was looking for you," said Cevat Bey, "they told me you'd headed this way."

Since arriving in Çatalca, Cevat Bey had a spring in his step, his soul was once again in ferment, his anger and ambition had reached a level that could conceal the doubts about the Committee that had been eating at his heart for some time, he was the kind of person who always had to fight and to struggle against an enemy, he couldn't fit into the small jigsaw puzzles of life, he couldn't find happiness and the power to live in the daily life of mortals, when he had no great goals or great battles he became doubtful, apprehensive, and uneasy.

Now he had regained his foe and his battle, because he was unable to live for himself, he was dependent on fighting for the happiness of others and this reminded him that he was alive, that he existed, his mission was to be among those who were preparing once again to save the empire.

"Come, let's smoke a cigarette."

They lit their cigarettes and leaned against the church wall.

"Mustafa Kemal Bey has gone back to Salonika," said Cevat Bey.

"Why?"

"Some say that he went back of his own accord when Enver Bey was appointed chief of general staff, but others say that Enver Bey wanted him sent back."

Both of them were aware of the frightful jealousy and conflict between Enver Bey and Mustafa Kemal Bey concerning the general staff. Even though, like everyone else, they appreciated Mustafa Kemal's skills, they found themselves more in tune with Enver Bey's unflinching courage and temerity.

"This time we'll drag that cursed old man off the throne," said Cevat Bey.

"They say Mahmut Şevket Pasha sent a telegram to the Sultan declaring loyalty."

"He did, but only to stall him, so that he doesn't support the mutineers . . . Also, should this miserable, so-called Sultan dare to call on our soldiers to join his ranks and defend the caliphate, we don't know what they would do."

Cevat Bey paused and sighed deeply.

"Ragıp, to tell the truth, even now I'm not sure about our men. It's not just me, no one is. We have no idea what they'll do tomorrow. If we can't crush the mutineers in the initial attack, every hour after that works to our disadvantage, the soldiers could switch sides at any moment. Be very careful tomorrow, never forget that this time the enemy is not just the other side, the men behind you could also be your enemy."

"Any man I go into battle with is my man, brother, I have to trust them."

"Don't trust the men, Ragıp, weren't these mutineers someone else's men? God knows, there are some among them who've gone into battle and fought with you many times. You know better than I do, but still, never forget, soldiers are like harvested wheat, they can scatter wherever the wind blows, take care of yourself."

"Don't worry, brother, tomorrow, God willing, we'll take Istanbul. There are no real officers leading the mutineers, they can't hold out long."

"I'm confident of that too, but you never know what this cursed Sultan might do, he has a lot of tricks up his sleeve."

Ragıp Bey looked at the village's silhouette.

"Forty years ago the Russian army was right where we are now."

Cevat Bey looked at his brother and tried to figure out what he meant.

"Destiny," he said.

"If it's destiny, what a strange destiny it is, we've come to capture our own city, I don't know what kind of destiny this is, brother, we're going to march against our own men tomorrow."

"They're not our men anymore, Ragıp, they're our enemies. How many officers have they killed . . . ? Who needs men like that."

Once again Ragıp remembered what he'd experienced a few days earlier.

"I know, how could I forget what happened, they made a

mockery of soldiering, you can't imagine how much I want them to pay for this, but it's still strange to me that the people who made me so angry were our own men."

Ragıp Bey stubbed out his cigarette.

"Whatever, I need to get back and check on the final preparations, it's not good to leave soldiers idle for too long."

The two brothers embraced.

Cevat Bey said, "May God be with you, Ragıp." Just as they were about to part, Ragıp Bey stopped, it occurred to him to entrust his mother to his brother, to say, "Take care of our mother."

"Is anything wrong, Ragıp?"

"No, God willing, we'll see each other tomorrow."

He walked along the shore, heading toward where his unit was among the sea of tents; soldiers sat around fires among the tents and murmured among themselves. The camp was fairly quiet. It was as if the tension preceding the battle suppressed all sounds, no one, not even the horses and cannon mules, made a sound.

The main part of the army was positioned at Çatalca; apart from the Third Army, there were Bulgarian guerillas against whom they'd fought for years, Greeks, Albanians, young students taking up arms for the first time, teachers and lawyers who had volunteered. They didn't in fact need these volunteers from a military point of view, but they gave the movement of the army that was on its way to dethrone the caliph the appearance of a people's army. The superiority of the Movement Army to the mutineers in weapons, numbers, and capability was indisputable, but the Committee worried that the Sultan might alter the balance with his words, those who'd come to end the mutiny might join the mutineers.

Ragıp Bey walked toward his unit past fires that smelled of wood and smoke and that made the shadows of the soldiers sitting cross-legged larger, he strode toward his men, gestured for them to remain seated when they started to stand, and called to the cross-eyed sergeant.

"How are the men?"

"There are no problems, commander."

Ragıp Bey examined the sergeant's face carefully.

"They're all strong, they're prepared, don't worry, they'll show those in the capital who disrespected our caliph what's what."

Ragıp Bey went into his tent and lay down on the narrow camp bed and clasped his hands behind his head, if all went well he'd see Dilara Hanım in the evening. He thought about his military high school history teacher from Aleppo, he'd said, "Discovering the taste of sugar ruined the Hunnic soldiers, an officer should stay away from the sweet side of life, he should abstain from sugar, drink, and women, otherwise, God help you, he'll end up like the Hunnic army." There was a smile on his face as he was somewhat absorbed in thoughts of Dilara Hanım, his history teacher, and the Huns when a soldier entered and said that there was a message from headquarters. Ragıp told him to come in.

The wizened soldier entered, saluted wearily, and gave Ragıp Bey a letter from the leather bag that hung from his neck.

"They said it was urgent, commander."

After he dismissed the messenger, Ragıp Bey opened the letter and saw that it was an order to move within the hour.

Headquarters, which had sent news to the Caliph telling him that he would not be touched and guaranteed that he would keep his throne, assessed that it would be dangerous to wait any longer and had decided to move.

Ragıp Bey went out at once and called for the cross-eyed sergeant.

"Come on, cross-eyed guy, tell the men to get ready, we're going, the fight is on."

The tent city started to ripple with movement, the tense silence gave way to loud commands, shouting, clanking bayonets, neighing horses; the order to attack had suddenly invigorated the troops. A unit that had received the order sooner passed Ragıp Bey in lockstep and moved toward Bakırköy, they would board a train there and move to Sirkeci.

Ragıp Bey rubbed his hands together and tightened his bandolier, a weight had been lifted from him, he felt lightened, almost cheerful. As he later told Osman, "The worst thing in war is waiting, it lowers the men's morale."

Fifteen minutes later they started to march toward Edirnekapı according to the order given to them. They marched along a narrow dirt road toward one of the largest cities in history, it smelled of wet soil and oregano. In the silence, he heard the stumbling of soldiers who were not yet fully awake; the metallic sound of rifle butts hitting the canteens on the soldiers' belts spread into the night. Toward midnight they reached the great walls of the queen of cities, this great and magnificent city that had been attacked by Greeks, Roman emperors, Byzantine Caesars, Bulgarian kings, Russians, Crusaders, Arabs, Ottoman Sultans, and rebellious generals and who made prisoners of whoever captured her, pitch-black and silent behind the walls, awaiting the newcomers.

Giant cypresses, centuries old, spread across the area between the road, paved with ancient Greek stones, and the walls, which seemed higher, blacker, and more threatening than usual, standing frighteningly still like celestial sentries that awaited the souls of those who died under the walls; the soldiers were frightened by the magnificence of what they saw, listening intently in case of a possible attack, and moved toward the walls, taking care not to make even the slightest sound.

Under the gigantic cypresses were thousands of stone dwarves with large quilted turbans, here and there among them flickered a few oil candles with strange flames that smelled of sorrow and death, in the long shadows cast by the small flames of these abandoned candles, some of the quilted stone turbans seemed to move, to lower or raise their heads.

The soldiers suddenly stopped.

When Ragıp Bey heard occasional whispers in the night he realized the soldiers were praying, they were afraid. He called to the men in a low voice.

"These are the tombs of Mehmet the Conqueror and the martyrs who conquered Istanbul. They watch over Muslim soldiers when they set out on a campaign. Recite the *al-fateha* . . . pray for an auspicious battle."

Even though the soldiers knew they might be attacked at any moment, they hung their rifles over their shoulders and recited the *al-fateha*, rubbed their faces with their hands, and sent their prayers to the souls of the martyrs and asked for mercy. They knew that when they went into battle there was no one but God in whom to take shelter, God may have agreed to share life with the devil, but didn't share death with anyone; this is what warriors believed.

Knowing that the men couldn't pass the tombs of the martyrs without reciting the *al-fateha*, he took the risk of allowing them to do so, then gave the cross-eyed sergeant an order in a low voice.

"We'll go through the gate in a double column, everyone keep an eye on the man next to him, no one is to make a sound, if anyone's rifle butt hits his canteen I swear to God I'll kill you first and then the man who did it."

They went through the high-arched gate carefully, as soon as they were through, each man found cover and lay down. Ragıp Bey turned his back to the inside of the gate, waiting for the men to pass through and glancing around. They were happily surprised when they realized no one was waiting for them. After they'd taken cover, the units behind them began to pass through the gate. At the same moment, the vanguard of the Movement Army entered Istanbul from four different points.

They stood at the foot of the walls and looked at the city.

This strong and unpredictable city, that had experienced innumerable bloody massacres, with its mosques, churches, palaces, domes, minarets, crosses, streams, seas, cypresses, plane trees, and people, was wrapped in the darkness of the night, it had turned off all its lights and quieted all its voices; not a single person in the city was asleep that night, but the houses of the city were darker and quieter than the cemetery outside the city gates. In that silence, the propeller of a barge sailing up the Bosphorus to the Black Sea could be heard in Edirnekapı, the entire city listened to the sound of this small barge at the same moment.

In the midst of this terrifying darkness, the Sultan's palace on Yıldız Hill shone like a ball of fire; the Sultan, who'd been afraid of the dark since childhood, had all of the lights of the palace lit that night as usual. The most frightened person in the city, shriveled by terror, had lit all of the lights in his house in such a way that it could be seen from everywhere and had placed himself in the middle of those lights. While his slaves hid in darkness, he hid in the light.

From within these lights, he too looked out at his city.

"Look at the capital of the empire," said the Sultan, "look at this inky darkness, was this how I was supposed to see my city, was it this gloom?"

Even the houses of the palace staff in the vicinity of the palace were empty and dark. When they heard the news that the Movement Army had reached Çatalca, most of the staff had abandoned their masters and taken their families and whatever they could carry and fled to Üsküdar by *caique*.

"Even the houses of the palace staff are dark, even they have gone. There's no need for Mahmut Şevket Pasha to enter the city, just hearing his name was enough to send people running."

As usual, Reşit Pasha looked for words with which to console the Sultan.

"In any event they'll come back, my Sultan. Didn't Mahmut Şevket Pasha declare his fealty to you, didn't he tell you many times that your throne is safe, that he didn't harbor any malevolence toward you?"

Very frightening and powerful people have a soft and loving face that they conceal from the crowds and that is different from their tyrannical face, they only show this face to those close to them, those who see it become attached to it, those who see this warmth become almost enslaved to it. The Sultan gave his fatherly, loving, but slightly condescending look that had always affected Reşit Pasha.

"You're a good doctor, but, as I always say, you're a child when it comes to politics."

The Sultan stopped talking and lit a cigarette. He put it in his cigarette holder. As he did so the look on his face changed, it hardened and solidified, the lines on his face, which had grown deeper of late, seemed to sag.

"Can a sultan who seeks assurances about his future from a pasha who is subordinate to him still be considered a sultan, doctor? Yes he can, of course he can, but is it really sovereignty?"

It occurred to the pasha to ask, "So why don't you stand up to them, why don't you do anything?" but even then he didn't have the courage to do this. With the intuition that had always frightened him, the Sultan answered as if he knew what the pasha was thinking.

"Then why don't I stand up to them, doctor, why don't I act while I'm still sitting on the throne?"

The Sultan stood, went to the window, and looked out at the city that has put out its lights as it waited in silence.

"Why don't I do anything?"

Then he answered his own question.

"Because there's nothing I can do . . . If I stand up to them, if I say, my sons, all Muslims, I have unfurled the flag of my caliphate, it's time for jihad, yes, they would come, most of my soldiers would come, but then what would happen, brother would kill brother, if I lose I lose everything, if I win, I will have made that vagabond Derviş Vahdeti my partner, instead of the soldiers, the mullahs will be demanding their rights. No one is aware of it, but an age is ending, doctor, here, tonight, we await the end of the Ottoman dynasty."

He went back to his armchair.

"Look, the state's army has come to conquer its own capital. They've tasted this, they don't want to give up this power . . . When soldiers get a taste of power, they don't give it up, this isn't like the Janissary uprisings. The Ottoman dynasty is ending, doctor . . . Ah, the Ottoman empire is ending."

"Why do you say that, Your Majesty, they won't touch you. Who can rebel against your power, the authority of the Caliph, what slave has that much power?"

"Perhaps, yes, I can keep my throne, but nothing will be as it was before. Moreover, I'm not even so sure about that, I'm not even sure they'll let me live. I'm not sure about anything, no one is."

For the first time the doctor realized so clearly how much the Sultan feared being killed.

"They wouldn't dare touch you, Your Majesty."

"I don't know, doctor, but if I go I'll take a few of them with me."

As the Sultan said this he put his hand in his jacket pocket. The doctor realized that the Sultan had a gun in his jacket pocket and that he was determined to kill anyone who came to kill him, he saw what desperation was, how it turned a sultan into a gunman. The old Sultan was thinking about fighting like a gang leader, he no longer trusted his soldiers, his people, his friends, the only thing he trusted was the gun in his pocket. Reşit Pasha told Osman, "That was the moment I realized it was over, the moment he put his hand in his pocket, after that moment, neither the state nor the angry and frightened Sultan would recover."

"Let's tell them to get the carriage ready," the Sultan said, "Go on home now." For the first time, Reşit Pasha found the courage to stand up to the Sultan.

"I would stay if you commanded me to, Your Majesty, you might need something."

The Sultan stood and patted the doctor on the shoulder.

"Go, doctor. This place isn't safe anymore, go home. From now on only God can help us. We should pray for the best, none of us has the power to change fate."

As the doctor walked toward the door, the Sultan called after him.

"Doctor."

"Yes, Your Majesty.'

"Her ladyship was coughing today. I told them to boil some lemon flowers . . . What do you suggest?"

"I would have suggested the same, Your Majesty, you found the appropriate remedy."

The Sultan nodded; even under these circumstances he derived a strange and inexplicable pleasure from showing off his knowledge of medicine.

"Yes, I thought so too."

As the pasha left the palace he noticed that the guards had disappeared, the palace was completely undefended. Most of the mutineering soldiers had gathered at the barracks, some had fled to join the approaching Movement Army. The physician knew the Sultan was aware of this; he was certain he'd weighed everything, he wasn't taking a stance because he knew he wouldn't win. If he'd thought he could win, he would have been prepared to burn down the world to do so, he wouldn't have cared if brothers shed each other's blood. Even though he knew this was true, it didn't diminish his love for the Sultan. When he thought that he was on the brink of death, this man who would do anything to hold on to power hadn't wanted his physician to stay with him, he'd sent him home so he would be safe.

As he rode through the pitch-dark, silent streets, the pasha wondered if this was because he was growing old. "Would he have fought if he was younger?" As he thought about this he rested his head on the quilted back seat of the landau, and suddenly he found himself dreaming about Mihrişah Sultan; he had no idea when his thoughts had drifted from the Sultan to Mihrişah Sultan.

Later he said to Osman, "That's how we men are, in difficult times we always think about women, we always want to take shelter in them." Osman could have said, "But you thought about her at other times as well," he also agreed that men always thought about women in difficult times and wanted to take shelter in them.

16

Once the Movement Army had reached Yeşilköy and it was clear that an advance on the city was inevitable, Mihrişah Sultan suddenly lost interest in what was going on. She couldn't tell anyone, but she even began to feel inwardly sorry that the Sultan was going to be dethroned. She too felt that an age had come to an end.

A period that had defined her entire youth would end with the dethroning of the Sultan, and she, along with everyone else, would pass into a new age through a newly opened gate, and she was secretly frightened by this. It was as if this fierce change was a sign that her youth and beauty had come to an end; she sensed she would not be able to pass through this gate with the youth and beauty she'd had before. She'd reached an age when the new worried her; sometimes she longed madly for something new, yet she was also frightened that it would make her older, or rather that it would make it apparent that she'd aged.

Of course this vague, nameless anxiety whose existence she would never accept wasn't the only reason her interest in these matters had lessened; like many beautiful women, she couldn't remain interested in anyone or anything for very long, she was soon herself again. Her beauty was like an attractive garden with high walls that it pleased her to stroll through; though she left it occasionally, when she was outside she only sought what concerned her garden, when she couldn't find anything she returned to her thick-walled garden and concerned herself with her own beauty. There was no room for anything but herself and her beauty; for her, her beauty was like a lover she couldn't renounce, a paramour she couldn't live without, she couldn't countenance anything coming between her and her own beauty.

Behind the selfishness of her passion for beauty there was a gentle sensitivity and humor somewhere in her thoughts that was even distant from her beauty, and it was this sarcasm that took aim at everyone including herself and her ability to discover the laughable that made her beauty attractive. But further behind this there was an empathy and a desire to love that was particular to the reclusive, that only emerged with difficulty, she looked at everyone to see if this was the person she could love, but after a time she wearied of this and gave up.

Mihrişah Sultan never said any such thing, but Osman liked to repeat it as if he'd heard it from her. "People who have difficulty loving are partial to people who are difficult to love." People like that loved murderers, madmen, dervishes, writers, rebels, seductresses; he pointed to Mihrişah Sultan as proof of this; she'd loved a father and daughter she should perhaps not have loved, Sheikh Efendi, who had no interest in carnal pleasures, who avoided sin, and who was impossible to tempt and difficult to approach, and who secretly loved another woman, and the rebellious, aloof, and sharp-tongued Rukiye, the daughter of Sheikh Efendi and the woman who had betrayed her only living son.

The love Mihrişah Sultan harbored for these two people lived, grew, and roosted in her because she saw one of them rarely and the other was always with her. She loved them the way she loved her own beauty, passionately, with the fear of losing them and occasionally growing weary of loving.

Loving taught her how to fear; she'd said this to Osman as well once: "If you love, you fear." This stately woman who was never frightened for herself, to whom it never even occurred to be frightened, would tremble with fear when it came to Rukiye, she couldn't stop worrying that something might happen to her. She told her everything she knew about men, life, and love, she wanted her to learn about life without the painful experiences, though she knew this was impossible.

This love showed her the sides of herself she hadn't known, that she was even surprised to see existed; she caught herself looking at Rukiye tenderly, or insisting she eat a bit more, she saw this not as a sign of love but of aging and became irritated with Rukiye and grumbled.

In addition, Rukiye was the visible side of her other love, which she wasn't able to see. She loved what she saw of Sheikh Efendi in Rukiye's personality, it was as if she had transferred her love for him to Rukiye; in a strange way she wanted to raise Rukiye well so that she would be a suitable daughter for Sheikh Efendi; when she saw a side of Rukiye she didn't like, she got angry not just because she didn't like it but also because it was something unsuitable for Sheikh Efendi's daughter. Sometimes, for whatever reason, mostly in the evening twilight as she stood by the window looking out over the sea as figures blurred and slipped into the shadows, she imagined that Rukiye was her daughter by Sheikh Efendi, she entertained dreams that embarrassed her, but even though she was ashamed she couldn't keep herself from enjoying these dreams.

As for Rukiye, she stubbornly refused to talk about her father.

Once, when Mihrişah Sultan told Rukiye that she should get to know her father better, Rukiye reacted almost angrily and said, "I don't want to talk about him, with your permission, let's not get into this subject at all."

"Pride," said Mihrişah Sultan, "is a feeling that belongs to the masses, what a noblewoman needs is not pride mixed with ridiculousness but a dignity that adds nobility to everything, even to behavior that seems to arise from lack of pride. You can do whatever you want, you can talk to whoever you want to talk to, as long as you do it with dignity . . . You can talk about your father too, you don't have to be so sensitive that it hurts your pride."

As was her wont, Rukiye gave a brief response to this long statement.

"I don't want to talk about my father."

"Because he doesn't reach out to you?"

"Isn't that reason enough?"

"Sheikh Efendi must have his own reasons."

Rukiye didn't answer; in fact she did want to talk about her father, she wanted to hear rumors about him, but she'd decided to go see her father and believed she shouldn't talk about him until she met him, she didn't want anything to influence her until she came face to face with him.

In any event, at the time a man other than her father occupied almost all of her thoughts and dreams, the interest in her that had recently been shown by an older man who couldn't resist the secret temptations had stirred her soul.

Her frightening honesty, the decisiveness so rarely seen in a young girl, her desire to see everything as clearly as possible, and her well-grounded tenacity had been shaken by this vague breeze of attention. If she'd been a bit more playful, if she'd been a more flirtatious girl, she wouldn't have been shaken like this, she wouldn't have been so moved the first time someone paid attention to her, but the curiosity that led her to want to bring every feeling and every word out into the open made her pursue and be swept up by this vagueness. Like a medium trying to find a lost soul, she thought about him constantly, trying to find signs in his every word and act, she wasn't interested in anything except him.

Life, consisting of thousands of sounds and images, was now filtered through Tevfik Bey like light rays focused into a single beam while passing through a prism, now war, soldiers, the Sultan, politics, fear, and worry only became real when Tevfik Bey spoke of them, otherwise they became scattered and didn't attract her attention.

When Tevfik Bey came to the waterfront mansion that night and said, "They'll make a move tonight," she was interested only in the way the man with the beautiful face said this.

Rukiye didn't worry about the news he brought because his kind voice and his sandy moustache softened even the most frightening subject. She didn't worry about anything that was defined and known.

With a curiosity that attempted to conceal her lack of interest, Mihrişah Sultan asked if he was sure.

"An officer friend told me, and I think the information is correct."

"This time they'll dethrone the old geezer."

"But your ladyship, in his letter to the minister of war, Mahmut Şevket Pasha gave assurances that His Excellency the Caliph would not be touched."

Mihrişah Sultan said, "As if," like all Ottoman nobles who looked down on the masses.

"Turks love to make promises they can't keep, they like to make promises but they're not strong enough to keep their promises."

"But Mahmut Şevket Pasha isn't like that."

"They're all like that, Tevfik Bey, you'll see that he won't keep his promise, they'll dethrone the Sultan."

"Won't they be wary of how the people will react?"

"Did anyone ever hesitate because of how the people might react . . . The Caliph won't get off the hook this time, he'll be lucky to escape with his life, that's all."

After Tevfik Bey left, Mihrişah Sultan ordered that the doors be bolted and the lights extinguished and had the lights in the living room dimmed as much as possible; for different reasons, neither of them felt sleepy. When Mihrişah Sultan saw that Rukiye hadn't gone to bed and had shrunk into an armchair by the window, she asked:

"Aren't you going to bed?"

"I'm not sleepy."

"Are you frightened?"

"No, not when I'm with you."

Mihrişah Sultan spoke as if she was grumbling to herself.

"I wonder if I should have sent you to your father, you would have been safer there"

Rukiye looked Mihrişah Sultan squarely in the face.

"I wouldn't have gone even if you had sent me, I prefer to stay with you."

"I know that you wouldn't have gone."

Mihrişah was more moved than she would have guessed that the girl had said she didn't want to leave her even at such a dangerous time; seeing her shrink like a little girl made her more sentimental, and she asked with an unaccustomed directness:

"Are you in love, Rukiye?"

"I don't know."

"That means yes."

"I really don't know, I'm just a bit confused."

"That also means yes. I'm worried that you might get badly hurt."

This time Rukiye was truly curious.

"Why?"

"If you knew the reason, I wouldn't worry about you being badly hurt, you'd be hurt anyway but it wouldn't be that frightening. You'll learn the reason, but will you be happy to learn the reason?"

Rukiye's honey-colored eyes were wide open as she looked at her with such serious curiosity that Mihrişah Sultan was truly frightened for this young girl; like a child breaking a watch to see what was inside, Rukiye was capable of breaking her life to see how it worked; her instinct to want to understand every detail, every feeling, every act would always make her impatient and meddlesome, she would occasionally tinker with the parts of life that should be hidden, that should not be seen, of which we shouldn't even be aware. She would never be able to look at a clock just to learn the time, she would always be curious about how it worked.

Perhaps it was because of the compassionate love she felt at that moment, perhaps because of her worries about the young girl's future, perhaps because of the heavy burden of the uncertainty of what that night would bring, perhaps because of all these things, Mihrişah Sultan did something she rarely did.

"Come sit next to me, Rukiye."

Mihrişah Sultan told the young girl about her own life, about the men she'd met, about her loves, about the duels that had been fought over her, her suffering, her anxieties and how she'd overcome them, which words meant what, all of these things as if she wanted to teach her everything that could be known about life in a single night, speaking in a soft voice, sometimes smiling, sometimes trying to conceal the slight roughening of her voice; the only thing she left out was Sheikh Efendi and the feelings she had for him.

They sat there not like a sheikh's daughter and a noblewoman, but as two women who were sad and worried about each other for no apparent reason; Rukiye asked questions and Mihrişah Sultan answered her.

On that unhappy and anxious night, they experienced a strange and restless happiness in their own way. Mihrişah Sultan tasted the unaccustomed pleasure of a motherly love she hadn't shown even to her own son and shuddered at the thought that this might be a sign of old age; for her part, Rukiye was disquieted by the thought that her love for Mihrişah Sultan rather than for her mother was a weakness that transformed her rebellious nature into obedience; but despite their disquiet, neither of them intended to give up the love they'd found, they were learning about the magnificent tranquility and the heavy price of powerful love.

As the gigantic tiled stove in the middle of the living room began to cool and the black water of the Bosphorus began to turn blue with the breaking of the pale morning through the clouds, Mihrişah Sultan stood and said:

"Let's go to bed, we're not going to get much sleep in any case."

As they were leaving the living room to go to their rooms, Rukiye took Mihrişah Sultan's hand with a gratitude to which she wasn't accustomed. "Your presence . . . ," but she couldn't finish what she wanted to say. Mihrişah Sultan caressed her face without saying anything; as she was making her way to her room she thought, "My presence is of no use whatsoever," on the day when her greatest enemy would face a strange and certain defeat, she too began to feel a strange defeat, and exhaustion.

While they were going to bed, the main units of the Movement Army had arrived at the edge of Istanbul; as dawn broke, the vanguard received the order to attack.

Twenty cavalrymen and an artillery battery had been added to Ragıp Bey's unit; with the cavalrymen in the lead and the artillery in the rear, they started to move toward Aksaray, their mission was to capture Babıali.

They arrived in Aksaray toward noon. They paused there to rest the horses and load the artillery.

The people who had sheltered in their homes in fear the previous night greeted the soldiers with applause and shouted, "Bravo, brave lads, welcome, courageous men." As for the mutineering soldiers, they were nowhere to be seen.

As they struggled up the muddy hill at Laleli listening to the sound of the Hungarian artillery horses, who sounded as if they were suffering and whose neighing resembled the snarling of a monster, they kept an eye on the houses on either side and pushed the cannon carriages as they slipped on the muddy road.

When they reached the Mahmutpasha tomb there were still no mutineers to be seen; it was as if the hundreds of thousands of people who'd been shouting in the squares, the dozens of turbaned mullahs, the many soldiers whose bayonets glinted in the sun had been swallowed by the earth and disappeared, the city had changed its identity, now only the people who were applauding could be seen.

As they moved from the tomb toward Babıali, they lost the cavalrymen in the narrow streets, they'd moved off into other streets, when they were passing the Iranian Embassy the cavalrymen emerged from another street and rejoined them.

When they were forty yards from Babıali, about a hundred and fifty mutineers deployed behind the iron fence of the government building suddenly began to shoot.

Ragıp Bey shouted at his men to position themselves at the foot of the walls. The cavalrymen's neighing horses bumped into each other as they tried to get out of range by retreating uphill.

The street was narrow and the soldiers had little room to maneuver against the well-positioned mutineers, it was difficult to take cover and shoot, if they advanced through the space between them they would suffer casualties.

Then Ragıp Bey gave the order for the cannon to be brought to the front.

The mutineers hidden in the ministry of public works just past Babıali and in the military club just below it began shooting as well.

The cannon, which were difficult to maneuver on the very slippery cobblestones, were aimed at Babıali and the ministry of public works and began firing; the windows in the buildings shattered from the sound of the cannon, the explosions echoed in the narrow street with a hellish cacophony.

The cannonballs brought down the iron fence in front of Babıali, opened a hole in the main gate, and the wall of a room to the right of the gates of the ministry of public works collapsed; the room, with its desk, chairs, coffee table and a sign on the wall reading "*Ya Allah*," was naked like a picture hanging on the middle of the building. The cannonballs ripped the branches off trees on both sides of the street.

At that moment Ragıp Bey saw a grenade that had been thrown from the top floor of the military club, it drew an arc in the air like a disembodied fist and landed on the ammunition wagon waiting behind the cannon. The wagon exploded with such a terrifying sound that Ragıp Bey watched its aftermath without hearing a sound, in a horrifying silence.

With that explosion it was as if every building on the street, every wall, and every person, had melted to their smallest particles and filled his ears like pressurized water; the carriage, engulfed in sulfur-colored flames, rose to the sky like a giant twister, spreading the smell of gunpowder; among the pieces of wood, grapeshot, and bullets there were chunks of scarlet flesh with green cloth on them; two soldiers waiting in front of the wagon had exploded with the wagon and been torn apart.

When Ragıp Bey felt the heat of the flames on his body and looked at his left side, he saw that his jacket's left sleeve had disappeared in the blink of an eye and that his arm, the hair on which had been burned off, was naked, he couldn't figure out if the smell of burned flesh was from the soldiers who'd been blown apart or from his burned arm.

He couldn't even hear his own voice when he shouted for the men to push the wagon down the hill. Five soldiers, moving in a strange, puppetlike manner, ran to the burning wagon and pushed it down.

The wagon careened down the hill, scattering yellow, blue, and purple sparks and trembling with exploding bullets, hit a wall, and continued burning there.

From the side of a printing works behind the military club, five to ten civilians began shooting in support of the mutineers; Ragıp Bey immediately deployed some of his men to lay down suppressing fire on the civilians.

There was a strong sense that the cannon fire had weakened the mutineers' resistance. Ragıp Bey was so absorbed in the excitement of the skirmish, he focused solely on his men and on the enemy, it was as if he had shed his entire life from his being and become part of the battle.

This was what he liked most, perhaps the thing he was madly in love with; that magnificent moment of fighting when he forgot life and death, in which he had no worries, in which he was not even aware of himself, in which his thoughts were subordinated to his instincts, in which he ran with a careful and merciless desire like a predatory animal in pursuit of its prey, in which he erased everything but his target from his mind . . . He gave one order after another, moved his men from one corner to another, changed the positions of the cannon depending on the direction from which they were being fired at.

Just then they saw a bulky man with a black beard running toward them past the Iranian embassy and waving his arms; without thinking, a few of the soldiers turned around and mowed the running man down, he was covered with large red spots that looked like red chrysanthemums, he stopped where he was, knelt, raised his head to the sky, and looked, then collapsed on the muddy pavement. Ragıp Bey, who had seen many battles and fought in many skirmishes, would remember the way the man fell for years; even though in every battle the move that made the least sense had a logic of its own, there was no logic, no reason for this man to run toward them with his bare hands; he always wondered if the man had been coming to tell them something.

When the crossfire became less fierce, they saw Hafız Hakkı Bey and a few volunteers coming toward them from below, ignoring the bullets speeding past them to the right and left. Just as his men were about to open fire on them, Ragıp Bey recognized his old friend and stopped his men from firing. Hakkı Bey approached Ragıp Bey as if he was watching something very amusing.

"Hey, commander, you're still alive."

Then he turned to the men and teased them.

"How are you lion cubs doing, are you having fun?"

A little later the surviving mutineers began to surrender and to come out of the positions where they'd taken cover.

After Ragıp Bey delivered the dead and wounded soldiers to the medical units that had been following them, he headed toward Sultanahmet Square with the cannon battery. When they reached the large square he saw that a crowd had gathered and was shouting, "Death to the Sultan," and applauding the Movement Army units and artillery batteries entering the square; a week earlier these people had been shouting "Long live the Sultan, long live sharia," in the same square.

Before he had the chance to position his units, which had just emerged from a skirmish, in a corner of the square he received word that the main attack was taking place at Taşkışla and an order to go there at once.

He took some Bulgarian guerillas with double bandoliers across their chests and Albanian volunteers with conical white caps and set out for Taşkışla. They made their way through the empty streets as quickly as possible and climbed up Yüksekkaldırım toward Beyoğlu; this time they were able to climb the hill faster because they had no cannon with them; in Beyoğlu, cadets from the military academy were patrolling and keeping order.

As they approached Taşkışla they saw Armenians from Tatavla pulling cannon from the Golden Horn to the top of the hill, Armenian women were tending to the wounded and distributing food to weary soldiers.

Major Muhtar Bey, commander of the unit that had surrounded the barracks, was lying dead on a corner in a pool of blood; he'd died from a wound he received during the fighting. By the Major's head, the Armenian patriarch, in his long, black robe, long cowl, long white beard and a heavy crucifix hanging around his neck, prayed and beseeched according to his own faith for this Muslim to go to his God purified.

After Muhtar Bey died, Enver Bey took command. As Ragıp Bey joined the forces besieging the barracks, his experienced eyes noted that the siege had been badly planned; there weren't enough men, because the terrain was rough the cannon were not well placed, there had been many casualties.

Most of the mullahs who'd been said to have stirred up this mutiny had disappeared, some of the soldiers who had joined the mutiny from Istanbul were dead or had surrendered.

The men who were defending the barracks were soldiers from Salonika who had in fact started the mutiny and they were good fighters; it was clear they had no intention of surrendering.

The fighting continued for a long time; twice, the men in the barracks attacked suddenly, sending out units of twenty-five to thirty men, and succeeded in capturing one or two light cannon and bringing them back into the barracks, but the forces of the Movement Army were strengthened by reinforcements from other districts of Istanbul, and new cannon batteries approached the barracks step by step.

At one point the men in the barracks flew a white flag, when some of the soldiers who saw this flag stood and began advancing they were cut down by fire from the barracks; this inflamed the anger and resentment on both sides.

Toward evening, Ragıp Bey was with the first units to enter the barracks, he didn't know that he would witness a second incident that day that he would never forget. They captured the barracks building by building and suffered many casualties due to fire from the barracks.

In the end the mutineers were confined to the last building. They could no longer either fight or flee.

Ragıp Bey saw some of the windows on the top floor being opened, just as he was telling his men to aim at these windows, a mutineer appeared on the windowsill. He stood for a moment with his hands spread, then allowed himself to fall into the void; as he hurtled towards the concrete floor of the courtyard, his fez flew off and glided after him like a red bird. Others followed the first jumper and allowed themselves to fall from the windows into the void one after the other. They heard the dull sound of the falling bodies hitting the ground and saw the soldiers shudder and die as blood spurted from every part of their bodies and their brains broke into pieces.

This strange mutiny that caused the entire nation to quake in fear and that was remembered darkly for a century as the "religious uprising" ended with soldiers falling through the air.

17

That morning, as the sudden warmth of spring brought out the smell of flowers, Sheikh Efendi stood on the shore of the Golden Horn, which lay like a faded, rose-colored velvet cloth, and watched the columns of ash-smelling smoke rise from the four corners of Istanbul into the hyacinth-colored sky that was swollen with layers of clouds.

The first order given by Mahmut Şevket Pasha, who would govern the empire and Istanbul like a complete dictator with an authority that no sultan had possessed for some years, was for the denunciations that had been collected in several buildings in Istanbul to be burned; millions of sheets of paper were piled into stacks and set on fire. There were so many of these terrifying letters of denunciation that had been accumulated over thirty-three years that it took a long time to burn them; these pieces of paper that had darkened the lives of thousands of people and that had nourished and increased the unjustified fears of an apprehensive sultan spread over the capital as ash and smoke like a pus that had accumulated in the collective bloodstream of an entire society, reminding everyone of their guilt and complicity.

No one objected to the burning of these documents, because among them there were even denunciations written by the officers who had come with the Movement Army to dethrone the Sultan. And Mahmut Şevket Pasha said he aimed to clear the past and save everyone from past fears by burning these documents that proved almost everyone had taken part in the tyranny of this period.

This city of rumors and legends, this city nourished by gossip, was not satisfied with this statement, it was already being whispered from ear to ear that the real reason the Pasha had ordered the documents to be burned was to destroy them before the denunciations he'd written were brought out into the open.

In any event, there were two main topics of gossip being discussed, one was the Pasha's denunciations and the other was the incredible amount of money the mutineers were found to have had. The Committee spread the word that the money had been distributed to the mutineers by the Sultan, but no proof of this was ever found; even though this was talked of for days, months, and indeed years, it was never clear who had given the mutineers this money.

Most of those who had stirred up the mutiny fled, and the peculiar strangers who'd been seen among the crowds before the mutiny disappeared. Apart from Derviş Vahdeti and a few of his cohorts, no one important was arrested for provoking the mutiny, and they awaited their execution in the dungeons of Bekirağa Division. The people knew that the gallows would soon be erected.

There was distress in Sheikh Efendi's soul, the nameless disquiet of someone who expected something to happen but who didn't know what it would be or how it would end.

The previous night he'd learned that Mehpare Hanım had returned to Istanbul with a fat Greek woman and had settled in a small wooden house in Aksaray that she'd inherited from her aunt.

One morning, after Constantine had gone to the city, Mehpare Hanım left the mansion with Sula, all of her jewelry, and the money she'd saved and set out for Istanbul; there hadn't been any fight between them, they hadn't even had an argument. Perhaps he was the man who'd made her happiest, he'd enriched their lovemaking with love games and desires that wandered through the darkest corners of savagery, he'd responded to Mehpare Hanım's carnal passions with passions and desires as strong as hers, none of it had been forced, he'd done it all instinctively, without thinking.

The reason Mehpare Hanım left Salonika without so much as a farewell, without even leaving a letter, was not that she was dissatisfied with their lovemaking or that she was bored with Constantine, it was just that she could no longer endure the alienation she always felt in that city, to which she'd never become accustomed. Lust alone, despite its power, was insufficient to ease that sense of alienation. She missed the smell of Istanbul, being among people who spoke her own language, and the life that seemed to be a natural part of her, when she could no longer endure this longing she made a sudden decision to leave Salonika.

They arrived on an evening when the city was wearied by the uprising that had just been put down. They arrived at the little house in Aksaray just as it was getting dark, got the key from the neighbor, and entered the house that smelled of cambric and dust.

They couldn't find a bakery or a grocery store that was open, so they went to bed hungry and tired. That night Mehpare Hanım experienced true regret and cursed her stupidity, she decided to write to Constantine at once the following day.

They got up wearily toward noon, and as they were tidying the house and uncovering the furniture there was a knock at the door.

A friendly-looking dervish asked for Mehpare Hanım.

"I am she; yes?"

The dervish handed her a pouch.

"They sent you this . . . And a mansion has been rented in Şişli, the rent has been paid."

The Dervish gave her a piece of paper on which the address of the mansion had been written with the pouch and left.

Mehpare Hanım was not at all surprised, she'd inwardly expected something like this to happen when she arrived in Istanbul.

She smiled as she went to Sula, who was cleaning the kitchen. She showed the pouch to Sula, who she loved because she was the only person she could talk to with the congenial feminine levity that she'd become accustomed to as a child in the rooms, kitchen, and garden of this house.

"This man is still in love with me."

"Which man?"

"The Sheikh."

Sula grumbled,

"He sent you that because he feels sorry for you."

Mehpare Hanım laughed.

"If he felt sorry for me he would have just sent money, but he also rented a mansion in Şişli."

"Is that what love is, renting a mansion?"

Mehpare Hanım sat in a chair with the air of a lower-class girl, an identity that had always been present beneath all of her other identities.

"Oh Sula, you're so . . . If he'd wanted he could have let me live here, provided for the basics, and left it at that. But he doesn't want me to just get by, he also wants me to be happy. He rented a mansion for me because he knows that living like this would make me sad."

"Will a mansion be enough to make you happy?"

"Oh, it's enough . . . I can find everything else I need in order to be happy, of course I'm not going to expect any of those things from the Sheikh, come on, get ready, I'm not going to spend another night in this house."

The mansion in Şişli, with its large garden, footmen, and servants awaited her, and Mehpare Hanım entered it as a lady, no one except Sula ever heard the voice of the lower-class girl from Aksaray, it was as if, in the carriage, as they passed through every neighborhood between Aksaray and Şişli, the voice from her childhood was masked, by the time they arrived in Şişli, that voice was once again lost beneath the many voices, expressions, and behaviors she'd learned. She was now ready for her new life as an Ottoman lady.

Sheikh Efendi knew that by doing his former wife this favor he was helping her to commit new sins, that he was enabling her to live a strange life that would make him burn with shame and jealousy every time he heard about it, that would cause him to be angry at himself, that he would be jealous about what Mehpare Hanım experienced before she even experienced it, but he couldn't bear for the woman he loved to be disgraced in a poor neighborhood by house raids, gossip, the impudent jokes of local shopkeepers, for her to be downtrodden; that woman was going to do what she did in any event, he preferred that at least she do so in a sheltered house, under sheltered circumstances.

The real reason for his disquiet was not his concerns about his former wife or the jealousy he felt concerning her, he expected something else to happen that day. There was no sign of what was going to happen, he just had a feeling that something would happen.

This feeling proved to be correct.

That afternoon an expensive, pitch-black landau with polished brass lanterns and well-groomed horses pulled up in front of the *tekke*, and the entire *tekke* suddenly fell silent.

It was as if everyone knew before they were told who the young woman in the lilac-colored abiya was who got out of the carriage, they brought her to Sheikh Efendi without asking any questions.

As usual, Sheikh Efendi was sitting in the dark *zikr* hall with two burning candles next to him; he stood without moving in his long black robe, with his long hair that seemed blacker with the three-inch-wide stripe of gray that swept back from his forehead like silver water cascading over his shoulder, the eyes in his transparent, white face like distant black lights that gazed into the depths.

The girl opened her abiya.

She asked in a voice hoarse from excitement.

"Do you recognize me?"

The Sheikh nodded.

"Yes."

That morning Rukiye had a sudden and irresistible wish to ask the question she'd wanted to ask for years, and she went directly to the *tekke* without telling anyone.

"Why haven't you ever reached out to me?"

The Sheikh's face became paler, his eyes deepened.

"Did you go to all the trouble of coming here just to taunt the sinner with his sin?"

"No . . . I came here to get a close look at the famous Sheikh who helped thousands of people but wouldn't lift a finger for his own daughter, who can't touch his daughter, who didn't want to see his daughter."

"I'm not one of those people who needs to see in order to love, I'm capable of loving without seeing."

"But I'm not someone who's capable of knowing she's loved without seeing, Your Excellency the Sheikh."

The Sheikh smiled slightly. Rukiye thought she was being underestimated and gave him a petulant look.

"Why are you smiling?"

"It's the first time someone has addressed me as His Excellency the Sheikh in order to punish me."

"What would you want me to say?"

"I've forgotten how to want, my child, I've forgotten what it's like to want."

Even though the young girl sensed the sorrow and loneliness in his voice she acted as if she didn't.

"Is that because wanting made you be like other people?"

"No, perhaps it's because I couldn't find anyone to want anything of, perhaps I didn't realize that not wanting was also arrogant, that it was a sin."

"Why didn't you want to see me?"

"Do you think I've never seen you?"

"I've never seen you."

Sheikh Efendi lowered his head and looked at the prayer beads he was holding.

"Someone who has spent his life believing in an invisible power might not have thought that to be seen was so important."

"I'm your daughter, not the sheikh of a neighboring *tekke*, why did you treat me like a sheikh who doesn't care about seeing or being seen, didn't it ever occur to you that I needed to see you, did you think the gifts that were left in my room and the little miracles in my life were enough for me?"

"Weren't they?"

Her answer was brief, definite and angry.

"No!"

The Sheikh smiled the melancholy smile that suited him so well.

"A sheikh, a saint, even a prophet can confess his mistake, but it's very difficult for a father to do this, to admit he's wrong in front of his daughter, but if this is what you want, yes, I admit that I wronged you, I knew I would pay for this mistake, for this wrong, but I never thought it would be my daughter who made me pay for it."

"Am I supposed to be ashamed?"

"No, what have you done wrong? You grew up and asked what you had to ask, but you're asking someone who doesn't know the answer, I don't know why I behaved that way, it was just that I wasn't strong enough, sometimes a person just can't do what he's supposed to do."

There was a long silence; Rukiye felt as if she couldn't

contain herself any longer, if they talked a bit longer she would lose the anger at this man that she'd been nourishing for years; even though she wanted to be free of this anger and to love her father, she couldn't accept for it to happen so easily and so quickly.

"I should go."

Perhaps for the first time in his life, the Sheikh asked someone to stay a bit longer in a pleading tone.

"Please stay a bit longer."

"I'm afraid that if I stay longer it will be more painful for you."

"Do you think your leaving will ease my pain?"

"Will it ease your pain if I stay?"

"Perhaps . . ."

The Sheikh changed the subject in a fatherly tone as if they'd been living in the same house for years, as if it was natural they would each know what the other liked.

"We have some of the pomegranate sherbet you like, do you want some?"

Rukiye felt that the very thin armor of anger that shielded the desire to love, to like and be liked, was being torn and that Sheikh Efendi had an indispensable place in her life, from his expression, his voice, and his words, even during this brief conversation, and was strangely distressed to feel that the anger she'd nourished and fostered throughout her childhood and almost made a part of her personality was dissipating.

She also recognized the chaos of life and of emotions. As she later told Osman, "To see that no emotion existed on its own, that they were always experienced in tandem with other emotions, sometimes even contradictory emotions, always surprised me and made me curious." It happened like this that day as well, an array of strange, contradictory emotions surprised her and wandered through her tangled thoughts as she tried to understand her feelings; as she regretted being so weak as to surrender so quickly, she was worn out like a child trying to catch a chameleon that changed color from moment to moment, the pride of having a father she could admire and the rejuvenating manner in which the road to love was being paved for her mingled with a sense of rejuvenation because of the departure of a vindictive anger whose authenticity she'd always doubted.

The fear that her tense nerves would break abruptly from the sudden movement of so many accumulated feelings and she would suddenly burst into tears there made her want to run away at once and find a quiet place to order and weigh her thoughts and emotions.

She said, "Thank you," with difficulty.

"I have to go now."

She closed her abiya and left the hall without waiting for the Sheikh to respond.

She knew she would return to this place.

The Sheikh also knew that Rukiye would return, but "sometimes knowing is of no use." Even someone who believed in the existence of God without seeing God, who had no doubt in his heart about that, could have difficulty understanding his own child's visible feelings and actions, as the sheikh never said, though at least it occurred to him for a moment, "A child's emotions are more complex and incomprehensible than God's existence."

The Sheikh closed his eyes and began praying, it was as if he was beseeching God to help the terrifying faith in him to fill the strange and melancholy void within him; it was as if this feeling of emptiness grew with his increasing love and longing for Mehpare Hanım, whom he was unable to forget, and now for his daughter from her. It was as if his feelings enlarged the void within him, he struggled to fill this void with his beliefs. He felt a deep anguish and loneliness after Rukiye left; despite his strength, an anxiety typical in weak people gnawed at his mind, he was afraid that something would happen to the young girl who was in such a hurry to leave him and that the pain he'd seen in his daughter's eyes would lead her into folly; for a moment, yes, only for a moment, he thought of asking Rukiye to stay, but there was a power that dominated him and that was larger than his emotions and wishes, under the influence of this power that gave him both strength and weakness he lowered his head and continued fingering his prayer beads, all he did was whisper, "God help me, help your humble slave, grant him the power to carry his sins with propriety."

When Sheikh Efendi looked up he saw Hasan Efendi waiting by the door in his unpretentious manner to catch his attention, he took off his cloak and put on something that was part coat and part jacket, of the kind that villagers wear, and that was too tight for him; his biceps, shoulders, and belly bulged out of it, making him look like a gigantic Jerusalem artichoke; no one dared to wear cloaks because the soldiers arrested all the hodjas with cloaks and brought them to the police station. During the first days the hodjas went out into the streets wearing their green cloaks, believing this would give them more immunity, but they couldn't escape being pushed around and insulted by cadets, and all men of religion who were seen on the streets were treated almost like traitors.

Everyone in the city was afraid, and an irritable mood predominated, hodjas either fled or disguised themselves, women didn't even look out the window, some of the aristocrats retreated to their summer homes; all of the non-Muslims went to milleneries and bought top hats; because they believed that if they dressed like this they could move about without being bothered, Pera, in particular, was filled with Greeks who walked around in tall, crow-black hats like gigantic crows on their way to a funeral.

Hasan Efendi put his Sheikh at ease.

"I assigned a man to follow Rukiye Hanım's carriage, they'll see her safely home."

Then he told him the important news,

"They're going to send the Caliph into exile."

"When?"

"Either this evening or tomorrow."

Sheikh Efendi expressed neither sadness nor joy. All he said was, "Let's hope it's for the best." Hasan Efendi left the *tekke* and headed for Yıldız Palace to keep a close watch on what was happening. He couldn't believe that the soldiers would overthrow the Caliph. He could forgive them for detaining, insulting, or even pushing and beating men of religion on the street, but he couldn't countenance them touching the Caliph, they were breaking the pillar of Islam, that was ingratitude. How could a mortal touch the Caliph, how could they step on the shadow of God on earth? None of the intelligence he'd gathered so far had turned out to be false, he'd heard about what was happening in the four corners of the vast Ottoman Empire, he'd transmitted all of it to his Sheikh, but he prayed that what he'd heard that day was wrong.

He knew that His Excellency the sheikh had never forgiven the Sultan for putting a spy in his *tekke,* that he'd always been suspicious of him, that he'd helped the Committee because he loved Ragıp Bey, but it saddened Hasan Efendi that he was so silent about the Caliph's circumstances. Still, his only shelter was in fact the Sheikh's silence, his indifference; he accepted his Sheikh as his guide, whatever happened he wouldn't consider being disloyal even for a moment. Now Sheikh Efendi's calm and unruffled stance was a consolation for his helplessness, he thought this might not be as great a disaster as he'd imagined. He would have liked the Sheikh to be angry, to be opposed, but still this silence was more bracing for him, more comforting, than the Sheikh's anger.

In any event, this was the advantage of being attached to

one person, to accept without question that his wisdom and his feelings were right, when you saw that he didn't suffer when you did, that what hurt you didn't hurt him, you didn't doubt his feelings, you doubted your own suffering, your own pain, and secretly believed that it wasn't something to be so upset about; occasionally when he realized they didn't share the same thoughts and feelings, a part of him was always content with this disagreement even though he was inwardly hurt and offended, because as long as the Sheikh didn't share his pain, his own pain always seemed imperfect and meaningless, Hasan Efendi was freed from the poison of his own feelings by Sheikh Efendi's heavenly silence.

As he approached Yıldız Palace the streets became emptier and quieter, and he realized that the houses that had been bestowed upon the Sultan's relatives had long been abandoned by their owners. The servants leaned out the windows and bantered with each other, eunuchs wandered on the grass in the garden without caring that they were stepping on the flowers, a few soldiers walked mercilessly through the large flower beds.

Occasionally carriages laden with furniture and carrying well-dressed ladies and men in bowler hats rushed past toward Ortaköy, non-Muslims and wealthy Turks in disguise were escaping toward the Black Sea with everything they could carry.

When he neared the palace he realized that it too was abandoned. There were no guards at the gate, a group of civilians who were palace servants were talking among themselves, occasionally a man in tattered clothes carrying a small bundle went out the palace gate, a few eunuchs in expensive clothes paced back and forth in front of the palace, in the shooting range next to the palace an officer rode a horse as a his stable hand ran beside him; a squad of soldiers from the Movement Army sat on chairs in the garden of a mansion further uphill, there was a melancholy air of an abandoned fairground at a summer resort.

As the flags were lowered at sunset, he heard a few people shout, "Long live the Sultan," according to custom, but there was no other sign that a sultan lived there.

It was growing dark, but the lights in the palace had not been lit, the electricity and the water had been cut off as well.

Not long afterwards he heard the sound of the first units of soldiers coming to besiege the palace with cannon batteries; the commander of the palace guards had summoned the soldiers to protect the Sultan; they were supposedly there to protect him but everyone knew that from now on the Sultan was nothing more than a prisoner.

In the twilight, the Sultan sat in his hall, where a few oil lamps had been lit, looking out the window at the arrival of the soldiers, there was an unusual, tense calm about him, contrary to his usual mood. In the next room, hafizes were reciting the Koran, the Sultan couldn't bear the darkness and had ordered that the Koran be recited constantly.

"They're here, doctor," he said.

Reşit Pasha didn't understand.

"Who's here, Your Majesty?"

"Mahmut Şevket Pasha's men."

The Sultan stroked his beard as he watched the soldiers surround the palace.

"The others will be here soon."

Once again the Pasha didn't understand.

"Which others, Your Majesty?"

The water and the electricity had been cut, the stoves hadn't been lit, and the palace was cold and dark. The Sultan was wearing an overcoat that came down to his ankles, his pockets were bulging, and it was clear that he was carrying guns.

"The people who'll announce what they've decided, of

course, since they've captured our capital they'll make a decision about us as well."

"No slave has the right to make decisions about his
Caliph."

The Sultan must have thought the doctor's attempt to console him made his humiliating circumstances even more difficult to bear because he didn't answer. Instead, he complained
about how the servants were running away.

"There's no one around except for a few of our loyal men,
and we can't even get them a bowl of soup, the ladies in the
harem are shivering with cold; can you believe it, I can't go to
the harem for fear that they'll ask what's going on."

Reşit Pasha was shivering from the cold as well, and trembling because of the uncertainty of the situation.

The Sultan said, "How dark it is, this is the first time in
thirty-three years that there have been no lights on in my
house, doctor, in your opinion, what else is this darkness if not
a sign of what the future holds?"

He sensed that despite his gloomy talk, the Sultan still had
hope; he'd been governing the empire for thirty-three years,
he'd managed to survive many difficult situations, he'd been
the nation's only master, and even though his mind told him it
was over he still expected good news.

"Doctor, you've placed yourself in danger by coming here."

"I've been coming here for years, Your Majesty."

"But throughout the years you've been coming here the
lights were always on, the stoves were burning, they're not
today, it's dark and cold . . . "

The Sultan suddenly smiled irritably.

"I've never liked darkness or cold, now it's as if destiny is
revealing my future to me . . . "

The Sultan paused for a while and then continued.

"I've grown old, doctor, when someone faces the fears he
had in his youth, he asks himself why he was so frightened

then. Like everyone else, I owe God a life, I'm not hesitant about paying that debt, but I don't want my children and my family to be made to suffer."

Just as the Sultan was saying this, a clerk from the chamber came in and whispered something into the Sultan's ear.

When the doctor saw the Sultan, who had just told him he was no longer frightened, stand abruptly and go pale, he realized that the "others" had arrived. The Sultan put his slightly trembling hands in the pockets of his overcoat and stood in the middle of the hall with his feet apart. The doctor realized that the Sultan had forgotten about him, he shrank further into his armchair and became almost invisible in the darkness.

"Show them in," said the Sultan.

The Sultan, who had decided the destinies of others throughout his life, would now have his destiny decided by others and would experience the terrifying humiliation of having his destiny dictated by someone else; this old man whose commands had determined the life of the entire empire was preparing to learn how the slaves whose lives he'd changed with his orders had felt.

The doors of the hall opened, and by the shadowy light of the oil lamps they saw four people standing in the waiting room. Both the doctor and the Sultan tried to figure out who it was that had come and looked at the faces that seemed like wax masks in the play of the dim light.

The doctor recognized Arif Hikmet Pasha and the Albanian Esat Pasha, then when he looked a bit more carefully he saw the Armenian Member of Parliament Aram Efendi and the Jewish Member of Parliament from Salonika Emmanuel Karasu Efendi. At that moment he understood what verdict they had arrived at. Later he told Osman, "I could never decide whether the Committee's decision to send two non-Muslims to dethrone the Caliph was rooted in their sense of humor or in the severity of their desire for revenge, but I never believed that they could send a delegation like this to represent all of the peoples of the empire."

The door to the waiting room was opened all the way, the Sultan stood in the hall looking at them, and the delegation stood in the waiting room looking at him. The delegation didn't come in, the dark expression on the Sultan's face and the way he chewed at his moustache made it clear that he was becoming impatient and excited, but the delegation didn't move.

He'd probably told others the same thing he'd told the doctor many times, "If I go I'll take a few of them with me," these words must have reached the Committee's ears. They didn't come in because they feared that the Sultan, who they knew always carried a gun in his pocket, would pull the gun on them.

Once the Sultan took his hands out of his pockets and let his arms hang free, they came in and lined up in front of him. Esat Pasha, who had once been one of the Sultan's most loyal slaves, announced the decision with a degrading anger, as if he wanted to erase his own past.

"According to the fatwa that has been issued, the people discharge you."

As the doctor was preparing to stand because he feared the Sultan might faint because his face had gone ashen and he was tensing as he stood, the Sultan corrected Esat Pasha, who had just told him he was being fired as if he was an ordinary civil servant.

"I think you meant to say dethroned."

By saying this, the Sultan wanted to remind the man standing in front of him that a sultan couldn't be fired, he could only be dethroned.

Then he asked the main question he had on his mind.

"Have any other decisions been made about us?"

He wanted to know if he was going to be executed. He'd lived his entire life in fear of a day like this, what he'd feared all his life was happening, but the Sultan asked calmly as if he was inquiring about someone else's future, as if his soul, which could not countenance this humiliation and this fear, had departed, leaving his body behind like a toy without emotions.

"There is no other decision."

"Where will we reside?"

"You will be informed later."

"We feel Çırağan Palace is appropriate. We allowed our brother to reside there."

"You will be informed later."

The delegation left without saying anything more.

After the men had gone the Sultan didn't move. The doctor thought he would light a cigarette, but the Sultan didn't move, he just stood there ashen-faced in his long overcoat, looking at the door that had just closed, his eyes sunken in their sockets, there was no telling what he was thinking.

The doctor heard the Sultan speak in a murmur.

"The ladies have grown accustomed to this place, it will be difficult for them to move to Çırağan now, what will they allow us to take, I don't know, will the dampness there make my rheumatism worse?"

The doctor looked at the Sultan carefully, he accepted the situation, he was worried about moving as if he was a director of land registry who had been assigned to another city, he was worried about what he would take with him and how his new residence would impact his health. Much later, the doctor realized that people took refuge in small problems when they were faced with great pain.

Before the Sultan moved, the clerk returned and the doors were once again opened.

This time it was soldiers who'd come. The officers were sterner and more distant than the delegation that had arrived earlier.

"Parliament has found it suitable for you to live in Salonika. You and your family will get under way this evening."

The doctor saw the Sultan press his hand against his

stomach and that he seemed on the point of falling down. This verdict was worse than being dethroned. Dethroning him removed him from politics but being sent into exile meant he was being expelled from life, all his hopes were destroyed.

"I told the delegation that we could live in Çırağan Palace."

The soldiers told him in an almost hostile tone that this was not negotiable.

"The decision has been made, we have no authority to discuss this matter further, start preparing at once, you're to set out this evening."

"How can we set out this evening, at least give us time to get prepared."

"These are the orders, you will set out tonight."

The Sultan realized that if he kept talking, they'd send him by force.

The doctor saw him go out the door toward the harem like an old man whose shoulders had collapsed and hunched. An hour later his two wives, his children, and the few things he was allowed to take with him were put into carriages, which had been difficult to find, and he was sent to Salonika, where he'd once exiled officers who opposed him. Those who had once been powerless were now showing the Sultan what it was like to be powerless.

That night, toward midnight, a man Hikmet Bey didn't know knocked on his door and gave him a message his father had written.

In the library, in front of the fireplace, he opened and read the letter his father had written hastily in illegible handwriting.

"Hikmet,

His Majesty the Sultan is going into exile in Salonika this evening. I have decided to accompany him. I know you will think my decision strange, but I made it for two reasons. Everything I've ever had in my life was given to me by the Sultan, I can't escape the thought that if I leave him on such a difficult day my life will have turned out to be a fraud.

Second, and perhaps you will think this even stranger, but this man is the only true friend I've ever had. Even though His Majesty the Sultan would be right to see it as arrogant that I speak of him as my friend I still dare to be disrespectful and see him as the only friend I've ever had. I don't claim that he's a good man who no one understands or that they think he's bad because they don't know him, I know this is not the case, I've been with him long enough to have seen his bad sides, but I think that friendship is like love, sometimes you can love someone without having a good reason to do so.

I will be leaving the city with him this evening. I leave the mansion and the management of my estate to you. When needed, you can send the amount I need to the address I will give you later.

There are ups and downs in life, I'm almost an old man now, this is why I've decided to tell you something I would have preferred to tell you face to face. I am proud of everything you've done so far, even though I was opposed to it at the time, just as it seems right to me to depart with the Sultan today, it seems right to me that you opposed him. You behaved like an honest and honorable man in all of the circumstances you encountered. Perhaps one day we will also have the opportunity to talk face to face.

I entrust your mother to you, even though she sees herself as strong enough not to have to be entrusted to anyone, she is a child, she was always a child and always will be, and she's also getting older.

I will write you a longer letter once I'm settled in Salonika.
I kiss your eyes.
May God help us.
Your father,
Reşit."

18

The following morning Hikmet Bey left early to go to the palace even though he knew his father was no longer there, just like someone who has lost someone close in an accident and wants to see the place where the accident occurred, to see the last place the person he loved had been, a curiosity that was difficult to account for drew him to the palace.

Soldiers were patrolling the streets, the streets were quiet, the city was in an introverted mood. Just after the mutiny was put down, the soldiers closed the Kurdish porters up in their rooms, they bastinadoed the volunteer firemen who swaggered around with their fezzes perched on their foreheads, they punished anyone who might be capable of causing trouble before they had a chance to do anything. Perhaps law and order was being enforced more fully than it ever had been in Istanbul, but the way it was being enforced was more frightening and oppressive for the people than the disorder itself had been.

It was as if all the sounds that made a city a city had been silenced; there were no arguments, no shouting, no laughter, no shopkeepers bantering from one side of the street to the other, no women talking from their windows, no hodjas dispensing advice. Martial law had been declared and it was even forbidden to run in the streets, people avoided walking quickly lest they be thought to be running, everyone made a point of walking slowly. The city was so tense, if someone were to run, people would uncoil like springs and follow this person and flee the capital.

The joy and enthusiasm at the proclamation of constitutional monarchy was long gone.

Within a few days, Mahmut Şevket Pasha, who had come with the Movement Army to save Istanbul, gained control of the city and indeed of the government of the entire empire, got the new Sultan completely under his control, and started to run the country as if it was a military headquarters. He gave sharp, severe orders, and the atmosphere of oppression that he created with extraordinary courts, death sentences, gallows, and torture in police stations frightened even the Committee that had brought him to power.

The people had become accustomed to the Sultan's tyranny, which had grown slack due to disorder and corruption, but with this new and disciplined tyranny, they disappeared like a rabbit disappearing in a magician's hat, but the Pasha, whose head stood a bit tilted on his neck and seemed longer than it was because of the rectangular beard that came down to his chest, with his sunken eyes and thick eyebrows, who was not showy, but an ordinary and stern commander, didn't know the city or its people. This city, whose harbors smelled of saltpeter, whose waterfront mansions smelled of jasmine, whose forests smelled of pine, whose back streets smelled of mud, which had garbage dumps behind each of its beauties and in which you could find beauty behind every garbage dump, which looked different from each of its hills, which didn't even have a climate and where depending on the wind you could experience both summer and winter on the same day, would emerge as death from the hat in which it had disappeared like a rabbit, and a few years later the Pasha would pay for his magnificent authority and he would be riddled with holes inside a carriage. He would not have enough time to realize that in this city, being victorious was as dangerous as being defeated.

As Hikmet Bey approached Yıldız Palace along empty, restless streets, he saw a procession walking under the guard of a few soldiers, all of the palace servants who hadn't fled because they had nowhere to go, eunuchs, footmen, cooks, gardeners, doormen were being brought in for questioning; even the Ethiopians' faces were white with fear.

As he moved through the streets he grew even more worried about his father, he hoped to find someone he knew at the palace and find out what was going on. The palace gates were open, the soldiers had withdrawn after the Sultan departed. He passed through the large main gate that the most important people in the nation, pashas, ministers, officers, spies, the Shayk-al Islam had passed through with a shudder and moved up the garden path paved with snow-white pebbles and reached the large chamber building, which had green Venetian blinds on its right side.

He'd spent part of his youth in that building, now it was completely empty; the carpets were in disarray and armchairs and large vases had been knocked over. He walked down the corridors, looking into the rooms whose doors were open, and reached the large hall where the Sultan had learned he was being dethroned the previous evening; perhaps because of the cold, the great hall seemed to Hikmet Bey like a place no one had been for years. He'd been in this large hall twice before, but his knowledge of the palace ended where the hall ended, he'd never seen anything of the palace beyond that point. There was a small room behind the large hall; he walked timidly toward that room, waiting for someone to call out to him, to rebuke him, to tell him to turn back, this was a very small, dark room where the Sultan had rested occasionally, the little window looked onto the harem, on the round table in the middle of the room was a dark brown medicine bottle with a label that bore the vague instruction, "a glass to be taken occasionally," there was another bottle next to it that looked like a liquor bottle.

The door leading to the rear sections which contained the

little secrets and human details of an emperor's life that no one had even dared to be curious about was in the back of the room; the two strange bottles on the table gave the first confidential clues to a life that might turn out to be simpler than expected.

Until he went into that little room, Hikmet Bey had a respectable reason, he was looking for traces of his father, but when he passed through the door at the far end this reason would no longer be valid, he would wander through those sections with a greedy curiosity; this would be an unscrupulous act, like deceiving a child to learn about his father's life or using someone's illness to hear their most deeply kept secrets. He hesitated briefly between good manners and curiosity, then his curiosity won out over his ethical concerns, he wasn't strong enough to turn his back on the inside scoop of a glorious empire when it was right in front of him, even though his father wouldn't consider this an act befitting an honorable man, he went through the door in the back.

He entered a narrow, windowless corridor. His father had told him that because of his fear of being assassinated, the Sultan had constantly either had doors walled up or doors opened in walls, and had had the corridors built so narrow that only one person at a time could pass; from this corridor he reached the room where the Sultan had slept for the last time before leaving the palace.

This room was also small and dark, the only window looked onto the inner courtyard, a velvet sofa that was also used as a bed stood against the wall, there was a disordered cotton quilt and five or six colorful silk cushions on the sofa, a wrinkled white nightshirt had been thrown onto an armchair next to the bed, by the head of the bed there was a little shelf for the Sultan to put the book he read at night, his coffee cup, and perhaps his gun, behind a folding lacquered screen in a corner was an alcove with a washbowl and a pitcher, and a Japanese painting hung over the bed.

When Hikmet Brey saw this simple, indeed scruffy room that was behind the magnificent splendor of the empire, he saw that the decorative Hassa regiment, carriages pulled by horses with silk harnesses, treasure chests full of emeralds and diamonds, velvet pouches full of gold that were given as rewards, uniforms that glittered with medals, all the betrayals, murders, uprisings, and executions were meaningless, he had the impression that it was all nonsensical theater. Had it all been for this, to sleep in a room like that?

He started wandering through the abandoned palace with some distress, hoping to find something that showed the reality of the life they'd lived, the pain they'd suffered; the narrow corridors were crammed with old furniture; closets, bedside tables, consoles, and brass beds without mattresses were lined up next to each other, on top of them were dusty packages that had been tied with string, it was like a forgotten, murky, dust-smelling antique shop on a dead-end street; all of the rooms were too small for a palace, there were only two large halls in the entire palace.

In one room he saw more than a thousand neckbands, fezzes, neckties, vests, incredible amounts of letter paper, and cheap American-made gilded wristwatches that had been thrown onto the floor. Someone had rifled through and disarranged all of these things, the drawers of the consoles in the corridor had been left open, shirts, socks, and underwear hung out of them, all of them grown old before they were even worn.

In a room on the top floor there was a glass case full of gold-covered weapons, and there were two stiff, silk-lined waistcoats on the floor, the Sultan had probably worn these to stop bullets if he was attacked, some of the carpets on the floor were torn or had holes in them, none of the furniture matched, French, English, German, and Japanese-style furniture had been placed randomly side by side.

In one room he saw the edge of a belt studded with

emeralds and pearls hanging among the disordered furniture, this was the only thing of value he'd seen in the palace, strangely he saw no other jewelry, everything that was useless had been left lying around, anything of value that could be carried had disappeared overnight, had vanished like a breeze into unknown hands.

The thing he found most interesting was that there was a piano in almost every room, some rooms even had three of them. In any event, the Sultan's fondness for music had long been known. The soldiers who'd seized the palace had found mostly pianos and guns; there were thousands of loaded guns everywhere, in rooms, drawers, on coffee tables, in the baths, next to the heads of beds, all of them loaded and ready to be fired. For years the Sultan had been prepared for an attack, but he'd had to abandon his palace without using even one of them.

On the lower floor he encountered a fairly large room with guns hanging on the walls, these guns were not inlaid, it was clear that the Sultan used that hall for target practice. At the far end of the room there were three dummies that he used for target practice.

When Hikmet Bey took a close look at the dummies, his blood ran cold for a moment, the three dummies that the Sultan shot at bore an incredible resemblance to the Sultan himself; he'd had dummies that looked like him made or the people who had made them had made them to look like him and the Sultan spent a considerable amount of time shooting at dummies that looked like him. Did the Sultan not see the resemblance or did he derive a morbid pleasure from shooting at dummies that looked like him and watching them sway and fall to the floor?

Perhaps for the first time, Hikmet Bey was curious about this man who was fond of music, carpentry, and guns and who shot at dummies of himself; what was the man they called

Sultan like, how did he live in these bizarre, dingy, unkempt rooms, in some of which the paint was peeling from the window frames in places, what did it feel like for him to live in a palace that was like a covered bazaar? He was surprised by the friendship between this man and his father. He himself could never have been friends with someone who lived in a place like this.

Didn't it bother his father that the Sultan he called his only friend had such a bizarre, ugly, even shabby life or did it give him secret pleasure to compare it with his own mansion, with its carefully chosen furniture, well-illuminated rooms that were decorated in style, uplifting halls, well-maintained walls adorned with the most distinguished works of master calligraphers, his closets full of good clothes made by the best tailors, and his life, which was the opposite of the Sultan's life and his palace, was this what made it possible for him to be friends with a man who had the power to destroy him at any moment and spend years by his side without being bothered by it? Did that palace give his father a secret, even devious sense of superiority, did the way the Sultan lived like an ignorant peasant with no taste even though he was an emperor from a six-hundred-year-old dynasty make it possible for Reşit Pasha to be so close to the Sultan?

As he continued to wander around, his mind full of questions about the empire, the Sultan, and his father, he came across a dark, damp-smelling bath next to the carpentry workshop where the Sultan made various pieces of furniture; it was like an old magician's alchemy laboratory, the carved marble shelves were full of bottles of healing water that nourished the hair, medicinal liquids that rejuvenated the skin, and creams that prevented wrinkles.

As he was walking down the corridor that led to the back garden, he was startled by shouts of "Long live the Sultan," from behind a door. He was both surprised and startled that there were people crazy enough to shout like this in the palace that day, he slowly opened the door from behind which the shouting was coming, in this foul-smelling room, where feathers of all colors floated in the air, thirty to forty parrots flapped their wings in panic, bumping into each other, flying in and out of cages whose doors had been left open and repeating the sentence they'd memorized, and which was now a serious crime, as they landed. Someone had put all these parrots in this room and left them there, the hungry animals pecked at each other and asked for help and food by repeating the only sentence they knew.

He recoiled in horror at the misery of the hungry parrots and closed the door immediately.

As he carefully picked his way among drawers that had been thrown on the floor, fallen underwear, closets that had been knocked over, he heard a loud, distant noise that sounded like moaning and he made his way toward it. There was a balcony that looked out over the inner courtyard, it was dark down below, there was a crowd packed so closely together they were almost a single being, kneeling down and moaning. When his eyes grew accustomed to the darkness, he realized these were hungry concubines in the cold palace where the electricity had been cut off; like the parrots, they too waited in hunger and fear, there was no one to give them food and no food to be given; the new government had contacted the Circassian villages and asked them to come get their daughters in the harem. After having spent years in the harem, these girls would return to the mountain villages and dusty towns where their families lived. They moaned as they waited in fear for their new lives.

When he found a door and rushed outside, he felt as if he'd fled a dark, smoky room, the old furniture that had been tossed about, the untidy drawers, beds without mattresses, tattered carpets in the gloomy corridors filled his lungs like muddy water. He took a deep breath. The white pebbles on the garden path seemed so shiny and real, he instinctively picked up a few pebbles just to see if anything was real and concrete and squeezed them in his palm, their cold solidity gave him a sense of security, indeed even of joy, after all the strange things he'd seen. When he told Osman about that moment years later, it was as if he was still surprised. "Which one was reality, the splendor and pomp of the empire, the sultanate, and those who killed each other for the sultanate or those narrow corridors and old furniture that darkened the soul, which face of life is real, or do we have to accept that everything we call fake is in fact a part of reality, if the fake is an essential part of reality, why do we divide reality into the real and the fake?" At this point as he was speaking he stopped and thought for a moment, then said, "Do you know, this worn-out question, 'what is life,' that has become so boring and that no one asks for fear of being mocked, it is that, I've always admired people who can remain calm at the moment we discover there is still no answer to this question, that we threw it away without finding an answer to it and that the question is still meaningful and we feel that we desperately need an answer to this question, I have to admit I was unable to become one of those people, life terrified me, I was always surprised, I always felt my helplessness, even questions about the lives of others became a personal matter for me, I couldn't escape them. I asked myself so many times who in fact that Sultan was, the man who'd sent thousands of people into exile and who shot at dummies that looked like him; in which face of that palace did my father's best friend live, was it the splendid side or the miserable side?"

He started walking down through the garden, past the flower beds that had been trampled the night before, the large trees, gazebos, small streams, there was not another person to be seen, even though the garden had been damaged by the coarseness of those who had captured the palace, it still had the splendor befitting an imperial palace garden. The sun warmed Hikmet Bey's neck, informing him it would be a nice, bright spring day and helping him forget what he'd just experienced; just then he came across the wrecked chicken coops, these had been the cages where the peacocks were kept, they were empty, the wires had been bent, the cages that had been full of animals of all colors were now empty.

A zebra emerged from the trees, Hikmet Bey had seen one of these striped creatures at the Paris zoo once when he was a child, but he was surprised to suddenly see one wandering free in the garden; when the animal noticed Hikmet Bey it turned and ran and disappeared into the trees.

A bit further along he noticed something white that looked like a large rock, when he approached it he saw that it was a dead white pig, there was a red hole in its forehead that looked like a third eye, blood flowed from its small ears and dried on the grass.

Someone had shot that pig in the forehead.

Hikmet Bey could no longer walk, he turned back and ran out of the garden. Throughout his life he'd seen so many people die, so many people being killed, but the killing of that pig frightened him more than all those murders and deaths; he felt as if he was surrounded on all sides by a low savagery that was crippled by blind rage and was seized by the feeling that he was being pushed out of this life, out of this country.

When he returned home in a panic and went to the library as if to seek shelter, he found Dilevser, who had no idea about life or what was going on outside, she was leafing through the books with her innocent white fingers. Hikmet Bey had told her she could use his library, and the young girl had begun to spend most of her time in that library.

When the young girl looked at Hikmet Bey as he came in, she sensed there was something wrong about the state he was in.

"Are you all right?"

"I'm fine," said Hikmet Bey.

He realized he was still squeezing the pebbles in his hand and put them in his pocket with concealed embarrassment without allowing the girl to notice, there were ragged, red marks on the insides of his fingers.

"I went to the palace this morning . . . "

The girl waited in silence for Hikmet Bey to continue.

Hikmet Bey realized he wasn't going to be able to tell the girl what he'd seen and how it had made him feel and stopped talking.

He said, "Let's have tea."

He ordered tea and when it came, while Dilevser pretended she didn't notice and turned her head away, he added cognac to his tea and asked the girl if she would like some.

Dilevser smiled and nodded her head.

"How do you manage it," asked Hikmet Bey, "how can you carry on with your life without having any interest at all in the lives of others, without ever touching those lives?"

"I don't know, perhaps people don't seem very relevant to me."

"People don't seem relevant to you, but I notice that you always prefer books that are about people."

Dilevser paused, she thought about Hikmet Bey's question and smiled.

"Yes, I probably expressed it wrong. I am interested in people, but I can only understand people in novels, I can't say I understand people in real life."

It was only after he'd asked the question that Hikmet Bey realized that he'd asked it in a reproachful manner.

"Why don't you ever try to understand them?"

Dilevser came and sat in one of the armchairs, holding a book in the fingers that seemed so innocent to Hikmet Bey.

"I don't think I'll be able to understand. When you asked now, I thought about it, I think I like someone to explain people to me, when someone explains I can see more clearly, I can understand the reason for any behavior, but it's not like that when you're living it."

Hikmet Bey didn't hesitate to say something that revealed his feelings, probably because of the courage that came from the shock he'd experienced that morning.

"I would like someone to explain you to me."

"I don't think there's anything about me that's worth explaining."

Dilevser had a kind of terrifying, self-abnegating modesty, it seemed impossible for anyone to get past it and reach the girl, she concealed herself behind a kind of modesty that surprised people, she put off anyone who wanted to learn what was behind this modesty by saying, "There's nothing there." Hikmet Bey couldn't understand why the girl behaved like this, why she erected a castle between herself and life with literature, why she concealed herself, why she never revealed her feelings, why she didn't have a connection with anyone, he thought the reason was hidden in an old wound that no one would ever talk about.

He stood and walked toward the girl.

"That's what you think," he said, "if I were a literary man you'd be the first person I'd want to explain; you're full of mystery, you don't give anyone the chance to discover even the smallest clue about you, it's impossible to find out what your feelings are, you're like shiny glass, it's as if there's nothing hidden, but whoever looks through the glass is faced with darkness, an impenetrable secret."

Dilevser shook her head.

"If only that were the case, but I'm afraid you consider nothingness to be a secret."

In the course of his life, Hikmet Bey had encountered all kinds of women, those who were very beautiful, volatile women who stirred up jealousy, sardonic women who used their intelligence like a merciless weapon, those who brought playing with men to the level of a pleasure-inducing addiction, coquettes who tried to render themselves unapproachable to increase their value, aristocratic women who shielded themselves behind an unsurmountable fence of nobility; with none of them had he felt the helplessness and disparagement he felt in the face of this girl's simplicity. Dilevser did nothing to make herself attractive, she said nothing to attract a man's attention. Hikmet Bey sensed that not making herself attractive was her way of telling people that she didn't find them attractive. When Dilevser rejected her own attractiveness she was in fact rejecting Hikmet Bey's attractiveness, and this added an irresistible attraction and allure for him.

Perhaps she was right, perhaps beyond that simplicity there was a void that came from lack of experience, a nothingness created by immature feelings, but Hikmet Bey could not endure how debasing it was that she made no effort to conceal this, that she ignored the person she was with.

It wasn't that there was a lovelessness in the way she treated Hikmet Bey, it wasn't indifference; she came to his library every day, leafed through his books, spoke about novels, when Hikmet Bey was disquieted or anxious or something was bothering him, she was interested in his concerns, listened to what he said, she shared his sadness, when he made a joke she laughed in a way that made him incredibly happy, but she never acted like a woman when she did these things. When they talked there was none of the exciting warmth, the unnamed but agreeable animallike presence, that occurs between a man and a woman. The only climate in which this warmth could exist was created by the rugged sea cliffs and shadowy nooks of the feminine soul, but Dilevser stubbornly remained straight and open; Hikmet Bey was afraid that their relationship would turn into an unhappy friendship.

He knew now that he wasn't going to be able to get past this girl, as long as this girl didn't accept his existence he would not feel that he existed with another woman in another place, that he was alive. This girl's innocence made him want to catch it, tear it apart, possess it, but even as he struggled to do so he became a prisoner of that innocence; it was easy to catch sinfulness, but innocence was too soft and indistinct to be captured. Later when Mihrişah Sultan learned about this and made fun of her son, "You're a fool, Hikmet," she said, "what man who knows himself wouldn't flee when he saw innocence."

"Dilevser, why are you so insistent on acting as if you're nothing, doesn't it make people who value you a bunch of nothings?"

It seemed to Hikmet Bey as if a small, playful light flashed for a moment in the girl's eyes. She immediately grasped what Hikmet Bey wanted to say and replied with a melancholy smile, "Sorry, I've never thought that."

In any case, this was what surprised Hikmet Bey, that Dilevser's mind had a quickness and agility that was out of step with the weight of her innocence, she immediately grasped even the most complex subjects that she'd never heard of, she immediately found the hidden meanings concealed in the very depths of the most complex sentences, but she answered them bluntly and without insinuation. When all of the words he uttered, words that seemed to carry all of the heaviness of life and that could scatter at any moment, plays on words that could mean almost anything, touched her fine-boned, innocent face, her dovelike eyes, her hands, whose index fingers were slightly splayed, they became so plain it felt as if life, with all its sounds, noises, colors, fights, loves had departed, leaving him alone in the midst of desolation, and he believed that in order for the accustomed sounds to be restored to life, Dilevser had to speak, had to participate in life.

She rejected life and people in such a calm, strong manner

it seemed to Hikmet Bey as if she was lying completely still on the bottom of a glittering lake, looking out of the water without ever taking a breath; you could pass the lake without even noticing Dilevser was there, indeed many people continued on their way without ever noticing her, but once he'd seen her there, lying at the bottom of the lake with her innocent eyes wide open, to move on, that is, it was impossible for him to move on.

Moreover, despite her appearance of clarity and simplicity, her soul was full of conflicts that were reflected in her actions; she had a pale but healthy face; she was innocent, but she was intelligent enough to give the impression that she was using this innocence as a means of entertainment; she wasn't interested in people but she talked about characters in novels as if they were real people and shared their feelings; she seemed indifferent to passion, yet she was passionate about literature; she didn't respond to what was going on, but she wept for Anna Karenina; she seemed indifferent to the blessings of life, but she was fond of clothes and food, she always dressed elegantly, she carefully chose dishes and asked her mother to have them prepared, but if these dishes were even slightly off she would complain that the cook was getting worse and worse lately.

As Hikmet Bey told Osman, "Innocence is a mystery, my good man."

He was soon wrapped in this mystery like a kitten wrapped in yarn while playing with a ball of wool, he was unable to unravel himself, to cut the strings, to escape.

But what unnerved Hikmet Bey most was her brief answers and long silences; this was like the games women with a lot of experience played to inflame men more, to make them talk more, this girl made this play naturally without even knowing the game; her brief answers and long silences left a man in such a large and empty space, the man felt obliged to fill this space with his own words; as there were no words that could fill a woman's silence he was dragged as if by a current toward the extreme, toward that which shouldn't be said, sometimes he even said things he didn't feel, made promises he didn't want to make.

When he spoke to Dilevser, he struggled with himself, put up an incredible fight, to not be drawn into that current, to not cross the line and say what should remain unsaid, to not fill the long silences with his words.

That's what happened this time as well; when she said, "Sorry, I've never thought that," and silenced Hikmet Bey, he wanted to walk toward the young girl and say, "I love you," to at least rouse her and force her to join the conversation, just so they would have something to talk about, he might even have said it if he wasn't afraid of a scandal or an embarrassing situation, but he bit his lip and remained quiet.

Even though he was so willing to say these words, he didn't in fact know whether or not he loved Dilevser. If this young girl were to open her soul to him, tell him she loved him, if she talked, told him her feelings, he might show no interest, might turn his back and leave. The girl's body didn't arouse in him a desire to make love, a passion, a fiery lust, but strangely it created a desire to embrace her. A soft embrace accepting that Hikmet Bey and the world existed was perhaps the greatest gift he expected from Dilevser, still, he also recognized that he wanted this soft embrace more passionately than he wanted all other types of lustful lovemaking.

A desire that was almost completely separated from the body and the skin, that was freed from the intense, magnetic, but confined passion of the flesh, that spread and grew in a restless manner without encountering any obstacles, it even surpassed Dilevser, it never encountered the opportunity to stop, to be satisfied, to calm itself down, it diffused itself into every particle of Hikmet Bey's soul like a cloud, a fog, like incense, its smell seeped into every part of his soul without giving his body any chance to give any comfort or satisfaction to the poor soul that had surrendered itself to this desire; it was as if even if he did embrace Dilevser, this embrace would not ease the longing he had in him to embrace her.

The April sun, fragmented as it struck the leaves of the trees in the garden, filtered through the large windows and spread through the room like shimmering yellow silk with black, leaf-shaped designs on it; the reddish brown of the cognac in the balloon glass was thinned and clarified by this yellow light's brazen assault and sat in Hikmet Bey's palm like fiery light that smelled of dried apricots.

Despite the tension Hikmet Bey felt, in this warm and well-lit room there was a somewhat acrid peace, a saddening calm that tasted like cognac; he sipped his cognac as if it was burning light, enjoyed feeling the warmth spread to his nasal cavity and his body.

In a strange and incomprehensible way, despite the tormenting questions it led to, Dilevser's presence intensified the peace, the soft warmth, and the light that also brought inner warmth to this room, it turned them all into real and concrete pieces of happiness. Either because he truly felt this at that moment or because he couldn't resist the urge to break the silence in a way that would get Dilevser's attention, Hikmet Bey said, "I believe in the existence of happiness." Then, waiting for the young girl's answer like a curious child, he added:

"But I suppose you don't believe in it?"

Suddenly a very meek and friendly smile that Hikmet Bey had never seen before appeared on her face.

"Yes, I do . . . I can even confess to you that I'm curious about that feeling, if one day I'm happy, will I know that I am?"

That little word, "confess," which might seem insignificant to someone else at another time, echoed in Hikmet Bey's ears, it was as if, after a long wait, the heavy, rusty iron gate behind which lay vast dream gardens had finally opened slightly, it was the acknowledgement of closeness and sharing that he'd awaited so long.

When he heard the word "confess" he really felt the happiness to which he'd just referred to in a somewhat forced manner. He stood and paced with a joy he couldn't resist; without being sure if this had come to mind at that moment or if he'd read it somewhere, he said:

"Whatever it is for nature to make diamonds from fossils, dried branches, and leftover bones, happiness is the same for people, to create something valuable from things that have no value, to create priceless jewelry from the sweepings of our souls. It's difficult and painstaking work, just as we can't find diamonds in every terrain, we might not find happiness in each person's soul . . . Still, even though it is rare, happiness does exist, just as diamonds exist."

With a tender smile, Dilevser watched this grown-up man, who to her seemed quite old, stroll around the room cheerfully like a little colt, drinking cognac from his glass from time to time. She was not impressed by the strange and almost laughable words Hikmet Bey was uttering in such a serious manner, but she was impressed by something else when she saw how childish and bewildered the man was, in his presence she felt like an adult, an intelligent woman, at that moment, for the first time, she glimpsed womanhood, from which she'd always felt distant, for the first time she looked at a man as a woman. While Hikmet Bey was busy trying to impress the young girl with his intelligent words, what opened a space, albeit a small one, for him in Dilevser's heart was how silly he looked.

Dilevser watched Hikmet Bey pace about the room and, with a gratitude and tenderness she couldn't fully comprehend, for a moment it occurred to her to go up to Hikmet Bey, hold his face between her hands, and say, "Stop for a moment, stop, calm down." At that moment she didn't understand what a dangerous feeling that urge was, but the young girl was learning to love without realizing that she was doing so.

Osman, who over time became more disrespectful and scornful toward his dead, stood before Hikmet Bey, of whom Mihrişah Sultan had said, "He's the most innocent of the innocent," and imitating his voice and manner when he'd said, "Innocence is a mystery, my good man," said, "Women are a mystery, my good man," then added with the snobbish pedantry that came from knowing both the past and the future of the dead, "What man can know that he is capable of impressing women with his silliness and weakness, my good man?"

Dilevser experienced the dizziness of the inwardly joyful but at the same time alarming lightheadedness that comes from the sudden breaking out of emotions that change form, from unnamed moods that are alien even to those who experience them, she didn't know what to do and how to control the warmth that was spreading through her, and, as women usually do when they first feel love, she wanted to run away at once, to be alone and think.

She stood hurriedly.

"If you'll excuse me, I have to go now."

And then she added immediately:

"I'll come back later, if that won't be an imposition."

"Please, Dilevser, what imposition . . . You've made this library rejoice, I haven't been interested in it for some time, I noticed the books again when you arrived."

"With your permission, I'd like to take this book with me."

When she saw Hikmet Bey looking at the book she explained:

"*The Demons* by Dostoevsky, I found a German translation here."

Hikmet Bey smiled.

"You've found a book appropriate for the frenzy our society is in, read what he has to say about insanity. Though I don't know if this book can tell you more about insanity than what's been going on in this city lately, but read it anyway, we can talk about it later if you like."

Hikmet Bey too, like Dilevser, wanted to be alone for a time; he knew that he couldn't feel more joy than he'd already felt that day, and he didn't want the young girl to cast a shadow on his joy by saying anything inappropriate.

After Dilevser left he continued pacing the room with the same enthusiasm, he whistled a French *chanson*, then looked out at the garden, at the newly sprouting leaves whose veins were swelling under the whiteish blue of the sky, the trees coming to life, the swelling buds that were reminiscent of nipples; he put his glass down on the coffee table and felt a deep and sudden weariness that stood in contrast to the cheery scenery he was looking at.

He realized how pathetic it was to be so delighted by a single word uttered by a young girl; in the same exaggerated manner in which he'd just experienced this joy, he felt suddenly emptied of thoughts and feelings; at that moment he wanted neither Dilevser nor anyone else, he didn't long for anyone, and this made him even more melancholy. As he thought about what a pathetic man he was, he remembered how his father had referred to him in his letter, as "an honorable man," these words now seemed like mockery, dark purple circles that looked like pansies appeared around his eyes.

His handsome face flushed with shame.

He stood abruptly, walked as rigidly and decisively as a landowner or a master, opened the heavy wooden door, and went into the hallway that was paved with unpolished diamond-shaped black and white stones and in the corners of which Louis Quinze chairs had been placed, looked around, and found what he sought leaning against the wall just outside the door he'd emerged from. Hediye, in a lilac-colored dress that swathed her body in such a way as to reveal her tall, thin figure and full breasts and that was decorated with small buttons from her neck to her waist and that had shiny lilac-colored flower designs, with her glistening hair gathered behind her neck, looked at Hikmet Bey with a sulking expression.

Hikmet Bey didn't even notice her expression, he just strode toward the stairs and said, "Come."

Without rushing, but also taking care not to fall too far behind Hikmet Bey, she climbed the stairs in her pointed, high-heeled slippers, which left her pink heels uncovered, as if she was gliding, after she entered the bedroom she closed the door slowly and, without looking up, started to unbutton her satin-covered, lilac-colored buttons one by one; she knew this would make Hikmet Bey suffer, and she did it every time with the sense that she was taking feminine revenge.

That day Hikmet Bey couldn't show his usual patience, he grabbed the collar of the dress and when he pulled it almost angrily, the small buttons fell with a tiny pattering and scattered about the room like lilacs; the dress fell to her feet in elegant folds, the girl freed herself from the folds of the dress around her feet as if she was stepping out of water and pushed the dress aside with her toes.

Because she was obeying Hikmet Bey's wishes and wore nothing under her dress, her body, which Hikmet Bey had likened to Carrara marble, appeared like a snow-white fountain gushing from the ground in the bronze, phosphorescent light that filtered through the closed curtains.

Hikmet Bey also pulled off his own clothes as if he was fighting, ripping and tearing at them, grabbed the girl by the wrist, and roughly pulled her into the bed.

He made love hurriedly, greedily, sorrowfully, as if there was someone he was pursuing and trying to capture, he bit the young girl's neck and breasts, hurting her, he mauled the magnificent body in his bed heedlessly without feeling any desire, without even hoping to feel pleasure.

She was still wearing her high-heeled slippers, as Hikmet Bey held her legs behind her knees, they rose and waved like wildflowers on a windy hill every time he moved.

Hediye didn't close her eyes as she did everything that he asked of her, she looked directly at Hikmet Bey's face, but Hikmet Bey, who treated the young girl as if she was part of the bed, a nightgown, a bedcover, a soft quilt, wasn't even aware of the eyes watching him.

After a time Hediye eased Hikmet Bey with her body as she surrendered tamely like white bubbles riding the waves, with soft touches and light kisses; they slowed down, when they started to make love again, maneuvering quietly and carefully like a ship approaching a harbor, Hikmet Bey was now aware of the woman he was with, of her body and her beauty, achieved the satisfaction of his full and patient lust, sensed the dark and spicy smell of pleasure.

The world closed them in like a door, they were alone together in a private darkness that enveloped them; like two lovers, they made love playfully, kissed at length, whispered dirty words to nourish each other's lust.

Then they moved on to games that Hikmet Bey never told anyone about, not even Osman, and which Hediye knew Hikmet Bey could play only with her, that she was certain the man she loved could only share with her, and which she therefore anticipated every time with desire and longing.

It was possible to see that Hikmet Bey, whose mother had referred to him as "the most innocent of the innocent," played games like this to forget his melancholic soul, searching in the deepest darkness into which he could dive, but Osman, who continued to believe in Hikmet Bey's innocence despite the strange lovemaking he was engaged in, thought that these games had been discovered in order to overcome the flames of lust that Mehpare Hanım had left behind, to extinguish that fire with another fire, to go beyond the unforgettable pleasures he'd experienced with his former wife and to find virgin fields of lust that belonged to him alone.

But neither was he certain about these ideas, once when he was gossiping about Hikmet Bey with Mehpare Hanım, Osman said, "Perhaps he was simply a randy and amoral man," and Mehpare Hanım, whose beauty even death had not been able to erase, smiled coquettishly to show that she agreed. Once, too, not bothering to rein in his recklessness, Osman said about Hikmet Bey that "perhaps he was secretly insane," but the other dead showed that they disagreed by turning and giving him strange looks; nevertheless, Osman always entertained suspicions of Hikmet Bey's insanity, the symptoms of which emerged under very special circumstances.

In a way that proved Osman right, the games he played in bed with Hediye, games it was impossible for him to speak of, constituted something similar to insanity. They left behind the reality of the world and time through whispers, acts, and touches, in bed they did what they could never do in real life, that it would never occur to them to do, and within the part of life and time that they fit into bed they tore apart and destroyed the most sacred taboos and created a dark home in which they could lose themselves completely.

There wasn't a single reality that dared follow them wherever they went; it was a long undressing full of delights, they began with their clothes, then they shed the realities of daily life, time, their identities, personalities, memories, morals, and finally their most sacred values, burned them all, and passed to another world without leaving any trace. The world into which they passed was so dark and unmarked, now even they themselves couldn't catch them, they shed themselves and everyone else, their completely liberated bodies were buried in the lust devil's paradise that smelled of human flesh, incense, and amber, they wandered recklessly on the edge of insanity, kissing at length, biting savagely, and touching frantically.

For Hikmet Bey, lovemaking was an uprising, an insurrection, a revolution that completely burned down this universe and established its own, that turned life upside down like an ailanthus, in which the counterfeit was real and the real was counterfeit, in which he was purified, in which he was freed from all his sins in order to commit new sins; compared with the seduction of forming a new universe, all other sins, even the worst sins, seemed insignificant to him when he made love, he didn't complain about sinking into and emerging from these sins, on the contrary, he derived a godlike pleasure from this devil worship that only the master of a universe could experience, a satisfaction that spread to every particle of his being.

At the end of an extraordinary adventure in which his body and soul were turned upside down, whatever he shed while making love could be replaced quickly, he returned to his former self, regained his sense of sin and shame, the morality of respect for the sacred; this was what made him so innocent, or "insane" according to Osman, that he could emerge from the most frightful sins without even a scratch on his soul, that he inhabited two different universes and had two different souls without damaging himself.

A sane person couldn't experience this, or if he did, there would be a wound in his depths from which he could never recover, but Hikmet Bey had no such wound; the wounds he did have were not the result of his own actions but of the actions of others.

When they returned wearily to life, breathing irregularly, and once again perceived their surroundings, the world, life, the light coming in through the window faded, that phosphorescent light was replaced by a broken redness.

Hikmet Bey embraced Hediye gratefully and lovingly

whispered the sentence he uttered each time they finished making love, and which he believed sincerely.

"Hediye, you're the only truth I have."

Even though Hediye was only allowed to be pampered in bed, she snuggled against Hikmet Bey without getting pampered, feeling the deep love she felt for her master, perhaps her reward was these loving embraces and caresses after lovemaking rather than the maddening lovemaking itself; at those moments she could suppress, even if only a little, the resentment that of late had become part of her and that she was never allowed to express, she could forget, briefly, the wounds of her grave defeat in a struggle in which she didn't have the right to make any moves.

Much later, when Hikmet Bey was experiencing the deep regret of not having considered that Hediye also had feelings, of not having been interested in her feelings, of not noticing the horrible desperation that grew daily like a pitch-black pearl in the woman next to him, he said to Osman, "Perhaps the truest love is the love of a slave."

This small woman, who in dark cellars, slave markets, and harem rooms had lost her pride, identity, personality, desires, the right to be pampered, the desire to see the reflection of her existence on life, who had been taught through the curses, threats, and insults of slave merchants, odalisques, and eunuchs how to be oppressed, how not to exist, how not to be recognized, who had learned that not doing what she wanted but doing what she was told was a virtue; ever since Dilevser had started visiting the mansion, she had suffered only because the man she loved had become distant from her, and felt it soon might be possible that he would never touch her again, but she didn't make it a matter of pride, never carried the shadow of being defeated, abandoned, seeing someone else chosen instead of her, that combined with the suffering of love, she carried this terrible sorrow alone and in silence.

Apart from the resentment in her eyes, which no one condescended to see, no sign of her pain was reflected to other people; if someone were to look into her eyes carefully, they would see that the silent loneliness and resentment was heavier and more traumatic than any of the other pains that had been spoken of.

She was from the class of people for whom suffering could even be considered insolence, she was a concubine, a slave, but she still could have found a comrade, a friend with whom to share the loneliness that deepened with her suffering, to console her and lighten the burden of her pain; there were a lot of people who were prepared to listen to her, if for no other reason than to have something to gossip about, but she possessed an inborn nobility that even the slave markets, the eunuchs who beat her couldn't take away, couldn't erase from her soul.

She found any kind of complaining unbecoming, sometimes when she felt very suffocated, when her loneliness and hopelessness became too heavy to carry, she withdrew to her room without letting anyone notice, leaned against the window, and looked out, at the garden, the trees, the coolness of the window on her forehead allowed her to forget her thoughts for a few minutes, and she accepted this brief moment without any thoughts as a gift from God; she couldn't even seek consolation, her greatest wish was to have a little time, just a few minutes, without thinking, because she was unable to free herself from her thoughts, her sorrow even haunted her dreams, she woke several times during the night, always with the same pain, and with the thought that Hikmet Bey loved that girl.

Her love for Hikmet Bey was the only thing she had in life; it wasn't that Hikmet Bey loved another woman that made her so desolate, but that another woman coming to this house could result in her being sent away, what made her so sad was the horror of knowing she would lose forever the only thing she possessed.

They had taken everything from her, they'd left her almost nothing that belonged to her, she'd given it all up without too much sadness, now she was preparing herself to give Hikmet Bey up, she felt this was inevitable; she wouldn't resist, but she wouldn't give up her pain, perhaps for the first time she would keep something that belonged to her, that pain; because she knew that this pain would be the only memory of Hikmet Bey that would remain with her.

She also learned the degree to which pain isolated a person.

She couldn't bear seeing anyone, she looked at people with a distant gaze, as if she was looking at a wall, she didn't take part in any conversation; everyone except Hikmet Bey distressed her soul, their existence disturbed her; she would wait silently outside the library for Hikmet Bey to come home, or if he was at home, to emerge from the library.

She felt something akin to happiness when Hikmet Bey embraced her after making love, she nestled against him gently for fear of interrupting these moments, she didn't even move as she wished he would utter that magical sentence.

"Hediye, you are the only truth in my life."

Sometimes she dreamed this was true, even though she knew she was deceiving herself when she thought that, at those times a smile appeared on her beautiful face, then that smile disappeared and the resentment returned to her eyes, and remained there.

As it grew dark, Hikmet Bey realized he was hungry, he hadn't eaten lunch.

Hediye wouldn't let anyone else serve him, she rushed downstairs, prepared a tray under the mocking gazes of the servants, and brought it up to him.

Hikmet Bey had already dressed, Hediye knew that for Hikmet Bey to have dressed was a sign that their relationship had turned into something else, she felt her heart sink, but the expression on her face didn't change. Even for Hikmet Bey to have his meal in the bedroom with her was something she was grateful for.

She placed the tray on the round table in the corner, pulled up a chair for Hikmet Bey, lit the lamps, and retreated into a corner.

Hikmet Bey sat hurriedly and started to eat greedily, praising the taste of the food. With the merciless selfishness of a master, he didn't even notice that Hediye wasn't eating, as his stomach became full, his mind drifted to other thoughts and there was a faraway look in his eyes.

At one point, though it wasn't clear whether he was speaking to himself or to Hediye, he said, "They even shot the pigs." Then he added:

"Is it time to leave this place?"

Hediye didn't understand the part about pigs, but "leaving this place" made her heart jump, to leave this place, to be far from that ugly duck who came and leafed through the books every day, to move to other lands, was such a magnificent dream, but it was just a dream, she realized this immediately after she experienced that little wave of joy. But still, this didn't stop her from thinking about how nice this would be, from adding this to the dreams she had when she was alone.

19

Ragıp Bey counted how many of them there were with an indifferent curiosity; he was a bit startled when he saw the first one, but after the tenth he was hardly aware of what he was counting, when he passed the last one in Eminönü, he'd counted forty-seven of them; what he was counting was executed mutineers hanging from gallows that had been erected from Sultanahmet to Eminönü, all in white shrouds, their death sentences written on large sheets of paper that had been pinned to their shrouds, their necks twisted and elongated, their bodies turning on the ends of the ropes in the wind.

These were the ones who had been found guilty in the first hearing, there were more of them to follow, Istanbul would become accustomed to these white-shrouded dead dangling on ropes hung from a tripod of logs, would even forget that these were dead people. Like Ragıp Bey, the city was at first be spooked by this and then grew accustomed to it.

The gallows and the dead became a part of Istanbul, turned into a kind of horrifying entertainment around which a few street children and idlers gathered and which old women passed muttering prayers.

Ragıp Bey didn't feel even the slightest pity for these people who'd been hanged, he only felt the kind of disgust he felt when a leech or a worm touched his body, disgust at what they'd done and how they'd died, these dead meant nothing more than this to him; if he'd been the one who had to decide what was to be done with these mutineers, he wouldn't have had the slightest hesitation to condemn them to death, the only difference was that he would have preferred for them to be shot, indeed he might even have done it himself.

When he passed the last corpse hanging from a gallows, he simply forgot them; for him they were not worth remembering; when he entered the *tekke* in Unkapanı, he felt a painful weariness in every part of his body.

Before setting out he'd thought he could go to Dilara Hanım on his first night back in Istanbul, but events hadn't unfolded the way he'd expected, it took days for the officers to send the soldiers who'd surrendered to prison, to send the wounded to hospitals, to station units in various parts of Istanbul, to distribute new ammunition, to count the bullets and the food in the warehouses.

When everything was finally organized and leave was granted, he went to the ministry of war to report on his unit, then hired a carriage, but he didn't tell the driver to go to Dilara Hanım's house, he gave the name of the *tekke* where his mother and wife were.

He could have gone directly to Dilara Hanım without seeing them, but he realized that if he did he would always be distressed and remorseful; despite his longing and his impatient desire, he decided to go to the *tekke* first so he could be at ease when he went to Dilara Hanım.

He found Sheikh Efendi wandering alone among the graves by the Golden Horn. The smells of seaweed, gunpowder, death, and everblooming roses mingled with each other. The Sheikh greeted Ragıp Bey as if he'd been expecting him.

"Welcome."

"Thank you, Your Excellency."

"You've been through some difficult times, how are you?"

"I'm fine, everything is going well, I might be a bit tired, but I'm used to that."

They started to walk together along the shore of the Golden Horn. Occasionally Sheikh Efendi stood next to a grave, looked at the flowers that had been placed on the grave, brushed the dirt off the stones with his hands. Ragıp Bey was surprised to see that his hands were still clean after he touched the dirt.

"Soldiers are beating hodjas on the streets."

Ragıp Bey made a face.

"I've heard that too, it bothered me a bit. But they need to realize that they have to stay out of sight for a while. The soldiers have just been in battle, they've seen the comrades next to them, their commanders get shot, it's not easy for them to stay calm under these circumstances, they see the hodjas as responsible for this, of course when I say hodja I'm not talking about scholars like you, but some of the mullahs bit off more than they could chew, they caused soldiers to kill soldiers."

Sheikh Efendi stroked his beard as he listened to Ragıp Bey.

"I don't approve of the way the mullahs got mixed up in this, no one from the ulema approved of this, but it's something else I'm afraid of, you know, politics always tries to find excuses for itself . . . "

For a time they continued walking as if they hadn't been talking about something important, then the Sheikh picked up where he'd left off.

"But religion shouldn't be an excuse for politics."

He stopped and looked at Ragıp Bey.

"Don't make the soldiers hostile to religion. Never forget that religion is the morality and conscience of a society, if a society loses its religion, it also loses its morality and conscience. In a society like that, no one can have the right to live. Religion exists to defend the powerless from the cruel, to protect the moral from the amoral. I respect the person who has no religion, I see him too as a precious slave of God, if he has lost his way, I try to hold as much light as I can, I try to show him the light of God that illuminates the Lord's fortunate slaves, but this isn't the point . . . A society losing its religion is not like a person losing his religion. Moreover if you create an army that's hostile to religion, you will darken this society's future; don't touch the people's religion, their faith, or their hodjas. I believe that those who respect are respected in turn. Don't confuse fake men of religion with genuine men of religion, if you do you will punish those who have committed no sin, the people will doubt your justice; if you become enemies of religion, the people will become your enemies. Don't divide the people from the army and the people from religion, it's easy to fight, but it's difficult to make peace, Ragıp Bey . . . Any bloodthirsty tyrant can declare war, but it requires someone with a great heart to make peace."

They started to walk toward the tekke.

Ragıp Bey thought about what Sheikh Efendi had said, but he didn't give an answer.

"I've detained you with my talk, I beg your pardon. You want to see your mother, she's fine and healthy, she's a good woman, I'm grateful that you gave us the opportunity to host someone like her in our tekke."

"Thank you, sir."

The Sheik, smiled suddenly.

"She's as tough as nails, too, God bless her."

Ragıp Bey knew what the Sheikh was talking about and smiled too; two men, two friends, despite the courage and reputation and power they possessed, tolerantly and tenderly admitted their timidity in the face of the woman who both frightened them and earned their love.

"Go, don't keep your mother waiting, I'm sure she's heard you've come and is growing impatient."

As Ragıp Bey was making his way toward the harem, Sheikh Efendi called out after him.

"Perhaps you should mention what we talked about with your older brother, I think it might be of more interest to him."

Ragıp Bey realized that a warning was being sent to the Committee through him. Perhaps Cevat Bey could understand the seriousness of this warning, but he was already certain that the Committee headquarters would not heed the warning.

He held the wooden bannister as he climbed the stairs. His mother, in her white headscarf, the lines on her face growing deeper, greeted him; first she looked him up and down to see if he'd been wounded, if he was sick, if anything was wrong. Her expression was resentful, she extended her hand to Ragıp Bey. As usual, her hands smelled of white soap; he could see her bluish veins, these were decisive and irritable hands. She asked her son if he was hungry.

"Yes, mother."

"Good, I had food prepared for you, I had the food sent to your wife's room."

"Thank you, are you well?"

"I'm fine, thank God."

His mother stopped, frowned, and looked at Ragıp Bey.

"You've overthrown the Caliph . . . You're beating hodjas on the streets."

Ragıp Bey took a deep breath, he was tired, and everyone he met told him the same thing, he was on the verge of getting angry, but he realized that all the officers might have been welcomed home in the same manner. Later he would tell his brother Cevat Bey:

"Brother, we're not fighting against hodjas but against our mothers, how could we win, is it possible to win a struggle like that?"

In a melancholy voice he said:

"I haven't laid a finger on any hodjas, I would have punished anyone I saw laying a finger on any of them, but they sowed discord among the soldiers, why are you only angry at us?"

His mother looked directly into his eyes, she'd said the same thing to her oldest son the previous day.

"Your great grandfather was a mufti, would you have allowed him to be beaten too if he was alive?"

"We didn't give orders for them to be beaten, this kind of thing won't happen anymore, sometimes misdeeds like this are committed in wartime, there's no need to blow it out of proportion."

The next question demonstrated that his mother's resentment was not just about the hodjas being beaten.

"Are you going to stay tonight?"

"I'm going to leave, I have to go back to the barracks, tomorrow I'll come and take you and Hatice Hanım to Göztepe."

"You spend too much time in the barracks."

"That's part of being in the army . . . "

"This much army isn't good, son, a man should put aside time for his family as well."

"You're right, I'll be back tomorrow, we'll go together. Do you have any complaints about the time you spent in this place?"

"No, how could I have, Sheikh Efendi didn't leave us wanting for anything, thank God, but still, there's no place like home."

"Is there anything you need me to do?"

"No," said his mother, "what could I need you to do, finish what you have to do so we can go home already and you can stop skulking around the barracks. There's no place like home, my son, if you stay away from home you're liable to get into trouble, don't forget that."

This indirect warning about Dilara Hanım was the limit to which mother and son could go, it wasn't possible for his mother to cross this line or for Ragıp Bey to say anything about it, both their traditions and their upbringing didn't allow them to be more familiar.

Ragıp Bey nodded to show he understood.

His mother extended her hand for him to kiss.

"Now go and see your wife and your child."

When Ragıp Bey went into the room, his wife was sitting by the window, holding her child in her arms. She didn't even move slightly when she saw her husband come in, she just glanced at him briefly and then turned back to the window. No one knew when the hatred between them had begun, on their wedding night or before then, when it was decided that they should marry, or later with the desperation that Dilara Hanım's presence caused in both of them; they couldn't remember, and none of the dead could say exactly when, but now they couldn't bear to touch each other or even look each other in the eye because of this hatred that was reminiscent of disgust. Ragıp Bey asked how she was in a dry tone.

"I'm fine."

Ragıp Bey went over to his wife and looked at the baby in her arms, with his eyes closed tight and his already prominent cheekbones he looked like a little Ragıp. He had a strange feeling he'd never had before, it felt as if he was drinking something warm that tasted very good. Just like all fathers, Ragıp Bey needed help from his friends and family to name the emotions he had for his son, to give them form, but because he was almost never home, he never had time to turn this warmth he felt into an established love.

For a moment he wanted to take the baby in his arms, but he was afraid he might drop him, his hands were too big and clumsy for a baby. He reached out slowly and touched his cheek with his finger, he was surprised by how soft the baby's skin was. When he reached out his hand, his wife held the baby more tightly and gave Ragıp Bey the sense that she didn't want to give the baby to him; he sensed that she saw the baby as her child, that she would not be pleased if her husband laid any claim to him. Just as when he sensed a bad omen, he saw his wife holding the baby more tightly as a sign that his son would be raised to be his enemy; his son would see him as an enemy, in the future his wife's hatred would turn this baby into his mortal enemy.

Ragıp Bey looked at the tray of food in the corner, there were shallow, copper-lidded frying pans, sliced bread, and a jug of water, he was starving, Hatice Hanım saw him looking at the food.

"Your mother sent food, have some if you want."

Ragıp Bey looked at the food once more.

"I have to go now, they're waiting for me at the barracks . . . I'll eat later."

"As you wish."

"How's the baby?"

"Well, thank God."

"Is there anything you need?"

"What could I need, we have everything, thank God."

"I'll come tomorrow and take you to Göztepe."

"Fine . . . In any event, I'm sure your mother has already prepared everything."

There was a strong resentment in the way she said this. She resented the way her mother-in-law acted as if she didn't exist and never left a single thing for her to do. She wasn't allowed to be the lady of the house, she lived in the mansion in Göztepe like a respected guest, but there was no love underlying that respect. Her intolerant piety, so different from her father's, was like a cold rock that destroyed the friendly feelings of anyone who approached her; as her faith and her belief grew, so did her anger at people, it was impossible for anyone to love her or for her to love anyone; she saw signs of unbelief everywhere, in every action, she showed this and made people of faith like her mother-in-law angry.

One of the main reasons she hated Ragıp Bey, apart from his betraying her with another woman, was that he was polluted because he'd committed adultery and he carried that sin into her house, into her bed; she feared that if she touched him she would touch sin, this was why she couldn't touch her husband. She turned the cleanliness of the soul into an obsession by washing her hands constantly and causing the skin on her hands to become irritated, her soul became irritated and lacerated by purification; no one could touch her anymore.

She didn't see people, she saw their sins and weaknesses, and as she fled these sins she also, without realizing it, fled the friendliness and love that were right next to those weaknesses. Sheikh Efendi was more saddened than anyone by his daughter's fanatical belief, which led her to reject human weakness, Sheikh Efendi sensed more than anyone else that this was not worship, not love of God, that it was a sickness. As he said to Osman, "You can't love God without loving people." But his daughter didn't love people, and this made her father sadder than any sinner could.

Sheikh Efendi wasn't the only one who was sad about this, Ragıp Bey thought that he was the reason for this spiritual odor that smelled of rotting fruit and that was diffused by a dying soul, he suffered from the sense of guilt he felt every time he saw his wife, and he hated this woman who constantly reminded him that he was a sinner.

He left the *tekke* as if he was fleeing, without even bidding farewell to the Sheikh.

When he went out the main gate he leaned his back against the wall and took a deep breath; it was as if he was leaving a cemetery, during his very brief visit with his wife he'd missed the cool smell of life. He inhaled the smell of seaweed, lilac, and roses along the Golden Horn, he looked at the undulating sunlight that glided like gold coins on the water, he wanted to light a cigarette, but his desire to get away from that place was greater; he strode down the street looking for a carriage, he wanted to go, to be with Dilara Hanım as soon as possible, to be free of the smell of suffering that clung to him.

When he arrived at the mansion in Nişantaşı, the distress his wife had created in his soul had turned into a weak shadow. They brought him into the living room as usual. A little later when Dilara Hanım entered the room almost at a run, the last shadow flew away from him, as Ragıp Bey felt himself trembling inwardly, he stood almost without moving, as for Dilara Hanım, she rushed over to him and gave him a big hug.

"Ragıp, thank God you're back."

She stepped back to look at him.

"You're fine, aren't you? There's nothing wrong? Lord, how I worried about you."

She hugged Ragıp Bey again and leaned against his chest. Ragıp Bey didn't move at all, he stood still because he didn't know what to do in a situation like this, he just lowered his head to smell her hair without letting her notice, this was the only loving thing he could do, and he tried to do it without letting her notice.

"Are you hungry?"

"Yes, I'm starving."

Dilara Hanım immediately had the table set for him, she served the food herself, she changed the plates herself, even though they usually never touched each other except in the bedroom, that day she caressed Ragıp Bey's hair as he ate, stroked his cheek, hovered over him like a little ladybug with the excitement of a woman in love.

At that moment she truly was in love with Ragıp Bey.

In any event all of Dilara Hanım's feelings were the feelings of a woman in love; she'd missed him as a woman in love, worried as a woman in love, was anxious like a woman in love, and rejoiced as a woman in love when she saw that he'd come.

All of these feelings were real.

She experienced each feeling, longing, wonder, anxiety, delight as a woman in love, but though these feelings of love were real when they were alone, when all of these feelings were felt together, love didn't emerge; Dilara Hanım didn't have the magnificent renunciation to hold these different feelings together and turn them into a real love, renouncing herself, existence, life. She was aware of herself and of her life at every moment, she never forgot them, as she confessed to Osman once, "Unfortunately love didn't emerge unless you forgot life, people, and yourself, unless you renounced them."

Despite all of her amorous behavior, the thing Ragıp Bey felt was missing but couldn't name or comprehend was the lack of renunciation, Ragıp Bey was never able to put a name to it; even if someone had told him, he probably wouldn't have understood what it meant. He had the same disquiet throughout their relationship, he saw love in everything the woman he loved did, but each time he parted from her it was with a strange, vague sense of loss.

After dinner she took him to the bathroom and washed him; with a painful patience that burned her skin, Dilara Hanım touched his entire body in that steamy bathroom without making love. As for Ragıp Bey, he didn't touch his woman even once, although his lustful body consented to allow the woman to wash him, his childish shame didn't allow him to move.

As Dilara Hanım washed him, she told him about the days of the uprising, the days they'd spent in Hikmet Bey's mansion.

Because she understood why Ragıp Bey's body tensed suddenly as he listened to this adventure, that he was jealous, she offered an explanation that would put him ease.

"I think Hikmet Bey likes Dilevser."

"How do you know?"

Dilara Hanım smiled.

"I just know."

"What does Dilevser have to say about it?"

"She's a bit confused, she's flattered, but she hasn't quite understood what's happening."

When they went to the bedroom after the bath and stretched out on the lavender-scented sheets and pulled the quilt over themselves, Ragıp Bey overcame his shame; the bed, like the battle field, was a place Ragıp Bey felt comfortable and self-confident.

They made love with appetite, like two healthy animals who'd met in the jungle, without talking, without playing any games. Dilara Hanım gave herself to the man with love and desire, there were finger marks, which later turned into bruises, on her hips, legs, and breasts, later she looked at them in the mirror in delight.

When they calmed down, and Ragıp Bey closed his eyes, which had seen hundreds of deaths, there was a happy expression on his face, just like the one he'd seen on his son's face as he lay in his wife's arms.

20

That year, summer arrived suddenly.

The city went to sleep on a cool spring night, in the morning it woke to the sounds and colors of a new season whose humid heat smelled of the sea; the playful sparkling of the sea was reflected on the entire city, Istanbul warmed suddenly like a colorful sea-stone. Shouting vegetable peddlers spread out through the city streets, baskets hanging from both sides of their donkeys, artichoke sellers wandered through neighborhoods of mansions with mocking smiles, shouldering wicker baskets of the vegetable that was said to be good for manhood, there was a proliferation of the voices that announced the arrival of the women who sold bedsheets and decorated cloths, there was satisfaction on the peddlers' faces.

The city was as silent as if it had fallen into a restless sleep under the hot, mother-of-pearl brightness that moved, spread, grew; it had not been able to overcome fear, but it had become accustomed to it. Perhaps the only entertainment the city experienced during this time of fear was the stories about how the new Sultan was afraid of Mahmut Şevket Pasha; there was a story about how when the Sultan was in the harem, reviewing the new concubines that had been presented to him, he dropped a handkerchief in front of the one he'd chosen, then hurriedly asked the people with him what Mahmut Şevket Pasha would say about it. People in the coffeehouses were still laughing about this.

When the Sultan gave him a very valuable horse as a gift,

Mahmut Şevket Pasha rejected it and said, "I don't have a stable worthy of such a valuable horse, Your Highness," adding a well-deserved respect to the fear the pasha inspired.

In this stagnant environment, the only segment of society that spoke with ambition, spirit, and passion was the officers. The officers were divided as to whether or not the military should engage in politics; the group led by Mustafa Kemal Bey and İsmet Bey held that "the military should get out of politics and get back to its actual job immediately," and the supporters of Enver Bey, who as Mahmut Şevket Pasha's deputy was involving the military in politics, claimed that the situation in the country would get out of hand and the religious fanatics would start stirring things up if the military retreated to the barracks.

A communique that İsmet Bey, who'd come to Istanbul with the Movement Army, wrote personally after convincing Mahmut Şevket Pasha stated that the military should no longer engage in politics, but Enver Bey's supporters didn't heed this demand.

The subject came up whenever two officers met.

Ragıp Bey and his brother Cevat Bey also discussed this matter frequently. At Ragıp Bey's insistence, Cevat Bey moved into the mansion in Göztepe at the beginning of summer; consequently Ragıp Bey felt more at ease when he spent the night at Dilara Hanım's mansion and was freed of his worries about his mother and his wife; as for their mother, she was happy to have both of her sons with her. The most surprising thing of all was that Hatice Hanım, who was completely puritanical, and Cevat Bey, who viewed religion with doubt, got along well with each other and managed to establish a close, friendly brother-sister relationship. Hatice Hanım, who never failed to see shortcomings and sin in religious people, never put Cevat Bey in the same category as other sinners; perhaps the way he brought his political beliefs to the level of religion, defended them puritanically, and lived like a hermit, avoiding women, adultery, alcohol, and entertainment, led her to love him; perhaps in the sisterly love she felt for an officer who was so different from his brother there was a reflection of the love for Ragıp Bey that her anger at his sins did not allow to emerge in any event; no one knew the reason for this love; what was even stranger was that Ragıp Bey's little son smiled at his uncle more often than he did at his father.

On the nights Ragıp Bey stayed at the mansion, the table was set under the large horse chestnut tree in the garden and the women decked the table with food the men liked in peaceful happiness. On such evenings there was a sense that even the hatred Hatice Hanım felt for her husband was lightened and diminished.

After dinner the women went inside and as the two men watched the fireflies that flew like sparks from a secret fire, the still water in the small pond that shone dully as if it had been polished with silver, and the dark green shade of the trees, they returned, to the accompaniment of the chirping of cicadas, the constant croaking of the frogs, and the smells of earth, flowers, and fruit, to the subject that preoccupied them most.

The statement that Mahmut Şevket Pasha had made at the beginning of summer to the effect that the military should not engage in politics had further inflamed the discussion between the two brothers.

As they were drinking their coffee, Cevat Bey turned to his brother.

"Have you read the pasha's statement?"

"Yes."

"In fact all of this is being done to sideline Enver Pasha, I don't understand how the great Pasha has allowed himself to be pushed into a corner like this, that is, if you keep the military out of politics, who's going to stop the religious fanatics, the reactionaries, and the enemies of civilization? We've only just put down an uprising, what would have happened here if the army hadn't intervened, think, Ragıp. Isn't it politics to say the military should stay out of politics, especially if the person who's saying this is a soldier?"

"Brother, to tell the truth, I don't approve of the military engaging in politics, as I've told you before, the Balkans are in ferment, even a child on the street can see that a war in the Balkans is now inevitable, you're not very aware of what things are like in the barracks, if we go to war in the condition we're in it will be one of the greatest disasters in history, the Ottoman forces would be crushed in that war."

Cevat Bey made a face.

"Ragıp, let's get ready for a war in the Balkans, fine, we're surrounded by enemies, I agree, but what about our internal enemies, the former Sultan's men are ready and waiting, if it wasn't for us they would already have risen up again and unfurled their green flags, really, don't you see this, you can catch the scent of our enemies in the Balkans but you can't see the enemy under your nose, I don't understand, how could you be so blind?"

"I passed on to you what Sheikh Efendi said to me, the ulema didn't support the uprising, in any event they didn't take part in the uprising, we can't be involved in politics forever just because of a few fanatics, if the army is so involved in politics, who's going to be involved in soldiering? The men are in a miserable state, their morale is low, they're tired, their weapons are old, there's no serious preparation because the pashas are all obsessed with politics."

"Ragıp, you keep going on about Sheikh Efendi this and Sheikh Efendi that . . . Don't put too much faith in these mullahs, it always ends in disaster, all they want is to sideline the military and seize the reins of power again . . . They bleed the people dry, where does the money for the *tekkes* come from, it comes from Muslims' pockets."

Ragıp Bey stirred restlessly in his seat.

"Sheikh Efendi was of great help to us, so many of our friends owe their lives to him, so many of the wounded were treated at his *tekke*. How can you be so harsh?"

"Fine, he helped us, but we can't change our political position just because a sheikh helped us. This nation is ignorant, Ragıp. You know that as well as I do, as soon as someone says that religion is under threat, they pour out into the streets."

"The people didn't take part in the mutiny, brother. If they had, we wouldn't have been able to put it down. On top of that, is it smart to be obsessed by a few mullahs among us when the Balkan nations have all of Europe's support and are preparing to move against us? Things aren't going well, brother, soldiers have forgotten that they're soldiers. Let the politicians engage in politics, let's do our own job . . . "

Cevat Bey stood, his shadow grew like a great tree trunk in the slippery light of the oil lamps.

"Our job is to protect the motherland against enemies, be they external or internal. Who else but the military can protect this country, you mention politicians, they would sell their own mothers for power if they could. If they came to power hand in hand with the reactionaries, do you think we'd be able to win wars, it would be worse. In history, have you ever seen a nation that's rotting internally win a war, believe me, we're in the age when the fate of the Ottoman Empire is going to be decided, if the army removes itself from politics the motherland will fall into the hands of the reactionaries."

"Brother, I'm a soldier, I entered my profession gladly and I perform my duties gladly, what I'm saying is, just let me do my job, but this isn't possible, in military circles no one talks about anything except politics, everyone is thinking about politics . . . The army is collapsing while you're talking about saving the motherland, why can't you see this? You say that politicians are prepared to do bad things to gain power, fine, then what's the difference between them and an army that's engaged in politics, don't you think about this at all? Look at Mahmut Şevket Pasha, he was a good commander, now he's a kind of sultan, Enver Bey was a brave officer, now he's more of a politician than the politicians."

"If it wasn't for Enver Bey, this army would never have acted so decisively, Ragıp. The young officers worship him, he earned this adoration rightfully. If you try to remove him from his position the army will rise up. As for Mahmut Şevket Pasha, you're right about him, I don't know what we're going to do about that pasha either, we brought him to where he is and now he's trying to sideline us. What are we going to do about the Pasha, I think about this too."

That summer night, the two brothers didn't know as they argued under the large chestnut tree that this subject would be discussed for a hundred years, and that within a few years the Ottoman Empire would suffer one of its gravest defeats in history in the Balkan Wars; even though they argued with all sincerity and conviction, they didn't quite grasp the full importance and weight of what they were discussing. Years later Ragıp Bey told Osman, "In fact Mustafa Kemal Bey and İsmet Bey were right, either because they were jealous of Enver Bey or they grasped it before anyone else, they talked about this a great deal, but strangely, when they came to power, they didn't keep the military out of politics. Even Mustafa Kemal's most ardent supporters chose to forget the opinion he once had on this matter."

When Cevat Bey said, "What are we going to do about the Pasha, I think about this too," he was laying the first paving stones for Mahmut Şevket Pasha's bloody end; later other Committee members would repeat these words frequently, each time these words were uttered, the wall between the Pasha and death grew thinner, each time this sentence was repeated, his future grew a little darker. Just like everyone who rises to the top, the Pasha never considered that little people and brief sentences could affect his destiny, but his destiny too was determined by those brief sentences uttered in gardens, coffeehouses, military circles, by people he didn't know or care about at all; the people he thought supported him were drawn away by these brief sentences, they left him unprotected to face the bullets alone.

That troublesome and quiet summer was a season in which many people determined someone else's life and destiny, many lives from different places mingled together, there were joys, disappointments, delights, weddings, and painful disappearances. As Reşit Pasha told Osman with the shy smile that suited him so well, "Everyone was someone else's destiny." After saying this, he added, "All of us have more influence on someone else's destiny than we do on our own, sometimes I think that if we could live a life and have a destiny others couldn't interfere with, we would all probably have much different lives, but unfortunately this isn't possible, it is as if the Creator connected us all to each other; when one of us moves, we all move."

As the two brothers discussed the future of the nation in Göztepe, Mehpare Hanım was in the garden of her mansion in Şişli, sitting in the gazebo to get a breath of air in this oppressive heat. Beams of moonlight filtered like fairies through the vines that covered the gazebo, and Mehpare Hanım felt like a little girl in an enchanted forest. Since she was a child she'd always liked disappearing, hiding in a secret place that belonged only to her, to dream in corners she shared with no one, but all of this was more appealing to her at times when there were people around who loved her, pampered her, admired her. And that night she was deeply distressed; because the city had retreated, the mansion parties, entertainments, and excursions had stopped because everyone preferred to hide than to be seen in public, Mehpare Hanım had been all alone in her mansion since she arrived.

This boredom spread like a feverish infection, sometimes it

424 · AHMET ALTAN

died down, sometimes it turned into a maddening crisis; at those times she missed Constantine, she ate her heart out, rushed from one dream to another, some mornings she woke feeling very certain that she smelled his smell, the smell touched her face and neck like a warm animal, she could swear that this smell was real. She remembered his wiles in bed, which she hadn't encountered in any other man, the piercing, crazy look in his eyes when he became savage, the way he kissed her body at length after they made love, the way he whispered her name in his Greek accent, his jokes, she set out on jarring journeys during which she swung like a pendulum between regret and dreams.

She realized that she'd become tense, irritable, and worn out by loneliness; but this led her to believe that all her feelings were the result of a nervous illness, which led her to doubt her longing for Constantine and all the pain she was suffering, led her to think that these things weren't real. The thought that they were the result of a nervous disorder didn't ease her longing, pain, distress, on the contrary, because she didn't believe in the reality of her longing and her pain, it shook the ground of her dreams and her hopes that new encounters would turn all of this into happiness in the future, when they lost the ground on which they existed, they receded behind a foggy curtain.

Then, without the consolation of dreams of the future, her pain and longing grew stronger. Being lost in uncertainty, to suffer desire and pain without even being sure about her desires and feelings poisoned almost every aspect of her life, it undermined the feeling she needed most in these times, her self-confidence.

The direct and natural Sula, who'd become her only friend and to whom she was connected by a bond of true love, was saddened to watch her suffer and asked her once why she'd left Constantine. Mehpare Hanım answered this question without pause, as if she'd been thinking about it for a long time.

"We were so much alike that I was frightened of him. I think I mistook this fear for boredom."

Once, Sula said to her in her motherly manner:

"Write to him, invite him to come here, believe me, he'll come running."

Mehpare Hanım gave her a pensive glance.

"Perhaps he'd come . . . But if what I feel for him isn't real . . . I can't stand that, Sula . . . If it was another time, I might, but not now, no, not now."

Then she made one of her strange requests.

"Dance the sirtaki for me."

Sula danced with an elegance not to be expected from such a large body, as Mehpare Hanım watched her dance, a number of memories and dreams floated through her mind, she did something that perhaps she'd never done, or at least that Sula had never seen, she started to weep.

Sula stopped dancing, sat next to her like a mother, stroked her hair, lovingly embraced this strange woman whose desires no one including herself believed were real.

"This is no way to live, Sula," said Mehpare Hanım. "This isn't a life. What is this? What am I living? I want a life the way everyone else does; I want to love and be loved. I want to trust. I want to be trusted . . . " Then she wiped the tears from her eyes and smiled. "I don't even trust myself, why should anyone else . . . "

She paused and took a deep breath.

"Still, I'd like someone to trust me completely. Who knows, maybe then I'd trust my own feelings. Everything would be so different."

These were sincere wishes, but just like so many other people, she wanted what she didn't have, she wanted to be in a mood other than the one she was in, even though she pursued her desires more recklessly than others did, her desires changed as soon as she had what she wanted.

She experienced brief periods of time during which what she possessed was also in harmony with what she wanted, during these brief periods she formed an idea about what happiness was like, but her restless soul couldn't live within the tranquility of happiness, satisfaction, and contentment, if an emotion became stable, even if this emotion was happiness, her soul began to stir in order to get moving again, to search, to seek new desires, to find new forms of happiness.

Now she had reached what could be considered the most dangerous point for a woman like her, and she knew herself. Now she didn't trust any of her wishes, she could not easily abandon herself to any of her longings, she doubted every feeling with an almost hostile anger. Like a runner who runs not to get somewhere but because he likes running, who, when he stops and asks himself where he's running realizes he no longer enjoys it, she too, when she was in pursuit of some nebulous wish, asked herself what wish she was pursuing, which wish was real, and stopped, wishing had also lost its charm.

When she realized that in fact there was no place she wanted to reach, the wind that her unsatisfied desires had created stopped, the dizziness of that wind ended, the sail of her life went slack without wind and hung there in a frightening motionlessness. When the thirst of wanting ended as well, what was left behind was a painful stirring up of multiple feelings whose reality was doubtful and which couldn't even dream of arriving somewhere.

Her pain and longing were real and true at the moments she experienced them, but to feel there was no longer any aim with which to satisfy these feelings, to know that her desires didn't have real aims, to realize that there was no destination at which to arrive in order to be satisfied, created an emptiness in her life, a sense that something was missing; these feelings, which didn't touch or make contact with anyone else, died in this void as well, they faded, and, strangely, became more bitter. Mehpare Hanım realized that for a wish to be real, it had to continue to exist once it had reached its aim.

That night in the gazebo, which in the moonlight seemed to be made of emeralds, she was confused, she was accustomed to being admired, it was like an opium addiction, and without this she was left alone with herself, she was left in the middle of a feminine reckoning that she was not accustomed to; she was even more saddened and surprised to hear rumors that Hikmet Bey had fallen in love with a young girl and wanted to marry her, to hear that someone whose admiration and passion for her she'd thought would last forever had freed himself from her enchantment.

Her wishes changed places so quickly that she was having trouble catching them, putting them in order, and separating the real from the counterfeit. She was on the verge of accepting defeat and loneliness, indeed she had already accepted them; now she was thinking about living a calm and quiet life in her mansion, closing the doors, spending time with her children, shedding her never-ending wishes, her burning, wounding lust; she would change the lifestyle that had given her so much pleasure but that had left an emptiness deep within her, though she didn't know what it was that was missing. She felt lonely and old; she would grow accustomed to not being admired, for Hikmet Bey to have moved on to someone else ended her pathetic struggle in complete defeat.

She leaned back in her wooden armchair with a strange inner peace and looked pensively at the bright moonbeams that played like silver birds at her feet. Her feelings changed so rapidly that when decisions she made in the flow of one of her feelings took form in her mind, her feelings changed as well: her thoughts were never able to catch up to her feelings, the moment she believed she'd accepted the mood of defeat and dejection, she suddenly clapped her hands, called a servant, and asked for a pen and paper.

She wrote a brief letter to Hikmet Bey, she could barely see what she was writing in the shade of the vines.

"Hikmet,

I must speak with you as soon as possible. The matter I wish to discuss is the future of our children. I will expect you tomorrow afternoon.

Mehpare."

She was unbelievably impatient, she couldn't wait until morning, she gave the letter to the carriage driver, if it had been possible she would have asked him to come at once, but she was able to realize how strange this would be.

The next morning she woke early in a dither, she inspected the entire house, gave the necessary instructions to the servants and the footmen, toward noon she had the fire for the bath lit and took a long bath, then she opened her closet and started trying on all of her dresses one by one; she called for Sula and asked her opinion about every dress she put on. Each time Sula said, "Very nice," she glanced at herself in the mirror, turned around, and looked back to see how it was from behind, took a few steps, then said, "This doesn't work," took it off, and threw it on the bed, the bed was covered with dresses.

Sula grew irritated.

"Girl, you're very beautiful, whatever you wear looks good on you. Anyway, he's not going to be looking at your dress, he's going to be looking at you, if someone asks him later he won't be able to say what you were wearing, he's a man!"

Mehpare Hanım shook her head.

"Hikmet will see, he has an eye for these things, you don't know him."

"I may not know Hikmet, but I know men. He won't see, when he meets you after such a long time he won't look at your dress, he wouldn't notice if you wore rags."

She finally decided on a yellow linen dress that no one would guess she'd gone to such pains to choose, she combed her hair, put on fragrance, looked at herself in the mirror once more, she considered putting a flower in her hair but then decided it would be too much.

She couldn't eat much at lunch despite Sula's insistence, she only took the heel of a loaf of bread, she was much more excited than she'd imagined she would be, she was very tense; she paced around the house and the garden and waited for time to pass.

As the time of Hikmet Bey's arrival approached, she started watching from the living room window. When the carriage she was expecting came in through the garden gate, she was able to control her excitement; Hikmet Bey would never know about the preparations for his visit, he would never know about any of it, he would never realize how she'd waited for him with her heart racing, Mehpare Hanım had erased all traces of this with a mastery only women could achieve.

When they met each other in the living room after such a long time, there was a silence. Hikmet Bey looked at his former wife's face, as usual he was surprised by the beauty he saw; just like all men who once again meet a beautiful woman who left them, he felt the pain of once again seeing how impressive the beauty he lost was and trembled inwardly in the hope of capturing her again, his palms were sweating, he blushed slightly.

"Please, have a seat," said Mehpare Hanım.

Hikmet Bey looked around the room, then sat in an armchair right next to him.

"You should sit by the window, you get a much better view of the garden."

Without saying anything, Hikmet Bey stood and went to sit in the armchair Mehpare Hanım had pointed to. He was terrified of the beauty he saw, how much he'd struggled to forget that face, how many days he had spent in pain trying to erase the images and recollections from his memory, how often he'd begged silently for all of the women toward whom he'd felt even a little closeness to help him forget that face; now that beautiful face, with all of its charm, was right in front of him,

430 - AHMET ALTAN

and Hikmet Bey realized he was prepared to sacrifice anything in order to be able to see this face every morning, to feel
he was once again loved by her. At that moment there was
nothing more precious, more important, than being loved by
Mehpare Hanım; he could give up his dignity, his honor, his
pride, his name, his past, even his future without even the
slightest regret. If he'd believed it would work, he would have
been prepared to drag her roughly by the arm, to lower himself by deceiving her with false promises, but he wasn't sure if
these things would help.

He hadn't slept since he received her letter, he'd reckoned
with his past, become excited, weighed his feelings, and had
finally left the house deciding that he'd forgotten Mehpare
Hanım, but now he could see clearly that he'd been mistaken.

"You seem a bit pale," said Mehpare Hanım.

"It must be because of the heat . . . "

"Yes, it's really very hot. Would you like something to
drink? Sula has prepared a very nice sour cherry sherbet, I
know you like it, would you like some?"

He gladly accepted the offer of something to wet his dry lips.

"I would like some, if it's not too much trouble."

In silence, they drank the sour cherry sherbet, which had
been brought in crystal glasses in ornate silver holders with
thin handles. He was both happy and embarrassed that
Mehpare Hanım had remembered he liked sour cherry sherbet. Later, he said to Osman, "You can't believe how desperate a person can be." Suddenly Mehpare Hanım said, "If you'll
allow it, I would like the children to live with me."

Hikmet Bey was truly surprised, as if Mehpare Hanım
hadn't said in her letter that she wanted to talk about the children. "Is that so?"

"Yes, Nizam is all alone in Paris, and to tell the truth, even
though he's happy to be there alone I'm a bit worried. As for
Rukiye, she's been a burden for Mihrişah Sultan for such a

long time, it seems a bit unsuitable for her to live with her ladyship when her mother is here."

"Have you spoken with Rukiye at all?"

"No, I'm afraid she's a bit resentful toward me. But that will
pass . . . To tell the truth, I'm worried that she'll grow even
more bitter the longer we're apart."

When he heard Nizam's name, Hikmet Bey blushed again.
He missed his son, his happy-go-lucky manner, his respectful
teasing, the amiability that made everyone love him, he'd given
a lot of thought to inviting him to Istanbul, but he was
ashamed to meet his son as a pathetic man who'd been
betrayed and who hadn't managed to kill himself, felt he
wouldn't be able to bear the look of reproof in his son's eyes,
even if it was just a little; like every father, he was frightened by
the thought that he could lose his son's respect.

He said, "As you wish. I too think that Nizam should come
here from Paris, I've missed him a great deal. You talk to
Rukiye, I can't make a decision about that, I think the two of
you need to sort this out as mother and daughter."

"You know that Rukiye sees you as a father and loves you
as such."

Hikmet Bey smiled.

"Yes, I know. I've always seen her as my daughter as well.
She's become a very intelligent young girl. I would like her
even if I had no connection to her, but in the end I'm not her
father, I have no rights in this matter."

"Then you don't have any objections to the children living
with me?"

"How could I, you're their mother . . . "

Even though it occurred to him to say, "Even though you
abandoned them . . . " he didn't, but they both stared straight
ahead as if these words had been uttered. Both of them were
ashamed when they considered what this situation meant for
the children.

The silence didn't last long, in a slightly bashful and flirtatious tone that suited her so well, Mehpare Hanım said, "Look, what I was going to say was . . .

"Let me show you around the mansion, let's see if you approve of my taste."

When Hikmet Bey raised his head and looked at his former wife's face, as soon as he saw that bashful look of her beautiful face he realized what she meant, he pressed his hands to his legs to keep them from shaking, he licked his dry lips and could only manage to say, "As you wish."

As they made their way to the living room door, Hikmet Bey noticed the piano, he hadn't noticed it when he came in.

"Do you still play?"

"Occasionally, when something's bothering me . . . But I don't enjoy it as much as I used to."

"What a shame . . . You used to play so well."

They toured the rooms of the lower floor quickly, Hikmet Bey murmured a few words of praise, then they walked to the stairs and climbed without speaking, tensed with excitement, maintaining a little distance between each other.

They entered the bedroom, the curtains were closed.

Mehpare Hanım said, "This is my room."

As Hikmet Bey was about to answer, he heard a sound. Mehpare Hanım had closed the door and leaned against it. In a scratchy voice she asked, "Have you missed me, Hikmet?" After that it was complete madness.

Even though people who have been in a long and fiery relationship forget what they experienced, or think they forget and suppress these memories, longing and desire hide in their skins, waiting for the day when they'll come back to life; from the first touch, their bodies remembered each other and they embraced each other with a longing that surprised even them, the desire hiding in their legs, between their legs, in their fingertips, and in their lips intensified at an unexpected pace, they began to make love as if they'd never separated.

They experienced perhaps the most magnificent, most unforgettable lovemaking of their entire relationship, as if they were betraying everyone in their lives, even each other, as if they were taking revenge on everyone, but without actually being aware of betraying or taking revenge, playing all the games they always used to play and from which they always used to derive pleasure, perhaps deriving more pleasure than in the past, they felt love and desire at every touch and at every moment, feeling as if they were washing away all of the pain, sorrow, and anger of the past, they made love until their souls and their bodies were too fragile and weary to contain anything.

In the evening when darkness fell and Hikmet Bey left the mansion, Mehpare Hanım, too impatient to get dressed, threw on a nightgown and ran to the kitchen, to Sula, and as she drank the sour cherry sherbet she served her, gave her the news that she herself was so pleased to hear.

"He's still in love with me . . . He's in love with me."

As for Hikmet Bey, he got into the carriage feeling tired and self-confident, he leaned back, he had the same feeling, he thought he was still in love with her.

Then something strange happened.

Hikmet Bey used to hear an echo within himself every time he said Mehpare Hanım's name or her name came to mind, some unknown thing was responding to that name, every time her name was mentioned a sound emerged from the depths. Hikmet Bey knew this very well, because he'd lived with this for years. That evening in the carriage, as he thought about Mehpare Hanım, he didn't hear that echo, that strange response; he was so surprised that he repeated her name out loud. There was no sign of the strange echo he'd become accustomed to, that sound, whatever it was, was missing.

Making love had satisfied all of the longing in his body, but it hadn't been able to reach the depths, it hadn't been able to reach his soul; just as this lovemaking had washed and cleaned their past, it had removed Mehpare Hanım from within Hikmet Bey and from his past; perhaps in order for him to realize that his love for his former wife was over, he'd needed to make love to her one last time, he'd needed to feel once more that he possessed her, no one could know why, but that magnificent, loving lovemaking had showed Hikmet Bey that this love was over.

Even though it had left a scar on his soul that would never disappear, the wound had closed; he realized this with a sense of relief, but also with a strange sorrow. This love that he'd thought would never end, for which he'd been willing to live as a sad and melancholy man, for which he'd even been willing to die, that he'd felt within him through so many lonely days and nights, had left him, taking with it all the pain, suffering, and melancholy. He didn't understand why he wasn't happy about this, but he didn't feel even the slightest joy. All he felt was weariness throughout his body and a pain in part of his soul that was difficult to describe.

He was afraid to return to the mansion and meet Dilevser in this condition; even though he realized that his love was over, he also felt something else, a feeling that was difficult to explain, it was as if, at this time, if he thought the wrong thought or was captivated by the wrong feeling, he would fall in love with Mehpare Hanım again, this time never to escape; to see Dilevser's ashen young face and innocent conversation after having beheld Mehpare Hanım's extraordinary beauty would serve no purpose other than to remind him of Mehpare Hanım's beauty. He knew he shouldn't see Dilevser now.

In order to erase the latest effects of Mehpare Hanım, he needed a woman as beautiful, intelligent, and scornful as his former wife, as usual he would take shelter from Mehpare Hanım in his mother.

He told the carriage driver to go down to the shore.

21

The doors and windows leading to the veranda that extended as far as the sea had been opened fully, and the iodine-smelling coolness of the Bosphorus, which flowed past constantly like a gigantic, burnished black leather strap with a swishing sound that the household had become accustomed to offered some relief from the summer heat that during the day had penetrated the wooden walls of the large living room. Mihrişah Sultan, Rukiye, and two ladies in waiting who had preferred to stay in Istanbul rather than accompany the others back to Paris after the mutiny were sitting listening to Tevfik Bey talk about daily political developments and rumors, about which her ladyship occasionally made sharp, witty comments that made everyone laugh.

Although she'd long since lost all interest in politics, Mihrişah Sultan pretended she hadn't for Rukiye's sake, and Tevfik Bey came every evening to give his daily report. This was like the worship of monks who'd long since lost their faith, but they continued without giving up and without taking it seriously, it became an amusement everyone had become accustomed to. Rukiye listened to Tevfik Bey's voice without talking and without caring about what he said; she'd grown accustomed to that voice, she became restless when she didn't hear it.

When Hikmet Bey entered the living room, they all turned and looked at him. With her usual pampered levity, Mihrişah Sultan asked, "What's the matter with you, Hikmet?

"Your face is like wax, you're so pale."

"It's just that I didn't get any sleep."

"Have you eaten?"

It was only then that Hikmet Bey realized he hadn't eaten anything since morning, but he didn't feel up to eating so he lied.

"*Merci*, mother, I've eaten."

"Good, then come, have a seat," said Mihrişah Sultan, losing interest in her son's health at once too and returning to what they'd just been talking about.

"We were talking about how stupid your Committee is, this is the second time they've made a military move but they still haven't been able to get into the government. They want to govern the nation but they're afraid to take responsibility. They're brave when it's time to kill, but they're cowards when it's time to take some responsibility. To tell the truth, sometimes I wonder whether or not the old geezer had more courage than these people."

Hikmet Bey answered as if he was grumbling.

"It's not my Committee, mother, I cut my ties with them a long time ago."

"It's not quite clear whether you cut your ties with them or they cut their ties with you . . . "

"Why are you being so offensive?"

When Mihrişah Sultan looked more closely at her son, she felt there was something strange about him.

"What's going on?"

It was impossible for Hikmet Bey to tell his mother what he'd thought and felt on his way there; the surprise he'd felt when he realized he was no longer in love with Mehpare Hanım showed him that he'd still secretly believed he was still in love with Mehpare Hanım during the time he thought he loved Dilevser, otherwise he wouldn't have been so surprised to realize he no longer loved his former wife. Throughout his trip there he'd kept asking himself the same question. "How could I secretly believe I loved Mehpare when I thought I loved Dilevser?" Moreover, he'd never noticed it . . . It frightened him to think that he didn't know his own feelings.

As he experienced the bewilderment of realizing he no longer loved Mehpare Hanım, he was unable to answer whether or not he loved Dilevser. He just knew he didn't want to see the young girl then. The innocence that had always impressed him would now feel like a heavy burden.

Because he knew he couldn't tell his mother any of this, he said there was nothing going on.

Thinking that there might be a private reason for Hikmet Bey to come at that hour, Tevfik Bey said:

"If you'll excuse me, I have to get going."

Rukiye stood up at once.

"Let me see you out."

As Tevfik Bey and Rukiye left the living room together, Hikmet Bey looked at his mother as if to ask, "What's going on here?" When Mihrişah Sultan turned and gave him a slight smile, Hikmet Bey realized that new feelings had emerged in his stepdaughter's life.

Every evening Rukiye saw Tevfik Bey as far as the garden gate as if this was very natural. During that time they exchanged a few words about what they would do the next day, and with the help of the signals contained in these exchanges they could occasionally "run into each other," they walked in the woods behind the mansion in the late afternoon and occasionally took a carriage ride to Kanlıca.

Despite Rukiye's impatience, Tevfik Bey was very cautious; he always kept the topic of conversation away from them, he didn't have Rukiye's boldness and recklessness. Rukiye slowly came to the conclusion that this relationship could go on this way forever, that Tevfik Bey would never have the courage to open up to her about his feelings, and that she had to take the

438 · AHMET ALTAN

reins. She knew now that soon she would talk to Tevfik Bey very openly, but there was no way she could know that a murder would bring the subject up, a murder would bring the man she loved into her life, but unfortunately another murder would take him away forever.

When Rukiye came back into the living room, Hikmet Bey immediately brought up the subject he wanted to talk about.

"I saw your mother today," he said.

Mihrişah Sultan looked at him in the mocking manner that always hurt him and carped:

"Now it's clear what happened to you."

Hikmet Bey acted as if he hadn't heard her.

"You mother wants you and Nizam to live with her."

Rukiye shook her head angrily.

"I want to stay with her ladyship."

Then she turned to Mihrişah Sultan.

"If you have no objection . . . "

"Of course I have no objection, on the contrary, I'd be pleased."

Hikmet Bey interrupted.

"But your mother has been very lonely, Rukiye, she wants to have her children with her."

Rukiye had never forgiven her mother's betrayal of her stepfather, she was determined not to forgive her, but Nizam had long since forgiven what had been done to his natural father.

"Nizam can live with her, I'm fine here."

Hikmet Bey realized that insisting wouldn't help.

"As you wish, Rukiye, but at least go visit your mother and tell her yourself. She is your mother, and nothing can change that fact."

"I'll write her a letter tomorrow."

"Please don't upset her."

Rukiye gave Hikmet Bey a scornful look for showing this tenderness to Mehpare Hanım after all that had happened.

"Don't talk as if you don't know my mother, nothing can upset her."

"Aren't you being a bit harsh?"

"Why is it harsh to tell the truth, but if you don't want to see the truth, then that's something else."

Hikmet Bey turned to his mother.

"With your permission, I'd like to stay the night here."

It was only then that Mihrişah Sultan noticed that Hikmet Bey was truly shaken, that meeting the former wife for whom he'd tried to kill himself had affected him.

"Of course, stay, it's very beautiful here in the morning, I really miss talking to you. You said you weren't hungry, but today they made some of the dishes you like, let me tell them to bring you some. Maybe you'll eat."

Hikmet Bey hungrily ate the food they brought and drank a bottle of French wine as well; as he ate, color returned to his face, his smile became vivacious, despite her hurtful manner, his mother's presence and her beauty, which made even Mehpare Hanım angry, reinforced the self-confidence that had been established again with that afternoon's lovemaking. As he said to Osman, "I don't know how she does it, but my mother gives everyone around her the feeling that they are the most important thing in her life, all of your problems seemed insignificant when you were with her."

After dinner he gave a long speech about the complexity and incomprehensibility of the soul, teased the ladies in waiting, as the women watched in surprise, he seemed to shift shape and become another person.

Mihrişah Sultan was irritated because she thought he was happy because of his reconciliation with Mehpare Hanım.

"I think you're drunk."

Hikmet Bey behaved like a pampered child.

"Oh, mother, you think that men are only cheerful when they're drunk, all of your friends must be depressed."

"Does it seem strange to you that I think people need a reason to be cheerful, as far as I know, only madmen and drunks are cheerful for no reason."

"I have reason to be cheerful."

Mihrişah Sultan became even more angry.

"Is that so? It must be something only you know about, I don't see anyone else being cheerful."

"You're here, Rukiye is here, these beautiful ladies are here, do I need any more reason?"

"We've always been here, but we weren't reason enough for you to be cheerful then."

"Mother, does it make you angry that I'm cheerful?"

"No, shame on you."

Before she'd finished her sentence, Mihrişah Sultan realized that her son was right, that his cheer did make her angry, but she preferred to ignore it.

"I just find it a bit meaningless."

As Hikmet Bey fluttered around himself like a snowflake caught in an air current, changing his expression and manner of speaking as he encountered a variety feelings and facets, he suddenly changed again, becoming the conceited Pasha's son in the salons of Paris.

"You think being cheerful is meaningless, I think, madame, that it's been a long time since you've read Rabelais, oh, madame, what a sin . . . "

Then he became a melancholy Istanbul gentleman.

"We have been unable to find anything but sorrow in meaning. Be lighthearted even if it is meaningless, don't think that being cheerful is too much for this poor slave."

That evening he parried his mother's innuendos, taunts, jibes, sharp witticisms, and mocking scorn and responded in kind; throughout their conversation he felt that this was what he really wanted, that motherly tenderness would have suffocated and killed him. Deliberately or not, Mihrişah Sultan gave her son what he needed most, to spar with an intelligent woman who was magically beautiful, just like a lioness teaching her cubs to hunt through games, she taught him again how to handle women, reminding him again how to make moves against beautiful women, succeeded in erasing Mehpare Hanım's extraordinary beauty and terrifying image with her presence, and showed him that this was possible.

After a deep and peaceful sleep, he woke the next morning to a lavish breakfast served by the sea and a tender mother. As much as he'd enjoyed sparring the previous evening, he would have found witty repartee tedious in the morning, but Mihrişah Sultan acted as if she sensed all of her son's wishes. As for Rukiye, she came over to him and kissed him on the cheek, as if to apologize for her rudeness the previous evening. They had their breakfast without much conversation, but with the complete warmth and love of a family.

Hikmet Bey kissed his mother's hand before boarding the launch that was waiting for him.

"Oh, mother, it's as if you give birth to me anew each time."

Mihrişah Sultan slapped his cheek softly and said, "Don't be silly."

But after watching Hikmet Bey waving from the back of the launch as it moved away from the dock, she eventually murmured to herself:

"Hikmet has suffered so much, I hope there isn't more suffering in store for him."

Rukiye waved without saying anything, but she made the same wish inwardly.

When Hikmet Bey arrived at his mansion in Nişantaşı, he found Dilevser browsing in the library.

"*Bonjour*, Dilevser, how are you?"

They met and spoke in the library almost every morning; it was as if the smell of old books showed them how meaningless time was and decreased the age difference between them, sharing the same taste, liking the same writers, being able to talk about the same characters established a solid bridge between them on which they could move safely. Over time they were able to speak more comfortably and freely; this was partly because Dilevser felt stronger among the books, in a world that belonged to her. When they talked about books, Dilevser abandoned the modesty behind which she concealed herself, she offered bold criticism and used sharp language to express what she admired. They grew accustomed to each other; they knew each other's taste in books and authors, they could now guess what books the other would like.

Whether it was because Hikmet Bey had said "*bonjour*" rather than "good morning" as he usually did, or because of the tone of his voice, or for some other reason, Dilevser sensed that there was something different about him that morning, that something about Hikmet Bey had changed.

And what she sensed was very true. That morning Hikmet Bey was very different from the man she'd seen the previous day, he was self-confident, he was aware that he had recovered from his wounds, he knew that he was strong enough to deal with women, he believed once again that he was attractive and he had made love to Mehpare Hanım; just like any man who had managed to emerge from a beautiful woman's bed without being wounded, he looked down on other women, how should this be put, he was somewhat arrogant and patronizing.

"Good morning, Hikmet Bey, perhaps I came a little too early this morning . . . "

She stopped and added softly:

"You weren't here."

Hikmet Bey understood that the phrase, "You weren't here," contained many questions, that the young girl was asking, "Where have you been, where were you, who were you with?" The previous morning he would have answered these questions at once, he would have told her where he'd been, but he didn't do so that morning.

"It looks as if it's going to be quite hot today, let me open these windows."

He went and opened the windows one by one. Dilevser watched him in silence, and it was clear she was still waiting for an answer to her question. And Hikmet Bey was deliberately slow, he took revenge for all the days he'd spent struggling to win her admiration by trying to make the young girl feel her jealousy more deeply. Even though he was ashamed of what he was doing, he couldn't hold himself back; a secret voice from his experience was also telling him that jealousy would help Dilevser grow up and become more of a woman.

When he turned back to Dilevser he acted as if he'd just grasped what the young girl had said.

"Oh, yes, I wasn't home last night, I stayed with my mother."

When he saw a faint flash of joy pass across Dilevser's slightly faded face, he knew that her interest had come to life. Later he complained to Osman, "I don't know why we treat some women badly, but why are some women more interested when we treat them badly, I don't understand that either."

He sat in an armchair and crossed his legs, and looked at the young girl arrogantly, almost scornfully, he was having trouble believing that this thin, pale, fragile creature was the woman who had caused him to spend weeks living in a misty, melancholy world that resembled a late afternoon in winter. The realization that he had freed himself from the poisonous effects of Mehpare Hanım's fateful enchantment was like an amulet that protected him from any woman's enchantment, power, and attraction and made him untouchable, unreachable, and invulnerable; he looked at those under whose influence he'd fallen, who'd wounded and saddened him, as if he was looking through the wrong end of a telescope, he found them small, distant, even meaningless. What he felt now toward almost all women was not anger or rage, but rather distance and scorn. That morning, the things he'd seen as beautiful in Dilevser he now saw as flaws; her faded face, the childishness of her innocent fingers, the thin, bony body in which there appeared no inklings of lust, the distant bashfulness in her eyes; someone had changed the angle of the light shining on her, the same person looked as if she was someone else, the shadows on her face suddenly moved from one place to another. Seeing her flaws gave him a strange, almost wicked pleasure.

Dilevser deliberately looked at the books with deep attention, taking out one after another, reading the back covers, leafing through them carefully as if she didn't want to see Hikmet Bey's arrogant and discomforting mood, the inner waves of which were reflected on his face; Hikmet Bey absent-mindedly watched the way her head bowed and her back hunched slightly as she took another book from the bookcase. This girl too had made him suffer, though not nearly as much as Mehpare Hanım had, she'd made him pursue her, she'd kept her shields of modesty raised against him in a way that had rattled his self-confidence; despite the closeness that had recently been established between them, Hikmet Bey always felt the taste of the embarrassing sediment left by the efforts he'd made to win the heart of a young girl who was the same age as his son.

He'd forgotten what a consolation her innocence and distance from the world had been for him just a few days ago, how comforting it had been for him to dream about her thin-fingered hands caressing the wounds Mehpare Hanım had inflicted.

When Dilevser tired of looking at the books so intently and turned toward Hikmet Bey with a book in her hand, for a moment she felt a real disquiet and avoided looking at the man sitting in the armchair.

"Why are you looking at me that way?"

"How am I looking at you?" asked Hikmet Bey in a condescending manner.

"As if you've caught me doing something wrong. Have I done anything to anger you?"

Then she put the book back into the bookshelf where she'd found it and walked toward the door.

"I'm sorry, I shouldn't have intruded on you at such an early hour, I was being thoughtless."

Hikmet Bey realized at that moment that she would never return. He jumped up, more in fear of being rude to a woman than of losing Dilevser.

"I beg your pardon, Dilevser, there's no intrusion, in this house your presence is never seen as an intrusion, if you say you don't know this then you can also say that I'm a bad host."

"No, of course not, I couldn't say that, the thought never even occurred to me. It was only today that I had the feeling I was intruding."

Hikmet Bey touched the girl's arm lightly.

"Please, sit down, let's have a morning coffee."

Then he couldn't resist and added with a mocking smile:

"You mother won't be angry if you drink coffee, will she?"

Dilevser answered in such a tranquil tone that Hikmet Bey couldn't be certain whether she was making fun of him or if she was serious.

"I didn't realize that you see me as a child."

"I beg your pardon, Dilevser, have you decided to shame me for everything I say and do, my dear?"

"I don't think you've done anything to be shamed for."

"Please, come. You haven't picked out a book today."

They went back into the living room together and sat down.

"I don't know, I couldn't find anything this morning. I think I'm a bit absentminded, I couldn't focus on books."

"Why are you absentminded, is there anything bothering you?"

The girl looked at Hikmet Bey with her large, clear eyes. "No."

She uttered only this one word, but she continued looking at Hikmet Bey's face, it was more as if she was trying to understand something than as if there was something she wanted to say.

They sat in silence until their coffee was served, the girl's serenity, the clarity of her eyes, her straight, open expression embarrassed Hikmet Bey a bit, caused a slight regret to move within him. He realized that Dilevser was hurt, even if she didn't say so.

Perhaps because he was ashamed of his ill-intentioned rudeness that morning, perhaps because he wanted to see himself as a man who was powerful enough to make the women around him suffer, he thought he saw a pain in the girl's eyes that was familiar to him, that was almost like a reflection of the state he'd recently been in; amid the fog and the inebriating cloudiness left behind after the experience of strong emotions, he thought he was seeing his own expressions, the unbearable pain he used to have, on the young girl's face.

His concern that he may have caused her to suffer made him blush.

"I haven't done anything to hurt you, have I?" Then he repeated the same question as if he was drunk.

"I haven't done anything to hurt you, have I?"

There was an almost pleading tone in his voice. Without changing her blank expression, she gave the same short answer again.

"No."

Hikmet Bey was surprised by her calm voice, the expression that despite its clarity revealed nothing of her, a single-word answer instead of a long explanation; he was unable to grasp what she was feeling and this disquieted him deeply. This disquiet once again shook the self-confidence that Hikmet Bey was quite sure existed, and the interest that he'd thought had ended was once again focused on her.

They drank their coffee without speaking. Hikmet Bey wanted to say something, to open a conversational door, to understand the girl's emotions, but somehow he wasn't able to speak, and Dilevser just remained silent.

When the young girl left, saying nothing more than good-bye and without borrowing a new book, she left behind her a chaos of emotions composed of curiosity, anxiety, the desire to love, and the disquiet of not understanding, showing Hikmet Bey that it was not easy to reach a new and tranquil mood after a great emotional upheaval and that these tides would continue for some time.

Hikmet Bey leaned back wearily, thinking about how he was always the one who was tired and defeated, and he saw a letter on the coffee table next to his armchair.

Reşit Pasha had written to his son to inform him that he'd settled into a mansion in Salonika, he'd sent the address and asked that money be sent to him.

Just as he did every time he felt defeated and alone, he rushed out of the library, said, "Come," to Hediye, who was leaning against the wall waiting, and as he climbed the stairs he thought, "My father is safe"; he had no idea what he was safe from or what he had made safe, but he believed that his pain had been eased and that leaving Istanbul had saved him.

And indeed Reşit Pasha had found a peaceful life. He rented a large mansion by the sea, close to the Alatini mansion where the former Sultan resided, he settled in, he'd brought his cook and butler from Istanbul and he'd restocked the harem he loved so much with new and beautiful girls. He woke early every morning, strolled in the garden, picked flowers, and then, after breakfast, went to see the Sultan, who was already up and waiting for him.

It was as if the friendship he'd longed for had been

established between them. When the Sultan, confined to a mansion surrounded by a battalion of guardsmen, suffered a breakdown brought about by being a prisoner after having possessed great power, experiencing occasional panic attacks and fits of hysterics, the doctor calmed him down, they established something beyond friendship, almost a father-son relationship, the doctor treated his former master as if he was a child, he calmed him down by speaking softly and reassuring him.

That morning he found the Sultan sitting pensively in the great hall. He'd become quite an old man, he'd lost almost all his teeth, he had only two teeth remaining. Because he had so few teeth, his jaw had caved in, his mouth was puckered like a drawstring sack, and this made him look more like an old man; despite his missing teeth, he was very careful about the way he spoke and the words he emphasized, he spoke in his magnificent voice without slurring any words.

He was happy to see the doctor.

"Come, doctor, I was waiting for you, Müşfika Kadınefendi had crisis of nerves last night. She was nervous when she was young too, what can she do, it's not her fault, that's her nature, she gets more irritable when she has her period, but her nerves are much worse here. I'm worried, doctor . . . In the old days she used to eat with me, she hasn't eaten with me since we came here, I suppose she's not being as careful about what she eats, she's put on weight, her body produces fat, it produces too much blood, then she becomes ill like this."

As he spoke he stroked the cat on his lap, a snow-white, silky-haired cat he'd brought from Istanbul.

"There are mosquitoes here too, I imagine you have them where you are, they're as big as my finger, they suck your blood all night, it's impossible to sleep. Lack of sleep makes her ladyship's nerves even worse."

He lit a cigarette, he chain-smoked all day, he offered the

doctor a cigarette, then he offered one to Captain Atıf Bey, who made a point of being present every time they spoke.

"As you well know, doctor, these mosquitoes carry all kinds of diseases, they're full of microbes, and what we refer to as microbes are the diseases themselves. Tuberculosis, for instance, is spread by microbes."

Reşit Pasha had learned that the Sultan always liked talking about medicine, illnesses, and treatment, and that this calmed him down; he was never boring even though he repeated the same things over and over, because even though he repeated it several times, he always added new details.

"The pine tree, it's a gift from God, it's very good for tuberculosis. Once they told me that there was no tuberculosis in the vicinity of Kastomonu, when someone contracts tuberculosis, they bring them to the pine forest and leave them there in a tent for some months. There's a substance that oozes from the bark of pine trees, they give this to the patient and if the disease hasn't progressed too far the patient is always cured."

He stopped and thought.

"Why am I talking about this, because a few days ago I was thinking to myself, and it became clearer as we talked, you see, the cure for many diseases exists in nature, we boil cinnamon, we boil lemon flowers, we use the juices of many plants, if you're seeking a cure for tuberculosis, you might suddenly find that it's hidden in a pine tree . . . This is what comes to mind, God created diseases, isn't it possible that he concealed the cure for each disease in nature, if the doctors look for it, can they find the remedy in nature?"

As was his wont, he stopped abruptly, turned to Captain Atıf Bey, and changed the subject.

"I asked for bergamot leaves, it's been more than ten days and they haven't arrived yet, can't something that basic be found in a city as big as Salonika . . . Even if it had been ordered from Istanbul it would have been here days ago. I see now that I'm not taken at all seriously."

With his complaint about the bergamot leaves he was returning to the subject that was really upsetting him, he didn't bother to establish connections between the topics he spoke about, he jumped from one topic to another with an almost pampered ease.

"And I don't understand why they don't give me newspapers here. What law prohibits me from reading newspapers? I'm a man who's interested in the state and future of the nation."

He hesitated for a moment and then, in fear of being misunderstood, offered an explanation at once.

"In fact I no longer have any political ambitions. But I want to know about the state and condition of the nation. It is my right to be pleased by uplifting news or, God forbid, to be saddened by bad news. Not even murderers and felons are denied this right, why are they denying me this right?"

The Sultan, who throughout his reign had banned foreign newspapers and Turkish newspapers that had been printed in Europe, who had not allowed his subjects to read what they wanted, was now complaining sincerely about not being allowed to read newspapers, he'd realized how painful this was.

Reşit Pasha tried to calm the Sultan.

"No one is being disrespectful to you, your majesty, I can see that every effort is being made to grant you even the smallest thing you ask for . . . Perhaps this is being done to protect you from criticism in the newspapers rather than out of disrespect."

The Sultan smiled faintly.

"I'm sure they're protecting me, and they're doing it very thoroughly . . . "

After they had lunch together, the doctor examined

Müşfika Kadınefendi, wrote a few prescriptions, then he returned to the Sultan and continued the endless conversations about medicine. The Sultan told him about his youthful adventures and about how he hadn't lost even an inch of territory throughout his reign.

Reşit Pasha saw that someone who had lost power was fond of talking about his past successes and couldn't refrain from defending himself and trying to prove he was right even though he knew there was nothing to gain from this, he listened to all of this with sincere sadness, feeling somewhat sorry for the Sultan. Throughout his life the doctor had faced occasional insults and threats from the Sultan, but he didn't feel even the slightest sense of justice that his master had fallen into such a state of powerlessness, it would be considered human for him to feel even slightly pleased, but on the contrary he was genuinely saddened.

A few days ago he'd witnessed this old man being forced to sign a document handing over a million in gold he had in German banks over to the army, he'd lost his teeth, he'd been imprisoned in a mansion in exile and had lost his wealth after abdicating, but the doctor was more moved by what he said as they parted that evening than by anything else.

"Will you come tomorrow, doctor? Please take good care of my wife . . . I've been living with her for twenty-three years, she's never once been mean or hurt my feelings. I want to do everything I possibly can for her."

He sighed sadly.

"Though in fact we don't have the power to do good deeds anymore . . . At least . . . "

The words were stuck in his throat, the doctor saw his lips tremble in the fear that something might happen to Müşfika Kadınefendi.

The man who'd been able to endure losing an empire couldn't endure the thought of losing his woman.

Without finishing his sentence, the Sultan extended his hand to the doctor.

Reşit Pasha shook his hand and left without saying anything.

As he walked away, he thought the man would die if he lost his wife. He repeated these words all night until the Sultan's pain mingled with his own.

22

On the ninth of June the city, which had abandoned itself to a soft heat that smelled of the sea, recoiled and tensed when a gun was fired in Bahçekapı.

Ahmed Samim, the twenty-six-year-old chief columnist for Sada-yı Millet newspaper, with his wire pince-nez, his thin moustache that was slightly twisted at the ends, thick hair that he combed back to reveal his gleaming forehead, this young journalist who had earned the love of his friends with his cheerful conversation and his stern articles, was shot and killed by a murderer who approached him from behind. He wrote the harshest criticism of the Sultan during the mutiny, he didn't hesitate to criticize the way the Committee governed after the mutiny either.

As was always the case, the killer fled and was never captured.

The city, accustomed to unsolved murders, turned to try to see the murderer's silhouette, they looked at the government and the Committee members in it with hatred, but, because its courage was not as great as its hatred, it bowed its head with a shame particular to cowards just as it did after every murder.

It was whispered from ear to ear that the murderer was Abdülkadir Bey, one of the Committee's infamous gunmen, but no one repeated this aloud.

That day Tevfik Bey returned earlier in the afternoon than usual, struggling to keep the tears from rolling out of his soft eyes, he broke the news of his dear friend's death to Mihrişah Sultan.

He had visited her waterfront mansion a few times, and Mihrişah Sultan had liked this courageous young man's talk and his perspective. She bit her lip when she heard the news of his death.

"This country is like a funeral home, death and more death . . . The dead change, but the mourning never changes. And it will never change. I can't bear this smell of death, this fascination with murder . . . "

She ordered her ladies in waiting in a stern tone.

"Start packing at once, we're returning to France on the first ferry. This country is killing itself, and my heart can't take watching any more of this. You too, Rukiye, get ready, start packing, we're leaving, I'll never come back here again!"

Rukiye remembered the young journalist talking about death mockingly during conversations in the waterfront mansion's garden as if it had happened yesterday. She'd listened to those words as if they were a joke, it had never occurred to her that such a lively young man would actually be killed. Just like anyone who hears unexpected news of death, she couldn't believe this unexpected news of his death, more precisely, she couldn't grasp the meaning of death, a person departing, never to return, never again to be seen among them. With the sudden arrival of death, the ground on which the meaning of life and of words stood had suddenly trembled, a gap appeared between words and their meaning, she experienced a strange semantic shift, yes, Ahmed Samim was dead, she understood that part, but she was unable to accept that he would never come to the waterfront mansion again. It was as if death and disappearance were two different concepts; people could die, but they didn't disappear; a person died, but then continued meeting his friends. Among all these shifting meanings, her heart could still feel the pain and meaning of death; the pain found its way through the blurred words and meanings.

Experiencing the deaf dizziness of the vibration of clusters of scattered, misty meanings and the pain whose sharpness increased in contrast, Rukiye didn't at first catch what Mihrişah Sultan had said, it was when she repeated it for the second time, mentioning her name and talking about leaving, that she realized they were going to leave and, just like Ahmed Samim Bey, she would never see Tevfik Bey again either; when the concepts of not seeing again and death were absorbed into the slippery, vibrating pile of meaning, she felt a strange feeling that made her tremble in terror, the feeling that Tevfik Bey would die as well, and she was seized by a kind of nervous crisis.

Either because of a nervous crisis, or the power of true love that continued to exist under all circumstances, or that in the midst of all this her curiosity was so strong she couldn't bear not getting an answer, she ran after Tevfik Bey, who was just going out the door on his way home.

At the main gate she caught up to Tevfik Bey, who'd been walking sadly through the garden that smelled of jasmine, raspberries, melons, and seaweed under a sky with reddish, lilac, and purple waves that was preparing for a summer night.

"Tevfik Bey!"

Tevfik Bey stopped, somewhat surprised, and turned back to see who had called him.

"Yes, Rukiye Hanım?"

Rukiye brushed back her hair.

She asked what she wanted to ask in a single breath, as if she was afraid she might change her mind.

"Do you love me?"

Tevfik Bey blushed in surprise and shame. Sheikh Efendi's daughter, the stepgranddaughter of the former Ottoman Sultan's physician, had done something that had perhaps never been seen before in any of the waterfront mansions of the capital of the Ottoman Empire, she had asked a man if he loved her. This was something that was difficult to speak about in the bedroom, let alone at the garden gate, but the young girl asked the question on her mind as if it was very natural, without hesitating, without giving a thought to what might be said about her.

Tevfik Bey, who was already bewildered by his friend's death, gave Rukiye a pleading look but didn't know what to say; for such a long time he'd loved this strange young girl who didn't recognize rules and traditions, who placed her will and her wishes at the center of her life, and who couldn't bear for any word, feeling, or subject to remain vague, but his upbringing would not allow him to speak of this openly, to open his heart to the girl of the house in which he was a guest.

For her part, Rukiye had no intention of being content with Tevfik Bey's pleading expression.

"Why don't you say anything? If you don't love me, tell me now and I'll go pack my things, we'll never see each other again anyway."

Tevfik Bey knew that Rukiye was decisive enough to do whatever she said; unable to endure the thought of never seeing her again, he sighed deeply and spoke in an almost moaning tone.

"I do love you."

"Enough to marry me?"

Tevfik Bey closed his eyes when he answered.

"Yes."

Rukiye took the young man's hand and they walked toward the house.

"Then come and ask Mihrişah Sultan for my hand in marriage."

Tevfik Bey immediately pulled his hand back out of fear of being seen.

"What are you saying, Rukiye, do you want Mihrişah Sultan to banish me from the house? I can't ask a lady for your hand in marriage right away, that's not the way it's done."

"Then how is it done?"

"I should send my mother."

"Then go and tell her to come."

"Rukiye, please, I beg you, don't behave like this. Let me speak to my mother so that she can come and ask for your hand in marriage in the morning, let's do everything the way it should be done."

Rukiye looked at Tevfik Bey, thought about what he'd said, and nodded.

"Fine, they can come in the morning, I'll go tell Mihrişah Sultan now."

Even though Tevfik Bey's mother remonstrated with him and told him how inappropriate it was to be in such a rush, she didn't deny her son's request. Of course Rukiye's father's fame and Mihrişah Sultan's wealth and the powerful social circles in which she traveled had an important role in influencing Tevfik Bey's family, despite the shameful shadow cast by Mehpare Hanım.

When Mihrişah Sultan heard the news she surprised the young girl by kissing her and saying, "You should have been my daughter," then she pulled herself together and said, "We should ask your mother and father as well." Rukiye immediately objected to this.

"Your permission is enough for me, if you give your approval, there's no need for me to ask anyone else. Do you think that my decision is fitting?"

Mihrişah Sultan smiled.

"Do you love Tevfik Bey?"

"Yes."

"Do you think that you can't live without him?"

"I can't countenance the thought of not seeing him again."

"Then I think it's fitting."

In the end Rukiye's will overcame all traditions and customs; with unprecedented haste, Tevfik Bey's mother asked for

Rukiye's hand in marriage, and Mihrişah Sultan consented. Because her ladyship didn't want to remain in Istanbul too long, it was decided that they would hold the wedding in a week's time.

After she'd spoken with Tevfik Bey's mother, Mihrişah Sultan called Rukiye, told her that the wedding would be held in a week, then added:

"There's one thing I ask of you."

"Please."

"Go to the *tekke* and tell your father you're getting married, get his blessing. Will you do this for my sake?"

"Of course, if you wish. I was going to go talk to him in any event."

Hasan Efendi returned from Aleppo on the night Ahmed Samim was shot. There, he had presented Yusuf Efendi's gifts for a Rufai Sheikh's son's wedding, attended the wedding in his sheikh's name, and then had spent several difficult days travelling back to Istanbul. He wanted to tell the Sheikh at once about what he'd seen but the Sheikh, in his usual forbearing manner, said, "Go rest now, we can talk tomorrow."

Hasan Efendi went to the harem weary from the long journey and terrified by what he'd seen in Anatolia, after taking the bath his wife had ordered be prepared, he put on a clean nightshirt, withdrew to his room, and found what he feared waiting for him in the bed. His dwarf wife, uncontrollably randy because he'd been away for days, attacked him, ignoring his objections of, "Stop for a moment, I'm exhausted." She climbed onto the gigantic man's body like a monkey, she moved all over him and once again Hasan Efendi experienced the horrible pleasure that was mixed with disgust and that filled him with hatred whenever he remembered it.

The following morning he wanted to speak with Sheikh Efendi at once to tell him what he'd seen and also to wash away the effects of the previous night, but because Sheikh Efendi had guests, he spent the morning strolling alone along the Golden Horn, thought about what he'd experienced in Anatolia, and decided that a state that had forgotten its religion was bound to collapse.

In the afternoon, when the heat of the summer day made its presence felt and everyone withdrew inside, he managed to get into the cool, dark room where Sheikh Efendi sat, he greeted his Sheikh and began telling him about what he'd seen.

"Anatolia is finished, my Sheikh," he began, "Anatolia is a cesspool. There is no religion or faith. There's corruption, extortion, and fraud everywhere . . . "

He talked about a district governor in the vicinity of Yozgat, the man sat in the garden outside his office in his night shirt, ignoring the people who came and went and drinking from morning to night; another district governor had lined bottles up on the garden wall and shot at them with a rifle from his office window, he did nothing but shoot at bottles.

"May God strike me blind if I'm lying, Sheikh, I saw an official who was a hundred and four years old, he rides a donkey, two men hold on to him so he doesn't fall off, that's how he goes to the government building, he's half demented, his mind comes and goes, but the man hadn't done anything wrong, as he himself said to me, 'I told the Shaykh-al Islam, if you're appointing me to this position, you would have appointed Noah if you could have found him, but he didn't mind, he just said we'll see what happens.' May God lead you to believe that Anatolia is off the rails. It would not be an exaggeration to say that there is no government, the people live in misery, you can't get a single document signed without paying a bribe. Along the way we saw many funerals, we saw sickness, epidemics, starvation . . . As I always say, if there's no religion, there's nothing left, sharia is no longer obeyed, I crossed the vastness of Anatolia without seeing any divine light anywhere."

Sheikh Efendi listened in silence, these were all things he knew, everyone who came from Anatolia told him the same thing.

He asked, "Did you see the monk in Sinop I told you about?"

Hasan Efendi smiled.

"I saw him, Your Excellency, he was all alone in a monastery in the middle of nowhere, on top of a mountain. May God grant that this infidel die in the correct religion, the man's an infidel but he's shrewder than any Muslim . . . But I think he has a screw loose. He dug a grave in the monastery garden, it's his grave, he lives next to his grave. While I was there, the governor came with his retinue, he was very fond of the infidel . . . The monk was very pleased by the Pasha's visit. When the Pasha was leaving he showed him the grave he'd dug, I remember what he said word for word . . . "

Hasan Efendi stopped, recalled the monk's exact words, and repeated them to his sheikh.

"He said to the Pasha, 'I'm one of the happiest creatures in the world, because I will spend this life that God has given me in the quietude granted to those who have conviction in a heavenly place, in forested mountains. When I die, I will be buried in a grave that I have become accustomed to seeing every day as if it was a bed. Because you are a great governor, a pasha, you will spend your short life, regardless of how long it is, in turmoil, you won't know where you'll die or where you'll be buried. To whom did the Lord who made you governor of a province and me a monk in a monastery grant the greatest blessing, think about it.' This is what he said to the governor pasha."

The Sheikh nodded.

"He's a good Christian. Did he send me anything?"

"He wrote a letter and gave it to me."

Sheikh Efendi took the letter and put it aside to read later.

Hasan Efendi was contemplating whether to tell him about

the meeting between Mehpare Hanım and Hikmet Bey, which he'd heard about as soon as he arrived and which bothered him, when both of them looked at the door in silence, they sensed that someone was coming.

Sheikh Efendi stirred restlessly because he sensed who was coming.

When he saw Rukiye come in and open her abiya, Hasan Efendi rushed to stand up, asked to be excused, and left.

"Welcome, please sit over here."

Rukiye sat on the cushion next to Sheikh Efendi.

She waited for a time in silence, looking straight ahead, and then, as was her wont, she took a deep breath, loaded the burden she was carrying into her father's mind, and briefly said what she had to say with a sharpness that freed her.

"I'm getting married."

In the way this short sentence was delivered, it was clear that she was not seeking her father's permission, that she was simply informing him.

Sheikh Efendi acted as if he didn't notice the tension in his daughter's voice.

"I wish you happiness. He's a good young man."

At first Rukiye couldn't grasp who the good young man was, then when she realized this was Tevfik Bey, she gave a smile that resembled Mihrişah Sultan's smile.

"Oh yes . . . I forgot that you hear about everything, that you know everything."

Sheikh Efendi looked at his daughter as if to shame her, but he didn't answer, he just asked a question that surprised her.

"Are you going to find peace in this marriage?"

Rukiye could guess that the question that was usually asked in these circumstances was, "Are you happy?" but her father had asked her if she was at peace.

"Why do you ask this?"

"I think you need peace, you have a restless, impatient

nature. My daughter, everyone finds happiness in different things, there are people who find happiness in anger, in fighting, there are people who find happiness in excitement, and some find happiness in love . . . I think that you will find happiness in peace, in order for you to be happy, you first need peace. If you had faith you could find this peace in belief, in worship, but I know your faith is weak, destiny has been cruel enough to find it appropriate for you to find peace not in the Lord but in his slaves, in unfortunate humans. For you happiness is concealed behind peace . . . I will always beseech the Lord in my prayers to give you peace."

Rukiye was more impressed by the touching compassion in her father's voice than by his words, she bowed her head. Sheikh Efendi continued.

"This is very difficult to confess, but I think I may be one of the reasons for your restlessness. Rukiye, there's a price for every misdeed in life, but sometimes someone other than the person who committed it ends up paying for it. I made the mistake, and you paid for it."

Sheikh Efendi smiled sadly.

"Of course this price naturally brings me my own share of suffering, but you were the intermediary. The child of a mother and father who were unable to find happiness also has difficulty finding happiness. Parents show a child the way to happiness, if we were unable to do that, how and where would you be able to find it? Then you might even think that there's no such thing as happiness, but this would also be a mistake. If you find peace, you'll also find happiness."

With difficulty, Rukiye said, "I'm not looking for anything."

"We're all looking for something, my daughter, some of us find it and some of us don't. Only those who've lost hope say they're not looking for anything. You shouldn't say this on the eve of a marriage, my child, you are looking for something, and with God's help you'll find it."

More out of tactless closeness than out of disrespect, Rukiye asked:

"What are you looking for?"

No one but his daughter could have asked Sheikh Efendi this question, and no one but his daughter would have received an answer.

"I'm looking for peace."

"You have the faith that you told me could help me, how is it that this faith didn't give you peace?"

Without realizing it, the Sheikh started to count his beads a bit faster.

"Why hasn't my faith given me peace? If I didn't have the faith, I wouldn't have found the strength to seek peace . . . The Lord showed me peace and light, but a time came when I was curious about darkness, I wanted to see what was hidden there. If you're walking in the light and you turn to look at the darkness, if you commit this sin, the darkness casts a shadow on your light and peace. All your life you try to get rid of that shadow, to find light and peace again, and this is more difficult than you can imagine."

It was only when she heard this that Rukiye was able to understand how much her father had suffered. She felt he wouldn't have told this to anyone but her, she felt that an incredible privilege had been granted her. When she felt this, it was as if the last knots within her had been untied, it truly gave her peace to be Sheikh Efendi's daughter and to know that he loved her. She asked in a soft, meek voice:

"Do you think this marriage is fitting, do you give your permission?"

Sheikh Efendi looked at his daughter.

"May God grant you happiness, my prayers are with you."

When Rukiye put her hand in front of her in order to stand up and asked to be excused, she suddenly started to cry; she sobbed, she wept breathlessly in a way she hadn't done since childhood; she tried to control herself but she couldn't, it was as if the knots within her, tied by all the things she'd experienced and hadn't been able to cry about, had been loosened, now, even though there was no apparent reason to cry she was crying about everything that had happened in her life. As she wept she murmured, "Forgive me, forgive me." From his seat Sheikh Efendi silently stroked his daughter's hair and allowed her to weep as much as she wanted.

She wept for quite some time, neither of them knew how long, then she wiped her eyes; she asked with a sarcasm that didn't match her swollen eyes and flushed face:

"Do you think I'm finding peace this way?"

"Are you?"

Rukiye became serious.

"I think I am."

Then she smiled again.

"But if I find peace like this a few more times I won't have the strength to experience that peace."

Sheikh Efendi smiled as well.

"You will, my daughter, you will."

"If you'll allow it, I want to come here with my fiancé before the wedding, so that he can kiss your hand."

"Of course, my daughter, I would be pleased."

Rukiye left that place with a feeling she'd never known, with a great trust in herself, her life, and her future, without all the nameless irritations and unaccountable tensions she'd suffered throughout her childhood, with the quietude her father called peace. It was as if a hoarder's room, full of junk, full of things whose purpose no one knew, no one could guess why they'd been saved, had been cleaned out, all of the unnecessary clutter had been thrown away; even Rukiye herself was surprised at the sense of rejuvenation she felt after this catharsis.

Sheikh Efendi, for his part, felt as if he'd been reunited with his favorite child, though she was his favorite for reasons he either didn't know or couldn't confess to himself, that his daughter had forgiven him and accepted him as her father, he was proud of her intelligence, her frankness, her honesty, and her rebellious soul, though all of these were considered disrespectful in the world of the *tekke*, he prayed softly for her peace and happiness.

After Rukiye left he called Hasan Efendi and, with a joy in his voice that surprised even him, gave him orders; a waterfront mansion on the Bosphorus would be rented for her, she would be given an income, all of Istanbul, and particularly the groom's family and Mihrişah Sultan, would know that this young girl, whose mother was remembered with curses, was not all alone, and that she was not indigent.

As the Sheikh was preparing for one daughter's wedding, he didn't know that another daughter was preparing to get divorced. It was as if destiny had determined that this man would not experience any joy fully.

The night Ahmed Samim Bey was shot, there was an angry debate between two brothers in the garden of the mansion in Göztepe.

Ragıp Bey was very angry.

He almost shouted, "What is this, brother?" his voice reached the women sitting on the mansion's veranda.

"I didn't object to men being killed for freedom, for the good of the empire, I myself killed people, I haven't doubted for a single day that what I did was right, but the men we shot in the streets provided guns and money to the Bulgarian guerillas, they were enemies of the empire. Why did you shoot this man? Why do you send this dog, Abdülkadir, after our people? Did this man sell guns to the Bulgarians, did he give money to the Greeks? Why did we fight for freedom if we're just going to kill our own people? A day will come when the entire population of this nation will be our enemy, can't you see this? This isn't soldiering, this is playing at being guerillas in our own capital, against who, against our own people."

Cevat Bey listened patiently to what his brother had to say.

"Ragıp, you're getting angry for no reason. You didn't read what he wrote, you don't know what he wrote, there's nothing he didn't stoop to saying about the organization, he wrote such garbage even a dog wouldn't eat it. Think about what it means to criticize the Committee. This man was buttering the fanatics' bread, as he attacked us, the religious fanatics jumped for joy. What will it lead to if everyone starts to criticize the organization like this, the fanatics will be revitalized, do you want us to go back to the old days, do you want the tyranny to begin again, do you want the religious fanatics to turn this land into a hell?"

"I saw what he wrote about the former Sultan, he had no connection to the religious fanatics. We have our own writers, why didn't you let them answer? I didn't become a soldier for this, I didn't become a soldier to kill my own people in my capital, they trained us to fight for our nation on the front lines, now everyone sees us as murderers with bloody hands. Yes, I am a murderer too, I've shot men, but I didn't kill anyone because they wrote articles, and I won't, I won't pull a gun on someone who has no interest in guns, when you start killing people who don't have guns you kill the army too, you're not giving any thought to the army's honor."

Despite his patience, Cevat Bey was beginning to become irritated.

"Ragıp, you're talking without thinking things through. You're expressing ideas about things you don't understand, do you think it's easy to govern a nation, is the enemy only at the front lines, don't you see that so many insidious enemies have infiltrated us, looking for ways to destroy us? What would happen if the Committee left the scene, tell me, who else but us can prevent the former Caliph from returning to Istanbul, who else but us can stop a return of those terrible days, Ragıp, you don't sound like the Ragıp I know."

Ragıp Bey sat up slightly.

"What do you mean, brother? Are you calling me a traitor as well?"

"No, that didn't even occur to me."

"Then what are you saying?"

"Istanbul has made you softer."

Ragıp Bey flushed deeply, he felt his brain numbed by anger, he understood what his brother meant, but he couldn't come up with an answer.

He clenched his teeth and could only say, "Is that so?"

Cevat Bet said, "Yes, that's so. Pull yourself together, the life you're living is preventing you from thinking as clearly as you need to be thinking."

If they continued talking even a little more, the relationship between the two brothers would be damaged for good, more frightening things might have happened right then and there in the fruit-scented garden, but just then they heard their mother's dry voice, it was clear she'd been listening to her sons from the beginning.

"Cevat, go to bed, you'll wake the child with all your noise. Ragıp, you go to bed too, you have to get up early in the morning."

The two brothers stood and walked inside like children. When Ragıp Bey strode in angrily and took off his jacket, he saw his wife sitting by the window; it was clear that she'd listened to the entire conversation. "Haven't you gone to bed?" asked Ragıp Bey.

"No, I was waiting for you, we need to talk."

"We can talk tomorrow, why not talk in the daytime, why do we need to talk so late at night?"

His wife's voice was cold, almost hostile.

"We have to talk now."

"What is it that's so important."

"I want to go back to my father's house."

"Fine, I'll take you back the day after tomorrow."

"No, you don't understand, I want to go back to my father's house permanently, I want to divorce you and never see you again."

Ragıp Bey had to get a grip on himself in order not to throw his jacket onto the floor, he sat in an armchair.

"Where did this come from?"

"From nowhere, I don't want to live with you anymore."

"Are you crazy, how could I do that to Sheikh Efendi, how can I leave His Excellency's daughter?"

"First of all, you're not leaving me, I'm leaving you, second, this has nothing to do with Sheikh Efendi, we're talking about our life."

"Hatice Hanım, how can we do this, what will people say, what will Sheikh Efendi think?"

"He'll think what he thought when you killed men, when you slept with other women, when you sank up to your neck in sin."

"You don't hear what you're saying, we're talking about your father."

"I know very well who I'm talking about, I hear what I'm saying."

Ragıp Bey sighed.

"As you wish. But with your permission, I'd like to speak to Sheikh Efendi first."

"You can talk to Sheikh Efendi when you take me to the *tekke*. I want to go tomorrow morning. If you don't, I'll take the child with me and go alone."

Ragıp Bey realized that his wife was determined and that she wasn't going to change her mind. If he didn't think he would be embarrassed before Sheikh Efendi he would have been very happy about this decision; to be freed from a relationship full of hate would, at the same time mean being able to live with Dilara Hanım freely and comfortably, without pangs of conscience, without being obliged to go to the mansion every other day.

His wife sat in the armchair by the window holding the baby all night long. Ragıp Bey lay on the bed in his clothes, he had a restless sleep that was interrupted often, sometimes by dreams of starting a new life with Dilara Hanım and sometimes by thoughts about what he would say to Sheikh Efendi.

The next morning they left the mansion without having breakfast, without offering any explanation despite his mother's questioning glances, Hatice Hanım didn't look back even once, they rode all the way to the *tekke* in silence.

When they arrived at the *tekke* he sent his wife to the harem and went directly to Sheikh Efendi. When he saw Ragıp Bey there at that hour, Yusuf Efendi realized he was going to receive bad news.

He said, "Welcome, I hope all is well."

"I'm afraid things are not well, Your Excellency."

The Sheikh waited for him to continue.

"I don't know how to tell you."

"Tell it as it is, that's the easiest way."

"Hatice Hanım wants a divorce, she wants to live here from now on."

"Oh."

"Yes, sir."

Sheikh Efendi stroked his beard.

"What do you have to say about this?"

"Your Excellency, how can I leave your daughter, how would I be able to look you in the face, but nothing I said would change her mind, perhaps you could talk to her."

Sheikh Efendi took Ragıp Bey by the arm.

"Let's go out into the garden."

They went out into the garden together and strolled among the rosebushes as they always did. The Sheikh spoke suddenly.

"Let's leave it as it is. I know Hatice, if she's made this decision, there's no way to change her mind. Perhaps this was a
mistake from the start."

Ragıp Bey had expected to hear bitterness in Sheikh
Efendi's voice, but there wasn't any, he only said what he
thought.

"But what will people say?"

"What is it to us, can a marriage be for the sake of other
people? Even if you manage to deceive others you can't
deceive yourself. It's better for this to end before it's too late, I
think that Hatice has made the right decision."

Ragıp Bey sighed. The Sheikh held his arm in a friendly
manner.

"Look, if you have any concerns about me, be at ease, you
weren't my son-in-law when I met you; I accepted you as a
friend, just as I saw you as a friend then, I will see you as a
friend in the same way. You have no fault in this, and neither
does Hatice. In matters of the heart, nothing can be forced,
Ragıp Bey. We don't look for sin where others find it, for us sin
is to harm what the Creator created and therefore to harm yourself. I know you never treated my daughter badly, not even for
a single day, you always treated her respectfully, this is enough
for me, anything beyond this is your problem. In my opinion,
you should let it go, you're young. Live a life that's better suited
to you. There's no need for you to suffer, trust me."

Ragıp Bey knew that Sheikh Efendi was aware of Dilara
Hanım, yet in spite of this he still treated him in a friendly and
understanding manner, and this made him feel even more
ashamed.

"I couldn't be the son-in-law you deserved, my Sheikh. I
know you forgive me, in your great heart there's no room for
anger or bitterness, but I can't forgive myself."

"Ragıp Bey, you're wearing yourself out for nothing, this
isn't something to forgive, it happens to everyone, it's a sin to

spend your life with someone you don't feel close to, you can't control destiny, if this is your destiny, this is what you'll live. Go and establish a life that suits you."

Ragıp Bey bowed and kissed Sheikh Efendi's hand.

"Don't forget to keep me in your prayers, I can't repay you for the good things you've done for me, but wherever I am, whatever the time, however it happens, a single command from you will be enough, I'll come no matter what it takes."

"I know," said Sheikh Efendi, "I know you. And don't hesitate if you need anything, just send word."

When Ragıp Bey left the *tekke*, the sun was already high and the heat had set in. There was a bluish mist drifting over the Golden Horn, the smell of roses mingled with the smell of the salty sea.

Talking with Sheikh Efendi had put him at ease, a heavy burden had been lifted from his shoulders. He wondered how Dilara Hanım would react to this news, how they would live from then on. He would finally be able to be with the woman he loved without any problems, perhaps for the first time he could establish a life with someone he loved.

He got into a carriage and lit a cigarette, as he told the driver the address of the mansion in Nişantaşı even he himself could hear the joy echoing in his voice.

The whole way he impatiently exhorted the driver to go faster, he wanted to arrive at the mansion at once, to tell Dilara Hanım what had happened, to celebrate that joy together, to embrace her. There would be no shadows, no doubt, no sense of guilt, no lies between them; the marriage that he thought had created the missing sentence had finally ended, and now there was a chance for both of them to complete the sentence.

He found Dilara Hanım having her morning coffee in the living room. When she saw Ragıp Bey, her beautiful face was lit up with joy.

"Welcome, what are you doing here at this time of day?"

Ragıp Bey embraced Dilara Hanım tightly

"I wanted to see you."

Dilara Hanım stepped back and looked at Ragıp Bey.

"What happened, there's something strange about you . . . I hope nothing's wrong?"

"It's good news, Dilara Hanım, it's good news. This morning Hatice Hanım went back to her father, she told me she wanted a divorce. I spoke with Sheikh Efendi, he forgave me."

There was a pensive expression on Dilara Hanım's face. She said, "I'm sorry."

Ragıp Bey was truly surprised.

"Are you sorry? Why?"

"But the end of a marriage is always sad, isn't it?"

Ragıp Bey looked at Dilara Hanım's face, squinting his eyes as if searching for a secret meaning, a hidden thought that he could only see if he looked carefully; Dilara Hanım didn't reveal the slightest sign of joy.

At that moment he realized that the missing sentence would never be completed, that the missing sentence would diminish his life too, that the pain would never cease. That missing thing was nourished less by the form of their relationship than by deeper, less visible places; he sensed this with sorrow.

He didn't say anything more about the subject, he made small talk, and as soon as he finished his coffee he left the mansion as if he was fleeing.

That day, right away, he submitted a petition to the ministry of war asking to be reassigned to a unit in Macedonia.

He knew the loneliness and the pain he would experience there on long, desolate winter nights, he already felt the infinite sorrow, but he could not stay here, in the city where Dilara Hanım lived, he couldn't stand to see the traces of that missing sentence that darkened his life wherever he looked. He knew only one way to heal a wound, he'd learned this on the front lines, and that was to cauterize it. Even though it was extremely painful at first, this was the only way to keep the wound from being infected and penetrating and crippling the body. He made this decision and cauterized his flesh, there was nothing left to do but clench his teeth and wait for the pain to pass.

A week later, without saying goodbye to anyone, just kissing his mother's hand, he left Istanbul. On his way to his unit he listened to the sound of the wheels of the train as it passed through steppes devoid of people, forgotten villages, he realized that the pain of cauterizing a wound was greater than he'd imagined, and he prayed to a power he didn't know for time to pass quickly and to be able to forget.

23

S eptember arrived with its crystal lights that flowed like
clear water and it matured all of the feelings and sharpened internal reckonings, after a summer spent in tense
frivolity, the city prepared to wrap itself in the melancholy of
this extraordinary season that had not yet lost its cheerfulness.

Hikmet Bey began playing the piano again with a sudden
enthusiasm whose source he couldn't understand, he spent his
days at the piano, playing with mad desire; he thought nothing
when he played, he forgot everything, it was as if he expected
his disordered feelings to be filtered through that forgetting,
for each of them to settle in him after being distilled in a still
made of crystal light by the sounds of ivory.

In the first days his fingers had difficulty responding to his
demands like traitors attempting to conceal a truth, sometimes
they struck the keys more weakly than necessary, sometimes
more heavily than they should, they couldn't keep up with the
measure, the sweet-souled sounds were broken by unpracticed
cracks, then the sound started to flow like light.

He stopped playing the piano only to speak with Dilevser
and to make love to Hediye, the traces left on his soul by this
lovemaking and these conversations were reflected in the
music he played.

That he returned to the piano, which had become a symbol
of the extraordinary love he'd experienced with Mehpare
Hanım and the scars of which he always carried, for the first
time since he'd separated from her, that he dared to do this

seemed to him like a sign of many changes, and of an ending and a beginning.

Sometimes Dilevser didn't leave after their conversation, she stayed, sat in a corner, and listened to him play the piano. Hediye, who spent every minute, day and night, waiting outside the library door, tried to fathom her master's mood from the sound of the piano, when he played sad pieces, she became saddened as well, and when he played enthusiastic pieces her heart ached.

It fell upon Hikmet Bey to play the role of the father at Rukiye's wedding. Even though Mehpare Hanım was invited, she didn't come and made the excuse that she was ill, because of the coldness of the invitation and the difficulty of her position, she'd wanted Rukiye to come see her before the wedding, but her daughter didn't go.

Although Sheikh Efendi didn't come, his presence was felt throughout, traces of him were everywhere, from the waterfront mansion he'd prepared for the young bride and groom in just a week to the helpers he sent to the mansion to work there permanently and to shoulder the preparations for the wedding, to the gifts for the bride from various *tekkes* and zawiyas, from the ulema and even from the palace. Mihrişah Sultan and Tevfik Bey's family played significant roles as well, but next to the sacred harmony of Sheikh Efendi's power their presence was drab.

Mihrişah Sultan prepared a wedding in the garden of the waterfront mansion that would be remembered for years, she cut no corners, she even managed to have a wedding dress brought from Paris even though there was so little time.

Despite all of the splendor, the melancholy shadow of the deaths, whose pain was still fresh, cast a shadow on the wedding, which wasn't as cheerful as weddings usually are. Rukiye didn't pay any attention to the concealed malaise of the wedding, perhaps she didn't even notice; what she realized was

that she was wrapped in the love and security she'd been looking for since childhood; she felt that Sheikh Efendi, her husband, Mihrişah Sultan, Hikmet Bey, and her brother Nizam,
who'd come from Paris for the wedding, all loved her, and she
had no fear that she might lose this love. She grasped what
Sheikh Efendi had meant when he told her about peace. The
only thing that bothered her, though she didn't say this to anyone, not even to herself, was that Mehpare Hanım wasn't
there, or rather that she'd become the kind of mother who
couldn't attend her daughter's wedding.

That night Hikmet Bey did everything in his power to make
Rukiye happy, he took an interest in all the guests, he felt what
it was like to be a father whose daughter had become a bride
and noticed that he'd come to another turning point in his life,
that he was a bit further removed from his youth and its freedom, that life had become a bit heavier.

He felt this the day before the wedding, when he and
Nizam met at his mansion for the first time in ages.

When Nizam came in, he stood restlessly and walked
toward his son, who was a young man now and looked at him
anxiously to see the expression on his face.

His son smiled cheerfully like a person who'd never known
sadness and never would, put out his hand, and said, "*Bonjour,
Papa.*" When he saw the light and love in his face, he
embraced his son instead of shaking hands, pulling him and
pressing him to his chest. Nizam was not accustomed to displays of affection, he awkwardly submitted to his father's
embrace, but he wanted it to end as soon as possible.

Hikmet Bey said, "You've grown up."

When he said this he felt as if his voice resembled his
father's voice, that it was almost exactly the same. They ate
together, they made small talk, Nizam told his father about
Paris, told him many amusing stories and jokes. As Hikmet
Bey listened to his son, he realized sadly that though he would

always love him, they would never have a deep relationship, that they were from two different ages, two different centuries. They would not have big fights, they wouldn't have differences of opinion, they would love each other only as father and son; they would have neither a friendship nor an enmity that would leave a trace.

In any event, despite his mother's insistence, Nizam didn't stay in Istanbul after the wedding and returned to Paris with Mihrişah Sultan.

That wedding night, perhaps because he was affected by the realization that he was a father whose daughter was getting married, perhaps because seeing that his son had grown up made him aware of the passage of time, Hikmet Bey experienced something else strange. When he raised his head and looked at his mother to say something, he saw something in Mihrişah Sultan's face that had not been there a moment earlier, that strange and indefinable mist, like the thin and transparent mist that appears on the sea on summer days, that appears on the faces of women who are growing older. Nothing was different, the lines were the same, her beauty was there, but it was as if, with a shift in her facial expression, her muscles revealed that they were having difficulty carrying her lines.

To understand what had created this impression that she was getting older, he stared at his mother and examined all the lines of her face one by one, he saw nothing in the details that was different from before, but in the whole there was the shadow of old age, when Mihrişah Sultan noticed that her son, who was looking at her so carefully, had gone pale, she asked in an irritable rush if he was well.

"I'm fine, why do you ask?"

"You suddenly went pale."

Hikmet Bey rushed to answer for fear that his mother might realize what he was thinking about.

"I'm fine, I just felt dizzy for a moment."

After Mihrişah Sultan looked at her son carefully, she smiled that magnificent smile that contained so many meanings and said in a sad tone:

"I'm getting older, isn't that it?"

"No, where did that come from?"

Mihrişah Sultan sighed, she knew that it would make her sadder to be consoled about this.

"I knew it would happen one day, in recent years I've expected it to come almost every day. Now it has come, it arrived suddenly. People think that things like this happen slowly, then they look and see that they've already happened . . ."

She stopped and leaned toward Hikmet Bey.

"But do you know, I'm not as sad as I thought I'd be, that is, I've become accustomed to the idea. But of course I'm not happy about it either."

She smiled.

"No, no, don't worry, I'm fine. Maybe, who knows, if you lose something you've been worrying about losing your whole life, maybe you relax. Whatever, we'll see. What a lovely bride Rukiye is, isn't she?"

They never spoke about this matter again, Hikmet Bey could see that they shouldn't, that it would be kinder not to console his mother. But Hikmet Bey was more saddened than his mother that this beauty had grown old, the shadow of old age was like a tiny cloud appearing in a summer sky and signaling a downpour. All of his life, Mihrişah Sultan's beauty had given him confidence, it had protected him as much as it could from Mehpare Hanım, when a shadow was cast on this beauty, he knew that he had lost one of his shelters.

After the wedding Mihrişah Sultan returned to Paris at once with Nizam, and Rukiye moved into her new waterfront mansion. Hikmet Bey felt a bit lonelier.

This loneliness grew steadily, enveloped almost all of his

days. Just like someone in pitch-black darkness walking toward the only light he saw, he walked toward the only light he saw in this loneliness, toward Dilevser, now, instead of feeling a desire to be admired by her, he talked to her, shared his problems, sometimes he would get himself the same book she was reading so they could read it at the same time, to find the warmth of closeness in the chest that had been created by his former desire, to find friendship, and to share his thoughts and feelings. Perhaps because Dilevser had become accustomed to Hikmet Bey over time, perhaps because this time the man approached her with genuine desire and need, the young girl demolished the walls between them one by one, stopped sheltering behind her modesty, and revealed the frightful treasure she'd concealed so stubbornly, revealed the intelligence that almost terrified Hikmet Bey,

During every conversation they had, Hikmet Bey was surprised by how that fragile body and that calm voice carried what was perhaps the most magnificent intelligence he'd ever encountered, each time he was frightened that this intelligence would crush and destroy her. Then he was able to grasp why she read the way she did, with an almost frenzied need, he realized that she had to feed the intelligence she carried, it was like a hungry lion that she had to feed in order not to be torn apart by it.

When people looked at their relationship, they thought he'd been charmed by a young girl, but he'd long forgotten Dilevser's age and her body, in which she moved like a thin branch in her elegant clothes, he was in pursuit of the mesmerizing glow of her intelligence. Later he said to Osman, "I don't know if I was interested in her because I noticed her intelligence from the start, or if I noticed it later."

Nor did he understand why the young girl concealed her intelligence from other people so jealously. As for Dilevser, she merely smiled at his comments and compliments about her intelligence and said he was exaggerating.

Hikmet Bey established a peaceful balance in his loneliness, he submitted his body to Hediye and his mind to Dilevser, he lived his life with a pleasantly satisfied lust and a mesmerized mind, and indeed he didn't want this to change at all. He believed he finally possessed the most magnificent balance and peace that was possible, but he knew that it was impossible for things to continue this way, he could see that one day something would upset this balance, that life would drag him to make a decision.

Hediye knew about his interest in Dilevser, but Dilevser didn't know what he experienced with Hediye, or at least she didn't appear to. This was clearly unfair, but Hediye bore this unfairness in silence, and as for Hikmet Bey, he wasn't aware that he was being unfair.

Despite all of the pleasure she derived from long nights of lovemaking, Hediye waited for her own little moment of sin amidst all of the sinful games, the moment after lovemaking when she could nestle against Hikmet Bey and he would embrace her lovingly, even if for a brief moment; when that moment came, she nestled softly against him, leaned her body toward his, and enjoyed the feeling of that moment. No one asked what she thought, but if anyone had asked, she would have said that those brief moments made it possible for her to endure that the man she loved spent his days approaching another woman with love.

She didn't complain about having to experience this moment without Hikmet Bey knowing, as if she was having an affair; in order to capture this moment she was prepared to do anything, to spend her life leaning against a door, waiting for the night, to accept being ignored during the day, to be seen as pathetic by the entire household of the mansion. But, like Hikmet Bey, she knew things would not continue this way for long, she knew they would take this brief moment from her, they would not let her have what was left over from a stolen life.

Despite her inexperience, despite her lack of knowledge about life, she could sense that no one, not even those who spent their lives with a great love and then lost their loved ones, would feel the pain she would feel when she lost that moment.

Some days, that moment grew longer, Hikmet Bey would lie embracing Hediye, absorbed in his thoughts; although she realized that the man embracing her had something else on his mind, this small, beautiful woman lay without moving, afraid even to breathe, she touched Hikmet Bey's arms softly with her fingertips, without letting him feel it. After nights like that, the mansion household saw Hediye smiling.

As Hikmet Bey and Hediye had sensed and feared separately, this peaceful and balanced life ended suddenly one night.

The telegram that Hikmet Bey had been awaiting with secret, inner shuddering, the same way Mihrişah Sultan had been awaiting old age, knowing that it would come one day, actually arrived.

It was composed of seven words:

"His Excellency Reşit Pasha has passed away."

When Hikmet Bey read this telegram he collapsed on the bed, then wept until morning, embracing Hediye and talking to her at length about his father and his own childhood; what was one of Hikmet Bey's most difficult nights was perhaps the happiest and most cherished of nights for Hediye.

One morning, as Reşit Pasha was making his way as usual to the mansion where the Sultan was residing, he stopped, leaned against a tree, had a heart attack, and died without suffering. Because it was summer and the weather was too hot, they could neither send his remains to Istanbul nor wait for his relatives to come, so Reşit Pasha was buried in Salonika as the exiled Sultan's physician in a silent ceremony attended by only a few.

If his father had been given a proper funeral or if he had been buried in Istanbul, where his son was, perhaps Hikmet Bey would not have suffered so much, he would not have been wounded by the feeling that his father had been left alone and neglected, would not have felt himself to be so alone and helpless, but that he had not even been able to attend his father's funeral remained a source of deep pain for him.

The letter his father had written hastily before departing for Salonika was always on his mind; the letter that had given him strength, that unforgettable letter. For his part, he had never told his father what he really felt and thought; Reşit Pasha had always lived with the thought that his son looked down on him.

Later Hikmet Bey told Osman, "I would like to have told him he was a hero, I've seen many heroes in my life, people who put their lives in danger, but they all demonstrated their courage for causes they felt and believed must be victorious, but my father sacrificed his final days for someone who had lost and who no longer had any chance of winning. I didn't have a chance to tell him that I have never seen greater heroism, I never told him how much I respected someone who stood with someone who had lost."

Now these words he had been unable to utter were added to his regrets in life, and for days he thought about his father and his deserted and lonely grave in Salonika. Even though he knew that it was irrational, he couldn't escape the feeling that his father was cold there all alone at night. Even though he and his father had had many arguments, conversations that had left behind traces of bitterness, he always remembered his father's witty, childish expression. In a strange way it was as if he was remembering not his father but his child.

It was not through his own will, not consciously, but instinctively, that he chose Dilevser, who shared her extraordinary intelligence with him, and not Hediye, who gave him a great love and a magnificent body; he started spending more

time with her, he found the consolation he sought in their conversations and in the warming brightness of her intelligence;
the balance between mind and body had been upset and his
lovemaking with Hediye grew colder.

Hediye saw what was approaching more clearly than anyone else and continued to spend her days leaning against the
wall outside the library without complaint.

Two weeks after his father's death, he received a letter from
Mehpare Hanım asking him to come. She said she wanted to
talk to him. Mehpare Hanım's voice, her image, even her handwriting had the same effect on him every time, suddenly everything and everyone in the world became insignificant,
Mehpare Hanım was in front of a pitch-black screen, alone in
a bright light that was shining on her face, and Hikmet Bey felt
the same excitement. When he read the letter he noticed that
he was so excited his hands had grown cold.

He started pacing around the room, he moved a household
ornament, straightened an ashtray, looked out the window,
struggled to calm the stirring within him.

When he sat in an armchair he was exhausted.

The excitement rained down on him like the heavy down-
pours that suddenly struck Istanbul on summer afternoons
and then disappeared with the same suddenness as they'd
begun, without leaving a trace; there was a deaf disquiet in
him, a lack of desire for anything.

When he didn't want Mehpare Hanım, he didn't want anything else either, anyone else, but he knew that just like the
excitement, this lack of desire would soon vanish and he would
become as he had been before he received the letter.

After burning desires, pains, jealousy, scorn, memories that
he relived constantly again and again, days and nights of suffering, he consumed Mehpare Hanım in his dreams; until his
dying day he would feel that same quivering excitement whenever he heard from Mehpare Hanım, whenever he saw her,

whenever he heard her voice, but each time he would wait for it to pass, knowing that it would.

That evening he wrote Mehpare Hanım a brief letter, informing her that he would not be able to come because he was busy, but that "if she had any request of him he was prepared to grant it."

He knew that with that letter, Mehpare Hanım would never return to his life; it wasn't that he didn't think about not sending the letter, but in the end he gave the letter to his carriage driver and sent it to his former wife, to the most extraordinary love of his life. But from then on he heard about every development in Mehpare Hanım's life, that she had an affair with a diplomat from the French Embassy, that Constantine came to Istanbul from time to time; even though his love was over, he continued to take an interest in her from a distance.

Now he waited for Dilevser every morning, talked with her at length about literature, books, writers, life, tried to wash away his past with Dilevser's intelligence, to purify and heal the wounds that had been left behind, and became increasingly attached to the young girl and her intelligence.

Literature was like a living soul that connected them to each other, it gave color to their conversations, they used books to say what they wanted to say to each other, to reveal their intelligence, to admire each other, to become attached to each other.

In her short, simple sentences, Dilevser said things the like of which had never occurred to Hikmet Bey, his surprise at and admiration for her mingled with each other; he thought he couldn't live without hearing her voice, without listening to her.

At night he encountered Hediye's love and silence, which were as terrifying as Dilevser's intelligence, he felt her softness, the strength with which she carried her desperation, the way she nestled against him, he felt their lovemaking occupied more and more of his life, became an essential part of his life. He said, "Hediye, you are the only truth in my life," and he believed this was true. No one in his life would ever be as real and as close as Hediye, no one would ever love Hikmet Bey as she did, effacing herself in her love.

Once he told Osman, "If my life had been something breakable, a glass or a vase or something like that, I would have given it to Hediye to hold, anyone but her might leave it behind for a moment absentmindedly, drop it, throw it in a moment of pain, but she would never, under any circumstances, let go of it."

It was as if God had given Hikmet Bey the woman he wanted, but the devil had divided her in two and made two women, now whichever of them he gave up, something would be missing.

Sometimes he wanted to marry Dilevser, to spend his life with that bright intelligence, educating that intelligence, nourishing it, giving it maturity with his own experiences, conversing with her, sometimes he wanted to do something crazy and surprise all of Istanbul by marrying Hediye, to travel with her, to please this little woman who managed to carry such a great love in silence, to see her be cheerful, to witness her at least once feeling safe enough to laugh sincerely.

One day during that time Dilevser said:

"My mother wants to invite you to dinner."

When Hikmet Bey went to his neighbor's mansion that evening, he found Dilara Hanım sadder than he'd ever seen her. Although he talked with Dilevser every day, he hadn't seen Dilara Hanım for a long time. She was as elegant and attractive as usual, but less talkative and less derisive.

At first she was happy that Ragıp Bey was gone, she felt as if she'd regained her freedom, that her colorful and flirtatious life had been restored, she felt rejuvenated by being freed of a bond that had no future, but then, as the days passed, she began to miss his wild and murderous soul, the security and the fear she experienced when she was with him. When she was with Ragıp Bey, she felt that no one, no power on earth, could touch her, that this man would protect her from everyone, it wouldn't even occur to anyone to harm her unless they were willing to kill or be killed; perhaps this was the ultimate peak of the sense of security a woman could experience, and no one but a murderer, someone who wouldn't hesitate to kill, could make a woman feel this sense of security in the same way. The fear she felt of the violence of this power that gave her a sense of security added an incredible excitement to that magnificent sense of security. While she was experiencing these emotions she began to find them ordinary, she thought that she could experience the same feelings every time, but a while after Ragıp Bey left, she felt the unfillable void the man had left behind in her life.

That was when she missed him. For a time she consoled herself with the thought that this longing was temporary, she invited new officers to the house, she experienced different lovemaking, with each man she longed for Ragıp Bey even more, in a strange way, the presence of other men increased the affect Ragıp Bey had on her. The more she compared the men she met to Ragıp Bey, the more attached she became to Ragıp Bey.

In the end she couldn't contain herself and wrote him a joking letter: "Are you so bored of Istanbul that you don't even consider visiting?" she asked; despite all of her longing she couldn't bring herself to write a love letter, even though she was angry at herself she found herself unable to do this.

Dilara Hanım waited for days, but she received no answer to that letter. Dilara Hanım never knew whether the letter had been lost in the mountains of Macedonia, in the hands of careless officials in isolated post offices, or whether Ragıp Bey hadn't written back because the joking style reinforced his belief that the thing that was missing from his life would only be felt more and he was too proud to accept a life from which something was missing.

All she understood was that she'd lost something she could never regain, and that for a long time she would look for what was missing in every man she met.

She decided to invite Hikmet Bey to dinner partly because she wanted to see the bond between Dilevser and Hikmet Bey, which was growing stronger by the day, with her own eyes, partly because she wanted to have a pleasant evening and ease her pain, and partly because she wanted her soul, which was suffocated by the sternness of the officers who came and went, to be refreshed by the behavior of an elegant man.

Although Hikmet Bey managed to make her laugh during dinner, and even though she enjoyed the courtesy she'd missed so much, Dilara Hanım realized it would be a long time before she could be as cheerful as she'd once been. When she saw the way her daughter and Hikmet Bey looked at each other, when she saw that they'd developed the habit of finishing each other's sentences, she sensed that the bond between them was more meaningful than she'd thought.

As for Hikmet Bey, the dinner had more of an impact on him than he imagined. Dilara Hanım's elegance, politeness, manners, delicacy, power, and wealth provided a sturdy frame for Dilevser's intelligence, which wandered like a lost cloud, in a strange way this enhanced Dilevser's feminine allure for Hikmet Bey, that night, perhaps for the first time, he felt strongly that he could marry Dilevser.

When he returned home, Hediye was leaning against the wall waiting for him.

After the impressive splendor of Dilevser's house, filtered through the delicacy particular to wealthy intellectuals, it made Hikmet Bey's heart sink to see how alone and helpless Hediye looked as she leaned against that wall. She had no family, no wealth, no past, not even a name; she stood there naked in her love, she asked for nothing, she didn't even have the courage to hope. She offered the only thing she had to offer, herself, and she did so body and soul, without hesitation, with incredible generosity, without leaving even the smallest shelter for herself in her life, without complaint she offered every part of herself to the man she loved, knowing he would never appreciate its value.

This girl demonstrated the same courage in the face of life that Ragıp Bey demonstrated in the face of death, in a different way she gave Hikmet Bey the same sense of security that Ragıp Bey gave Dilara Hanım. Later, Hikmet Bey told Osman, "A sense of security is such a strange thing, the ease you feel when you have it can make you undervalue the sense of security itself."

When Hikmet Bey saw Hediye leaning against the wall in the room in which most of the lights had been doused, he was ashamed of what he'd felt in Dilara Hanım's house, at that moment, even if only briefly, he fell in love with the girl's desperation, he considered renouncing his own life and marrying Hediye simply to give meaning to someone else's life, he considered this as seriously as he'd considered marrying Dilevser.

They didn't make love that night. Hikmet Bey embraced Hediye tightly, he buried his head in her neck and repeated the same sentence until he fell asleep.

"Hediye, you are the only truth in my life."

That night, as she experienced what she'd most wanted in her life, the night Hikmet Bey embraced her with such love she realized, with an intuition much stronger than Hikmet Bey's, that the horrible end was approaching, that she was on the verge of losing the man she loved. She waited until Hikmet Bey was asleep, gently eased herself out of his arms, went to the other side of the bed, and, pressing her head into the pillow so that no one would hear her, wept until daybreak. At dawn, she turned the pillow over so no one would notice it was wet, got dressed, and went to her room. Hikmet Bey thought she'd been very happy that night, he never knew she'd wept the way she did.

The following morning Hikmet Bey woke with the irresistible desire to play the piano.

He played the piano for days.

All of the mansions, the neighbors, passersby, indeed the entire city listened to Reşit Pasha's son Hüseyin Hikmet Bey's pain, longing, sorrow, indecisiveness, joy, hope, memories, and dreams as sonatas, suites, and concertos; occasionally striking the keys softly, occasionally with strong, angry staccatos, he sought his truth and his future in the sound of the music he played, he looked to the ivory keys for all the answers he couldn't find in his feelings and thoughts.

Every time he touched the keys, something went missing from his life and something was added to his life; no one, perhaps not even himself, knew what he thought and what he felt when he played the piano, but in those sounds they heard death, loss, betrayal, pleading, struggling, courage, fear, hope, and hopelessness, they heard a person and his entire life; during those strange days Hikmet Bey managed to turn himself into sound, into music.

Toward the end of September he woke one morning feeling worn out and exhausted, while Dilevser was talking to him about Balzac, he interrupted her.

"Dilevser, if you'll forgive my presumption, may I ask you something?"

"Of course."

"Will you marry me?"

Dilevser went over to the open window, looked outside, then turned around.

"Yes."

What they said during this brief conversation surprised

both of them, in their surprise they resumed talking about Balzac as if they hadn't just been talking about something else.

This quick, silent conversation between them, which would have been difficult to notice, exploded in the mansion with a great noise. It was as if everyone in the mansion had heard the words "Will you marry me?" with their own ears, there were excited whispers, laughter, rumors spread immediately.

Then everyone in the mansion turned and looked at Hediye.

Hediye went pale, her face trembled, her eyes closed for a moment, when she opened her eyes again there was no emotion on her face, she was standing by the wall where she always stood.

That day Hikmet Bey passed her a few times, but he couldn't find the courage to talk to her. He thought they could talk that night, he would console her, he would tell her that he was going to buy a house for her and take care of her for the rest of her life. Hediye stood where she stood every day as if nothing had happened; there was no bitterness or pain on her face, once, when he was passing her, Hikmet Bey smiled at the woman, and she smiled back. This smile made Hikmet Bey think that Hediye would not be affected very much, that she would not suffer as much as he'd feared.

When dinner was being prepared, they noticed that the girl was nowhere to be seen, they sent one of the servants to her room to check.

Hediye had undressed completely and was lying under the quilt.

There was no sign of death on her sad face, she died as she'd lived, in silence, without ever becoming ugly. They never knew when or how she'd found the poison, or where she'd hidden it.

She didn't leave behind a note or a letter.

Hikmet Bey was the only one who saw the white silk dress she'd worn the first night they met folded neatly on the bed.

The letter that became an ache that was never soothed for Hikmet Bey, that he carried everywhere he went, that made him rebel and ask, "Oh God, is there no joy without sorrow," was nothing more than a white dress.

24

A crescent moon thinner than any Osman had ever seen appeared in the sky like a golden eyelash.

From the window of the old mansion, he looked at that crescent moon and felt the movement of his fragile and transparent dead.

He knew that Hikmet Bey was happy with Dilevser, but that for the rest of his life he never forgot Hediye.

He knew that the uprising in the city had been put down, that it had ended, but he also knew that the city would see new uprisings, coups, assassinations, wars, occupations, and disasters.

He saw the lies of the living and the reality of the dead.

He was seized by a feeling, as if it was a sorrow he'd inherited from his own past.

Sheikh Efendi said, "We're all helpless, we all suffer, the Lord carries all of our pain for us, he suffers for all of us, he is the one who heals the pain, he is the one who offers consolation, I would like to suffer as much as he did, to feel the pain of all humanity, then I would have been able to bandage the wounds as he does, I could stop the pain, but no slave can suffer as much as his God. I think that the lack of remedies and consolation lies in the lack of pain."

When Osman asked him if he needed to suffer more, Cevat Bey had a different answer.

"A person's consolation is people, my boy, people find pain, and they find consolation, but people don't give themselves a chance to find the remedy."

Sula laughed at all of this, without raising her voice too much, she asked Osman in her playful, flirtatious voice, "What are they saying? What are they saying?"

His dead spoke beneath the very thin crescent moon.

They each had a story, a pain they complained about, a way to offer consolation.

Only Hediye was silent.

She was silent in death just as she'd been throughout her life.

She was like a white silk dress among the dead.